Madeline House

Maggie Christensen

Published by Cala Publishing 2016
Sunshine Coast, Qld, Australia

Cover and interior design: J D Smith Design
Editing: John Hudspith Editing Services

Dedication

In memory of Maxine, who was the inspiration for Maddy

Also by Maggie Christensen

Oregon Coast Series
The Sand Dollar
The Dreamcatcher

Sydney books
Band of Gold
Broken Threads

Sign up for the author's mailing list – keep up-to-date with news and new releases and get a FREE copy of *The Sand Dollar, Book One of the Oregon Coast Series.*

http://maggiechristensenauthor.com/

One

Beth Carson sighed and moved restlessly behind the wheel. She'd been driving for two days now and was becoming weary. Having left behind the wide stretches of Californian beaches, today she'd driven through the dense forests of Oregon. Stopping for lunch in Eugene, Beth found the city landscape couldn't provide the refuge she was looking for, so she'd driven towards the coast again, seeking some sign, some sense of recognition. Once she'd left the city of Eugene behind, the scenery changed, and Beth was surprised to see how flat much of the land was, with fields stretching out on both sides of the road and dotted with small wooden houses. It was all so vastly different from what she was used to. Beginning to wonder if she'd made a big mistake, Beth frowned, but kept going, driving through more forest and a couple of wide tunnels, before turning onto the road leading to the coast. When water appeared to the left side of the road, Beth began to feel more relaxed. Maybe, just maybe, this would prove to be the right thing to do.

The *City of Florence* sign appearing on her right seemed to welcome her. It made her think of that other Florence where she'd spent her honeymoon all those years ago. Images flickered behind her eyes – the Uffizi Gallery, the statue of David, the Ponto Vecchio, the Basilica of Santa Crocce, the palaces, the piazzas. Then there was the Tuscan landscape itself, the trattorias where they'd enjoyed lazy lunches. Beth shook her head to dismiss the images. That was a happier time. Those days were gone, long gone. She was ready to begin again, even though a niggling voice in her head asked her how she thought she deserved a fresh start, how she could shake off all the negativity she'd been surrounded with for so long.

Beth touched her new short hair. It felt sharp and spiky, different. But it would grow again, and this time it would be in her natural gray. No more blonde locks for her. Looking down at the casual pants and fleece top, purchased in a Walmart on her way up the coast, Beth grinned. No one would recognize the elegant Sydney socialite, even Bryan would hardly recognize his elegant wife in this garb. Good. She had no desire to be known as the vapid socialite, wife of the local surgeon. She was going to be herself, Beth Carson, of no fixed abode.

Beth drove along the wide stretch of Highway 101 into town and stopped at the first motel she came to. The white-sided two-storied building was set around a central courtyard and looked inviting. She'd been traveling non-stop for two weeks and needed to find a base, to put down some roots. It was a strange sensation – to be alone. She felt naked, as if part of her was missing, as if she'd waken up any moment and everything would be back to normal. She'd be in her oversized bed, with the Sydney sunshine streaming in the window, and the tall sophisticated man she'd married would be fussing with his tie and expecting her to go to the kitchen to prepare breakfast. She trembled at the memory of Bryan. What would he be doing? How would he explain her absence? She shook her head, parked the car, and entered the motel office.

"Can I help you, ma'am?" The blonde ponytailed receptionist looked up from the book she'd been reading, holding a finger in the page to keep her place; seemingly Beth was an unwelcome interruption.

"Do you have a room?"

"Sure. A double? How long will you be staying with us?"

"Umm, two weeks?" Beth was still unclear as to her next move, but two weeks should give her time to work something out.

"Name?"

"Eliz… Beth, Beth Carson," she said firmly.

Elizabeth Flynn was gone. She'd left her behind in Australia.

"And how will you be paying?"

"Cash." As she drew the notes out of her wallet and completed the registration form, Beth remembered she must set up a bank account.

The cash she'd brought with her wouldn't last for long, and she'd need to organize a credit card and a checking account. Thank goodness she'd retained a passport in her maiden name. Along with her social security card, that should be sufficient identification.

With her room key in her hand, Beth unloaded her one small case from the car. Once she'd made the decision to leave, she'd thrown together a few essentials, some personal mementoes and several changes of clothes. The rest she could buy as necessary. Once inside the room, she stretched out her arms and twirled round. She'd done it. She was here. The double bed with its white candlewick bedspread looked comfortable. Beth sat down on the bed and patted the surface. She sat there for a few moments, contemplating what she'd done, how far she'd come, then picked up her purse and headed back to the reception desk.

"Do you have a map of Florence? And can you recommend a good place for coffee?"

"Here you are." The young woman put down the book she was still reading and handed over a colorful folded sheet of paper. "I'm Trudi. Are you on holiday? I don't recognize your accent."

"Thanks." Beth ignored the question and accepted the map.

"You might want to go to Old Town. Just follow the road down to the river. You'll find lots of places there. It's where most of our tourists like to go. Let me know if you need anything more."

Beth smiled her thanks and walked outside into the sunshine. She stood for a moment looking at the map to get her bearings, then headed to the area marked Old Town. After going down some winding streets past small wooden-sided houses, she reached the river. There was something relaxing about the long boardwalk bounded by its white railings, the placid Siuslaw River flowing along, and the tall bridge spanning the watercourse. She felt as if she'd come home, had the weird feeling she fitted into the place, belonged somehow. It was odd to feel that way when she'd only just arrived, but it was a good feeling.

Finding a seat overlooking the river, Beth breathed in the fresh air. She felt free, free at last. "Thank you, Mom," she whispered. Without her mother's legacy this trip would never have been possible, and she'd still be trapped in Sydney in an unhappy marriage. Despite the warmth from the sun, Beth shivered as if an icy wind had blown in from the river. She wrapped her arms around her body, rubbing her hands up and down her arms to dispel the chill.

Deciding to explore, Beth strolled along the street, enjoying the sight of the old timber-clad buildings, so different to the Sydney streets she was used to. Halfway along, she thought she recognized a building from one of the postcards in her mother's effects. The white wooden siding, the dormer windows and the red roof all seemed familiar. Florence was the place named on the postcards, though Beth wasn't sure her mother, Audrey, had actually visited the town. But its location, here on the west coast of Oregon, was far enough away from her home in Sydney to make Beth feel safe.

Could Audrey actually have come here? She'd never mentioned it to Beth, so it seemed unlikely. But then how did her mother get the cards? The day was too lovely to worry about something she'd never know the answer to, so Beth continued along, till she spied a neat bookshop on the other side of the road.

She pushed open the shop door and found herself in a veritable Aladdin's cave. The sunlight, beaming in through the window, left shadows on the wooden floor and shone directly onto a display table. The air was sweet with the scent of honeysuckle, and she was surrounded by shelf upon shelf of books interspersed with deep, comfy chairs. She paused, awed by it all, then, moving to the table, she picked up one of the books. It was by an author she hadn't heard of, a local guy judging from the blurb on the back.

"You enjoy thrillers?"

Beth turned in surprise. The tall Native American woman had approached so silently she hadn't heard her.

"Oh! Sorry, I didn't know you were there. I was just looking…"

"I apologize if I startled you. I heard you come in. I was in the back office. I'm Ellen. Welcome to The Reading Nook. You're new in town."

"I'm Beth."

The two women eyed one another: one short and slim, with spiky gray hair, blue eyes and a faded appearance, the other tall and imposing, her long dark plait thrown over her shoulder. We're like chalk and cheese, Beth thought, but she was shaken by a sense of familiarity.

"It's good you came – to Florence."

"It is?"

"You'll find peace here. You've been troubled."

Beth fidgeted. She looked away.

"Don't be afraid." The mellifluous voice was kindly, not at all threatening.

Beth licked her lips, moistening their dryness.

"Who are you?" she said at last, wanting to leave, but feeling an irresistible pull towards this woman.

"Ellen. Ellen Williams. This is my shop. And that's my husband's novel you're holding."

Looking down, Beth saw she was still gripping the book she'd picked up. "Travis Petersen," she read and raised her eyes to meet Ellen's.

"I kept my maiden name. It's what I'm known by, and I didn't want to give up my identity when we married, the way some women do."

Beth gulped. This was too close to the bone for her to deal with right now.

"I'll take this one." She paid for her purchase and left, clutching the package to her chest.

Hurrying from the shop, Beth almost tripped on the curb, throwing out her hand to maintain her balance. She didn't understand what had spooked her, made her need to leave right then, rather rudely. The owner, Ellen, had been polite, not over-friendly. But there was something about her…

Seeing a coffee shop across the road, Beth headed over. With a seat on the deck giving a lovely view of the river and the bridge, a large mug of the local brew and an enormous cinnamon roll on the table in front of her, she began to feel better. Mum would have loved this. Her eyes misted over. Her mum was gone too soon, though it had been a merciful release. Living in pain in the nursing home was no life. But Beth missed her, missed her daily visits, missed the tales of her youth, missed her encouragement. A small bird hopped onto the table. Beth broke off a piece of her bun. Tossing it to the little creature, she remembered the last time she'd seen her mother alive.

"I don't have long left now."

Beth turned from the window, her eyes brimming with tears as the feeble voice reached her. Although she knew the words to be true, she was sad to hear them. She went to the bed and took her mother's hand.

"Mum?"

The older woman's hand tightened in hers.

"It's you I worry about. You must leave. Take your chance. You will, won't you?"

Beth bit her lip. They'd had this conversation over and over again. But how could she do what her mother wanted?

Audrey was the only one left who called her Beth. She'd shed that persona with a lot of other things, when she'd met Bryan. Now she was the sophisticated Mrs Elizabeth Flynn, wife of the respected surgeon, well known by all in Sydney, Liz to only a few close friends. Beth, the carefree young girl who'd grown up on the farm, determined to be her own person, to change the world, was long buried and forgotten.

Beth squeezed the hand in hers and gazed out of the window, trying to figure out how to reply. While she wanted to reassure her mum, she'd never lied to her and didn't intend to start now. But the view of treetops swaying in the breeze did nothing to help her decide.

"I…" she began, then turned back to the figure in the bed and the hand in hers went slack. The even breathing told Beth her mother had fallen asleep. Releasing her hand, she gently stroked back the silver hair from Audrey's forehead and dropped a kiss on her cheek. She sighed. How many more conversations would she be able to have with her mother before the end?

Beth could still recall her anguish when she finally arrived at the nursing home later that evening. The nurse told her Audrey had passed away peacefully in her sleep, and that patients often chose to go that way – to wait till their family had left. But that did nothing to assuage her guilt. Bryan's callous attitude had further inflamed her and made it easier for her to pack her bag and leave when she learned of the small legacy Audrey had left her.

Beth drank the last of her coffee and gazed out over the slow-flowing river. Its sluggish movement seemed to be sending her a message, a message to slow down, to take life as it came. She gathered her belongings and wandered out onto the street. The bookshop across the way didn't appear so threatening now. She felt lighter, as if a heavy load had been lifted from her shoulders. Beth had the strong impression her mother had wanted her to come here, but she had absolutely no idea why.

Two

The tall, broad-shouldered man in the red polo shirt, faded jeans and black leather jacket slid into the booth at The Little Brown Hen and picked up a menu.

"Your usual, Tom?" The waitress wiped the table and poured him a coffee as she spoke.

"Mmm, good stuff," he said, taking a gulp of the coffee. "Sure. I'll have the crab melt with onion rings."

"Make that two." A lanky man with faded blonde hair, neat moustache and beard, slid in opposite. "Mind if I join you?"

"Don't usually see you in town at this time of day."

"No. I got my last chapter under my belt, and Ellen suggested I might catch you here."

"What's up?" Tom was surprised Travis had chosen to waylay him over lunch instead of coming to the office, but decided to hear him out, and enjoy the company. All too often he ate alone, and although he didn't know him well, he'd heard good things about Travis Petersen.

"It's Ellen's mom." Travis cleared his throat. "She should be talking to you about this herself, but she thought, they thought…" He hesitated as if trying to find the correct words. "She's in perfect health right now. Well, as perfect as anyone in their eighties can be." He paused as two brimming plates were placed on the table and their coffee mugs were filled. "Thanks," he said to the waitress and continued, "Anyway, seeing what's happened to the old man, she wants to be sure that if she… Hell, this isn't an easy conversation."

"Are you talking about a living will?" Tom asked, trying to help his companion out.

"You got it." Travis sounded relieved. "Ellen heard that Maddy, her cousin's godmother, had one set up. Seems it's quite common. I hadn't heard of it till now."

"Very common in Florence where there's an aging population. You'll be referring to Madeline De Ruis. I didn't draw hers up. I think that was my old buddy up in Waldport."

Tom saw Travis exhale slowly.

"So you know about them?"

"Sure do. There's also the possibility of a revocable trust. Most folk want that in place too. It'd be best if Rita could come in to the office herself, or with Ellen, if that's what she'd prefer."

"Think she might. Rita spends a lot of time at the nursing home with Dick these days. He doesn't know her half the time, but she can't seem to let go." Travis pulled on his beard, then scratched his ear. "Tough when it gets to that stage. Ellen wants to help, but there's not much she can do."

"Yeah." The two men paused to dig into their meals. When they'd finished eating, Tom changed the conversation.

"So how's Ellen treating you?"

"Couldn't be better. This town – and Ellen – have saved my life."

"You were married before?"

Travis' face closed up, and Tom regretted the question.

"Better go." Travis tossed some notes on the table, rose and left. Tom scratched his head. What had he said? He'd no idea the man was so sensitive. Writers – they were a different breed. Why, the man didn't even hunt or fish, just seemed to sit at his computer all day, or rode around on that bike of his.

Tom wiped his mouth with a napkin and called for the check. He had a mountain of work to get through before he could go home. On the way to his pickup, his cell rang. He checked it. Blast! What did Simone want now? Since Janet died five years ago, it seemed Simone kept tabs on him almost every day. Sometimes he wondered whether it was her own neediness rather than concern for her dad that prompted the calls.

"Hi sweetie, what's up?" He juggled the phone and his keys as he opened the pickup's door and turned on the engine, immediately transferring the call to the vehicle's speaker. As he drove back to the office, he let Simone's voice wash over him, listening to one word in ten and uttering platitudes in response to her remarks. They seemed to satisfy her, as when he finally reached the office and said, "Honey, I need to go now. I've an appointment," she merely said, "Take care, Dad," and hung up.

It irked him that both the kids imagined he was useless on his own, but whereas Brad left him to his own devices apart from the odd email, Simone pestered him with calls about nothing. He should be grateful he guessed. She missed Janet too, probably more than he did. He sighed. Janet's death had come as a release. Her final illness had taken its toll on both of them. She'd been ready to go, and he'd had time to come to terms with her death. But Simone still found it difficult to accept and wanted more from Tom than he was able, or prepared, to give.

It was a relief to walk into the familiar office.

"Hey Tom, your two o'clock's running late. Can I get you a coffee?" Gwen, his receptionist greeted him as he stepped through the door. Tom smiled and shook his head. The plump middle-aged woman had been his office assistant since he set up this office some twenty years ago. He didn't know what he'd do without her.

Tom walked into his inner sanctum and sat down at his desk, the solid wooden piece of furniture and round-backed chair welcoming him like a comfy old shoe. His gaze roved around the room, moving over the case of stuffed fish, the photos of him and the guys with their guns, pretending to be big-time game hunters, when the most they ever managed to shoot were a few deer, or ducks in the season. He remembered that day as if it had been yesterday. He'd come home to find Janet curled up in pain. She'd had the photo framed in one of her bouts of remission. Her caring was all around him, in the neat arrangement of photos, the runner on the top of the credenza, the special blue vase Gwen kept filled with fresh flowers, just as Janet used to. But instead of bringing him grief, it comforted him, wrapped round him in a protective coating. Shit, he was getting sentimental in his old age. He rubbed his eyes, his elbow catching on a pile of books and knocking them to the floor.

"You okay in there?" Gwen called through the doorway. "Need anything?"

"I'm fine." As he replaced the pile, Tom cursed his clumsiness. Travis' request had got him thinking. A living will and a revocable trust was something he recommended to all his elderly clients. Maybe he needed them too. You never knew what was round the corner, and he wasn't getting any younger. He imagined Simone's reaction if he tried to speak with her about it. She'd no doubt imagine he was at death's door and she was about to lose another parent. Instead of which it was just good sense to think ahead.

Tom stood up and went into his washroom – another innovation Janet had insisted on. "You need somewhere private right off your office," she'd said, and before he knew it, the builders were in and it was done. Feeling slightly foolish, he examined himself in the mirror. Six foot something, wide shoulders, still pretty trim, only a bit of spare flesh around the midriff. He pulled his stomach in. That looked better. He frowned. What on earth was he up to? Who cared what he looked like? A sixty-two year-old man checking himself out as if he were in his twenties. Just as well Gwen hadn't chosen now to pop in. She'd be calling the madhouse to cart him off.

Sitting down again, he leaned back in his chair, tipping it up on its back legs – a practice Janet always said would make him come to grief – when he heard the outside door open and close. A woman's high-pitched, breathy voice followed.

"Is he in, Gwen?"

Damn! He'd forgotten his first appointment for the afternoon was with the local man-eater. She'd set her sights on him, and made him squirm with her gushing and simpering. What did she want this time?

"Go right through," Gwen said, giving Tom only seconds to regain his equilibrium, pick up a pen, pull some papers together and pretend he was engrossed in studying a document. He was conscious of the slim figure hesitating in the doorway, and waited a moment before looking up and rising, hand outstretched.

"Mrs. Walker."

"Yvonne, please," she simpered, an odd sort of behavior for someone who'd never see this side of fifty again. She sat down, and Tom averted his eyes from the expanse of thigh visible through the slit in her skirt, and the cleavage revealed by the low cut blouse. Did the woman have no shame? But then what did he know? Maybe this was the latest fashion. If so, he had no taste for it.

"What can I do for you today?" Tom fiddled with his pen, hoping this wasn't going to take long. His old buddy, Alan Thompson, was planning to drop by to talk through some idea he had about low-income housing.

"Well, Tom." She smiled and crossed her legs. More flesh. Hadn't she the sense to see he wasn't interested in having a new woman in his life. And if he was, it certainly wouldn't be one as obvious as this one. He'd heard the term sixteen-sixty a while back. Fitted her to a tee. She was close to his own age and dressed and acted like someone in her late teens. He tried to concentrate on what she was saying.

"So you see," she concluded, pouting, and reminding him of a five year-old Simone when she wasn't getting her own way. "It's only fair that Greg increase his payments, isn't it? I deserve it, and if he can afford to pay for his trip to Europe with his new bimbo, he must have more than he's revealed. What do you think?"

Tom sighed. "I'll look into it, Mrs… Yvonne." He checked his watch, hoping she'd take the hint.

"I'll make another appointment, shall I?" She rose and took two steps forward. Tom winced at the thought she was going to lean over the desk, but she turned toward the door. "You must come to one of my little cocktail parties, Tom," she said coyly. "You know what they say – all work and no play makes Tom a dull boy – and we can't have that, can we? I'll be in touch."

Tom waited till he heard the external door close before striding to the outer office. "Did she…?"

"She sure did." Gwen grinned. "Next Tuesday, as usual."

Tom groaned.

Three

It was Beth's second week in Florence and she was beginning to find her way about. She'd spent the previous week driving around, getting to know this sleepy town, and had discovered some really quiet streets and quaint homes. It had been an easy decision to buy a house here. The town was a place where she could settle down, relax, make a new life.

Beth was humming to herself as she dressed in what had now almost become her uniform – jeans topped with a tee-shirt, long-sleeved shirt and a waterproof jacket. She'd found a good little clothes shop in Old Town and had managed to replenish her wardrobe. Downing a cup of her new favorite tea – a licorice concoction she'd found in the cafe by the river, which was now a special spot for her – Beth grabbed her purse. She had an appointment with her realtor at ten. The system here had been a surprise to her. Unlike Australia, here in Oregon, both buyers and sellers had an agent, and the agents negotiated with each other.

"Morning, Beth, ready to go?" The buxom blonde, wearing a pair of faded jeans and a long striped sweater topped by a padded waistcoat, her curly hair lying loose on her shoulders, didn't look anything like the realtors Beth had known back home. But neither did any of the other business people she'd met here. Florence was a casual place, and all of its inhabitants seemed to have embraced its casual dress and lifestyle.

"Hi, Julie. What have you for me today?" Beth had already inspected a few properties, but so far, none of them had been quite right. She was glad the prices seemed to be pretty low compared to home. The inheritance from her mother wouldn't stretch far. She'd need to find a job too, but she'd think of that later. The house came first.

"This one has just come on the market. I think it may be exactly what you're looking for. Ron listed it yesterday, so you'll be the first to see it. Deceased estate, so it's a bit tired. But the old lady who owned it looked after it really well. It's a well-loved home."

Beth looked at the flyer describing the house and examined the photo. It appeared to be like one of those she'd admired driving around. A rush of excitement flooded her.

"We'll take my car," Julie leant over the counter and grabbed a set of keys. "Let's go." Following the realtor outside, Beth hopped into the passenger seat of the pickup. Soon they turned off the main drag into the side streets, Julie keeping up a running commentary about the neighborhood as they went.

"This is one of the older parts of town," she said, swinging the vehicle around a corner. "It was mostly built in the 1970's. The one we're going to look at was originally part of a nursery. Lovely garden. Just wait till you see it. I guarantee you'll fall in love with it."

Beth wasn't impressed. The ebullient Julie had said that about every house they'd seen so far, and Beth had failed to fall in love with any of them. However, this one did appear promising. She wriggled in her seat, eager to reach their destination.

Beth peered out through the windscreen. Some of the homes they were passing looked pretty run down. A few had a limp American flag taking pride of place in the front yard, while others had well-kept gardens, and carefully mown lawns. Julie drew to a halt in a concrete driveway. "This is it."

Beth gazed at the house. The white painted exterior with four steps leading up to the front door appealed to her. There was an old wooden bench sitting under a window to the side of the steps, and a couple of hanging baskets with a collection of brightly colored blooms swung from the edge of the overhanging roof. Stepping onto the driveway, she stopped to admire the various rhododendron bushes in the front yard, then raised her eyes to the house again. It had a welcoming look about it, as if it was asking her to come in, to take pity on it. She tried to imagine living here, coming home each night to its welcoming warmth. She looked up and down the street. It was quiet. As she looked, a woman walked out of the house across the road and waved. Friendly, too.

"Ready?"

Beth turned back to Julie and smiled.

"Yes, please."

Julie opened the door and stood back, allowing Beth to enter first.

Walking in, Beth was amazed to discover she could look straight through the house to the garden out back. She walked across to the sliding glass door and, pushing down on the catch, slid it open. A breath of fresh air wafted in, and a white cat rubbed itself against her legs.

"Oh, you sweetie." Beth bent down to stroke the cat. "Does he come with the house?" She turned to Julie.

"I think the old lady fed it. May be a stray."

"And this garden!" Beth looked around at the well-groomed bushes, the birdfeeders hanging from two large trees, and the large gnome sitting reading on the lawn. "The owner must have loved it. Did she do it all herself?"

"I think she had a gardener, but she did love it. You can tell."

"Mmm."

"Ready to see the house now?" Julie's question startled Beth, who'd been lost in thought imagining herself spending lazy summer afternoons reading in the shade of one of the trees.

"Sure." Already in love with the garden, Beth allowed herself to be shepherded inside, where she dutifully examined the old-fashioned kitchen, the large open living area and the three bedrooms. When they came to the master bedroom, she stopped in surprise. Where she expected to find an ensuite, there was a sunroom instead, full of hanging plants and windows looking out onto the garden.

It was chock-full of white cane furniture, and walking into it was like stepping into a conservatory, with the sun warming the whole room.

"No ensuite, I'm afraid," Julie began, "but…"

"This is perfect." Beth walked back through the house and sat down in a large green armchair. From there she could see through the whole house – all except the bedrooms. Her eyes roamed around the room with its heavy wooden furniture, out to the front yard and through the kitchen to the garden. She was home. This house had been waiting for her.

Beth sat there for a full five minutes luxuriating in the feeling of peace and contentment the place brought to her. She closed her eyes, and it was as if she could hear her mother's voice, telling her she was making the right decision.

"I'd like to make an offer."

While they were completing the paperwork, Beth was wondering about the furniture. Much of it was exactly to her taste and suited the house so well. "What happens to all of this stuff?" she asked. "You said it was a deceased estate. I thought the family would have…"

Julie referred to the file of papers she'd been carrying. "Says here it's to go to an estate sale."

"What's that?"

"What it says. We have a few companies in town that deal in deceased estates. They set up the house for the sale, and buyers come along on the day and bid for items. A bit like an auction. It's big business here, with so many old people."

"So, if I want to buy any bits and pieces, I need to come to this sale?" Beth stroked the arm of her chair. It already felt familiar. And the heavy wooden sideboard, and the … She looked around imagining how she would rearrange the room. She had to have some of these pieces, they belonged here. "And the plants?"

"Them too. Everything goes."

"Everything?"

"Everything people will buy."

"Wow. So, do you know when this sale will be?"

"When the house is sold. The family wanted to wait till that happened. If this goes through, Jo'll set up the sale."

"And Jo is…?"

"Runs Green Heron Estate Sales. Been doing it for years." Julie paused to think for a moment. "Wouldn't be surprised if she'd let you have a look before the sale, put your name on the pieces you want, you know."

"Really?" Beth couldn't believe her ears. To be able to move into this house, to turn it into her new home, with much of the existing furniture. It was a dream come true. She was so busy picturing herself living there, that she had closed her ears to the sounds around her. Breaking out of her reverie, she became aware Julie was speaking again.

"Sorry. What did you say?"

"I was just asking about your own furniture. This is pretty old-fashioned. Will yours fit with it?"

"I don't have any. And this suits me." Beth saw Julie's eyes widen and hoped she wasn't going to enquire further, but the realtor had clearly met a heap of different situations because her only response was, "Right."

"So what happens now?"

"I submit your offer to the family's agent. If it's accepted, the contracts are drawn up and we're away. Shouldn't be a problem. Ron and I work together. We'll see you right."

"How long will it take?" Beth was conscious of her dwindling resources and the costs she'd incur by remaining in the motel for much longer.

"Shouldn't take too long, provided your offer is accepted. I think it will be," she added as Beth's face fell. "Then they just need to set up the sale with Jo."

"Jo. Can I go talk with her?"

"Don't see why not. I'll let you have her contact details and give her a call to expect to hear from you. Have you seen all you need?"

"Yes." Beth gave a lingering glance around the room before following Julie to the door. Once outside, she stood still again, examining the exterior of the building. A glow of happiness infused her for the first time since her mother had died. Mum would approve of this house, and Bryan would hate it. She was tempted to chuckle at the thought of what he'd say if he could see his elegant wife, dressed in such casual gear, with short gray hair and no make-up to speak of. A chill swept over her, making her shiver despite her warm outfit, at the thought of her husband. But she was safe. He'd never find her here.

*

After a quick lunch, Beth was still excited about the house she'd seen. She drove by it again, stopping on the road outside and peering at the white wooden building and the lush garden. Even though the sale was still to be agreed upon, she already felt the thrill of ownership. She'd never owned her own home before. It had always been Bryan who chose where they lived, usually in order to impress others rather than somewhere she'd be happy. As a result, she'd become mistress of what she considered to be ugly monstrosities. Well, he could have them. She'd be happy with this cute little timber-sided cottage.

Beth drove off again before the neighbors became curious, but she was unsettled. She needed to do something to cement the place in her mind. Almost without thinking she made her way to the address Julie had given her for the estate sales. To her surprise, the route took her, not to an office as she'd expected, but to a warehouse filled with furniture and other knickknacks. Pushing open the door, she was greeted by a stocky woman, not much taller than herself, her dark hair pulled back untidily from a cheerful face.

"Jo?" Beth asked warily.

"You must be the Australian lady Julie spoke about. She said you'd be dropping by. Beth isn't it?"

"That's me." Beth said, trying to hide her surprise. It seemed news traveled fast here. The thought that there would be no secrets caused her a frisson of alarm, but it was soon stifled by Jo's obvious friendliness.

"Coffee?" Jo led the way to a back office where a pot of coffee bubbled away. Beth smiled to herself. They seemed to drink an awful lot of coffee here. She wondered if she'd ever get used to it. Back home she'd enjoyed her morning cappuccino in the local café, or when meeting friends, but tea was really her beverage of choice. However, she accepted a mug of the strong brew and took a seat opposite Jo.

"Julie tells me you're buying the Browning place. Interested in some of the stuff in the sale?"

Beth nodded. "I… I didn't ship over any of my own things," she said, hoping that would be sufficient explanation. But Jo didn't appear curious.

"Some good pieces there. I was just drawing up the inventory yesterday. Since you're the buyer, I can take you through before the sale day. We can mark the pieces you want as sold, and they'll be left when the house is cleared. We clean up after ourselves too, so it'll be ready for you to move in. I have a sale tomorrow, so how about the day after, if there are no hitches?"

"That'd be good." As they walked out, Beth stopped to look around the warehouse. "You have some lovely items here," she said, reverently stroking a cream leather armchair, "and it sounds as if you're kept busy."

"Sadly, yes," Jo replied. "There are a lot of old people in the community, and when they die... Well, let's say the families don't always want to go through their effects."

"So you do all that?" Beth's eyes widened. She'd spent several days doing just that with her mother's belongings, both before she went into the nursing home and after she passed away. "I can't believe they wouldn't want to do it themselves. When my mother..." Beth's eyes misted, and she rubbed them with her knuckles. "Sorry."

"You lost her recently?" Jo's voice was gentle.

"Yes, before I left." The two stood silently, Jo in respect for Beth's loss, and Beth remembering her mother.

"Do you have a lot of staff here?" Beth asked in an attempt to change the subject, worried she was going to break down completely.

"I had a good assistant, but she's recently left town. I wonder..."

Beth felt Jo's eyes studying her.

"You wouldn't be looking for a job, would you?"

"A job? Me?" Beth could hear a squeak in her voice. "I most certainly would. Do you mean...? But you don't know me."

"I'm a good judge of character. And you've been through it. You'll be able to relate to families selling up their parents' beloved possessions. This business is as much about empathy as it is about sales. I can tell you'll be a fast learner. Bet you used your brain for something back there in Australia."

Beth gave a tight-lipped smile and looked away. Jo would never guess she'd been an ornamental wife whose life was spent at charity functions and other social events to support her husband's ambition. "I trained to be a teacher," she said after a long pause.

"There. I knew it. We'll soon knock you into shape."

While Beth was still reeling from surprise, the door opened, and a large man with a thatch of thick, faded blonde hair pushed in.

"Hi, Jo! Just wanted to check on the result of the Hart's sale. The son is hassling me. Wants it all finalized yesterday."

Beth shrank back. The man didn't appear to have noticed her.

"Tom! Mind your manners. The Hart stuff will go through this week. I'll email the details to you as usual, and his money'll be in the bank by the weekend." She turned toward Beth. "This is Beth Carson."

Tom's eyes swiveled around to focus on Beth, now trying to become invisible behind Jo. "She's moving into the Browning place, and she's going to be joining me here. Now that Maureen's left, I needed to find someone to help."

Beth took the outstretched hand and looked up into twinkling blue eyes in a careworn face. This man seemed to be the total opposite of her husband. Dressed in jeans, a yellow polo top and a padded jacket, it was difficult to work out what he might do for a living.

"Tom's our favorite local lawyer," Jo said with a grin. "Keeps us all on our toes. Isn't that right, Tom?"

Beth felt a tinge of something she couldn't quite identify.

"I wouldn't know about that." The big man smiled – a wide, sunny smile, with just a hint of sadness to it, then it was gone.

"I'll see you Thursday, then," Beth said, slipping out.

*

"So the Browning place went quickly," Tom said, stroking his chin. "I'm not acting for them. Got some fancy lawyers down from Portland. And you've got yourself a new assistant?"

"Yes. Made the decision on the spur of the moment, but I'm pretty sure she'll work out. She…"

"She's the sort to fit in," Tom finished for her, pulling on his ear. He'd only caught a glimpse of the woman before she left, but he'd sensed something vulnerable about her, with an underlying core of steel.

"She's from Australia. Lost her mother recently."

"Australia? That's a fair stretch." For a fleeting moment he wondered what had brought her across the world. Maybe she had connections here. If she had, Jo would soon find out. Not what you'd call a snoop, Jo had a way of gaining people's confidence. But she wouldn't spread it around. She could be pretty tight-lipped, something he'd had reason to be grateful for himself, more than once. "Well, better be getting along. I was just passing."

"Before you go…"

Tom stopped in the act of opening the door, and turned with a rueful grin. With Jo, there was always one more thing.

"Sunday. The fair at the church. You'll be there?"

Shit! He'd completely forgotten. Looked like the weather would be fine, and a day on the lake – just him and his rod – was what he was planning. His doubt must have shown on his face, because Jo laid a hand on his arm.

"Rob could sure do with a hand at the barbecue," she said in the winning tone not many men in Florence would refuse. Rob was a lucky guy.

"You've twisted my arm."

Tom mentally farewelled his lazy day on the water. Maybe he could manage a few hours in the late afternoon. Saturday was out as Simone had indicated she'd be driving down from Portland to 'make sure my old dad is doing okay'. This meant a grilling over every detail of his personal life, plus her rummaging around in his cupboards to ensure he was 'looking after himself properly'. While he was grateful for her concern and enjoyed seeing her and the boys, he'd dearly like some time to himself.

"Great. We'll see you at eight. I'll let Rob know."

"Hmm." Tom knew he'd be seeing Rob himself before that. They were both members of the gun club and would be having their usual session at the clubhouse the following evening. Rob could have asked him then. But that wasn't the way it was done. It was the women who made the arrangements and the men fitted in as best they could. This is where he missed Janet. If she'd been alive, Jo would never have mentioned the fair to Tom. She and Janet would have made all the arrangements. And I'd have ended up there at the barbecue just the same, he thought.

Tom took his time walking back to the office. From memory, his next appointment was with Rita and Ellen Williams. Odd Ellen hadn't changed her name when she and Travis married. His Janet would no more have retained her maiden name than… But Ellen and Travis were well into their fifties. Maybe that made a difference. If he were to re-marry, would…? No, he wouldn't go there. He wasn't interested in another wife. He spent enough time fighting off the local biddies who were on the prowl. He laughed to himself, imagining them like cats in the night, howling for a mate. It wasn't too far from the truth, and they'd be out in force at the fair on Sunday.

Ellen and Rita were sitting in the outer office when he arrived and made to rise.

"Give me a minute," he said, gesturing to Gwen to follow him in.

She closed the door behind her, and referred to the notebook in her hand. "Two calls from Mrs. Walker, wanting an urgent appointment. I managed to stave her off, but she'll be on again this afternoon I'll be bound. A call from your daughter to remind you about Saturday. She said to tell you your grandsons are looking forward to seeing Grandpa Tom, and Matt Robinson rang to see if the fish were biting tomorrow. That's all." She looked up with a smile.

Tom rubbed his hand over the top of his head. All? It was enough. And damn that Walker woman. Did she think he had nothing to do but listen to her whinging and whining, coupled with her revealing more than someone of her age ought? But Matt's call was a welcome one. He must have read Tom's mind.

"Tomorrow," he said. "Can you check the diary?"

"Already did, and managed to reschedule a couple of things. You're good to go."

"Thanks, Gwen." She proved her worth to him over and over again. A day's fishing tomorrow would break up the week nicely and almost make up for his commitment on Sunday. "You can show Ellen and Rita in now."

When the two women entered, Tom was sitting behind his desk, but he immediately came around it to shake their hands, before encouraging them to be seated and returning to his own seat.

"Now, ladies. Travis mentioned you'd like to arrange for a living will, Rita?" He met the older woman's eyes, noting she appeared unsure.

"Well, I thought… with Dick…"

"How is the old rascal?" Tom asked to help Rita relax. He could see her twisting her hands in her lap.

"Some days are better than others. But on his better days…" Her eyes dropped to examine her hands.

"He wants to come home," Ellen finished for her, taking one of her mother's hands in hers.

"It's a raw deal he got," Tom said picking up his pen and twirling it. "Falling off his ATV like that. A mercy your Travis found him," he added, looking at Ellen.

Ellen blushed, but said nothing. Rita seemed to pull herself together. "It was all of the same thing," she said. "His mind was beginning to wander even before… Now, let's get this done. We came to get this living will stuff sorted out, and Travis said you mentioned something about a reversible trust?"

"A revocable trust. That's right. Many of my clients who put a living will in place, also choose to set up a revocable trust. It's a way of transferring assets to your heirs without it going through probate. Speeds the process up."

"And is that what Maddy has?" Rita spoke to her daughter, who looked at Tom.

"It surely is." He waited, knowing from experience there was no sense in hurrying this process.

"It's your decision, Mom," Ellen said, still holding her mother's hand.

"Maybe you'd like to think it over?"

"You've got the papers there?" Rita asked, dragging her hand back from Ellen's grasp.

"Right here." Tom pulled a sheaf of papers towards him from the side of his desk.

The next half hour was taken up with Tom explaining the documents, and the two women signing them.

"Now what about Ron?" he asked. Your son should be a signatory too, as he's mentioned here.

"Will it be all right if he comes in by himself?" Ellen asked. "Mom spends most days with Dad at the nursing home, and Ron being up there in Yachats – he doesn't often get down this way."

"That'll be fine." Tom gathered up the papers, and putting them into a file, dropped them into his filing cabinet. "They'll be right here when he comes, and I sure hope we don't have to activate any of them for a long time yet."

"But it's best to be sure. I feel better about things now, knowing that...." But Rita couldn't finish her sentence.

The two women rose to leave.

"Will we see you at the church fair on Sunday?" Rita asked.

"Wouldn't miss it for the world," Tom said, tongue firmly in his cheek.

23

Four

Sunday dawned fine and sunny. Tom stretched his arms above his head as he stood by the window and gazed out at the lake, calm and smooth in the bright morning light. He poured his first coffee of the day, a sense of well-being infusing him as he sipped what was to him the nectar of the gods. It would be glorious out on the lake today. He could feel the sun on his back, hear the warbling of the birds and the slap, slap of the water against the side of his boat. For a moment he was tempted to ignore the fair and take the boat out. Spend the day alone. But common sense prevailed. He knew he couldn't let old Rob down.

Breaking a couple of eggs into the pan and sliding a few strips of bacon around them, he began to whistle. Maybe it wouldn't be so bad. At least Simone wouldn't be there to nag at him. He thought back to the previous day, when his daughter had arrived with her two boys in tow.

"Dad! Are you sure you're looking after yourself?" was her greeting, and it had gone on from there. Apart from some fun playing with the boys, Tom had been subjected to her nagging and carping for the duration of her visit. "Why are you still burying yourself here in Florence?" "Why don't you come to live near us? You could set up practice anywhere." "Why do you still need to work? Surely at your age, you can take it easy?"

When Janet had been alive, there was no mention of them 'Burying themselves in Florence'. Simone seemed to enjoy getting away from the city and visiting them by the ocean, taking time to relax. But now…

Tom suspected his daughter really wanted him close by, so she could use him to babysit while she and Ed went gallivanting, or she spent time in her endless charitable endeavors. Well, that wasn't going to happen. He was settled here. His business was here, his friends were here. What would he do in a city like Portland?

Rinsing out his plate and mug, and placing them to drain by the sink, he glanced over at the dishwasher. Simone had left it full of dishes last night, and it had taken him ages to empty it this morning. Living alone, he found he didn't use many of the gadgets Janet had loved. His meals were simple, and one plate and mug did him. He couldn't see the point of dirtying a whole lot of stuff when it just had to be washed anyway.

Tom hopped into the car and drove off. His route took him along the lake, which glistened in the early morning air. As he drove past the boatshed, he saw a few of the guys getting ready to set off. Half their luck!

He soon reached the main road, and his mind turned to the task ahead. He wasn't a church-goer, but Janet had always supported it. Seemed to be the same for most of the women. They'd be out in force today, the married ones with their husbands trailing behind. It was for a good cause, though. He'd read in the paper that this year's proceeds were to go to the new women's shelter. He shook his head in disbelief that there was a need for such places here in Florence. He'd always considered it to be a safe community, but everywhere had its bad apples, and women had been victims over the centuries. Florence was no different, really.

All too soon he arrived at the park where the event was to be held. Even though he was early, the tents and stalls were already being set up, and the banner at the gate proclaimed the fair open. Finding a place to park, he headed towards the far end of the field where he could see Rob and a couple of other guys setting up the barbecue.

"Hey, Tom. Good to see you." Rob strode forward, hand outstretched.

"Doesn't look as if you need me after all," Tom replied, indicating the two behind Rob.

"I certainly do. These two are only helping set up. Matt's doing the tombola and Bert is down for the lucky dip barrel. It's just you and me, pal. Hope you're up to it."

"Right." Tom heaved a sigh. For a moment he'd thought he could slip away, but it looked as if he was stuck here for the day.

"Here you are." Tom's eyes bulged at the sight of the large apron emblazoned with a pair of women's boobs and a tiny G-string.

"You expect me to wear that?" He gingerly took hold of the offending garment with the tips of his fingers, as if it might bite.

"It's all for a bit of a laugh. I have one too." And Rob proceeded to don his own garish outfit.

"Okay." Tom held the apron against him, slipped the loop over his head and tied the strings behind his waist. Maybe he could offer to do all the cooking. That way he'd have his back to everyone, and they wouldn't see what a fool he looked.

"Loosen up, man." Rob slapped him on the back. "It's not about you. It's about the women we're raising money for – abused, alcoholic, homeless. We have too many of them, and the money we're raising is going to provide some much needed help."

"You're right. I need to chill." Tom rubbed his hands together. "Where do you want me to start?"

*

Beth slid her car into what appeared to be the last parking spot and gazed around. It seemed everyone in Florence was here today. She'd read about the fair in the local paper and decided to pay a visit. The cause was one dear to her heart, and it would give her a chance to suss out the locals. So far the only people she'd spoken to, bar a few shopkeepers, were Julie, her realtor, and Jo at the estate sales.

Stepping out of the car, she grabbed her purse and began strolling towards the first row of stalls. As she wandered along, picking up and discarding several items of giftware and clothing, she could hear the shouts and yells of children, enjoying the various rides. She was examining some jars of homemade chutney and trying to decide between the mango and chilli and the apple, cranberry and orange, when a warm voice from behind startled her.

"How are you settling in?"

Beth turned round so quickly, she almost over-balanced. A firm hand steadied her. Beth's eyes met a pair of concerned brown ones.

"Sorry if I surprised you. We met a few weeks ago. In the bookshop."

"Yes, I remember. Ellen, isn't it?"

"And you're Beth."

Unlike their earlier meeting, Beth felt a warmth in Ellen's presence, or maybe it was only the sun shining on her. She smiled. "I'm getting to know the place, thanks. I've bought a house and found a job. I've been meaning to come back to your shop, but…" *Now why did I say that? If I've thought of her shop at all, it's been with some misgivings. I got real spooked last time.* "I'm enjoying the book. I think you mentioned your husband wrote it? It's a real page-turner," she said.

"He's pretty good, isn't he? He should be around here somewhere. We came over on his bike, and I left him to park it." She gazed around. "Oh, there he is," she said in a relieved voice, pointing to a blonde man with long hair, beard and moustache, wearing jeans and a shabby fringed jacket. "Do drop into The Reading Nook again soon. You need to talk." She strode off, a magnificent figure in her tight jeans, loose cheesecloth shirt and red boots, her plait swinging on her shoulders.

Beth looked after her in amazement. Had she heard correctly? Did Ellen really say 'You need to talk', not 'We need to talk.'? And what would they have to talk about anyway? Books? Shaking her head in bewilderment, Beth looked down at her hands, which were still gripping the two jars of chutney. "I'll take both of these," she said, handing them to the stallholder and rummaging in her purse for some cash.

Swinging the bag with the two jars in it, Beth continued wandering among the stalls. She collected a cute owl ornament and a couple of books about the Oregon National Parks, before the scent of frying onions and sizzling meat drew her to where a line was forming in front of a barbecue. Joining onto the end, Beth prepared to wait while enjoying the chitchat of the two women in front of her.

"Tom's ripe for the picking," twittered one. "Janet's been gone five years now. That's quite long enough for a man to be on his own. He'll be missing home-cooked food. I'll be bound."

"I think he's already taken," the other replied archly. "Yvonne says…"

"More than her prayers," her friend laughed. "But she does seem to have her foot in that particular door."

At that point the line moved on, and the two women moved out of range. Beth idly wondered who the poor man was. Seemed the gossip mill was alive and well here in Florence. Not much different from home.

By the time Beth reached the front of the line she was really hungry, and the burger with onion rings looked like ambrosia. Seeing the sign *Burgers $4,* she pulled four dollar notes from her purse, and looking up, did a double take at the wild apron in front of her.

"Sorry about this." The man waved a spatula at the garment. "All part of the fun. Burger, ma'am?"

"Yes, please." Beth handed over the notes and studied the man turning away from her to fetch the burger. He looked familiar. But she didn't know anyone here, so how…?

"Here you are. Enjoy."

As their fingers almost touched, he seemed to observe Beth more closely. "Aren't you the lady who bought the Browning place – and who's going to be working with Jo?"

How did he…? Then Beth remembered. Of course, he was the man who'd arrived just as she was about to leave Green Heron Estate Sales. She felt a blush rise to her cheeks, remembering how she'd tried to hide behind Jo, then had slid quickly out.

"Yes, that's me," she said, dropping her eyes and beginning to turn away.

"Good to see you again. Enjoy the fair." Beth rushed off, found a bench and took a deep breath. She was shaking and not sure why. The guy was only being polite. If she remembered correctly he was a local lawyer, a pillar of the community, no doubt. But so was Bryan, a little voice reminded her. She bit into her burger, the ketchup squirting out onto her chin. She wiped it with her other hand and munched slowly. It tasted good. Different from those back home, but good, nevertheless.

*

Tom's eyes followed the diminutive figure walking quickly away. Seemed he'd scared her off again. He'd been surprised when she'd left Jo's so soon after his arrival, now this. He scratched his head. He wasn't used to women avoiding him. It piqued his interest. Her feisty little gray-haired image stayed in his mind for the rest of the afternoon as he served burgers and joked with the patrons. He wasn't sure why, but he was intrigued by this Australian woman. She wasn't much to look at, but he sensed there was more to her than what appeared on the surface. Slap on a bit of make-up and put her in one of those fancy outfits, and she'd give anyone a run for their money. He stopped short. What was he thinking? He spent most of his days avoiding women. How was it that this one – who seemed determined to avoid him – had made such an impression?

"Thanks, Tom. A good result, eh?" Rob punched him gently on the shoulder, as the crowds began to disperse. "I think we're done here."

Tom removed the apron with relief. But it hadn't been too bad – got a few laughs and sold a few more burgers. He got started with Rob to clean the barbecue, before packing up for the day.

"Stay for a beer?"

Tom hesitated. He'd been hoping to get home in time to have a couple of hours out on the lake. Just him and the fish. Maybe he could snag a trout for dinner. He'd not had much luck on Wednesday with the guys, but Matt had managed to draw in a couple of perch.

"Just a couple," Rob persisted. "What d'you have to go home to?"

Tom winced. That was the trouble with people. None of them could understand that he actually enjoyed his own company. He was trying to work out a reply that wouldn't offend old Rob, when he felt his cell vibrate.

"Just a mo', Rob." He took it out, seeing Brad's face beaming out at him. Must be something serious for his son to be calling him. Usually Brad restricted his communication to the odd text or email.

"Hi there. What's up?"

"Dad." Brad's voice bubbled with excitement, unlike his usual measured tone. "There's someone I'd like you to meet. I'd like to bring her over. Tonight?"

"Tonight? You want to drive over from Eugene now?" Tom checked his watch. It was close to six, so they'd arrive around seven. Bang went any chance of fishing. He sighed. Another takeaway dinner.

"Dad, are you still there?" Brad's voice broke in. "Brooke and I…"

"Brooke. Is she…?"

"We'll tell all when we arrive. See you then."

Tom regarded the now silent cell with suspicion, then met Rob's curious eyes. "Looks like I'll have to give the beer a miss. Young Brad's on his way over with a lady friend." He shrugged at Rob's raised eyebrows and made his way back to the parking lot. This was a turn up for the books. First Brad actually calling his father, then wanting to bring over a female to meet him. Over the years, Tom and Janet had debated their son's lack of interest in the female of the species. A successful lawyer in his own right, Brad had chosen to enter local government in Eugene rather than join his father's practice, or set up his own office. Now he was a valued member of the City Prosecutor's Office and had high hopes of becoming a judge. But women had never featured in his life. At least, not any he cared to share with his parents.

Driving home, Tom recalled the many times he and Janet had tried to talk with Brad about his love life. He'd neatly evaded all such discussion – to such an extent they'd sometimes wondered if their macho son was gay. Now, here he was at the ripe old age of thirty-five bringing home a girl. Brooke. The name conjured up a picture of an old-fashioned girl, one such as his mother would have approved. Tom felt a touch of moisture come to his eyes. How Janet would have loved to see her. What a pity Brad hadn't managed to find himself a partner before his mom had died. But these matters couldn't be rushed. He'd have a quick beer himself when he got home, then heat up one of these chicken pot pies he'd picked up at Fred Meyer and throw some salad on a plate to accompany it. He'd snacked on a few burgers at the fair, so that should see him through.

Having a quick shower to remove the sweat of the day, it suddenly occurred to Tom he should make some sort of preparations for Brad and his Brooke's visit. As he toweled himself dry, he took a mental inventory of the contents of the pantry and fridge. Since Janet had gone, he'd stopped stocking up on those little delicacies women liked: the fancy biscuits, the cheeses, the sweet cakes. He'd maintained a supply of beer, wine, and Coke and the corn chips he favored himself. Plus, he thought he remembered seeing a packet of chocolate biscuits in the back of the pantry, but god knows how long they'd been there. Probably should be thrown out. He was still thinking about this and pulling on a fresh shirt and pants, when he heard a car pull in. Christ, they were here already! Dragging a hand through his hair, Tom walked down the stairs to greet them.

"Dad, this is Brooke." Brad pulled forward his companion, and Tom gasped. This girl was in her early twenties. Almost as tall as Brad and slim, her long black hair rippled down her back, and a wide smile beamed out from a pale white face. Her knee-length flowery skirt combined with a skimpy top made her look like a model from one of those fashion magazines Simone used to pore over.

"Mr. Harrison. Brad's told me so much about you."

"Tom, please call me Tom."

She stretched out a hand, a sparkler on the engagement finger, and, as he grasped it, her lips brushed his cheek lightly. It was a long time since Tom had felt the touch of a woman's lips, and he was conscious of a flowery fragrance that reminded him of Janet.

"Pleased to meet you. You have the advantage on me. I can't say Brad's mentioned you."

"I was waiting till…," Brad blustered, blushing. "I didn't know… That is…"

"Silly boy." Brooke wagged a finger at him. "You knew how I felt about you. But it took him so long to come to the point, Mr… Tom. Has he always been so slow?"

Tom laughed at that, then led the pair into the house. Well, no shrinking violet here. Brooke might be almost half Brad's age, but she sure had his measure. What would Janet think of her? And Simone?

"Does your sister know?"

"No, not yet. We thought…" Brad twisted his hands in an action developed as a young child. He'd always been in awe of his older sister, who liked to think she knew what was best for her little brother. Seemed some things never changed.

"Well, come on in. I see celebrations are called for." He noted Brooke glance down shyly at her ring. "I'm afraid I haven't many supplies for…"

"We brought this." Brad leant into the car and pulled out a bottle of pink champagne with a flourish. "I thought your drink supply might not stretch to bubbly."

"Hmm. Seems you've thought of everything. I do have some corn chips. Maybe…?"

"That'd be lovely, Tom." Brooke smiled and followed him into the kitchen, where he managed to find three champagne glasses from the set he remembered making an appearance every Christmas.

"Good old Dad. Let's go out to the deck, and you can see the lake." Having deposited the bottle on the kitchen bench, Brad led his fiancée outside and threw an arm around her shoulder, pointing out the scenes from his childhood.

Tom set the bottle and the three glasses on a tray and opened a packet of corn chips, emptying them out into a bowl, before joining the others outside. It was a few moments before they detected his presence behind them, giving him time to study the pair. Seeing them there, so young and happy, their whole life ahead of them, brought back memories of when he and Janet had moved here. The children had been little then, and purchasing this house on the lake had been a big step. They'd taken the risk, hoping his practice would grow to support the huge mortgage they'd incurred. The risk had been justified, and now he could relax. It was all his, and held so many memories. Simone didn't seem to understand that. Maybe Brad did.

Brad turned and just for a second, with the evening sun lighting up his hair like a halo, Tom was reminded of the little boy who had enjoyed playing right here on the wooden deck. Then it was gone, and the grown-up Brad was speaking. "Want me to pour, Dad?"

"Sure." Tom sat down, and the two young people joined him.

"So," he began, unsure what to say next, but he needn't have worried. Brooke had plenty of words. He leant back and listened, taking occasional sips from his glass. She babbled on about how she and Brad met – at a jazz concert – her job – as a buyer in a fashion store – and their plans for an autumn wedding. They weren't going to waste any time.

"And Mom's widowed, just like you. Dad died when I was little, so she's had the challenge of bringing me up by herself." She paused, and her glance took in the house, the deck, the view. "You must get lonely rattling around here all on your own." She gave Tom a sly look over the top of her wineglass.

"I think Dad likes it that way," Brad said.

"You're right, son. I miss your mom, of course. But I've gotten used to doing for myself. I enjoy the solitary life here." Tom sighed and drained his glass.

By the time the young couple finally rose to take their leave, it was completely dark, the moon hidden behind clouds.

"Good to see you, son, and to meet you, Brooke." Tom hugged Brad and was surprised to have Brooke envelop him in a warm hug too, her cheek soft against his own, rough from a day's growth.

"We're going to be family soon, Tom," she said. Why did he feel Brooke was being overly familiar? She was right. She was going to be his daughter-in-law. But still…

"So, you'll let Simone know, Dad?" Brad hovered in the doorway. Tom blinked. He hadn't expected this.

"Won't you want to talk with her yourself?"

"Sure, but if you can pave the way, that'd be great."

Tom frowned. He was being used as the go-between again, just like when the kids were little and he'd been called upon to settle an argument. "If that's what you want."

"Thanks, Dad. Knew I could count on you."

"And we must get you and Mom together." Brooke's voice carried over the still evening air. Then they were off, and Tom was left scratching his head. Something was going on here, something he didn't understand.

Five

"I have a sale today. Why don't you come along? You'll learn more about what we do there than you will sitting here in the warehouse."

Beth looked up in surprise. The first week in her new job had consisted of her familiarising herself with the goods on sale and trying to get an idea of the prices of the various objects and pieces of furniture. Jo had been out 'on-site' as she called it, setting up and pricing items for her next sale. She'd assumed today would be another day spent in the warehouse, so Jo's invitation was unexpected.

"Are you sure? I don't expect I'll be much help."

"Of course you will. It's a matter of being empathetic and dealing with cash sales. I'd like you to sit with the cashbox while I do the actual selling. Most people have an idea of what they're looking for, apart from the few neighbors who just want to see what's there, and the lonely ones for whom it's a day out."

Beth gulped. How morbid to think there were people who took pleasure from peering at a deceased person's belongings, but there was no accounting for tastes. She wished there had been a business like this back home. When she'd had to sort out her mother's belongings, it had been a matter of having a garage sale or advertising the larger items. Beth had taken what she viewed as the easy way out and had called one of the large charities to pick up most of the stuff which had accumulated over the years. It was sad how one person's treasures became another's clutter when the owner was no longer there to value them. She'd kept a few mementoes of Audrey and had brought them with her – a china rose bowl, a delicate figurine and a favorite metal trivet, but all the rest had gone.

"You ready?" While Beth was musing, Jo had been picking up a box.

"Sure. Can I take something?"

"Get that box over there. And don't forget your purse. You may see something you like in this sale too. We'll take the pickup."

Beth followed Jo out and, dumping the heavy carton in the back, settled into the passenger seat.

By the time they reached their destination, quite a crowd had gathered, reminiscent of the home auctions, or garage sales of Beth's experience. The pair had to push their way through, with Jo reminding everyone that the sale didn't start for another half-hour.

"Is it always like this?" Beth asked as they carried the boxes in.

"Pretty much. This is a big one, so it's drawn a lot of attention, but the estate sales are quite an attraction around here. Now you can set up with the cashbox right here at the door." Jo pointed to a card table strategically placed in the doorway. "I'll get the show on the road."

To Beth's surprise, Jo set up an iPod and soon the house was filled with soft music. She then moved around the room, lighting a number of candles. By the time she'd finished, the place resembled a church more than a deceased estate.

Her surprised expression must have given her away because Jo touched her lightly on the arm. "It's important we're respectful."

"Mmm." Beth couldn't think of anything else to say, but she knew right there and then that she'd made the correct decision in accepting the position with Jo and Green Heron Estate Sales.

The day passed peacefully, with many of those who came telling Beth how much they had liked the old lady who lived there. When the last of them had gone, she helped Jo check out the remaining items against the inventory.

"What happens to these?" she asked.

"The good stuff goes back to my sale rooms, the rest will be picked up by the owner's nominated charity." Jo checked her file. "In this case it's the Florence Goodwill Store. Most choose that one. Now let's get started. We can probably fit all the stuff we need to take into the back of the pickup."

There wasn't much conversation while the two lifted the remaining items into the vehicle, but once they were on their way, Jo turned to Beth. "Well, how did you find the day? Think you can handle it?"

"I loved it." Beth smiled. "But, are there just the two of us? How did you manage to get everything set up so beautifully?"

Jo laughed. "No. We'll be the mainstay. But I have a few other women who help out from time to time. Cicely and Betty are an elderly pair who have a real feel for that part of the work, and my daughter Marie helps out in the shop when she can. With two little ones, she can't get away as often as she'd like. This is all down to Cicely and Betty."

"And are you the only estate sales business in town?"

"Dear me no. There are a few of us, and plenty of business to go around. I have a sale most weeks, and that's enough to keep me in business. Don't they have businesses like this where you're from?"

"Not that I'm aware of. We have the usual charity shops, but nothing on this scale."

"Here we are." Jo drew into the parking lot outside the warehouse. "Fancy a coffee? We can unpack later."

"That would be good," Beth replied, even though she knew the coffee would be strong and black. If she was going to live here, she might have to get used to it.

The two were settled in the back room of the store with large mugs of strong black coffee – just as Beth had foreseen – when Jo uttered the last words Beth wanted to hear, "Now, tell me about yourself." Beth took a large gulp of her coffee to delay her reply, but Jo's curiosity couldn't be ignored for long.

Holding her mug in both hands, Beth gazed into the dark liquid for a moment, while working out what to say, before looking up to meet Jo's eyes.

"I lost my mother recently. I think I already told you that. Well, when I was going through her belongings, I found these postcards of Florence. I wouldn't have known where they were from, but on the back of each was written Florence, Oregon." She took a sip.

"Did she come from here?"

"No. Australian, born and bred. Her parents were from the States, but I never heard her mention Florence. I don't know if she ever came here. She always encouraged me to travel, so I decided on this trip, and here I am."

"But it's not just a trip, is it? You've bought a house."

Beth blushed, gave a tight-lipped smile and looked away. "Yes. I heard from Julie today. The sale should go through this week, so I'll be able to move in."

"She was in touch with me too. We've scheduled the estate sale for next weekend. Would you like to be involved – or would that be too weird?"

"I'd rather not." Although she'd enjoyed the sale today, Beth couldn't imagine sitting in what would be her own home, hearing the soft music and seeing people turning over all the items for sale. It would be a bit like sitting in a church, then moving into it.

Beth could see Jo was going to say something else, but at that moment her cell rang. "You get going," Jo said as she picked up the phone. "See you tomorrow."

Beth walked out. As she closed the door behind her, she noticed the still laden pickup and almost went back in to offer to help unload. She hesitated, then moved off. It was safe enough there, and if Jo had wanted help, she wouldn't have sent her off. It was too early to go home – Beth was still trying to get used to these long light evenings – so she wandered further into Old Town and stopped in front of The Reading Nook.

She remembered Ellen's words at the fair. It was as if something was drawing her here. Beth pushed open the door.

"Hello," Ellen's voice greeted her. "So you decided to come?"

Beth didn't reply immediately. She hadn't consciously made a decision. She'd been drawn here, as if by some unseen force.

"I…"

"It's almost closing. Why don't you join me across the road for a coffee?" She pointed to the coffee shop Beth had found on her first day in town.

"I… I've just had a coffee." After the strong one with Jo, the last thing she felt like was another of the same.

"That's okay. They have some great herbal teas there, too. Have you tried their Licorice Spice?" Ellen's eyes met Beth's with an intensity she couldn't look away from. "I know you need to talk with me," she said, repeating the words from the fair, which had perplexed Beth then, and did so even more now. The two women walked across the road together.

"I'll get them," Ellen said, leaving Beth to find a spot on the deck. She sat gazing at the river while Ellen placed the order. What was she doing here? Was she in for yet another interrogation? She'd managed to deflect Jo's questions, but had a feeling Ellen's wouldn't be so easy to avoid.

"Here we are." Ellen placed two large cups on the table along with a plate of cookies. Beth could smell the spicy licorice wafting towards her, and looked gratefully at the cookies. She hadn't taken time for lunch. She braced herself for Ellen's questions.

"So you're from Australia?" asked Ellen. "I have an Australian cousin. It's a long story, but she's living here right now – up at Seal Rock with her partner. Which part do you hail from?"

While relieved to be spared more intrusive personal questions, Beth tensed at this news. Someone else from Australia? Here? What if…?

"Sydney," she said shortly, beginning to tremble.

"That's somewhere in New South Wales, isn't it? Jenny's from Queensland. Noosa?"

"Yes, it's a lovely holiday venue. I haven't been there." Beth drew a sigh of relief. There was little chance this Jenny would know anyone she or Bryan knew.

Ellen reached across to cover Beth's hand with hers. "You've had a challenging time," she said. "And it's not over yet, but there *is* a silver lining. You're stronger than you know and you'll get through this. Don't ignore your chance at happiness when it comes, Beth. Make sure you recognize it. Don't be afraid to take a risk."

Beth's eyes were becoming wider and wider as Ellen spoke. When she finished and removed her hand, Beth gripped both of her own under the table. "What…? I don't…"

Ellen laughed gently. "I'm sorry. I know I can sometimes freak people out."

"But how do you…?"

"How do I know? I see things, sense them really. It's something I've grown up with, learned to live with. I don't see details, just get a general impression. And I'm always right," Ellen smiled.

"Now," she said, leaning her elbows on the table. "What have you been up to here in Florence? I know you went to the fair yesterday. What else have you been doing? Are you settling in?"

Relieved Ellen seemed to be acting normally again, Beth gradually loosened her grip, picked up a cookie, took a bite, and chewed carefully before replying.

"I love it here," she smiled. "I've bought a house and found myself a job."

"Already? You've been busy."

"I started work a couple of weeks ago – at Green Heron Estate Sales. Do you know it?"

"With Jo? You'll be fine with her. She's had that business for years. Have you experience in that sort of thing?"

"Not really."

"But you lost someone recently. Someone dear to you."

"My mother." Beth was beginning to feel edgy again and started fidgeting in her chair. She picked up her cup and drained it. "I really must go," she said, rising. "Thanks for the tea and cookie. It's been good meeting you again." She hurried out of the café and walked briskly back to the motel. What was it about the woman that made her uncomfortable? She was perfectly nice and polite, but she had this way of getting right under Beth's skin.

*

Tom held the phone away from his ear. He wished he'd never agreed to share Brad's news with his daughter.

"Simone! Calm down. Brooke seems to be a nice girl. She's a bit more outgoing than Brad. May be good for the lad."

"I'll bet. Twenty-something, you say? Sounds like a gold-digger to me. And it seems she pulled the wool over your eyes, too. We've got to stop this, before it goes too far."

"Steady on. The pair are engaged. Planning an autumn wedding. What do you think you can do to stop it?" Tom walked over to the fridge as he was talking, tucked the phone into his shoulder and opened a can of Coors. He knew he should have refused and let Brad do his own dirty work, though why Simone was so incensed, he couldn't imagine. Taking a mouthful of beer, he laid down the can and rubbed his jaw. It had been the same since Janet died. Simone had taken on her role in the family. But it was time he put a stop to it. Bad enough she tried to organize Tom's life, but Brad was a grown man with every right to make his own decisions.

"I'd better meet her. I can do next Saturday. I won't bring the boys. Greg'll have to miss his golf for once. Make sure they're available. I'll be there for lunch."

Tom sighed and scratched his head as the call ended. Picking up his beer, he wandered out onto the deck. Bang went another Saturday's fishing. When had life gotten so complicated? Unbidden, the image of the little woman who'd bought the Browning place appeared in his mind's eye. Now that *would* be something for Simone to worry about. He grinned to himself as he downed the rest of the beer and went to the fridge for another.

Six

The fish'll be jumping today, Tom thought as he opened his eyes to the sun streaming in the window. But no. As his feet hit the floor, he remembered this was the day Simone had agreed to come to meet with Brad and his lady and Tom had promised to provide lunch for the trio, so fishing was out. Still it was early, maybe he could fit in a few hours on the water before they arrived. Simone had promised to bring something for lunch, and while it irked him that she seemed to consider him incapable of providing a suitable repast, he was glad to be spared the trouble.

He wandered downstairs, scratching his head and trying to decide what to have for breakfast, when the sunlight shining on the wooden floor caught his eye, revealing dust that he could swear wasn't there the day before. He filled a bowl with his favorite cereal, poured in a generous serving of milk and set the coffee-maker. He ate standing and looking out at the lake shimmering in the sun, feeling the familiar pull of the water. He wished the children weren't coming today, but Brad had been insistent, and once she'd heard about Brooke, Simone had sounded impatient to meet her. He hoped the meeting would go smoothly. Simone had always believed she knew what was best for her brother. Meeting Brooke would be a real test of her open-mindedness, something she wasn't renowned for. Brooke seemed a nice kid, but not one to be trifled with. Tom rubbed his chin. Perhaps Simone would meet her match, despite the difference in age.

A quick tidy up – surely the girls wouldn't expect too much from him, and Brad wouldn't notice a few specks of dust – and Tom was out on the water. This was where he could forget the worries of the week, put his work life behind him, and enjoy the peace and solitude of his favorite sport. It was also where he found himself talking with Janet without fear of being overheard and thought mad. When she was alive, Janet had often joined him on these fishing expeditions, and as the children grew, it had been a time to discuss their offspring's various schemes.

Today, he cast his line into the still water and watched the ripples form. Simone was sure to arrive full of curiosity and not a little upset that Brad had chosen to share his new love with him first. She'd never actually said so, but he knew his daughter and was sure Simone felt she and Brad had a special relationship, one which would demand he share something as special as his new love with his sister before anyone else, even his dad.

"What do you think, Janet?" he asked aloud. "How do you think our girl will cope? She's always seen herself as the chief go-to person for her brother. How will she handle the fact he's found his future wife all by himself?" Tom remembered Simone's reference to Brooke as a gold-digger and sighed. "I wish you were here, sweetheart. You'd know how to handle our girl, how to ensure Brooke feels welcomed into the family, not put through the inquisition Simone may have in mind. Though…" Tom smiled. "I suspect Brooke can give as good as she gets. Our boy has chosen a bride not unlike his big sister in nature. It might be amusing to see the resulting interaction."

Tom continued in this vein, imagining what Janet might say to reassure him, till a glance at his watch told him it was time to return, unless he wanted to be caught out here. He hadn't managed to catch anything, hadn't even had a bite, but that didn't concern him. It was the conversation, thinking things through aloud, that helped him relax. He returned to the jetty and tied up his boat feeling more prepared for the meeting to come.

He was still standing under the shower, allowing the water to pour over him, when the ringing of his cell phone forced him back into the bedroom. Dripping water onto the deep pile of the carpet, Tom was surprised to see Brad's face on the screen.

"Hi, son. What's up?" Tom patted himself ineffectually with a towel, while holding the phone in his other hand.

"Dad." Brad's voice was tentative, as if the call hadn't been his idea. "Brooke wants to know what we should bring. She thinks…," he hesitated. "She wants to help." There was a pause, and Tom could hear a female voice in the background. "Brooke wants to know what you're planning for lunch."

"Not me, son. It's Simone's show. She's bringing some stuff down from Portland. You know your sister. Wants to make an impression." *Or show who's in charge*, he thought as he finished the call. This could be amusing.

By the time he'd dressed, made his way downstairs and opened a bottle of Coors, he heard Simone's car and opened the door in time to see it throwing up dust along the road. It was a perfect Oregon morning. The air was clear with just a hint of overnight frost, the warbling of water birds filled his ears and the sun shone down, making the grass sparkle like diamonds. The vehicle drew up in a flurry, and soon Simone emerged struggling with a basket and a large box.

"Welcome, honey." Tom tried to hug his daughter, but was hampered by the box she was carrying. "No boys today?" He looked around expecting Tommy and Sam to appear from the back of the car.

"No, I told you, Dad. Ed's doing parent duty today. He promised them a trip to the park, and I think his folks are dropping by. I thought it best not to inflict them on Brad."

Tom hid a smile at this sudden concern for her brother and asked, "Can I help?"

"Just let me get this into the kitchen," she puffed. "There's more in the back."

Tom walked around to the back, stunned by the amount of food Simone had brought. "Did you empty your cupboards?" he joked as he hefted a cooler into the kitchen and placed it on the bench beside the others. "Looks as if you're planning to feed an army."

"It's for Brad. We have to show his… whatever she is… that we know how to put together a good lunch. It's what Mom would have done."

Tom bit the inside of his mouth and tried to hide his amusement, but all he said was, "Brooke's her name, and she's Brad's fiancée."

"Well, it's the first time he's brought someone…"

To his surprise, Tom could see his daughter was close to tears.

"Come here." He drew her into his arms, resting his chin on her head, just as he had when she was a little girl. "She's only a girl, a young one at that. I'm sure she's not coming to judge you – us. More likely the boot's on the other foot. She's going to be joining our family. She'll want to impress us." Though even as he said it, Tom wasn't entirely sure that was the case. He recalled the cool, self-possessed young woman he'd met the previous weekend. She may have set out to impress, but the word which came more readily to mind was 'charm'.

"It'll be just fine," Tom said, squeezing her shoulders. "Now what have you brought?" He released Simone and opened the flap on the closest box, drawing out a roll of what appeared to be a tea towel.

"Careful, Dad." Simone took the package from his hands and laid it gently on the table. "This goes in the fridge. It's for dessert."

"It's not…?" Tom suddenly recognized it as something Janet used to make on special occasions.

"Mom's pumpkin roll. Yes. I tried to think what she'd make and…"

"She most certainly would." Tom swallowed, trying to rid himself of the lump which had formed in his throat. The pumpkin roll was Janet's special recipe, made for Thanksgiving, Christmas and other family celebrations. His mouth watered at the memory of the spicy cake filled with delicious cream cheese and walnuts. It was something he hadn't tasted since his wife passed away, something he'd always associate with her. "Good choice, hon." He turned away to hide his emotion.

Oblivious to her father's reaction, Simone started unpacking the icebox. "I cooked up some roast beef last night," she said in a worried tone. "And there's a few salads. Do you think that'll be okay? She won't be expecting a hot meal?"

"Sweetheart, whatever you have will be a hundred times better than anything I could rustle up. Left to me it'd have been a takeaway or ready cooked meal from Fred Meyer. And it's your brother, remember. When has Brad cared what he ate?"

"Dad!" Simone's exasperation was noticeable in her voice, but there was a touch of laughter too this time. Tom was glad to hear it. Sometimes Simone was too serious for her own good.

"What can I do?" he asked, looking around. Simone appeared to have taken over his kitchen. "The table?"

"That'd be great. I'll manage in here, Can you…?"

"I think I can set the table. Why don't we eat on the deck?"

"Good thinking."

Tom could see Simone was eager to get him out of her hair. "Right. I'll get on, shall I?"

There was no reply, so Tom headed out to the deck wondering what all the fuss was about. Brooke was just a girl Brad had decided to marry. In fact, Tom wouldn't be surprised if it had been her idea. He shook his head. What on earth was Simone up to? He couldn't help but think she had some ulterior motive. He remembered her initial comment about a gold-digger. Just what was Simone's plan?

When Brad and Brooke arrived, Tom was at the door to greet them.

"Dad."

"Brad."

The two men shook hands, then Brooke stepped out of the car, coming right up to Tom and kissing him on the cheek as if they were old friends, or already family. He breathed in the same scent as before and couldn't stop his hand from reaching up to touch the spot. Brad had certainly found himself a feminine girl. She grasped Brad's hand, swung it and looked around, whispering something into Brad's ear.

"Simone?" Brad said, meeting Tom's eyes.

"Inside. She's…" But at that moment, Simone appeared.

Tom blinked. The contrast between the two women was stark – Brooke all frills and flounces, decked out in pastel colors, her long hair swinging down her back, and Simone in her neat black pants teamed with a pink and white striped shirt, her thick blonde hair so like Tom's forming a neat cap.

Simone seemed to take in the scene, and a forced smile appeared on her face.

Brad smiled in return. "This is my sister, Simone."

"Simone. I've heard so much about you. It's lovely to meet you at last." Tom saw Brooke move forward to give Simone the same treatment he'd received, only to be thwarted by Simone taking a step back and holding out her hand.

"So you're Brooke?" Simone raised her eyebrows, making Tom wonder what was going through her head. Did she approve of Brad's choice, or was Brooke still being judged?

Brooke appeared to have no such qualms. She smiled and tossed her hair, grasping Brad's arm, her diamond ring twinkling in the sunlight. "And you're Brad's big sister, soon to be mine too. I never had a sister. It's been just Mom and me for so long. Now we're all going to be a family."

Tom rolled his eyes behind Brooke's back, meeting Simone's startled gaze. Definitely still judging and perhaps finding wanting. "Come along in," he said. "We're eating on the deck. Simone's prepared a feast for us."

"Just a simple lunch," Simone muttered as she followed the others through the kitchen.

"Beer, son?" Tom asked, gesturing with his own bottle, but before Brad could reply, Brooke interrupted.

"Oh, I think we'd prefer a white wine. We have a bottle, don't we?" She tilted her head towards Brad who smiled at her indulgently.

"It's still in the car. I'll fetch it."

Brooke released her grip and turned to the other two. "Brad can be so forgetful, can't he?"

Simone snorted. There could be no other way to describe it, Tom thought.

"There's a cold bottle in the fridge." As he spoke Tom extracted a bottle of Sauvignon Blanc from the fridge. "Wine for you, too. Simone?"

"I'll have a beer with you, Dad."

So that's how it was going to be. Tom fetched another beer and poured the two wines, then joined the girls on the deck where Brooke was enthusing about the view.

"You're so lucky to have grown up here," she was telling Simone. "When we left last time I told Brad the same. Mom and I lived in the city, and now Brad and I do."

"Brad and…" Simone's mouth fell open, and Tom realized he'd forgotten to provide his daughter with the crucial piece of information that the pair were living together already.

At that moment Brad returned flourishing a bottle of wine. "Put it in the fridge, will I, Dad?" he said, seeing the already filled glasses.

When Brad joined them again on the deck, the conversation revolved around how Brad and Brooke met and their future plans, mostly relayed by a voluble Brooke. Brad seemed content to listen and to nod occasionally when she turned his way. It wasn't till lunch was almost over that Brooke turned to Simone and asked, "And you, Simone? Brad tells me you have two little boys. They're not with you today? I was hoping to meet them." Her mouth turned up in a small pout, as if Simone had deliberately chosen to disappoint her.

"Obviously." Simone's lips tightened, then relaxed slightly. "They're with their dad. I thought it best to come on my own this first time – not expose you to the whole family at once."

"But I'd love to have met them."

"Maybe next time," Simone said, as if realizing there would be a next time, many next times. Brooke was here to stay.

When the pair finally rose to leave, it was Brad who hugged Simone, and Tom heard his son mutter, "You'll like her when you get to know her, sis, I know she comes on a bit strong, but I love her, and she's good for me."

Tom and Simone waved the pair off and turned to each other. "Well?" Tom asked. "What do you think of Brad's choice?"

"She's very young," Simone said carefully. "But," – she paused – "I think she may be good for him. She's…"

"Not a gold-digger, then?"

"No…." The word was drawn out. "I don't think so. She seems pretty well-heeled herself, if she's to be believed. And I think she really loves him. She'd better, and she'd better treat him right, or she'll have me to deal with," she finished grimly. "Now how about we finish that wine they brought?"

Tom winked as father and daughter linked arms and made their way inside.

Seven

"I'll just pop down and check on Maddy." Jenny finished stacking the dishwasher and drew a light shirt on over her tee. "She's been a bit low these last few days, since Mary-Lou went off on her trip."

"She didn't look well, yesterday, when Ben and I walked past. She was out in the garden as usual – doing some weeding, I think," Mike said.

"I wish she'd leave it to us. She shouldn't be doing all that bending and stretching at her age."

"You'll never persuade her to stop," Jenny's husband replied. "Your godmother is a law unto herself, always has been, and always will be."

"Hmm. You're right there," Jenny said, lifting her face for Mike's kiss. "Won't be long."

She stepped out the door and walked quickly down the track to Maddy's home. There were only two houses on this track in Seal Rock. Jenny's godmother had lived here since she was a young woman and lost her sweetheart in the war, while the house Jenny and Mike lived in had been a holiday home for Mike and his first wife, Mary. When Mary died after suffering from Alzheimer's for many years, he had retreated here to continue his research into the local Native American tribes. The couple had met when Jenny, smarting from an unexpected redundancy, had traveled from Australia to visit her godmother a few years earlier, and now they spent six months of each year here, the other six months in Australia.

As Jenny approached the house, she could see the curtains were open and breathed a sigh of relief. She knew Maddy sometimes slept late and was afraid of disturbing her, while keen to make sure all was well.

"Hello, Maddy, it's only me," she called, pushing open the door and walking into the large open living area. "Are you…?" There was no answering greeting, no lively Maddy hurrying to welcome her with a warm hug. Jenny stopped in her tracks. Something wasn't right. There was a calmness in the house – as if time had stopped. Her heart leaping into her mouth and an unwelcome twisting in her gut, Jenny stepped further in. Maddy was sitting in her favorite chair, but she was still – so still.

"Oh, no! Maddy!" Jenny froze, swallowed hard, then the tears streamed down her cheeks. Maddy was gone. She must have passed away in her sleep, right here in her favorite chair. Jenny's legs buckled, and she dropped to the floor beside the chair. She took Maddy's hands in hers. The wrinkled hands speckled with age spots were cold. What was she going to do without Maddy? Ever since she met her again as an adult, Maddy had provided a guiding hand. It was she who'd steered Jenny in Mike's direction, had helped her realize she could trust again and find love. Jenny sobbed and sobbed, till her throat ached. Then she rose, patted her godmother's hands, gently kissed her cheek, the skin fine as tissue paper, and whispered, "Goodbye, darling Maddy. I'll miss you so." Jenny looked around. Everything was in perfect order. She couldn't think straight. She walked into the kitchen to get a glass of water, and there, lying on the bench, was a bundle of documents. Gulping down the water, Jenny's eyes blurred. Fresh sobs overtook her, and she sank down into a chair.

"Anyone home?" The words were followed by the patter of small feet, and Jenny felt a wet tongue licking her hands. "You were gone a long time, so we came looking…" Mike's voice died away as he obviously took in the scene. "Oh, Jenny!" He hurried forward to take her in his arms. Jenny melted into the hug, tears streaming unchecked down her cheeks.

"I'm sorry. I…" She felt Mike's rough beard on her cheek, its familiar coarseness bringing her back to the present. She drew herself out of his embrace and wiped her eyes with the back of her hand.

"She went as she'd have wished," Mike said, still holding Jenny gently by the shoulders.

"I know. It's just that… she was all alone. I wish…"

"It's what she wanted. She died as she lived – fiercely independent."

"Yes," Jenny sniffed. "You're right, of course, but…"

"Stay here. You need a cup of sweet tea."

"Tea!" Jenny was outraged. "You can talk of tea, when Maddy's…" She couldn't bring herself to say the word. Maddy would have had coffee bubbling away in the kitchen. The room should have been redolent with coffee and cooking. Instead the whole house had a strange feel about it, a sense of emptiness. Its heart had stopped beating.

Jenny cupped her hands around the cup of sweet tea. She was beginning to feel better. She realized Mike knew her better than she knew herself. Knew exactly what she needed at this time – tea, not coffee. "If only… if only I'd called in last night, when we got back from the fair."

"We were tired, and Maddy's light wasn't on. No one can blame you."

"I can blame myself. I hate to think she died alone."

Sitting opposite, Mike opened the folder lying on the bench. "Oh, my God!"

"What is it?" Jenny placed her cup down carefully. She'd had enough shocks this morning. What now?

"It's all Maddy's paperwork." Mike flipped through the contents of the folder. "Her living will, revocable trust, what to do with her …" He put his hand over his eyes and said in a breaking voice, "She was ready, Jenny. She knew. It's all here."

Jenny's hand crept over to cover Mike's, now lying on the closed folder. "What do we do now?"

Mike seemed to rouse himself. "There are people to contact – her doctor, lawyer, the police."

"The police?" Jenny's eyes widened.

"Maddy died alone. We need to call the police to certify there was no foul play."

"She'd have hated that."

"Maybe not. She always did like being the center of attention."

Mike picked up the phone, while Jenny gazed out into the garden. She wasn't conscious of what she was looking at, only a dull blur of color. Ben laid his head on her lap and her hand automatically dropped to stroke him.

In no time, the house seemed to be filled with people. First to arrive was the doctor, who offered condolences, signed the death certificate and removed all of Maddy's remaining medications. While he was still there, the police arrived and, after a brief discussion with the doctor, contacted the coroner's office.

"What will happen now?" a still weepy Jenny asked Mike.

Putting an arm around her shoulders, he replied gently, "The undertakers will pick up Maddy's body. It's out of our hands now. The best we can do for Maddy is to make sure her wishes are carried out."

"Her wishes?" Jenny raised a teary face. "How do we know her wishes?"

"I've been looking through the papers she left on the table. It's all there. She doesn't want the fuss of a funeral. Her wish is for her ashes to be buried in her plot."

"She has a plot?" Jenny was startled. While she knew her godmother had planned ahead, this was all a bit too much.

"She does. Bought it a few years ago. Probably around the same time she set up her living will and the trust. She's stipulated which funeral director she wants us to use and how she wants all of her belongings to be dealt with."

Jenny walked over and picked up some of the papers, but her eyes were too blurred for her to see properly.

Mike followed her and took the papers from her hands. "Look, honey. This is going to take some time. You don't need to be here. Why don't you go home? Take Ben with you. I'll join you when it's done."

"I don't think…" Jenny hesitated, but finally, at Mike's urging, she called Ben and made her way up the track.

Once there, she couldn't settle. She kept seeing Maddy sitting there, so peaceful and so still. She was standing outside, arms wrapped around herself and quivering, when her cell vibrated. Seeing her cousin's face, the tension left her.

"Something's wrong. Are you okay? Is it Maddy?"

"How did you know?" But even as she asked the question, Jenny was in no doubt how Ellen knew. Her cousin's gift of second sight was now familiar to her. "She…she's…" Jenny still couldn't say the word. "We found her. Oh, Ellen, what'll I do without her?"

"You'll do what you always did. She's still with you. It's only her physical presence that's gone. All of the wisdom she's shared with you is still there, with you. As long as you remember her, she'll be alive in your thoughts, yours and Mike's."

A warmth began to spread throughout Jenny. She was still sad, but whereas before, there had been despondency, now there was… She wasn't quite sure what, but something akin to *hope*.

"Thanks, Ellen. As always, you've hit the right note. I feel as if Maddy is talking to me, telling me to 'soldier on'." Jenny heard Ellen chuckle.

*

"How do you feel about going it alone?" Beth was sorting through a crate of books when Jo spoke to her. She looked up, frowning. She'd only been working here for just over a month and was still finding her feet.

"It's a new estate up at Seal Rock. Madeline de Ruis. Lovely lady. Her goddaughter has inherited the estate, and the old dear nominated us to do the sale."

"You think I'm ready?"

"I do, but it's more that I'm tied up for the rest of the week, and Jenny's keen to move on it. She's from Australia too, so the two of you should get on."

Beth gulped. Not another one. She racked her brains. What had Ellen said her cousin's name was? But she came up with a blank. That whole conversation had been so weird she'd avoided the bookshop ever since.

"Sure," she said, though her heart began to beat madly. What if it wasn't Ellen's cousin? What if it was someone from Sydney? Someone who knew Bryan, who'd recognize her. Who'd… She gave herself a mental shake. What were the chances of meeting one person from back home in this isolated place, never mind two? Her heartbeat returned to normal. "When do you want me to go?"

"I said you'd go up there tomorrow." Jo looked apologetic. "I'm afraid I assumed you'd agree. You know I need you to…"

"Fill in when you're busy," Beth finished. "I know. I'm just a bit stunned you'd trust me on my own so soon."

"You're fitting in well. I bless the day you walked through my door."

"Works for me, too. Now I'm really settled, I'm beginning to feel I belong here."

"That's what we like to hear. Though.as far as most of the locals are concerned you'll probably always be an incomer. I've written down the details for you. It's just a matter of getting a feel for what's there and completing the initial paperwork. We can both go up next week and do a proper inventory, then we'll schedule the sale for the week after, when I have an opening."

*

The sun was shining when Beth set off next morning. Closing her motel room door, she thought how glad she'd be when she could finally move into her own home. The estate sale had been last weekend, and the owners agreed she could rent the place until everything was finalized. She knew it was a bit of a risk, but she already owned the remaining furniture, and it would save her motel bill. She couldn't wait.

As she drove up the highway, the road dropping away to a wild ocean on one side, she was struck, not for the first time, how different this scenery was from the familiar Australian landscape. Back there, the ocean had been a place for leisure, for basking in the sun or surfing for the more energetic. Here, she shuddered at the thought of putting any part of her body into those fierce waves. Instead of being inviting stretches of smooth white or red sand, the beach had a grayish tinge, appeared rough, and was peppered with protruding rocks and bleached pieces of driftwood.

Out of the corner of her eye, Beth spied a rough track going off to the right, with a couple of mailboxes at the edge of the road. This must be it. She turned in and bumped up the track to where a large weathered house stood, door wide open, a black Labrador lying across the entrance in a pool of sunlight. When she drew up and stopped, the dog lazily rose and ambled over to greet her, wagging his tail and sniffing at her feet, before wandering off again to reclaim his spot in the sun.

Beth walked over to the door, stopping to pat the dog as she passed. "Hello," she called, stepping through the doorway.

To her surprise, it wasn't a fellow Australian woman who came to greet her, but a bearded man, at whose arrival the dog immediately rose to his feet again.

"Not now, Ben," he said, then turning to Beth, "You must be from the estate sales."

"Beth Carson." Beth held out her hand tentatively. She couldn't tar every man she met with the same brush as Bryan, but she *did* find it difficult to trust the male of the species. "I'm from Green Heron Estate Sales. Jo made the arrangement with Jenny?"

"My partner. I'm Mike, Mike Halliday. Maddy was her godmother, and my dear friend and neighbor. We live just up the track a way. Jenny wasn't sure she could handle it. She's still grieving."

It was obvious from his dejected expression that he was too, and this immediately put Beth at her ease.

"I'm sorry," she said, cursing herself for the inanity or her response. "I know it must be difficult. I…" She stopped. He didn't want to hear about her own loss, and she had a job to do.

Mike seemed to collect himself at the same time.

"Let me show you around. Everything still here will go. Jenny and I have taken the bits and pieces we want kept. Do you need to…?"

"I can go around by myself if you wish. I just need to get a feel for what's here, and there's some paperwork. I guess it'll need Jenny's signature."

"Thanks." Mike subsided into a nearby armchair, while Beth began to move through the house.

At first, Beth felt as if she was prying. This was someone's beloved home. It wasn't the same feeling she had when inspecting a house to purchase, or when she'd helped with other sales. This still felt like a well-loved home, and she was conscious, as she almost tiptoed around the rooms, that the owner had been a warm and loving person. The scent of dried herbs and another more elusive fragrance Beth couldn't identify flooded her nostrils. She noticed that several pieces of furniture had already been removed, their legs leaving indentations on the carpets of the bedrooms and scratches on the wooden floor of the living areas. Similarly, she noticed faded spots on the walls where photos or paintings had once hung. Her own new home seemed an empty shell in comparison.

Beth was admiring the view from one of the bedrooms and reflecting that Jo would be pleased – there were still lots of interesting pieces left, including lots of the little knickknacks that proved so popular, when she heard voices from the other end of the house. Maybe Mike's partner had arrived, and she could get the paperwork done. Hurrying out with a smile on her face, prepared to greet the Jenny she'd heard about, Beth stopped in the doorway at the sight of two men, one of whom had his back to her.

"Oh, hi Beth. This is Tom Harrison, our lawyer. He's taking over from Maddy's guy, George, who's overseas. Seems there's some paperwork I need to sign as one of the executors of Maddy's estate."

The man turned to face Beth. Her breath caught in her throat. It was the same man – the one she'd avoided at the warehouse and met again at the barbecue. A shiver ran through her. Why did his presence disturb her? Taking a deep breath, she forced her trembling legs to move forward and took his outstretched hand.

"We meet again," Tom smiled. Beth's hand felt warm as Tom's large one enfolded it. She looked up to meet his eyes. He was a big man. Maybe that's why she'd felt intimidated when she'd first met him, found his bulk threatening. But she felt different this time. Maybe it was the atmosphere in this house. Standing beside Mike, the two men emanated a sense of warmth, security. Beth flushed as if they could read her mind. She'd thought Ellen was weird. Now she was having these strange moods herself.

"So you have some paperwork?" Mike's words brought Beth back to the present.

"Yes. Right here." Beth opened the folder she'd been carrying around with her. "I need a signature on each of these. Are you sure…?" She looked from one of the men to the other. "Jo expected Jenny…" She hesitated, then handed the papers over. Surely everything was okay. Mike was Jenny's partner, and Tom her lawyer. What could go wrong? "I need signatures here and here." Becoming all businesslike, she indicated the spots Jo had highlighted. "One of these is your copy."

Mike did as she asked and handed back the signed copy.

"Thanks, I guess that's it. Jo will be in touch regarding the inventory and the sale. We'll need access both of those times."

"We're just up the track, and Tom'll have a key too. Best to call first."

"Jo knows where to find me," Tom said.

"Right, I'll be off."

"Good to meet you again – properly this time. Maybe…"

But whatever Tom had intended to say was lost as Beth whirled out of the door. Enough was enough, and she'd done what she came here to do. But as she left, she was struck by the memory of the conversation she'd overheard at the fair. Wasn't it Tom someone the two women had been gossiping about? Was this him? In that case he was spoken for, though why that would concern her, she had no idea.

*

The two men stood looking at the departing figure.

"Very businesslike lady," Mike muttered. "Reminds me of what Jenny was like when I first met her."

"I think she's afraid of something." Tom rubbed his chin. "Bumped into her a couple of times, and she's always rushed off. This is the first time I've actually had a conversation with her."

"Not every woman you meet is going to fall at your feet," Mike laughed. "By the way, what's happening with Yvonne Walker?"

"Don't ask. The woman makes a weekly appointment and is forever inviting me to dinner or some such."

"Why don't you accept? Might frighten her off."

"What if it didn't? No, think I'll leave things the way they are. I'm not about to replace Janet. Not that anyone could."

"No. I never met her, but seems she was a pearl above price."

"She was that." For a moment, Tom stood, lost in his memories. Then he shuddered. "She passed before you moved up here. She would…" He paused. "She'd have liked you – you and Jenny."

"Maybe…"

Tom could see Mike was struggling with what he wanted to say.

"Out with it, man."

"When Mary died… She was my first wife." Mike paused as if unsure how to go on. "She left me a letter."

Tom fidgeted, shuffled his feet. He wasn't sure what his friend was trying to tell him, or if he wanted to hear it, but Mike continued, "She told me if I found someone else, she'd be happy for me. Didn't want me to go through the rest of my life alone."

"And how did you feel about that?" Tom was curious.

"Sad. Resentful, even. All I wanted to do was to bury myself up here with my research and writing."

"And…?"

"And I did. Then I met Jenny."

"Hmm." Tom thought he could see where this was leading. He didn't want to hear any more. "I manage okay. There's a lot to be said for the solitary life."

"I thought that too. I'm not suggesting you take up with any of these women who chase after you, like Yvonne or her cronies. But keep an open mind. There are other sorts of women out there. Women who have faced their own challenges. They're not the ones who'll do the chasing. In fact," Mike pulled on his beard, "they'll probably do their best to avoid you. They may be damaged, have something in their past they want to hide. Or they may be recovering from some hurt. Beth Carson strikes me as one of those. She may be hard to get to know, but the man who manages to open her up may well find a treasure."

Tom looked down at his feet. How did he reply to Mike's outpouring? It wasn't like his friend to bare his soul like this. In his experience, men didn't talk this way. He shuffled his feet again. "Well, better be getting on," he said, moving toward the door. "Be seeing you."

Tom drove back to Florence along one of the most scenic highways known to man, but today, he saw little of the deep green forests or the wild ocean panorama. His eyes focused on the road ahead. He was turning Mike's words over and over in his mind. Maybe his friend was right. Maybe he should consider… what? Again the image of the short gray-haired woman who had left so abruptly came to mind. As he'd told Mike, she did seem afraid. Afraid of him? Afraid of men in general? What had happened to make her so reticent? She didn't appear to be a timid woman. In fact, he had the impression she had a backbone of steel, but there was a reserve about her, a definite 'no entry' sign. Mike had talked about women who were damaged in some way, who were hiding some hurt. Beth Carson had come all the way from Australia to this little one-horse town in Oregon. She didn't appear to know anyone here, but she'd upped sticks and moved here at her age.

She must be close to his own age, a time when most women were set in their ways. He knew it was none of his business, but he'd dearly like to know the reason.

Eight

By the time Beth returned to Green Heron Estate Sales with the paperwork from the Madeline de Ruis estate, she was beginning to feel hungry, so was pleased to find the door closed. There was a note from Jo attached asking her to meet at Mo's for lunch. Reflecting how laidback this whole community was – that a store owner could leave such a note on the door for an employee – Beth set off to walk down to the river and the boardwalk.

When she reached her destination, she stopped for a moment and stared at the long, low wooden building, set out on pilings over the river. Although she'd passed it several times already she'd never gone inside, but had heard about its famous clam chowder. With a lightness in her step, she entered and searched the tables for her employer. A hand waved from a booth in the far corner, and she hurried to join Jo, who was sitting by a window looking out onto the river.

"What a glorious spot," Beth said, sitting down and gazing out at the water, where several birds which she thought were herons, were strutting and flaunting themselves close to the side of the restaurant.

"Aren't they…?"

"Herons. Yes, blue herons."

"We have them back home – blue and gray. But you called your business Green Heron Estate Sales. Are there really green herons? I've never heard of them."

"There certainly are. They may be unique to this part of the world. I'm not sure. The green heron is smaller than the blue or gray variety. It's a short, stocky bird with a loud call. Rob says that's me!" she chuckled. "They're pretty much nocturnal, so you won't see them around like these ones." She indicated the birds they'd been watching.

"Interesting. Jo, I…"

"So, how did you get on at Seal Rock?"

Beth opened her mouth to answer, but was interrupted by a plump waitress asking for their order. "Oh, I haven't…" Beth said, flustered and picked up a menu, only to have Jo put a restraining hand on her wrist.

"If this is your first visit to Mo's you have to order clam chowder. People come from all over for their signature dish."

"Okay. I was probably going to order it anyway. I've heard so much about it."

"I suggest a bowl, then we can have peach cobbler to follow. Not much I can do about my size now." Jo glanced down deprecatingly at her solid figure. "And you could do with a bit more flesh on you."

"Hmm." Beth had always been careful about her weight, but she knew that, since leaving home, she'd lost quite a few pounds, and supposed it wouldn't do her any harm to indulge.

When they'd placed their orders, Beth began again, "I had a good look around, and it should provide a decent sale. There are several pieces of old furniture – solid – and lots of little ornaments, the sort of things you said are popular. And I got the contract signed. Mike Halliday signed it. I didn't meet Jenny. I hope that's all right? Your friend Tom Harrison was there too." Beth wasn't quite sure why she mentioned Tom's name.

"Mike's signature will be fine for starters, but I'll probably need Jenny's at some stage. I guess she's too upset right now. Sometimes happens." Jo took a sip of the water which had been poured for each of them, and the conversation stalled while two large bowls of chowder with side baskets of crackers, were set in front of them.

"Wow!" Beth was still getting used to the generous servings of food here in Florence. No wonder there were so many large people around.

"It brought it all back," Beth said, almost to herself. "Walking through the house. It reminded me…" She shivered, remembering how empty her mother's house had seemed when Audrey had entered the nursing home.

"Do you want to talk about it?" Jo's voice was gentle, her eyes full of concern. Suddenly, Beth found she *did* want to talk about it. At the time she'd had no one to talk with. Bryan didn't want to know, and she had no women friends with whom she could share confidences, only those hand-picked by her husband – wives of men who could further his career.

"Yes, I think I do." Beth leant her elbows on the table, pushing away her now empty bowl. "Mum lived in the country, in the house I grew up in. She'd stayed there when Dad died – even though the house was much too big – and leased out the land to our neighbor. When she took ill, Bryan – my husband – insisted she go into a nursing home in the city, to be close to us. It was the sensible decision, but…" Shit, she hadn't meant to mention Bryan. She hoped Jo wouldn't ask about him – where he was, why he wasn't with her. Her companion's next question reassured her.

"It meant her home had to be closed up?"

"Right. Once Mum was settled, I went back down. The house was like a mausoleum, empty, populated with ghosts. Bryan didn't want any of her things, though I did manage to salvage a few mementoes. I have them with me." Beth looked down, her eyes misting. "I don't know how I managed to do it. I called the local charities, who took most of the furniture, but the little things, the things that she used every day, these were the hardest to deal with. Seeing that house today, I could feel the warmth of the last inhabitant – Maddy, I think they called her. It brought it all back. I can understand how her goddaughter feels. They must have been close."

"You were close to your mother?"

"Yes." Beth wiped her eyes. "Sorry, I don't usually blub like this."

"And your mother was American?"

Beth was surprised at the question, though it was a logical one for Jo to ask. She'd actually expected more questions earlier, but the production of her social security number had been sufficient for her to gain employment. Now Jo was curious. It was understandable.

Beth took a long drink of water before replying. She was loath to divulge too much about her past, but surely her mother's history couldn't do any harm? After all, the individuals were all dead. "My family comes from here. Mum's dad, my grandfather, taught in university in Minnesota. Was a bit of a livewire by all accounts. In the McCarthy era Grandad became known for his left-wing politics, and his university position was in jeopardy – maybe even his freedom, according to Mum. The result was he brought his family to Australia. Got a job there. Mum was born there, married a local farmer, and that's where I grew up."

"And they never came back?"

"No, none of us did, not till now. But my grandparents retained their American citizenship – never became Australian – and they made sure Mum and I had dual citizenship. Hence my ability to come here and work."

"And you've never tried to find any American family members?"

"As far as I know there aren't any. Grandad and Granma were only children. I don't know about any extended family. But it was all so long ago."

"And why Florence? Why now?"

"When Mum died, I needed to get away, start afresh. I found some postcards of Florence among her papers – the ones she'd taken with her to the nursing home. It seemed like a message. I don't know." She drew her hand across the top of her head, ruffling her still short hair. She'd never verbalized that before, never admitted, even to herself, her reason for driving up the west coast of the United States to find this small town.

"Anyway, I'm glad I did. I like it here."

"Coffee, ma'am." Beth looked up to see the waitress hovering with a coffee jug.

"Thanks." She hoped this would be the signal for Jo to change the subject. It was, but her next topic of conversation was no more welcome.

"So you met Tom Harrison again, eh?"

"I did." Beth took a sip of the coffee, cursing herself for mentioning the big man's name. That's how Beth remembered him – big in every way. He was tall, wide-shouldered, solidly built, big hands, big smile, big voice. Altogether larger than life. "Mike said he's their lawyer, and he's acting for the de Ruis estate at the moment."

"That'd be right, with young George away. Not that he's really young," Jo laughed. "He's well into his sixties, but he took over the practice from his father and will always be 'young George'. I think he and his wife have gone to visit your neck of the woods. I understand they've been picking Jenny's brains."

"Australia?" Beth heard her voice come out in a squeak. She'd come as far away as she could from home, and references to her native land seemed to pop up wherever she turned.

"So what do you think of him?" For a moment Beth was lost. Was Jo talking about this young George?

Jo must have grasped her confusion, because she immediately added, "Tom."

"Oh, he's… he seems…," she stammered.

"A lot of man there." Jo didn't wait for a reply. "Can seem to be a bit of a charmer. But don't be misled. He hasn't looked at a woman since Janet died, five years ago now. Seems to enjoy the solitary life up there by the lake. Part of the local hunting and fishing brigade. That appears to keep him busy. That and his work, not to mention a son, an overprotective daughter and two grandsons. But that's not to say the local ladies haven't tried to get their claws in. He's pretty good at evading all overtures." Jo smiled.

Too much information, thought Beth, though it did put him in a better light – not the aggressive predator she'd first imagined.

*

"Has she gone?" Jenny greeted Mike as he walked in the door. "I know I should have come with you. I just couldn't bear to see someone pawing over Maddy's things. I wish…"

"It's okay, honey." Mike took her in his arms in a tight hug. "But we've been over this before. We can't house everything here. We've taken the pieces you felt were special, and Maddy left clear instructions for the rest."

"I know. Ignore me."

"That's pretty hard to do when you're right here and you're the light of my life. Is there anything I can do?"

"The fact that you're here is enough. I don't know what I'd do without you." She thought back to the person she'd been only a few years ago. That person would have derided her dependence on Mike. How she'd changed, and Maddy had been instrumental in that change. She sighed. "I suppose I'll have to meet her sometime – this Australian Beth Carson."

"She seems a nice woman, and there was no pawing that I saw. In fact, she seemed very respectful. Tom thought so too. She and Jo will need access to do an inventory and set up the sale. There's probably no need for you to be involved, though it would be good if you could sign the paperwork too. But they can get the key from Tom."

"Yes." Jenny was distracted, trying to work out how she could avoid seeing these people in Maddy's home. "Maybe I can meet them in town?"

"That's a good idea. Why don't we go down this afternoon? You really should sign the contract too."

"I know." Jenny twirled a strand of hair in her fingers, then made a decision. "I'll go this afternoon. No need for you to come. You've already spent time on Maddy's estate, while I've been moping here. I can do this myself. Down near Old Town, isn't it?"

Mike threw his arm around Jenny's shoulder and gave her a warm hug. "You're a resilient woman, Jenny. I know Maddy's death knocked you down, but you'll bounce back. You'll see. Maybe you need an infusion of Ellen's common sense."

"Ellen? Of course. Why didn't I think of her? I'll go to this Green Heron place first, meet the Australian woman, sign the contract, then pop in on Ellen." At the thought of Ellen's soothing presence, Jenny felt better. Strange how even thinking about her psychic cousin could bring a spring to her step. "Let's have some lunch first, then I'll be off."

*

Jenny tentatively pushed open the door of Green Heron Estate Sales, wondering how she could have missed this building in all of her visits to Old Town. Looking around, she was impressed by the layout and the care which had clearly gone into setting out the pieces to their best advantage. Something inside her stilled at the thought that any remaining items from Maddy's would receive the same care.

"Can I help you?" a short, slim gray-haired woman came hurrying towards her. It took only a moment for Jenny to recognize the Australian accent.

"You must be Beth," she said, holding out her hand. "I'm Jenny. I…"

"Ms de Ruis' goddaughter," the woman said. "Yes, I'm Beth, and I'm so sorry for your loss."

Jenny thought she saw a tear in the woman's eye, but she blinked, and it was gone. Maybe a trick of the light? "Mike told me you need my signature too, so here I am."

"Please take a seat, and I'll fetch the paperwork."

Jenny looked around, seeing only pieces for sale. She felt awkward sitting on one of these, but Beth indicated an armchair upholstered in a bright floral pattern.

"They're all well-loved pieces," she said, as if reading Jenny's mind. "It's okay to sit on them. You can't do any damage."

Jenny sank into the chair with relief, wondering why she suddenly felt she'd found a friend. Maybe it was the accent, which reminded her of home.

The papers signed, Jenny felt a sense of release. She leant back in the chair while Beth gathered the papers together and stood up.

"That's all we need for now," she said, hesitating as if she expected Jenny to leave.

"Right." But Jenny remained seated, suddenly unwilling to make a move. "Do you mind if we talk for a bit?" She thought she saw the other flinch, but Beth gathered the papers to her chest and sat down again, albeit on the edge of her chair. *What was the woman afraid of?*

"It's nice to hear a voice from home," Jenny said to break the silence, which was becoming awkward. She wasn't quite sure what she wanted to say. She just sensed this woman needed her company. As soon as the thought crossed her mind, Jenny dismissed it. She wasn't Ellen, her cousin who had second sight. She was Jenny, the pragmatic one, but she did sense her companion's distress and wanted to try to alleviate it. Maybe talking of home would help.

"We Aussies should stick together," she said at last. "I'm from Noosa. What about you?"

"Sydney." Beth fiddled with the bundle of papers, giving Jenny the impression she didn't want to talk. But Jenny persisted.

"Didn't get down there much. A bit too cool for us Queenslanders." She laughed. "And now I spend half the year here. But we do try to avoid the Oregon winter. My husband is involved in research, so he can work anywhere, and I'm part-owner of a bookshop in Noosa. I think you've met my cousin who has the bookshop here?"

"Yes." Beth let the papers fall into her lap and relaxed in her chair. "She seems a bit…"

"Odd. I know. I thought that too when we first met. I didn't know she was my cousin then. It's a long story. Maybe I can share it with you some time. I'd love to catch up with you again. Are you living in Florence itself?"

"I've bought a house." The words came out slowly, as if Beth was loath to give too much away. "I move in at the weekend." She paused, then it seemed as if she'd made a decision that Jenny could be trusted. "I'm really looking forward to having my own place. I feel I've been living out of a suitcase for so long." She sighed. "I'm growing fond of Florence, even though I feel I'm surrounded by strangers. It's a surprise to meet someone from back home."

And not altogether a pleasant one, Jenny surmised, wondering what the woman was running away from or trying to hide. "Well, let's meet again. I'm always popping down here for one thing or another. Maybe we can meet for coffee next time?"

"Maybe."

Both women rose, and reaching into her purse, Jenny found a piece of paper and jotted down her phone number. "Now don't be a stranger, as Maddy would say." Jenny's voice almost broke on her godmother's name. "And I guess I can find you here?"

Beth nodded and stood silent as Jenny left.

*

Beth watched Jenny depart, the door banging behind her. She seemed so sure of herself, so at home in her skin. Beth envied her. She felt afraid of her own shadow. What if Bryan found out where she'd gone? She could imagine his fury over her departure. She didn't fool herself he still loved her. His frequent outbursts of anger, his cruel taunts that she was no longer attractive, that he only married her out of pity, often followed by flowers next day, had worn her out. Sure, they only happened when things had gone wrong at work – when he lost a patient or was in a temper about a co-worker's perceived incompetence. But these occurrences had become more and more frequent. When they first married, they were events they'd discussed over a glass of wine, and she'd rubbed his shoulders and taken him to bed. But in recent years, he'd refused her comfort, preferring to berate her instead, to blame her when there was a glitch in his perfect life.

"Are you still there?" Jo's voice interrupted her memories and brought Beth back to the present.

"Sure. Jenny came to sign the de Ruis papers."

"Lovely lady." Jo appeared from the back office. "Met her a few times with that attractive man of hers. She came to Florence on her own a few years ago. Seems she was going through a difficult time and needed some space. Certainly plenty of that here." She laughed, then her voice became more serious. "She met Mike up there at Seal Rock. I don't know the details, but everyone says she's a changed woman. This place can do that to a person."

"Mmm," Beth muttered, laying the papers on the desk. "Here are the signed copies. Is there anything else you need today?"

"No, you go off. I'm sure you have a lot to do before you move in at the weekend."

That was the trouble, Beth thought as she drove back to the motel. Right now besides work, she didn't have anything to do. But that would all change when she was in her own home. She had lots of plans for it and couldn't wait to get started. She couldn't forget Jenny, the woman she'd just met, the woman whose life had changed right here in Florence. And she remembered the strange words of Ellen, the bookshop owner. "You'll find peace here." Maybe, just maybe, she would.

*

As Jenny hurried along the street towards Ellen's shop, the conversation with Beth, repeated over and over in her head. What was the woman afraid of? It seemed that, instead of being pleased to meet a fellow Australian, she'd been nervous. At least, until Jenny mentioned she came from Queensland. Then Beth seemed to relax somewhat.

"Hi Jenny, I thought I'd see you today." Ellen's voice broke into Jenny's thoughts. She'd reached The Reading Nook already, and her cousin was standing outside the shop, coffee in her hand.

"You did?" But Jenny's voice held no element of surprise. She'd long since ceased to be amazed at Ellen's uncanny awareness.

"I expect you want to talk about Maddy," Ellen continued. "Come on in. It's quiet today, so we'll have time for a chat. Would you like one?" She held up her takeaway drink.

"Love one. I'll just pop across the road."

When Jenny returned, she was balancing a coffee and a bag containing two cinnamon rolls. "In honor of Maddy," she said, smiling sadly. "She loved them. It'll seem to bring her closer if we're eating them while we talk."

"She's never far away," said Ellen, accepting one of the sweet pastries. "Now, how are you managing?" she asked, as the two settled down.

"So-so. Some days are better than others. I miss her so much. She was the last link with Mum. Even when I was in Australia, knowing she was there, at the other end of the phone or on the internet, it gave me…" she sniffed and wiped her eyes. "She was a comfort," she finished.

"And she still can be. She's still with you – her memories, her words, her presence. Don't you feel it?"

"Ye…es, but… It's not the same as having her there. I can't hear her voice, feel her warm hug, see her smile." Jenny's voice grew quieter and quieter, and her eyes became misty.

"Close your eyes."

Jenny obeyed.

"Now, visualize Maddy as you remember her – feisty, loving, all the things you love about her." Ellen paused, letting silence fill the room. "What would you like to say to her?"

Jenny's eyes flew open. "Oh, Ellen!"

"Just try," Ellen encouraged.

Jenny closed her eyes again, blew out a breath, and began to speak.

"Maddy, I do miss you so. Why did you have to go so suddenly? We didn't even get to say goodbye. I wanted… There are so many things I want to say to you… to ask you." She sniffed.

"And you can," Ellen said. "There's no reason why you can't still talk to her, tell her things. You won't hear her voice reply, but you may sense what she wants to say to you."

Jenny opened her eyes again. She sighed. "I wish I had your faith, but I do feel… calmer somehow, lighter. It's as if…"

"As if Maddy's here with us," Ellen finished for her.

"Yes. Do you really think…?"

"She *is* with you, Jenny, though not in her physical form. She'll still be there to guide you, to listen to you, to comfort you. You just have to let her in."

"Mmm." Thoughts were whirling around in Jenny's head as she tried to process what she was hearing. She wanted to believe her cousin, but her old pragmatic self kept rearing up and telling her it was a load of old codswallop. "Maybe," she said, rising and grabbing her purse. "Thanks, Ellen. I *do* feel better, though I don't know…"

"Ask Mike," Ellen said.

Jenny stopped halfway to the door and stared at Ellen. "Mike?"

"As you know, he lost someone dear to him not so long ago. Ask him if he talked to her, was aware of her. You might be surprised to hear what he has to say."

Nine

It had been a busy day, but Beth relished it. She was loving her new job and the variety of her daily tasks. Today she'd accompanied Jo to meet a new client and had a lesson in valuing. She knew it would be some time before she developed the skill to do this on her own, and had been astonished at Jo's grasp of the task.

Home again, and after a quick meal Beth opened up her laptop to check her emails. She'd been in her own home for a couple of weeks now and checked each day, even though the only person to have her new email address was her mother's lawyer in New South Wales. Not expecting to see anything in the inbox, she was surprised when not one, but two emails from Ann Beattie appeared.

Beth's stomach plummeted. What could be happening back home to make Ann email twice in the one day? She opened the first one, relaxing when she discovered it was merely a record of the outgoings from her mother's estate and a confirmation that the residue of the monies had been deposited to her new account with Oregon Pacific Bank. Breathing a sigh of relief, she scrolled down to the second email, sent only an hour after the first. She gasped as she read the words,

Had a formal request from your husband re your whereabouts. He hasn't made it official at this stage, but is threatening to contact his lawyer and the police. He's accusing you of taking off with a large sum of money and jewellery. I know you haven't done any such thing. He's obviously tried everyone else to find out where you are and has fixed on me. As you know, I'm not easily intimidated and can fob him off for a bit. But if he brings in his legal guys and the police, I might not find it so easy. I wanted to let you know, so you can be prepared.

My best,

Ann

Beth's hand went to her mouth. She should have thought of this. She knew Bryan had Ann's details. He'd dealt with her when Audrey entered the nursing home. But she'd been hoping he'd forgotten. How could she have been so stupid? Bryan never forgot anything. She'd learned that the hard way. Slumping back in her chair, Beth remembered.

"I don't forget," Bryan roared, as Beth shrank away from him. "Did you think I would? You promised never to see those women again. Didn't you realize I'd find out? Sydney isn't such a big city as you imagine. You were seen. I won't have it. I won't have you disobey me. Do you hear?"

After that, she'd done as he demanded – dropped all of her former friends. But he couldn't make her stop seeing her mother, even though he'd bad-mouthed Audrey at every opportunity. He'd even had the hide to say he was glad she was dead. Beth knew then she couldn't stay with him, but it wasn't till she learned of her mother's will that she had the wherewithal to leave. She was sure Bryan knew nothing of this. As far as he was aware, the cost of the nursing home had eaten up all her mother's savings plus the value of the family home. He'd be assuming she was staying with friends, penniless and destitute, ready to return to him, ready to become his metaphorical punching bag again.

Unable to settle to anything, Beth shrugged on a jacket and set out for a walk. Maybe in the fresh air she could calm down and put everything into perspective. She walked along briskly, head down, barely noticing the houses on either side, skirting the trash cans positioned on the edge of the sidewalk. By the time she was out of breath, she looked around, mystified. Where was she? In her haste, she'd crossed roads and turned corners, and was now in a part of town she didn't recognize. How was she going to get home? Well, at least it gave her something else to worry about. Beth saw a figure in the garden a few houses down and broke into a run. She could ask this person the way home. As she drew closer, the figure began to look familiar. It was…

"Hello there. Out for a run? Lovely evening for it." The woman stopped in the midst of her trimming, a pair of secateurs in one hand.

"Ellen?" Beth stopped in her tracks. "You live here?" She looked at the house behind Ellen, which was almost a replica of her own.

"Sure do. Are you living somewhere nearby?"

"Yes. No. I'm not sure." Beth felt a fool, but she needed to find her way home. "I've recently moved, and I've been walking around for so long, I'm lost." She gazed around seeing the old water tower she'd used as a marker still in the distance.

"Well, seems to me you need something hot. Come on in and I'll put the kettle on. Hope you don't mind herbal tea."

As the women entered the house, there was a shout from the driveway, followed by the sound of a bike starting up.

"That's Travis," Ellen said. "He often goes out for a ride at this time when he's been stuck in front of his computer all day. We'll have the place to ourselves."

Beth followed Ellen into the kitchen, sat at the scrubbed wooden table and looked around. It had the same open feel of her own house, but there the similarity ended. Whereas her own new home was still pretty much an empty shell, this house was lived in. The tall dresser held a collection of Delft plates, and the table itself was strewn with books and papers. A large bowl of fruit took pride of place in the center, and a vase of rhododendrons had been pushed aside to make room for a laptop computer.

"Excuse the mess," Ellen laughed, picking up some of the papers and placing them on a chair. "Travis was busy in the office when I got home, so I set up my laptop in here." She pulled on her hair. "We don't usually live in such chaos. Now, tea."

While Ellen filled the kettle, set out a couple of mugs and slipped some slices of cake onto a plate, Beth wondered why she'd accepted the invitation. She'd agreed without thinking, and now she was here, she wasn't sure what she had to say.

"So you met my cousin, Jenny?"

"Yes." Beth was relieved. This was something she could talk about, something non-threatening. "She seems nice. She suggested we get together again – two Aussies away from home." She laughed, but was conscious it came out uneasily.

"Why do I think you're not altogether happy about that?" Ellen placed the two mugs on the table and sat down.

To avoid answering immediately, Beth picked up her mug and took a gulp. The lemon and ginger tea left a pleasant tang in her mouth, giving her a sense of well-being. The trepidation she'd previously felt in Ellen's presence had disappeared. She looked into Ellen's eyes and realized that, like Jenny, here was someone she could trust.

As if reading her mind, Ellen spoke. "You can trust me. I've been privy to many secrets over the years. I can keep my mouth shut. Is there something you want to talk about?"

"I..." Beth bit her lip. Could she really tell this strange woman what was bothering her? It would be a relief to unburden to someone. She'd thought maybe Jenny was the one, but she had connections in Australia. Ellen was completely objective. She met the other woman's eyes again, and something she saw there helped her make the decision. "I need to talk to someone," she began, "I came here when Mum died." Beth gazed into space picturing her mother's face. "She was a strong woman. Growing up on a farm, she tried to instil independence and self-reliance into me. And she did. Growing up, I was ready to take on the world. But I left home, moved to Sydney, to university, then a teaching position. I knew what I wanted to do with my life, where I wanted to go. Then I met Bryan." She hesitated, took another sip of tea and met Ellen's sympathetic eyes. "I met him at uni and couldn't believe the handsome young English doctor was interested in me." She smiled sadly, remembering the heady excitement of those days.

"You married?" Ellen asked gently.

"Yes. I gave up all the dreams I had, dreams of volunteering overseas, helping children in underdeveloped countries. He was a few years older than me and persuaded me I should support him in his career. At first I assumed we'd have our own children, but that didn't happen. Bryan's career always came first, and over the years I became 'the doctor's wife', then 'the surgeon's wife', then just 'the wife'. It was as if I lost my identity. Beth Carson disappeared, along with all of my old friends, to be replaced by Elizabeth Flynn, someone I didn't recognize. The old Beth only reappeared when I visited Mum and Dad in the country. Then Dad died, and Mum became sick. Bryan insisted she move into a nursing home in the city. She was never happy there." Beth rubbed her eyes to stem the tears which threatened.

"And now she's gone?"

"It was a peaceful end. But she knew what my life was like. She'd been telling me to leave Bryan for ages, but how could I?"

Beth picked up her cup again, expecting Ellen to say something, but she remained silent.

The pair sat still for a few moments, the only sounds the hum of the refrigerator and a dog barking somewhere outside, then Ellen prompted Beth, "Bryan?"

"He was never violent. Nothing like that, but…"

"There are other types of violence besides physical."

"So I've read now, but I didn't know at the time. I think Mum did." Beth hesitated again.

It had preyed on Beth's mind – something Audrey had said, something about not all violence being physical. It had made Beth take stock. She'd never considered Bryan's behavior could be classed as domestic violence. He'd never raised a hand to her, never physically assaulted her. All his behavior had been controlling, 'for her own good' or 'to protect his reputation'. That's why she'd accepted it for so long, considered herself at fault, tried so hard to be the sort of wife he demanded. Domestic violence didn't happen to people like them, like her.

But what if she'd been wrong? One evening she opened up her laptop and typed in Domestic Violence. In the long list of articles, she chose one titled *Forms of Abuse –Domestic Violence* and poured herself a glass of wine while she waited for it to boot up. She might need some Dutch courage for this. Once the page opened, Beth read down the list incredulously. Initially it referred to fear as being a key element in the way a perpetrator – could Bryan really be called a perpetrator? – exerted control. He had certainly exerted control, but… Beth read on, shivering as she began to recognize her former life in which she had felt powerless as described. As her eyes scanned the list she began to relive much of her life with Bryan: verbal abuse? – yes, emotional abuse? – yes, social abuse? – yes, financial abuse? – yes, controlling behaviors? – most definitely. She leant back, her eyes blurring. According to this article, she'd been the victim of domestic abuse, and as it stated, she'd come to accept Bryan's behavior as normal, while living in fear, fear of displeasing him, of disappointing him, of being a bad wife. How foolish she'd been. But it was easy to be wise when there was an ocean between them. Before reading this she'd have laughed at anyone who suggested she was a victim of domestic violence. Her mum tried, but didn't know the correct terms. She only told Beth she should leave, then in her death gave her the means to do exactly that.

"She heard how he spoke to me on the few occasions they were together, but she didn't… she never heard…" Tears began to trickle down Beth's cheeks, and Ellen handed her a tissue.

"He said some dreadful things. It was only when he'd had a bad day, lost a patient, or when one of his staff acted incompetently. He couldn't stand incompetence. He couldn't stand failure."

"What sort of things did he say?"

Beth looked down at the table and spread her fingers. "He told me he hated me, that he'd never loved me, he should never have married me, that I was useless, unattractive, a rotten housekeeper. He'd turn his back on me in bed." She raised her eyes. "Then, next morning it would all be over. He'd be back to the sunny disposition, kissing me good morning and planning his day. It was as if he were two different people," she said in wonder.

Ellen smiled encouragement, placed her hand on Beth's, but didn't speak.

"When Mum died, he was glad. He said maybe now I'd spend more time at home, looking after his needs. Then, when I learnt of the money Mum had left me, I knew what I had to do. I left."

"Just like that?"

"Just like that. I don't know how I found the courage, but I packed a bag and left. And here I am, in Florence." Beth smiled.

"Wow." Ellen leant back in her chair. "But there's something upsetting you now, something that made you walk until you became lost."

"He's trying to find me. Spreading rumours. Saying I stole from him."

"Why would he do that?"

"It's how he is. He can't bear anyone getting the better of him. He'd want me back, so he could punish me." Beth broke down in harsh sobs. "Sorry, I don't know what's come over me to go on like this. I barely know you and…"

"Hey, no problem. I tend to have that effect on people." Ellen smiled. "Who knows you're here in Florence?"

"No one. Ann, my mother's lawyer has my new email address, but I didn't tell her where I was going. As far as she knows I'm still in Australia. Bryan's threatened to bring in the police if she doesn't tell him where I am. Do you think…?"

"I think you're worrying unnecessarily, though I do see anxious times ahead for you. Your troubles aren't over yet, but you'll come out okay. It'll just take time. Meantime, can I suggest you look for new opportunities?"

"What…what do you mean?" Beth was bewildered. She remembered Ellen telling her she could sense things, but this was altogether too weird.

"You'll see," Ellen said and rose. "Another cup?"

Feeling she'd prefer something stronger, Beth agreed and the conversation moved from Beth's worries to more mundane issues relating to the town. Just as she was beginning to feel relaxed and ready to return home, Ellen asked a question, a question which floored her.

"And I understand you've met our friendly local lawyer?"

"Umm." Beth played for time. "You mean…?"

"The handsome Tom Harrison."

Beth played with her teaspoon while she tried to think of an appropriate answer. Why did the man's name keep cropping up?

"We met at Ms. De Ruis' place up at Seal Rock," she said eventually, realizing her hesitation might give Ellen the wrong idea. Tom Harrison hadn't given her the impression of being particularly friendly, or at least no more so than any of the others she'd met here.

"He's led a pretty solitary life since his wife died," Ellen continued. "Needs a good woman to put him straight." Then she laughed. "Listen to me trying to pair him off. Before I met Travis, I'd have shot anyone who tried to do that with me."

"I'd better go now." Beth rose. "Thanks for the tea and chat. If you can point me in the right direction, I'll make my way home."

Ellen led Beth to the door and pointed out directions. Beth felt a tad foolish when she realized she'd almost walked in a circle and her new home was only a couple of blocks away.

"What a fool you must think me," she said, only to have Ellen assure her it was a common mistake to make and that, to a stranger, all of these small streets must look alike. Reassured, Beth set off, determined to memorize the street directory before leaving home again.

By the time she reached home, Beth was ready for bed. She found herself humming as she undressed. The visit with Ellen had worked its magic. Already she was feeling better. However hard he tried, surely Bryan would never find her here?

Ten

Ellen stood still and gazed into space, hand to her throat.

"What's up?" Travis reached around her to grab a mug. "You look as if you've seen a ghost."

"Not quite, but close." Ellen turned slowly to meet her husband's eyes. "I had the strangest feeling… about Beth – the Australian woman I met."

"The one you've got lined up for old Tom?"

"I never said that." Ellen accepted a coffee and joined Travis at the table. She took a sip before continuing. Travis' warm hand covered hers on the table and gave her the confidence to go on. "It's odd. I'm getting mixed messages about her." Travis remained silent.

Ellen was grateful for his understanding. In her experience most men –let's face it most people – had little patience with what they called her flights of fancy. But Ellen knew her visions were real, and it was only a year ago she and Travis had shared the same horrific nightmare. But this was something different.

"It doesn't make sense," she said at last. "There's sadness tinged with relief, then a dreadful shock which rocks her new life."

"And…" Travis' hand tightened on Ellen's.

"I can't see any more. I can't see a resolution." Ellen closed her eyes in an attempt to bring back the prophecy, then shook her head. It had gone. She wasn't really surprised. She'd never been able to conjure up the future at will. These premonitions came in their own time and disappeared the same way.

"Will you…?"

"Tell her? I'm not sure. I don't like giving bad news. I'd only do it if I thought it would help her be prepared. Though for what I'm not clear. No, I won't say anything – unless she asks me," she added.

*

Tom hung up the phone and took his coffee outside. He stood on the deck and gazed over the lake, trying to work out what it was about the call that had disturbed him. Then it dawned on him. Simone hadn't been her usual bossy self. She'd seemed distracted, hadn't asked any of her usual intrusive questions, and answered his in words of one syllable. He took two steps back inside to return her call, then stopped in his tracks. If she didn't want to talk, another phone call wouldn't make any difference.

He downed the rest of his coffee and headed back inside, shaking his head when he saw the weekend papers lying around the floor, and the remains of last night's dinner congealing in the sink. Checking his watch, he realized he'd better get a move on. It was almost nine o'clock, and he was still in his PJ's. Simone's call had interrupted a leisurely breakfast, but Brad and Brooke, along with Brooke's mother were coming to lunch. Tom sighed.

It had been Brooke's idea to get the two parents together to discuss the wedding. "… and I know you'll just love each other," she'd enthused while Brad shuffled his feet in embarrassment, and Tom reluctantly agreed. Though he was stumped if he knew how he'd come to agree to them all traveling up here and to his providing lunch. He rubbed his chin. Better have a shave, too. He could light the barbecue when they arrived, and the fridge was full of the salads he'd picked up in town yesterday. Brooke had promised to bring dessert.

Walking upstairs, Tom wondered what this mother of Brooke's would be like. Probably an older version of his future daughter-in-law. That would make her a middle-aged fashion plate, maybe another Yvonne. Please God not! Louise was going to become part of his family, albeit through marriage. They'd be linked through Brad and Brooke and future grandchildren. He hoped they could find more in common than the young people. Still, Brad seemed to like her. That was something. She and Brooke had taken his studious son out of himself, and now there was this wedding to plan. His worries about Simone forgotten, Tom hummed as the shower water flowed over him. He owed it to his son to be polite to Brooke's mother, even to like her, if at all possible.

At exactly twelve o'clock, Tom heard a car stop in the driveway. Putting down the beer he'd been sipping, he headed for the door in time to see a tall, slim dark-haired woman emerge from the back of Brad's car.

"This is Mom – Louise." Brooke came forward to give Tom a peck on the cheek, while Brad gave his arm to the stylish woman dressed in tailored black slacks and blue pin-striped blouse. Her hair was the same black as her daughter's, cut in a bob.

"Hello, Tom." Louise's voice was high-pitched and sharp – a lady used to getting her own way. She peered at Tom over the top of a pair of half-glasses, an affectation if ever he saw one.

"Louise. Welcome." Tom held out his hand to find it enveloped in both of hers.

"I'm so pleased to meet you. Isn't it delightful these two have found each other? And Brad tells me you're a lawyer too?"

"I have a small law practice in town."

"Dad." Tom turned to his son with relief, and the two men hugged. "Where shall I put this?"

Brooke appeared, carrying a covered plate of something smothered in cream and fruit.

"In the kitchen, honey." Brad led her into the house, leaving the older couple to follow.

"This is a lovely spot. Lived here long?" Louise appeared intent on making conversation as they headed through the house to the deck.

"My wife and I built it when the kids were small. A long time ago, now."

"Yes, Brad said you were a widower. How many…"

"Janet died five years ago." Tom answered shortly, but it didn't deter his companion. He felt a hand on his arm.

"I'm sorry. I lost Brooke's dad over ten years ago. It's been hard." She seemed about to continue in this vein, then shrugged, tightened her grip on Tom's arm and dragged him to the edge of the deck. "Now tell me about this lake."

Back in his comfort zone, Tom proceeded to fill her in with the history and wildlife of the local area, till they heard Brad call out from inside.

"Dad, where have you hidden the beer? And do you have anything for the ladies?"

"Sorry." Tom disentangled himself from Louise's grip. "I'm forgetting my duties as host. Take a seat," he said, indicating the heavy wood setting. "I'll be right back."

"Here you are, son." Tom extracted a couple of bottles of beer from the fridge in the garage. "There's some white wine in the kitchen fridge. Will that suit you and your mother?" He looked around, but Brooke had gone outside to join Louise on the deck.

"Her name's Louise, Dad. Brooke's keen for you two to get along." Brad didn't meet Tom's eyes as he wrestled with opening the wine bottle. "You're both…" He hesitated, as if noticing the shock on his father's face. "It's not… I mean… shit, Dad, Mom's been gone a while now. Maybe it's time… Brooke thinks…"

"I'm not looking to replace your mother, whatever Brooke might think."

"Of course not, but… Hell, you're stuck out here on your own. You run your practice as if…, you only ever see your hunting and fishing buddies – and Simone and me. It's no sort of life for any man."

Tom bit the inside of his cheek to prevent him bursting out laughing. This, from a son who until recently had no social life whatsoever, who lived and slept his job, and who barely made time to visit his dad or his sister. Brooke had certainly influenced him in the short time they'd been together.

"It may seem solitary to you, but I'm happy with my life," was all he said, and without further ado, they joined the womenfolk outside, Brad carrying the two glasses of wine, while Tom ferried the beer, plus a basket of corn chips he'd found in the pantry.

While Tom fired up the barbecue, he could hear the others babbling on. It was mostly the women who did the talking, with Brad mumbling agreement from time to time. It might not bode well for Brad's married life – to be caught up in the net of a wife and mother-in-law – both ambitious and needing a man to complete their lives. But the boy seemed happy, and that was all Tom wanted for him. It would probably be good for Brad to have a woman's influence in his life again. He'd been the child who was closest to Janet, and missed her terribly when she died. Maybe a mother-in-law could take away some of his hurt.

"Can I help?" Tom's thoughts were interrupted by a gentle voice at his elbow and the delicate fragrance of... Turning quickly, he found himself staring into a pair of gray eyes, not two feet away from his own.

"Umm." Tom took two steps backward, almost falling over, and racked his brains for something he could say to make her move away, without sounding rude. "Salads," he said, remembering. "Yes, there are salads in the fridge – back in the kitchen. Maybe you could...?"

"Sure." And off Louise went.

Tom felt the sweat bead on his forehead and wiped it off with a tea towel. He was sure it wasn't all related to the heat now rising from the barbecue grill. By the time he'd cooked the steaks, Louise had not only brought out the salads, but had evidently been poking around in the kitchen. The table was now set not only with bowls of salad, but also cutlery, the earthenware plates he and Janet had picked up in Vegas, and a set of linen napkins he hadn't seen since Janet died. For the first time, Tom felt a twinge of regret for his solitary existence, but it disappeared as soon as it came. No, he didn't need all this fuss. It was okay for the womenfolk – made them feel comfortable. But when it was just him – or him and Brad – he didn't need it. Why, even Simone didn't make such a fuss when she visited. This made him think of the conversation with Simone that morning. His forehead creased at the memory. He must call her back.

"Here we are," he said, carrying the plate of steaks to the table.

"Sorry, Dad." Brad had the grace to look shamed. "I should have offered to help. Brooke and I got caught up."

"It's okay, son. I managed, and you and this lovely young thing have a lot to talk about. I remember what it was like when your mum and I were..." He stopped, figuring out this probably wasn't the best avenue to pursue.

"Dig in." Tom sat at one end of the table and picked up the beer he'd abandoned to start cooking. It felt empty. He was about to rise to fetch another, when Brad anticipated his move.

"I'll get them, Dad."

"And bring out the wine bottle, honey," Brooke smiled at Brad.

Left with the two women, Tom wasn't sure what to do. Neither of them had touched the food, and he was loath to be the first.

"Brad's a lovely boy," Louise said. "You must be so proud of him."

"Yes." Tom wished the 'lovely boy' would hurry back. "Do help yourselves," he said, offering the platter of meat to Louise.

"Thanks. I've always said it takes a man to barbecue a steak."

Tom was at a loss for words. He realized he'd been alone so long, he'd lost the art of polite conversation, conversation without a purpose. With the guys down at the club, it didn't matter. They could communicate with silence and the odd grunt. At work, there was something specific to discuss. Then it dawned on him. The wedding! That's what they'd got together for, wasn't it? To discuss the wedding.

"So," he said. "How are the wedding plans going?"

There was an awkward silence. Brooke and her mother looked at each other, as if each willing the other to speak.

"Here you go." Brad's return broke the silence, and the two women turned to him in obvious relief.

"Your dad's asking about the wedding plans, Brad," Brooke said. "Maybe you…"

"The girls here," Brad began.

Girls? Brooke, maybe – but Louise? Tom realized Brad was continuing to speak.

"They thought. We thought. Well, after out last visit, Brooke suggested…"

For God's sake, what was he rabbiting on about? It wasn't like Brad to be so tongue-tied.

Louise smiled at Tom and interrupted. "When Brooke saw what a lovely place you had, nothing would satisfy her but to have the wedding here."

You could have heard a pin drop. The wedding? Here? Tom gulped. "Umm."

"And now I've seen it for myself, I agree. Absolutely. This huge deck, the view, the lawn leading down to the edge of the lake. It's perfect." She smiled at Brad and Brooke who were holding hands, Brooke's face was screwed up anxiously awaiting his response.

"Oh, do say 'yes', Tom."

Tom's gaze followed theirs across the deck to the 'lawn' and down to the lake itself. The grassy area had been left to its own devices for some time and was now almost knee-high. He kept meaning to get it cut, but no one used it these days, and it provided perfect cover for the water birds which lived in that part of the lake. A small row boat lay unused on one side, the grass below it no doubt yellow and dead. A couple of old green plastic chairs lay on their sides nearby, left over from long-forgotten picnics, while his Chris Craft took pride of place at the side of the jetty. Out of the corner of his eye, Tom could see the remnants of what had been Janet's vegetable garden, untended since her death, any remaining plants long gone to seed. He could see her now, pottering among the beds, kitchen scissors in one hand, basket over her wrist, glancing up towards him with a smile from time to time. She'd reproach him to see it so neglected.

"Dad?"

"Well… it would take some work," was all Tom could think of to say.

"Oh, thank you, thank you." And before he knew it, Brooke had risen and thrown her arms around his neck. He inhaled her perfume, before she moved off and reclaimed her seat.

"I'm so glad that's settled," said Louise. "Now you and I can start planning in earnest."

Tom began to cut into his steak, then realized she was looking straight at him. She meant… She couldn't mean… "You and I?" he asked weakly.

"Well, you can't expect these two young things to plan their own wedding. That would never do. And since we're both on our own, it makes sense for us to combine forces. Don't you think?"

No, he didn't think. Or not that they should combine forces anyway.

"Brad said his sister was married from here," Brooke's voice broke into his musings.

But that was when Janet was alive. It was customary for the bride's family to arrange the wedding, and Janet had been in her element. Nothing was too good for their daughter. She and Simone had planned it all between them. All he had to do was provide the funds. He suddenly had an unworthy thought. Was this what it was all about?

Were they expecting him to stump up for the whole thing?

Louise must have read his mind.

"I'll pay for everything, of course. Alexander left me comfortable, but we'll need to liaise on the arrangements – marquee, lights, setting, tables, all the things that make the day special.

There hadn't been a marquee at Simone's wedding and Tom didn't remember lights and settings either. Maybe there had been, but he hadn't needed to be involved. Why on earth did he need to be involved this time?

Again it seemed Louise had read his mind.

"I know it's usually a woman's task, but since Brad's mom isn't with us, I thought we two could put our heads together. Hmm?"

"Maybe." Tom realized they'd all been eating while they talked, and there were now four empty plates on the table along with the empty salad bowls.

"We'll clear, Dad. And Brooke will bring out the dessert. You can stay here and make plans with Louise."

"Well!" Tom spread his hands on the table. "Seems we've a bit of work ahead of us if they want to have the wedding in…"

"We thought September, late September."

"So soon?"

"They're both well-placed financially. There's no reason to wait. Brooke has already moved into Brad's condo."

Tom hadn't been surprised when he heard. He suspected Brooke's gentle manner hid gloves of steel. She'd always get her own way, a bit like her mother.

"We should pencil in some dates." Louise opened her purse and drew out her cell phone. Tom watched with amusement as she tapped the face to find her calendar.

"Now, when are you free? I'll contact the celebrant, and once we have a wedding date we can get moving."

Shit, the woman was serious about this. Dates? Free? Who did she think he was? He didn't set dates. Gwen kept his calendar. That was it! Gwen!

"My assistant keeps my diary," he said. "Gwen. I'll have her contact you." Anything to keep Louise off his back, and Brad too.

"Oh!" Louise's mouth turned down, and for a moment, Tom

thought she was going to sulk. Then she smiled. "That'll be fine. Brad can give you my details. Here are the two lovebirds, now."

As she spoke, the pair emerged from the house, Brooke bearing a plate with the cream concoction she'd brought, while Brad had a tray containing four glasses and a bottle of champagne.

"I know we've already celebrated with both of you separately," he said, "but we wanted to do it with the four of us, now we're family."

"To us."

"Brad and Brooke."

The four voices chimed in unison, as they drank the toast.

"Coffee?" Tom asked, when dessert was finished, only to be told that the others would need to leave. Evidently the young couple had another engagement that evening.

"But we'll see each other again soon," Louise said as she stepped into the car.

However, it was Brad's final comment that stuck in Tom's mind. As he hugged his father goodbye, he whispered, "We knew you two would get on, Dad. You've both been alone for too long."

Eleven

Beth's mind was in a whirl. She couldn't think straight. Her face felt clammy, and her hands couldn't stop shaking. Bryan was dead! Not only that, but he'd died leaving gambling debts for which she was deemed responsible. It couldn't be true. Was it one more ploy to get her to return to Australia? Well, that wouldn't work. She loved it here.

She re-read the email from Ann. Evidently Bryan had suffered a heart attack in the hospital parking lot, and his colleagues had been unable to save him. Instantaneous, Ann reported. It had taken Bryan's lawyer a few days to locate Ann's contact details. He knew she'd been Audrey's lawyer and begged her to contact Beth. I'll bet, Beth thought, remembering the narrow-minded old school friend of Bryan's who'd often come for dinner with his equally narrow-minded wife. At least Ann didn't know where she was, but her friend was urging her to come home to take care of things. Things? What things? Bryan's effects, and the house itself, could go to the bottom of Sydney Harbor as far as she was concerned.

Beth picked up the mug of coffee which had grown cold while she was on the computer. She grimaced, checked her watch and rose. She couldn't do anything about Sydney right now. It was close to midnight there, and she had to go to work. She and Jo were driving up to Seal Rock to value the de Ruis estate today. She was looking forward to it, feeling a sense of ownership as she'd been first on the scene. She shut down the computer, grabbed her purse and got into the car.

"You're quiet, today. Something up?" Jo shot a sideways glance at Beth as they drove up the coast.

"Mmm," Beth muttered, dragging her eyes away from the magnificent view of the ocean dropping away on one side and the thick forested slope on the other.

"Want to talk about it?"

Did she? Beth wavered. It was pretty personal stuff. Jo didn't even know she was married – widowed, she corrected herself with a shudder. She still couldn't believe it was true. "No," she said. "Just some unexpected news from home."

"Right." Fortunately, Jo wasn't one to pry, but Beth knew she had to talk to someone. She cast her mind over the people she'd met here. The only ones with whom she felt comfortable to confide in were Jenny and her cousin Ellen, the weird bookshop owner.

"Here we are." Jo turned into the long driveway and pulled up outside the house. "Got all the papers?"

Beth held up a folder, and the two women got out of the car and headed to the door which stood open.

"Jenny said she'd open up for us," Jo said, but Beth had a strange feeling walking into the now empty house. It was as if she was expecting to find the owner, this Madeline de Ruis sitting there waiting for them. As they walked in from the sunshine, the house seemed to close around them, and Beth started when she saw an empty armchair sitting facing her.

"Is that…?" she asked, taking a step back.

"I think that was her favorite chair – where she died. You're not spooked are you? You were here before." Jo sounded so matter-of-fact, Beth stifled her unease.

"It was different. This time it seems so empty, as if she's really gone." As soon as she spoke, Beth realized how silly she sounded. The woman was dead. Of course she was gone, but she couldn't easily dismiss the feeling that had come over her. It was different from the warmth she'd felt on her last visit. It was as if the house was trying to tell her something. She gave a shake, telling herself not to be stupid. It was just a house, an old, well-loved house, a house whose owner had recently died.

By the time they'd spent a few hours sorting and valuing, Beth had forgotten her initial feeling, but when she found an old wooden box at the back of a large cupboard, the sensation came back again.

"What have you there?" Jo paused in her own work to help Beth drag the box out.

"It's quite heavy," Beth said. "It seems to be full of papers."

"Let's see." Together the two women pulled off the lid. Inside were indeed a lot of papers and on top was an envelope with the name Richard Turner printed in black ink.

"Richard Turner. I wonder who he is, or was?" Beth said, sitting back on her heels. She realized this was one of the surprising moments in her new job. While their task was to prepare the estate for sale, they often came across valuable items the family had missed. She'd been surprised when Jo instructed her to shake every book on the shelf, telling her she'd once found a recent will in one such book causing the family a lot of upset. Another time it had been some share documents hidden away for safekeeping.

"Looks like family. Best keep that one for Jenny. Leave it by the door, and one of us can take it up later."

Hiding her disappointment, Beth did as she was told and continued with the task of going through the other items. It was close to lunchtime when Jo called a halt, and they sat down to eat the picnic she'd prepared. After consuming a couple of ham and cheese sandwiches washed down with some mineral water, Beth was ready to keep going, but Jo had other ideas.

"We're almost done here. Why don't I finish off, and you can take that box up to Jenny? I'll help put it in the car, and you can come back down when you're done. No hurry. Take time for a chat. I'm sure the two of you have lots in common."

Not really, Beth thought as they lifted the box into the trunk of the car. Why does everyone here think Australians must have a lot in common? But I did like Jenny, she remembered, and it might be nice to have a break. While not physically demanding work, it was heartbreaking to sort through a deceased person's belongings. A bit ghoulish.

"See you soon," Beth called as she drove off up the track.

"Hello," Jenny greeted Beth at the door. "Are you and Jo finished, then?"

"Not quite. Jo's just finishing off. We found a box, which we thought you might have missed. It looks like personal family stuff. It's in the trunk. It might take two of us to shift it."

"Pity Mike's not here, but I'm sure we can manage."

They lifted the box out and into the house, but once there, Jenny didn't appear to be in a hurry to open it.

"Time for a cuppa, or do you have to rush back to help Jo?"

"No, she said…" Beth replied awkwardly.

"She said we'd have lots to talk about, didn't she?" Jenny laughed. "Everyone here seems to think Australia is one small speck on the map, and we all know people in common."

Beth smiled in reply, though inwardly wincing at the similarity to her own feelings. But she followed Jenny through to the kitchen and watched in silence as she took a couple of mugs from a shelf and filled them with coffee.

"I know," Jenny smiled. "I've fallen into the local habit – coffee always on the stove. It was always ready at Maddy's house, and it reminds me of her." Beth saw Jenny wipe away a tear. "Sorry, I still can't quite believe she's gone. Silly of me I know. But to have coffee always on the go with its enticing aroma, and her favorite cookies…" Jenny popped a couple of macadamia nut cookies onto a plate and placed it on the table. "It keeps her close. But enough about me. How's Florence treating you? Are you finding it easy to make friends?" Jenny wrapped both hands around her mug and contemplated Beth.

Beth flinched under the direct scrutiny and dropped her gaze. Jenny was still grieving for her godmother, just as Beth had grieved for her mother. Now Bryan was dead too. Her eyes filled with tears, not for Bryan, for herself. How was she to cope with the fact he was gone and had left her in debt?

"I'm sorry. Is something wrong?"

"No. It's…" Beth could feel the sobs welling up and took a gulp of coffee to hide them, but the coffee went down the wrong way, and she began to choke. At least that'll explain my tears, she thought, as Jenny poured a glass of water.

"Thanks." Beth put down the water and smiled through her tears. "I'm sorry. You have enough to worry about with your own loss."

"Jo mentioned you'd lost your mother. Was it recent? Maddy's been almost like a mother to me. My last link with my own mum." Jenny waited patiently for a reply while Beth tried to work out how much she could confide.

"Fairly recent, but it's not only that. Can I…? Can you keep a confidence?" Beth sniffed up her remaining tears and took another sip of water.

"Of course."

"It's like this," Beth started, wondering where to begin. "When I came to Florence, I was running away. Oh, I haven't done anything wrong, committed any crime," she said quickly, seeing Jenny's surprised look. "I left an unhappy marriage. My husband was a control freak. It took me a long time to realize it, and when I did, I had no way of leaving, nowhere to go, no money of my own. But when Mum died, I came into some money. Not a lot, but enough for me to make a new start."

"So you're safe now?"

"I thought I was, but now…"

Jenny raised her eyebrows.

"I heard this morning. Bryan's dead."

"Oh!"

"And he's left debts, gambling debts, for which I appear to be responsible."

"And you'd no idea?"

"I knew he gambled, but almost everyone we knew had a bit of a flutter at the races. And I knew he sometimes visited the casino, but I never imagined…" She took a deep breath. "My lawyer wants me to go back, but I can't do that. And I don't have any money to repay what is his responsibility." Beth felt a familiar flutter in her gut, not unlike the one she used to feel when Bryan came home in a temper. She'd thought he could never hurt her again, but it seemed he could still hurt her from the grave. She felt the blood run from her face at the very thought, and the room began to spin. The next thing she knew Jenny was forcing a fiery liquid through her lips. It burned all the way down.

"What?"

"Jack Daniels. Mike's favorite tipple. Feel better now?"

"I think so." Beth put a shaking hand to her forehead, "Did I…?"

"Out like a light. Scared the pants off me."

"Sorry, I don't know what came over me."

"Panic. Fear. I'd most likely have reacted the same way in your shoes. Seems to me you need some help. Lawyer-type help."

"Ann…"

"Is that your lawyer in Sydney?"

"Actually, she's in Wagga. She was my mother's lawyer. The Sydney one is a friend of Bryan's. I couldn't contemplate using him."

"What about someone here?"

"Here? Oh, I don't think…"

"There's Tom Harrison, not a stone's throw away, and you've already met."

Beth had a vision of the big fair-haired man whose presence, while apparently dependable, had provoked such odd sensations. She wasn't prepared to tell him her sordid little tale, but he appeared to be a good friend of Jenny and Mike, so she thought it best not to dismiss him out of hand. All she said was, "I'll give it some thought. Thanks for the suggestion."

*

It was the day of the de Ruis estate sale. The previous two weeks had passed without any further communication from Australia, and Beth was beginning to believe she'd been worrying unnecessarily. Maybe if she ignored Ann's email, it would all go away. After all, she was on the other side of the world. Could the legal arm of Australian law reach her here? But a niggling thought in the back of her mind reminded her of her innate honesty. If she owed a debt, she should pay it. But how was she going to find the money? Maybe the Hunters Hill house could bring in enough. Before she left, Beth dashed off a quick email to Ann with this suggestion. The house was in Bryan's name. He hadn't permitted her to own anything. So surely it could be sold without any input from her.

The de Ruis house looked different with everything tastefully displayed by Cicely and Betty. There had been so many items that Jo had hired a marquee, which now sat outside the front door, its flap open in welcome. Inside, the atmosphere was exactly as Beth remembered from the first sale she'd attended. It was like a church, the fragrances of lily of the valley and lilac filling the air and the soft music playing in the background.

"Will you do the cash again?" Jo asked as soon as Beth walked in. "I have a few things to see to, and the crowds will be here soon." She'd barely finished speaking when Beth heard the first few cars draw up.

From then on, it was non-stop action, and by the time the last buyers had left, it was close to five o'clock.

"Wow, we didn't stop!" Beth ran her hand through her hair which was now beginning to resemble a bird's nest. Reminding herself to find a hairdresser soon, she pushed back her chair and surveyed the empty marquee. She'd been sitting at the entrance, so hadn't been inside the house all day, but had seen lots of large and small items move past her as their new owners paid. "Is there much left?" she asked.

"Not a lot. It's been one of our best days," Jo replied, wearily. "I think we'll manage to load it all into the pickup. Save us coming back. We can drop the key in… Damn, no we can't. Shit! Jenny left me a message. They've gone out of town for the weekend. Didn't want to be here when it all went, I guess. I don't blame them."

"So, the key? Can we leave it somewhere?"

"They want it dropped off to Tom." Jo scratched her head. "He's probably out at the lake by now, if not on it. I'll need to take the stuff back into town. Could you…?"

"Tom?" Beth heard a shrill note in her voice. That bloody man again! She seemed fated to keep seeing him.

"Would you? It'd be a great help. I'll give you his address." Jo proceeded to jot it down on a scrap of paper.

*

Half an hour later, Beth was driving along the side of a large lake. It was a part of the region she hadn't visited before and the diversity of the landscape and the wide variety of water birds, swooping and even seeming to run across the surface of the water, surprised her. In the distance she could see a couple of small boats with heads bobbing up and down. Wasn't Tom Harrison supposed to be a fisherman? Maybe he'd be one of those out there, and her trip would be in vain. She wasn't sure whether she hoped for that or not. Probably not. She had to get the key to him some time or other, and the sooner the better.

Beth checked the torn piece of paper once again and drew up outside an imposing shingle-sided dwelling on the edge of the lake. The two-story home was set back from the road, its gray shingled roof gleaming in the thin sun of the late afternoon. The four dormer windows winked at her from their elevated position while the white fencing of the front veranda was almost hidden by greenery. It looked like a well-loved family home, a little battered by time, quite unlike the glossy Hunters Hill house she'd left behind. It had never been her choice, bought to satisfy Bryan's urge to big-note himself in the medical fraternity. This one looked as if it had a lot of stories to tell. It had seen a lot of living and loving, and had stood the test of time.

Grasping the key in one hand, Beth made her way to the wooden front door and knocked lightly. She wasn't sure she wanted to meet this man on his home territory. Maybe there would be no one home. But her unspoken hope was in vain. She heard a thump and a muffled curse from inside, then, the door opened to reveal Tom, barefoot, hopping on one leg and holding a bottle of beer. She wasn't sure which of them was most surprised.

"I...," she stuttered, holding up the key.

"Come on in. Sorry for this." He pointed to his upraised foot. "Stubbed a toe on the bottom of the stairs."

Beth stifled a grin. "Are you all right?" Tom looked like an overgrown schoolboy or a shaggy Old English Sheepdog. His hair was awry, his feet were bare, and he was dressed in long khaki shorts topped with a shirt the color of tomato soup.

"Ah, Maddy's key." Tom stretched out his free hand and attempted to balance on one leg, then, almost toppling, used the hand to steady himself against the doorjamb. "You'd better come in."

Beth was about to decline, when Tom turned his back and headed off.

Still clutching the key, Beth pulled the door closed behind her and followed Tom through a long hallway into a large open-plan room. At one end was a kitchen which looked out onto a large deck, and further to a wide expanse of lake. She stood in the middle of the room, unsure what to do next. Maybe she could drop the key on the table and leave.

But Tom pre-empted her. No sooner had the thought crossed her mind, and her hand moved towards the kitchen table, than Tom seemed to regain the use of his right foot. Putting his beer down, he hobbled towards her.

"Thanks," he said. "Look, you've driven all the way out here. The least I can do is offer you a drink."

Beth looked at the bottle of Coors he'd been drinking. Her face must have revealed her thoughts, because Tom immediately said, "I *do* have a bottle of white in the fridge. Can I tempt you?"

The word 'tempt' shook her for a moment, but the thought of a glass of wine was attractive. "I…"

"Go out to the deck, and I'll bring one out to you."

Grateful the decision had been taken for her, Beth dropped the key on the table and went through the French doors which opened onto the deck. She walked straight across to the rail and gazed out onto the still surface of the water. The small boats were no longer visible. Maybe the occupants had decided they'd caught enough fish for the day, or had given up in disgust, empty-handed. A trio of the birds she'd noticed earlier flapped their wings and seemed to race across the surface of the water. Leaning her arms on the rail, Beth checked them out. They were unlike any she'd seen before.

"Enjoying the local birdlife?" Tom's voice startled her, and she turned abruptly, almost bumping into him. They both laughed, any tension she might have felt in his presence, broken.

"Here you are."

Beth grasped the glass in both hands, the condensation dripping onto her fingers. "What are they?" she asked, "They seem to be running on the surface of the water."

"They're grebes. See, here come some more." Tom pointed, and sure enough, another pair came flapping by, heads erect, their webbed feet running so fast on the surface of the lake they sent up waves

"Amazing!" Beth said, taking a sip of her wine and thinking how astonishing it was that she was standing here drinking wine on the deck with this man and feeling… How exactly *was* she feeling? Beth tried to analyze it. Relaxed – yes, comfortable – yes, and – just a tad – excited. There was a bubble of something akin to pleasure rising up and threatening to overwhelm her.

"The lake's a home for many of our water birds," Tom said, leaning on the rail beside Beth, his arms so close to hers she could almost feel the hairs on them touch her skin. She shivered involuntarily and moved a fraction sideways, away from his disturbing presence.

"Look over there." Tom pointed to a clump of grass at the edge of the lake, right next to a well-worn jetty. Beth peered in the direction of his finger, but at first she could see nothing. Then a small stocky green bird came into view.

"Is that…?" she asked, a touch of excitement in her voice.

"A green heron."

"Wow! Jo told me it was a short stocky bird."

"A bit like her." They both laughed.

"Her very words," Beth agreed.

"They're fairly solitary birds found in shady spots like this. In the mating season they perform for each other – a delight to watch if you're lucky enough to have the opportunity."

"And they nest right here?"

"They sure do."

The pair stood silently for a moment, then, "Let's sit down," Tom said, leading Beth across to the heavy wooden table.

Perched tentatively on the edge of a bench, Beth carefully placed her glass on the table and folded her hands in her lap. One part of her wanted to know more about this man, find out what made him tick, another part wanted to rise and flee. She'd just erased one man from her life, and the last thing she wanted or needed was another. Beth's brow wrinkled as the warring thoughts flashed through her mind.

"Problems?"

"No… yes." Beth's fingers tightened under the table, as she remembered her present dilemma. Here she was, sitting opposite a lawyer, the very lawyer Jenny had suggested she talk with. Her stomach churned. She untangled her fingers long enough to take a sip of her wine. Tom was gazing at her, one eyebrow raised. She needed to say something, before Tom had her classed as a crazy woman.

"I need some legal advice," she said after a long pause, "but maybe this isn't the time or place. Your office…," she muttered, fearful he'd think she was asking for a free consultation.

"No time like the present." Tom put both hands, palms down, on the table and leaned forward. "I'm all ears."

Beth winced. She'd walked – or talked herself – right into this one.

She hesitated, then made a decision. She *did* need advice, and she *was* sitting opposite a lawyer, and he *had* offered. Her tongue seemed to be stuck to the roof of her mouth.

"More wine? It can't be that bad." Tom disappeared into the house, giving Beth time to compose herself. When he emerged again he was carrying a wine bottle. While he was topping up her glass, Beth licked her still dry lips, then took a gulp from the now brimming glass.

"It's my husband… in Australia… he's dead."

If she'd thought to shock her companion, she'd failed.

"Recently?" Tom asked, taking a swig of beer.

"Recently. But it's not that simple." Even as she said it, Beth realized that death is never simple. "He's left debts… and I'm liable."

"And?"

"And I can't pay them. I didn't know…"

"So, he was in Australia, and you're here?" Tom's forehead creased as he tried to figure it out.

"I left him." The words sounded so stark, so cruel.

*

Tom heard the break in Beth's voice. Was he really ready for this? He'd offered to help – to listen – without thinking, his only impulse to take the worry away from behind Beth's eyes. He'd known there was more to her than appeared on the surface. What had brought her all the way from Australia to Oregon, leaving her husband behind? But now wasn't the time to ask that particular question. He leaned back, prepared to listen, and focused on Beth's face, noting the changing expressions that crossed it as she told her sad tale.

"I married young," Beth began. "I won't bore you with the details, but things didn't work out as planned." Her eyes began to fill with tears, which she angrily wiped way with the back of her hand. "Sorry, I didn't mean to fall apart on you." Beth gazed into space as if remembering. "But until recently, I didn't have the wherewithal – or the guts," Beth's voice dropped to a whisper, "to leave."

"What changed?"

"My mother died. I received a small legacy. Enough to move here, buy a house, begin again."

"Then your husband died. Will you return to Australia?"

"No!" Beth spat out the word. "That's what… That's what they want me to do."

"They?"

"Bryan's lawyer. The creditors – the loan sharks, I guess."

"They've been in touch?"

"They don't know where I am."

But instead of looking pleased, Beth appeared downcast at this admission.

"Then, how…?"

"Ann. My mother's lawyer. They've been in touch with her." Beth rubbed the top of her short cropped hair with one hand, making hardly an impression on its surface. "Before Bryan died, they contacted her. Bryan claimed I'd stolen from him – money, jewellery…"

"And you hadn't?"

"Of course not! The bastard just wanted to find me – to drag me back. Now his lawyers are at it, too. Ann has my email address and passed on the message."

"Hmm." This was becoming more complicated than Tom had expected, though he didn't know exactly what he'd expected. He ran his hand through his hair and rubbed his chin.

"What would you like from me?"

Beth's lower lip quivered.

Oh, God. Surely she wasn't going to cry. He'd seen her eyes fill earlier, but she'd stemmed the tears in time. He wasn't good with weepy women. Janet had rarely let him see her cry. He'd always managed to comfort her when she did, but she was his wife, and that was five years ago. He was out of practice.

Wordlessly, Tom rose, went into the kitchen and returned with a box of tissues.

"Thanks." Beth took one, wiped her eyes and sniffed. "Sorry, I'm not usually like this. You… I… I guess I'd like to know what my rights are, and what I can reasonably be expected to do. I'm not trying to evade anything, but I definitely don't want to go back." She shivered, although the sun's rays were still warm.

Tom was trying to work out the implications of Beth's situation, and his lack of knowledge of the Australian legal system, when he heard a car skid into the driveway. There was the crash of a car door closing, the patter of footsteps and a blonde-haired woman followed by two small boys burst through in the doorway.

"Simone?" Tom half rose.

"I've left. I need somewhere to stay for a few days."

Twelve

"Who's she?"

At the words, Beth looked up to meet an angry pair of blue eyes. "I'd better go. I'll make an appointment." She grabbed her purse and fled, ignoring Tom's halting explanation and request for her to stay. What was she doing here? She'd come to return the key, not to join him in a glass of wine, not to spill her guts, not to be found weeping by… who was she?

Driving back to Florence, Beth regretted her hasty action. Surely she could have stayed? It would have been the polite thing to do, but the woman had made her feel like an interloper, as if she had no business being there. And she hadn't. Once she'd recovered her equilibrium, Beth could think more rationally. The woman and the two little boys. She looked young enough to be his daughter. Damn! She probably *was* his daughter – his daughter and grandsons. She clearly hadn't expected to find Beth there – to find any woman there. Beth's embarrassment turned to amusement as she imagined the conversation Tom was having now.

It had been good to unburden herself to Tom, felt right. But nothing was resolved. Beth was still left wondering what to do. She'd have to make an appointment with him at his office, as she should have done in the first place. As her thoughts swirled, Beth stopped herself from stepping hard on the gas. This was a steep, winding road. She didn't want to be the next casualty. It was with relief she saw the lights of Florence twinkling ahead and realized the sun had begun to set.

Breathing more easily, Beth decided to treat herself to a takeaway. She could pick one up on the way home. It would save cooking. She could feel the effect of the two glasses of wine she'd consumed. She probably shouldn't be driving. But, now she'd left the lake and Tom's place behind, Beth felt encased in a warm glow. He wasn't what she'd expected. Not sure what that had been, Beth didn't probe too deeply.

*

Tom felt, rather than saw Simone's eyes follow Beth and him through the house. When he returned to the deck, it was to discover she'd poured herself a glass of wine and was gulping it down while the boys wrangled over a toy car one of them had found lying in a corner.

"Who is she? I'm…"

"She was returning a key for a client," Tom spoke more sharply than he intended, angry that he felt he had to account to his daughter for a visitor to what was *his* home. "But what are you doing here on a weekend. Where's Ed?"

"I told you. I've left him."

Tom's eyes widened. Not what he expected. "You mean…?"

"For a few days. Till I get my bearings, and he comes to his senses. Can I stay here?"

Tom scratched his head, unsure how to deal with this new wrinkle. He was fond of Ed, didn't want to be seen to take sides in what was clearly a domestic dispute of some sort. He was well aware how difficult Simone could be, and suspected the pair often had their differences, but this was the first time it had come to this.

"Well, can we?"

Tom realized some time had passed since Simone's question. "Of course, it is your home, always will be," he said, trying to hide his dismay that his sanctuary was going to be invaded, albeit by his beloved daughter and grandchildren.

"Good. Come on, boys." Simone put down her now empty glass. "Grandad will find you drinks while Mommy gets our stuff out of the car."

"Do you need a hand?"

"No. You take care of the boys. Milk would be good, and they're probably hungry too. We left in a rush."

By the time Simone eventually joined Tom in the kitchen, the boys had demolished large glasses of milk along with some cookies saved from their last visit and were playing happily on what Louise had called the lawn with a couple of balls.

"Coffee?" he asked, holding up his own oversized mug, emblazoned with the slogan *Honey Do List* and a row of empty lines. It had been one of Janet's last gifts to him and was a favorite.

"Just a small one, Dad." Simone drew out a high stool and plopped herself down, elbows on the benchtop.

"So, are you going to tell your old dad what's up, or keep me in the dark?" Tom asked as he poured coffee into a more ladylike mug and added a generous spoonful of sugar.

Simone took a sip of her coffee before replying. "I need time out."

Time out? Tom had never heard of such a thing. Separation –yes, divorce – yes, but time out? "What do you mean? How long do you…? What's happened between you and Ed to bring this about?"

"Oh, Dad. You wouldn't understand. You and Mom never argued. She always gave into you, did things your way. It's not like that with Ed and me."

Tom felt his hackles rise. Wouldn't understand, indeed. He and Janet had been married for close to forty years. Of course they'd had their disagreements, but they'd always managed to come to some arrangement and put their differences aside. The love they had for each other was far greater than any differences they might have had. They'd had a strong marriage, because they'd worked at it, and it had become stronger over the years, until he'd lost her. But how to explain this to his daughter, who it seemed, had come running home at the first sign of discord in her relationship of less than ten years.

Simone looked up and met Tom's eyes. "I can see it in your eyes. You're blaming me, but it's not my fault. Ed's so…" She twisted her mouth into a grimace. "You weren't there. You didn't hear."

"Try me," Tom said gently. Simone had always been the feisty member of the family, always taking on the offensive in an argument. He had difficulty in believing that the mild-mannered Ed could be at fault. Most likely it – whatever *it* might be – was a figment of Simone's overactive imagination, some imagined slight or other.

"Okay." Simone drained her coffee and put the mug down with a thump that made Tom wince. "It's been building up for days, weeks. Tommy will be going to school in a year's time. I want to book him into one of the private schools in town, but Ed won't hear of it, says the public system was good enough for him, and the money could be better spent on other things."

"Well it was good enough for you, too," Tom reminded her.

"See? I knew you'd take his side. I don't know why I came here. And I find you cavorting with a woman right here on the deck!"

Tom hid a smile. Cavorting, indeed. He decided to let that comment slide, and holding up his hands, replied, "I'm not taking sides. This is between the two of you, but if it's only about money…" Doing a quick calculation, Tom reckoned he could stretch to school fees for his two grandchildren, because if Tommy went to a private school, then young Sam would too.

"No. That was just the beginning," Simone said bitterly. "Then we got onto the multiracial mix or lack of it, quality of teaching, exam scores, the importance of honesty, humility, integrity. I called him some dreadful names," she admitted. "So I thought it best to leave to give us both time to cool off."

"Mmm." Tom poured himself another mug of coffee while he took time to digest all of this. Seemed the fiery six year-old who'd bullied her younger brother still wasn't far from the surface of this elegant thirty-eight year-old. But Ed wasn't Brad, and a marriage wasn't a sibling relationship in which the parents could step in and make everything right. Simone would have to sort this one out herself. All he could do was offer advice. But right now, she was in no mood to listen to his advice, let alone accept it.

"Sorry, Dad. I'm boring you."

"No…"

But Simone had already risen and was making her way to join the boys by the lake. Tom shook his head and gathered the dirty mugs and glasses, reflecting he'd have to continue this discussion another time, when Simone might be more receptive. And maybe he could give Ed a call too.

*

Beth sat in the car, stomach churning. Her eyes flickered over the well-maintained flower garden surrounding the parking lot. It struck her as unusual for a lawyer's office, more like a private home. Maybe there was more to this Tom Harrison than appeared on the surface.

She drew a deep breath, hands clenched in her lap. The appointment was for two o'clock. It was five minutes to. Picking up her purse, Beth opened the car door and stepped out. The afternoon sun beat down on her, and the scent of lilac filled her nostrils. She breathed it in and tried to relax. What was she afraid of? She'd come here for help – for legal advice. *She* wasn't in trouble, not the sort of trouble that usually required a lawyer. Shrugging her purse strap over her shoulder, Beth made her way towards the entrance of the building.

"So, we meet again?" Tom rose from behind a large wooden desk. Although it was a business day, he was dressed as casually as ever. Today with his long khaki shorts he sported a blue polo shirt, which enhanced the deep blue of his eyes. "Take a seat. I'll have Gwen bring in some coffee."

Beth opened her mouth to refuse – she couldn't get used to the endless cups of coffee – but before she could say a word, he'd ordered it.

"So," Tom, repeated. "Sorry we were interrupted the other day. My daughter…" He dragged a hand through his hair before drawing a pad towards him and picking up a pen.

"I… I…."

"Coffee for two and there's a couple of your favorite cookies, too." Gwen pushed through the door and placed a tray on the desk, interrupting Beth's train of thought.

"Help yourself," Tom said.

Beth picked up a mug, shook her head to the offer of a cookie, and wrapped both hands around her drink.

"Well, as I told you…" she began.

"Best start again, and I can take down the details."

By the time Beth ended her story, Tom had finished the plate of cookies, and his pad was full of what looked to Beth more like doodles than notes.

"So, I don't know what to do," she concluded. "I don't really want to go back to Australia. There's nothing for me there. Can it all be sorted out from here? And what'll happen if I can't pay Bryan's debts?"

Tom leant back, balancing his chair on two legs and rolling his pen in both hands. "First things first. We need to see your husband's will. Find out exactly where you stand. You say you own," – he checked his notes and corrected himself– "*he* owned a large house in Sydney. I presume it'll be part of the estate and may well cover the debts."

Beth bit her lip. Jenny had thought that too. She wasn't so sure. Bryan had always been so secretive about finances. And now there were these gambling debts. What if…? But Tom was speaking again.

"You have his lawyer's details?"

"Ye …es." Beth's voice was almost a whisper. "John Blackwood. He has an office in Sydney, in the city. I'm not sure exactly where. But do you…?"

Tom didn't reply, but wrote on his pad. "I'll contact him, and we can go from there. And to answer your question. No. I don't imagine you'll need to go to Australia. We should be able to handle it at this end. The debts…" He rubbed his chin. "I'll need more information. Maybe this fellow Blackwood can fill me in on that. Don't worry," he added, as Beth's eyes began to fill with tears. Beth wasn't sure why, maybe relief someone else was willing to help her. "I'll be in touch when I have more information." Tom rose, and Beth figured their meeting was at an end.

Although she'd dreaded coming, Beth was now reluctant to leave. While she was here, in this room, she could imagine that the mess her life had become was shut outside, gone. But Beth knew her worries would return as soon as she left.

"Don't worry," Tom repeated, coming around the desk to shake Beth's hand, which he held for what she considered was a few seconds longer than necessary. "Maybe… maybe we could have dinner sometime?"

*

Shit! As soon as the words were out of his mouth, Tom regretted them. What the hell was he doing? She was a woman, a client, new to town, and here he was inviting her to dinner. He hadn't invited a woman to dinner since Janet died, and not for years before that either.

After he and Janet got together all those years ago, she'd been the one to issue the invites, not him. And to crown it all, he felt as nervous as a schoolboy on his first date. He saw Beth's eyes widen.

"I don't…," she began.

Tom spoke quickly, suspecting she was about to refuse. Bad enough he'd issued the invitation, but to be refused… Suddenly it was important to him that she accept. "Nothing flash. Mo's does a good clam chowder." He saw her eyes glaze over. "Or we could take in an early dinner out at the casino. Have you been there?"

Hell, here am I babbling on, he thought. A casino's probably the last place she wants to go. Tom closed his lips tightly together. Let the woman answer.

Beth raised her eyes, and Tom saw they reflected the smile that now sat on her lips. "Maybe," she said.

His hopes soared. "I just thought," he said. "You're new to town. It can't be much fun doing everything by yourself." Since when have I been concerned about that before, he wondered? "Tomorrow?"

"O…kay." The word was drawn out as if against her will. "I've been to Mo's."

What did that mean? She'd been there, done that, didn't want to go again, or…

"The casino, then, Three Rivers. They do a fair buffet." And they were less likely to bump into Yvonne and her ilk.

"I saw it on my way into town." Beth seemed as surprised at her acceptance of his invitation as he was at having given it. What a pair they were. They stood silent and motionless for a few seconds, then Tom collected himself and, opening the door, ushered her out.

"Pick you up around six?"

"How…? Oh, of course. You have all my details."

As Beth walked away, Tom stood watching her cross the parking lot and slide into her car.

"Smitten?"

He turned with a start to meet Gwen's amused grin.

"Hits you hard at your age," she said.

"Stuff and nonsense. I'm only entertaining a client, a newcomer to Florence. Anyone would do the same."

But Tom wasn't being completely honest. Returning to his position behind the desk, he twirled his pen in his fingers and considered what he'd just done. "What do you think, Janet?" he asked the portrait of his late wife. "Am I making a fool of myself? They say there's no fool like an old fool, and I can certainly fit that category. But you'd like Beth. She has a steely determination under that vulnerability. She's had a hard time. I want to see if I can help bring a smile into her eyes more often. Seems to me she hasn't had much to smile about lately."

Having convinced himself – and hopefully Janet's photo – of his honorable intentions, Tom settled down to compose an email to John Blackwood in Sydney.

*

What had she done? Beth drove home, her mind in a spin. She'd agreed to dinner without thinking. Tom had been so helpful, it had seemed churlish to refuse, but dinner? It was almost like a date. No almost about it. It *was* a date. This wasn't what she intended. It wasn't what she wanted, but… What the hell. She deserved to have some fun.

Once back in her own house, Beth felt a sense of release. She hummed to herself as she prepared a simple salad for lunch. Deciding to put the promised dinner to the back of her mind, she concentrated instead on the fact that she'd now put everything into the hands of a capable lawyer. She dashed off a quick email to Ann, letting her know that a Tom Harrison might be in touch, then freshened up.

Checking herself in the mirror, Beth paused. Who was this woman who looked back at her? She was barely recognizable as Bryan's wife – or widow, she reflected. Her hair was beginning to grow, and she now had a waving cap of gray, which made her look… She turned from side to side as she tried to work out exactly what she looked like. A frowzy woman past her first youth, she decided at last. No. Tom Harrison couldn't be interested in her as a woman. He was only being kind to a new client, to someone new to town. She should be relieved, but it was with a feeling more of disappointment than relief that she gave her hair a final pat before turning away from the mirror, and deciding to visit a hairdresser soon.

She'd promised to visit Jenny up at Seal Rock that afternoon. It would be the first time they'd met as friends, without having to discuss estate business, and Beth was looking forward to it.

The trip up the coast seemed to be quicker than before. She must be getting used to it. The sea was wild today, waves crashing against the rocks, and the trees swaying in the strong breeze. Before long, Beth turned into the long track, up past the de Ruis house to where Jenny and Mike lived.

"Hello, there!" Jenny was at the door to greet her, the black Labrador frolicking around her feet. "Come on in. Mike's gone down to Florence to catch up with Travis, so we have the place to ourselves. How about tea? I'm sure you're tired of all the coffee."

"That'd be lovely," Beth laughed following Jenny through to the kitchen, where she parked herself on a ladder-backed chair. "Is that…?" she asked, pointing to the pile of papers and photos lying on the table.

"Yes. I finally got round to delving into that box you found at Maddy's. It's so sad. She had his photo on the wall, you know. But I wasn't aware of all of this. He was a handsome fellow, a real romantic. Makes you think."

But Beth didn't hear what it made Jenny think. She was gazing in surprise at the photo of the young man in army uniform. She'd seen him before. He was the man in the photo Beth's mother had kept hidden away along with the postcards of Florence.

"What's the matter? You look as if you've just seen a ghost." Jenny placed two cups down on the table along with a platter of cookies.

"I have." Beth took a deep breath. "The man in the photo. Who is he?"

"Richard Turner, Rick. He was the love of Maddy's life. Killed in the war. She never forgot him. I never knew much about him. She didn't say much, but it's all there – photos, letters, the whole shebang. Listen to this." Jenny picked up one of the letters and began to read aloud, but Beth heard none of it. Her head was filled with a humming noise. What could it mean? What was this Richard Turner to her mother, and why had his photo been among her effects?

Thirteen

"Are you okay?" Jenny suddenly seemed to notice Beth's lack of attention.

"Yes. Sorry. It's just that… I've seen his face before. In Mum's things." Beth breathed deeply and took a drink of tea before continuing. "There were postcards too. That's what brought me here. I didn't…" Her voice broke. "I didn't know what they meant, where they'd come from, who he was. The cards were signed with an R. It could have meant anything. But as far as I know, Mum was never here. Could…?" Beth wasn't sure what she was trying to say.

"A mystery?" Jenny's eyes lit up. "Drink your tea first, then you must tell me all you know. There has to be some connection with Florence, maybe even with Maddy."

While Beth drank her tea, Jenny gathered up the papers, putting all the photos together in a pile. "Now, let's look through them," she said, placing them on the table one by one.

"That one." Beth pointed to one of a young man dressed casually in flannels, open-necked shirt and patterned pullover. "That's the one I have – Mum had."

The two women looked silently at the snapshot as if it could tell them its story, and the link between Rick and Maddy here in Florence and Audrey back in Australia.

"You said your folks came from here, didn't you?" Jenny asked at last. "Maybe…"

"Not here, not Oregon. And it was my grandparents who emigrated to Australia from Minnesota. As far as I know no one's been back here since. Maybe…, maybe this Rick was a pen pal, or…" A bubble of excitement began to fizz up inside Beth. "Maybe we're related. Could Mum's family have relatives here in Oregon? He did live here, didn't he?"

"One thing at a time," Jenny smiled. "To answer your last question first – yes, Rick did live here in Florence. According to what I've read so far, Maddy and he met before the war, but they didn't have much time together before he went off to fight. As to your other question, I suppose anything's possible. Do you want to try to find out?"

"I'm not sure where to start. And Mum never mentioned him. Surely…? What if…?" Beth's imagination was working overtime. What if she didn't like what she found out? Wouldn't it be better to let sleeping dogs lie, as they say?

"Your call. I'm in the midst of going through all the stuff in the box – letters, photos, even dried floral bits and pieces. Maddy kept everything. I never knew. She had his photo on the wall, but all of this…" Jenny waved her hand over the pile on the table. "He meant a lot to her, and the letters… They're so romantic. Poor Maddy. What a loss she suffered."

The two women sat in silence contemplating the devastation the war had wrought on those who had lost loved ones.

Beth was conflicted. While she was keen to find out more about the mysterious R in her mother's life, who now appeared to be Madeline de Ruis' deceased fiancé, she was wary of sounding too eager. "Maybe some other time," she said. "He's not going anywhere, is he?" Then, aware her words may have sounded too flippant, she quickly added, "I mean there's plenty of time."

"Did you contact Tom?" Jenny asked, clearly intent on changing the subject, but this was one Beth wanted to keep off limits too.

"Yes," she said, hesitating as she wondered how much to reveal. Jenny was becoming a friend, but Beth had reservations about sharing too much. "He's going to contact the Sydney people, see if he can get more information, then…"

"Oh, good," Jenny interrupted, saving Beth from any further explanation. "Tom'll get it sorted for you. So there'll be no need for you to go back, then?"

"No." Beth was sure about that. Although the house was warm, she shivered in fear at the thought of returning to Australia. "He didn't think so." She sipped her tea and wrapped her hands around the cup, thinking quickly. Jenny had been living here for some time. She and Mike seemed to be close to Tom. Maybe she could find out a bit more about him.

"He… he seems kind," she said, feeling her way and wondering how to ask the questions she wanted answered without giving too much away.

"He is. He doesn't say much, but he…" Jenny paused as if unsure of what she was about to say. "He's helping us – Mike and me – set up a trust."

"A trust?"

"Yes." Jenny bit her lip. "When I… When Maddy invited me to visit a few years ago, she wanted to set things in place so that I could have her house when she…" Jenny took a shaky breath. "Well, when Mike and I got together – not completely without Maddy's encouragement, I might add – when that happened and she could see I was firmly ensconced at this end of the track, she had to rethink what was going to happen to her house. We only decided a few weeks before she passed," Jenny said, her eyes filling with unshed tears. "So there wasn't time to put everything in place. She'd have hated that." Jenny smiled. "Maddy always liked everything cut and dried, but this time… Anyway, we knew her wishes, so Tom is helping make them reality."

"And?" Beth was curious. She'd felt drawn to the de Ruis house, to its comforting ambiance, the sense of years of happiness – an almost spiritual feeling about the place.

"It's to become a women's refuge. We already have a couple in town, but one up here away from everything will be different. It will give the women who live here a sense of space."

"And Tom's helping?"

"He's been wonderful. He understands not only the legal issues involved, but the importance of it to the community – to the women."

"Hmm." Beth digested this new insight into Tom. He was definitely a far cry from the man she'd left behind in Sydney, the man who'd seen women as people to be controlled, used to bolster his own ego, and to show off as the occasion might demand. She wanted to ask more, but all she said was, "The fair, wasn't that…?"

"Yes. The fair was in aid of the refuge in town. This one – we'll call it Madeline House – will be funded from the trust."

"What a wonderful legacy." Beth could feel her own eyes beginning to fill. If only… She drew in a shuddering breath. No, even if she'd been familiar with such places back in Sydney, she could never have… Bryan would have… "And the women…?" she couldn't help asking. "Do they…? Are they…?"

Jenny seemed to know what she wanted to ask. "Some have alcohol or drug problems, but most are victims of domestic violence. They come from all walks of life. And the abuse isn't always physical. The other types aren't so easy to see. Oh, I'm sorry," she said, clearly noticing the stricken look on Beth's face. "Of course, you know all about that." She fell silent.

"It's okay. Really." Beth waved a hand in the air as if by doing so, she could wave away decades of emotional abuse. "It's over for me. But these women are still suffering. What a magnificent bequest. I'd like to help." The words were out before Beth had time to consider the implications. Did she really want to help abused women? Would it bring it all back? Remind her of all those occasions when she'd felt helpless, unable to answer back, to fight back? She stretched her neck and lifted her head, meeting Jenny's bewildered eyes.

"Are you sure? I mean…"

"Yes," Beth's voice came strong and determined. "I am. I know what it's like to feel helpless, to wonder if it's my fault, to finally recognize there may be a way out, but to be scared to take it."

"Oh, Beth!" Jenny reached both hands to grasp Beth's firmly. "That would be so great. You'd be able to add something special – your own experience. Something none of the rest of us have."

"The rest of you?" Beth drew her hands back and clasped them together. What had she just let herself in for?

Jenny's face lightened, and she began to speak quickly in her eagerness, "We've formed what I guess you might call an interim committee." She laughed. "It all sounds very formal, but believe me it isn't. Only, Tom insisted that we do everything by the book, so…" Jenny stretched her arms wide as if to encompass the extent of Tom's influence.

"A committee? Oh, I don't think…" Beth wondered how she could back out now. When she'd offered to help, it had been a spontaneous response to the idea of a women's refuge, but a committee? That sounded all too much of a commitment, one she wasn't sure she was ready for.

Jenny seemed to understand her reluctance. "Don't worry. We're not really that organized or formal. So far, we've just had a couple of meetings here over a few glasses of wine."

"Who?" Beth risked asking.

"Well, Mike and me, of course. And Tom with his legal brain. And Ellen and Travis. Oh, and Jo's keen to be involved too."

Beth felt her breathing become easier. These were all people she already knew. All except Travis, that was. And she'd read his book, so felt she had a bit of an acquaintance with him. More importantly, the women at least were all already familiar with her past. That meant she wouldn't have to go over it all again for strangers.

It seemed Jenny had been watching closely and had noticed Beth's imperceptible sigh of relief. "You'd be okay with them, wouldn't you? We're meeting here again next Monday at seven. Why don't you join us? No obligation. Just come along and listen in, then you can decide if you want to be part of it or not." Jenny tilted her head to one side as if waiting for an answer.

Beth looked down into her now empty mug, realizing that, now she'd offered to help, it would be churlish to refuse to attend what was really a simple get-together of people she was already beginning to regard as friends. "Okay. That sounds good," she said reluctantly, then looked up again. "I mean, thanks, I'd love to come."

"And I'll keep a look out for anything that links Maddy and her Rick to your mum, shall I?"

"Oh, yes please." Beth had all but forgotten about the curious coincidence. "That'd be great. And I'll…" But she wasn't sure what she could do in that regard. While it would be nice to discover what the link was between her mother and this beautiful spot in Oregon, she could live without knowing – or could she? Now she'd discovered one piece of the puzzle, she had a feeling it would nag away at the back of her mind till she found more.

By the time Beth rose to go, Jenny had filled her in on her own story, giving her an inkling of the happiness that could be found in later years. Jenny was very clear that neither she nor Mike had been looking for or had wanted the complication of a relationship, but as Jenny put it, 'Fate had a way of getting in the way, helped along by Maddy's inimitable instinct'.

"So, you're okay about meeting Tom again?"

Beth stopped in the act of lifting up her purse. How did Jenny know?

"Tom?"

"Next Monday. He'll be here. I get the feeling you shy away whenever his name's mentioned."

Beth felt a blush rise from her feet right up to her cheeks. Was she really so transparent? "No, that'll be fine," she said, glad she hadn't mentioned her forthcoming dinner date. That would really have given Jenny – and no doubt Mike too – something to talk about.

*

"Bet it's nice to have a proper dinner, Dad," Simone greeted Tom when he returned home from the office. He sighed as the two little boys, already in pyjamas, started to run around his feet, whooping with delight at his return. Although he loved them dearly, all he wanted to do was to put his feet up, grab a beer and catch up with the day's news on Sky Channel. A piece of pizza or slice of bread and cheese was his usual fare at this time of day. He often ate out at least one meal each day, and he'd had lunch out with some of the guys.

He dragged his hand through his hair, eyes taking in the carefully set table, as the aroma of a roast assailed his nostrils. Simone had pulled out all the stops. He wondered if Ed got the same treatment back home. He doubted it, suspecting a quick and easy meal was more common.

"I fed and bathed the boys earlier. They've only stayed up to say goodnight, and maybe you could…"

"A story, Grandpa Tom," they chorused, little Sam stammering in his excitement.

Seeing any hopes of a relaxing time in front of the television was out of the question, Tom hoisted one child on his shoulder and, hefting the other under one arm, carried them upstairs, making noises he hoped sounded like an engine.

"Broom, broom," echoed little Tommy, while Sam erupted in a fit of giggles.

They were far from sleep, but such is the unpredictability of children, by the time Tom had read the two stories demanded, their little eyes started to close, and he was able to return downstairs.

Once there, it was clear Simone was making an effort to ingratiate herself. She'd poured him a beer, the ice cold glass awaiting him on the deck where she was sipping a glass of wine.

"I heard you close the door," she said in explanation of the beer, but not of the wine bottle, which Tom noticed was now half empty. "Dinner will be ready in half an hour. I thought…" She twirled the glass by the stem. "I thought you'd appreciate a homemade meal. There wasn't much in the pantry, so I did a shop. I… It's good to be home," she finished.

Tom sighed. Simone was his daughter, but he felt he was being taken over. Exactly what he'd been trying to avoid. It had taken a while, but he'd come to terms with living alone, moved through the awkward stage of missing his lifelong companion to enjoying his solitude. He'd never forget Janet, never get over her death completely, but over the years he'd made a life without her, evaded the machinations of the local women, and developed a routine. Now Simone had arrived to disrupt what had become to him an orderly life.

"That's good of you, hon." He sat down, took a long swig from his glass and wiped his mouth with the back of his hand. He reflected how, since Janet was gone, he'd become accustomed to doing without the niceties of using glasses, instead drinking straight from the bottle – saved washing up was his view.

"Seems you've been letting things go," Simone began. "I noticed…"

Shit! Tom tipped his chair back and regarded his daughter with jaundiced eyes. So she'd been doing a bit of snooping while he was at the office. He thought back. Yes, this would be the first time she'd been here alone with time to pry. Not that he blamed her. She probably felt she had a right. She'd grown up in this house, no doubt still regarded it as her home, even though she hadn't lived here for years. But it was *his* home, his refuge from the world, and it was exactly as he liked it.

"It suits me," he said. "No need for all the fancy stuff when I'm on my own."

"So I see."

She appeared to be about to say more, but Tom interjected, "How was your day? What did you and the boys do besides checking up on your old dad?"

Simone's face twisted up in one of the expressions he remembered from her teenage years – not one of her best habits. He used to say her face would stick that way, but couldn't say that to her now she was an adult. He satisfied himself with a rueful smile.

"I'm only trying to help, Dad. Why don't you get a housekeeper? I could ask around while I'm here."

And have someone else poking and prying around? No thanks. Tom decided it was best to ignore Simone's suggestion. Instead of replying he asked, "Did you talk to Ed?"

"No. I'm giving him time to reflect. To see how he likes it with us gone. He'll come to his senses soon." Her tone belied her confident words, and Tom noticed her mouth turn down. So she wasn't as self-assured as she wanted to make out.

"And how long do you think it'll take?" Tom drained his glass while he waited for Simone's reply.

She twisted her glass in one hand, and stroked the table with the other, refusing to meet his eyes. "I don't know. I can stay here, can't I?"

"It'll always be your home," Tom said, knowing as he said it that the last thing he wanted for was Simone to stay for any length of time, while obligation to Janet's memory insisted he agree. Simone's fleeting visits were one thing, and although he enjoyed the boys, he was always glad when they left and he could return to his peace and quiet. For her to be staying for an indefinite period… He pushed his hands through his hair. "But your place is with Ed – you and the boys," he said at last.

He was prevented from saying more by the bleep of the oven timer. Simone jumped up.

"That's dinner ready. I hope you're hungry. I used one of Mom's old recipes."

The meal of pot roast accompanied by mashed potatoes and green beans passed pleasantly. It wasn't until they were relaxing with a final cup of coffee that Tom found himself floundering in difficult waters again. "That was a real treat, Simone," he said, having eaten more than he'd thought possible. "You've got your mom's touch when it comes to cooking." Pleased to see her bridling with pride at his words, Tom was unprepared for Simone's next utterance.

"I'll do another for us tomorrow. I bought a nice piece of pork today. Remember how you loved the way Mom used to do it?"

"Hmph. Tomorrow. Can't do tomorrow, hon. I won't be home for dinner."

Simone's face fell. "Won't be home? Where else would you be? After all the trouble I'm going to, I thought…" Her face began to crumble, and although he wanted to make things right for his daughter, Tom was darned if he was going to change his plans.

"I'm meeting a friend for dinner."

"A friend? Maybe he could come here? There'll be plenty." She looked across expectantly.

Realizing the fat really would be in the fire if he revealed who his dining companion was going to be, Tom thought quickly.

"Not a good idea. We'd planned on going to the casino. Play a bit on the machines." He coughed to hide his embarrassment at lying and rose quickly lest his face gave the game away. It would never do for Simone to guess who he was taking to the casino. Tom was conscious of an unwelcome feeling of guilt, which he immediately suppressed. Simone wasn't here at his invitation. He didn't really want her here. But now she was here, he wasn't going to change his life around to accommodate her. She'd have to realize he had his own life to live.

Fourteen

As they entered the bistro, Beth looked around her in surprise. The dining area was quite large. A chef manned a bain-marie along one wall, while a collection of salad platters and desserts were laid out on the other to entice the diners. They'd had to pass through a mass of clanging slot machines on the way in, and she'd kept her eyes downcast. This wasn't her scene. She was beginning to feel distinctly uncomfortable and wondering why on earth she'd agreed to dinner here of all places.

"I'll get us some drinks," Tom said as Beth took her seat at one of the few empty tables. "White wine?"

"Thanks." She examined the other diners, noting several large groups obviously celebrating some family event, interspersed with smaller groups of older people, mostly women. The noise from the slot machines penetrated this area, even though it was set off to the side. It brought it all back – the gambling, the debt, Bryan's deceitfulness, his…

Her thoughts were interrupted by Tom's return. He placed a large glass on the table, taking his own seat opposite, and raising a beer to his lips. "Well," he began, smiling, "what do you think of our casino? Sorry you came?"

Beth felt her face redden. Had he guessed her thoughts? "I…" she looked around her. "It's not what I expected."

"Not what you're used to?"

"It's not that. We have clubs in Australia – Returned Soldiers,

Sports. It's a bit like one of those, with all the poker machines."

"Poker machines? Oh, you mean the slots?"

"Is that what you call them? Well, yes. I guess I expected… from a casino… something more…" Beth couldn't figure out how to say it without sounding rude.

"Something a bit more glamourous?" Tom's smile widened. "It's all here – Roulette, Craps, Poker, Blackjack, Let it Ride, Pai Gow, No Limit Texas Hold 'Em, plus the old favorites keno and bingo. We bypassed it coming in. I didn't think you'd want to be reminded."

"No." Beth began to relax, though it was a bit disconcerting that Tom appeared familiar with the games, most of which she'd never heard of. It was *her* decision to come here. They could have been sitting in Mo's by the river with no grim reminders, but she'd wanted to see what…? To see what had attracted Bryan, she supposed, but this wasn't what she'd expected, this friendly, noisy, almost family atmosphere. Just as she was figuring out how to explain this to her companion, there was the loud sound of bells ringing followed by cheering.

"Jackpot," Tom said. "And I'm not as familiar with all these games as I sound. Living here, I hear a lot, see more than I'd like of the results of gambling on families." His face lost its cheery smile. Beth was conscious of his feet shuffling under the table. Tom's hands moved on the table, and for a moment she thought he was going to take one of hers. She automatically drew back, but she needn't have worried. Instead, he picked up his glass and took another gulp of beer. "I'm sorry. Maybe this wasn't such a good idea. It must remind you…"

"No, it's fine." And surprisingly, it was. Tom's company was comforting, his bulk reassuring. "I can't avoid places like this just because of Bryan's history with them. I need to move on. It seems a popular venue."

"It is that. A few of my old dears…" Tom coughed. "Clients, I mean. Elderly ladies who've been widowed or divorced, on their own. This is their only bit of fun. They come here a couple of times a week play the slots, have lunch or dinner. They're not serious gamblers, you understand. I guess it gets them out of the house, provides a bit of company."

"Mmm." That would explain the groups of older women Beth had noticed earlier. It made perfect sense when Tom said it, but it was so far from her own experience she couldn't help but be somewhat shaken. It wasn't something she could imagine doing herself. Her mother, too, had shunned the club scene back home. This would have shocked her to the core. But somehow, looking at the women around her, it seemed an okay thing for them to do, an okay place for them to be. Beth let out a breath she hadn't been aware of holding. She guessed it was a matter of degree. They weren't here to gamble away their savings, only to enjoy the company and maybe win a few dollars.

"You okay?"

Beth realized Tom was looking at her strangely.

"It's a lot to take in. It's so different."

"Little old ladies don't gamble in Australia?"

"I guess so, but none I know." She laughed.

"Not all gambling's addictive, you know. Your husband… he didn't seem to know when to stop."

"No." Somehow, Bryan and Australia seemed so far away.

"Hungry? It's a buffet, so we can go up anytime, and as often as you like." Tom grinned, and Beth had the impression he often ate here and was in the habit of making several trips to the buffet. "Shall we?" He rose, indicating she should do the same.

Beth followed him, and soon the pair returned to their table with plates heaped with food, Tom's much larger than hers. As she was picking up her cutlery, Tom began to speak.

"I guess I owe you an apology."

Beth raised her eyebrows, and waited.

"Simone. My daughter. She's not the politest member of the family. She…" Tom ran a hand through his hair, a habit Beth had noticed he had when anxious.

"You did mention… in the office…"

"Right. Thing is… She's staying with me for a bit." He began to cut into his roast beef, and speared a potato on his fork.

"Problems?"

"I think *she's* the problem," Tom said, with a rueful chuckle. "She's always liked getting her own way. Now she's not finding it so easy."

"Her husband…?" Beth asked cautiously. She didn't want to intrude on Tom's personal life, but he had started the conversation. Also, she was wary of becoming involved in discussion of someone else's marriage. Her own was more than enough to be dealing with.

"Ed's a lovely guy. Usually lets her run all over him. Needs a bit more backbone, I sometimes think. But this time, seems he's dug his heels in."

"Mmm?" Beth muttered, her mouth full one of the delicious salads she'd selected, not sure she wanted to be part of this conversation.

Tom laid his cutlery down, clearly determined to be open about his family problems. He sighed. "It's about the boys. Their schooling. You don't have children?"

Beth felt a tightness in her stomach at the question. She looked down. How she'd have loved children. "No."

"Well, not an argument you'd be familiar with, then. Sorry to bother you with this." He ran his hand over his hair. "Sometimes… sometimes I need someone to talk to."

There was silence as they finished eating, both lost in their own thoughts. It wasn't till they rose to check out the desserts, that Tom spoke again, this time it was on a different topic.

"Have you been on the Dunes yet?" he asked, as Beth was trying to decide between the rhubarb pie and the strawberry ice cream.

"The Dunes?" she asked. "Isn't the whole place built on them? There certainly seems to be enough sand around." She was remembering the homes she'd seen on her walks which seemed to be built on floating foundations, and the sand that had blasted her on her way into the supermarket one especially windy day.

Tom smiled as they made their choices, Beth opting for the ice cream which she thought might be less filling than the large helping of pie Tom had added to his plate along with a generous serving of ice cream. "You're right, of course. Florence was originally a sandspit, and the dunes stretch for forty-two miles along the Oregon coast. They're a popular tourist attraction. Probably why you've not come across them. People go out on them on horseback and dune buggies."

"By people do you mean you do?" Beth was pleased she was beginning to find out more about this man. She tried to imagine Tom racing across a wide expanse of sand in one of the ATV's she'd seen in pictures, and failed miserably.

"From time to time," he replied. "Fishing's more my bag, but they're worth checking out. Travis Petersen is the one to talk to. Bikes and

ATV's are very much his thing. Ellen Williams' husband. You've met Ellen?"

"The bookshop owner. Yes, and I've read her husband's book, but I haven't met him."

"You will. We're a close-knit community here, and it looks like we're mixing in the same circles."

Beth dipped her spoon into the ice cream, and took a small mouthful. It was strange to think that she'd already become part of a circle of friends. A warm tingle spread through her. It was as if she belonged. How odd. She counted back. It was only two months since she'd left Sydney, and already it seemed like a different world. She'd been a different person then. Now, it was as if a weight had been lifted from her shoulders, Beth felt free. Until she remembered the debts Bryan had left. How could she have forgotten?

"Penny for them?" Tom's voice interrupted her thoughts.

"Sorry. I was miles away."

"Back in Australia?"

"No, not really, I was counting my blessings. I really have felt welcomed into the community here, even though I still haven't met many people. Those I have met have been lovely. Jo, Jenny, Ellen." She paused. "And you," she added in a quiet voice.

"I certainly hope you consider me a friend," Tom said, with such a wide smile that Beth couldn't help but smile back.

"I do." A good friend, she decided. He was the first man she'd felt able to trust since she left Australia, since way before then, too. Beth shivered at the realization of how Bryan's behavior had affected all of her dealings with the opposite sex. From the happy-go-lucky girl she'd been when they first met, Beth had turned into a cautious and suspicious person. She'd drawn into herself, become unrecognizable, only thawing out in the presence of her parents, latterly only her mother.

Beth sighed. "I'm glad I came here," she said. "Jenny…"

"She tells me you're going to join us in the Madeline House Project."

"Yes." Once again Beth wondered if that had been the right decision. It was still all too close. What if it brought it all back? All the memories she'd managed to push to the back of her mind. Could she bear that? At least Tom was unaware of her real reason for leaving

Bryan, but what if he found out? Would he think any less of her? And did that matter? She was beginning to think it did – that his good opinion was something she'd value. He'd been remarkably tactful so far in not asking her reasons for leaving Bryan, but he must be wondering.

"And why Florence?" Tom asked, clearly unaware of her thoughts reeling from one question to another.

"No reason," Beth said quickly, her old persona automatically reasserting itself, before she pulled herself back to the present. "No, sorry, that's not quite accurate. When my mother died, I was sorting through her effects and I found a photo and some postcards. The cards were from Florence, so I guess my subconscious brought me here. I didn't deliberately set out to come to Florence. I just drove up the coast and here I am."

"Well, I'm glad you did," Tom said, raising his glass, "To your subconscious!"

Beth clinked her glass with his. What a lovely man.

Fifteen

Beth stepped into her car and set off for the meeting at Seal Rock. She wasn't sure if becoming involved in this women's refuge project would prove to be a big mistake. Driving up the winding road with which she was becoming familiar, Beth had time to think, to remember. How had she managed to survive all those years of being abused by Bryan, who had claimed to love her? He'd never hit her; his abuse had taken different forms. How did those other women survive? Those who suffered a more physical form of abuse. Was she really like them? One of them? Her foot pressed down heavily on the accelerator as her anger rose. As the car almost ran into the bank, she came to her senses and eased off, slowing down to a safer speed. How could thinking of Bryan still have such an impact on her? He was dead. He could never hurt her again, never make her feel so insignificant she wanted to curl up and disappear.

But a tiny wisp of something reminded her once again of the debts he'd left behind. Maybe he could still reach her from beyond the grave. She shivered and wondered how soon Tom would have an answer from Sydney. Then another wave of anger swept through her. She was tired of being a victim. No, if she could help other women, save them from their brutes of husbands, she'd do anything she could.

She'd be meeting Tom again tonight, too. Their dinner at the casino had gone well, even though she'd been a bit stunned at the noise. Beth had been curious to see what had attracted Bryan to such places, but the Three Rivers – at least the part they'd eaten in – was more of a family place than those Tom assured her Bryan would have frequented.

Tom had been good company, telling fishing stories she was sure were greatly exaggerated, but had made her laugh. His presence was comforting, his bulk reassuring. She'd felt safe – that was a word she hadn't used about herself in recent years. She'd built a strong shell around herself for protection. But this was a different world, she was a different person. Anything could happen here.

It was nightfall when Beth arrived at Jenny and Mike's home. Noting the three cars already parked outside, she drew a deep breath. They were all here already. She didn't relish walking into a room full of people, visualizing them all turning to look at her. Beth stood for moment and looked up into the sky, enjoying the silence of the evening. It was easy to feel insignificant in the light of such vastness. She took another deep breath, grabbed her purse from the car and stepped briskly across the driveway. Before she reached the door, it flew open, a beam of light streaming across the path, and the black Labrador Beth remembered came running out, tail wagging in excitement.

"Thought we heard you pull up," Jenny appeared and greeted Beth with a hug. "Come on in. The others are all here already, and we've started on the wine."

Once inside, and with a glass of white wine in her hand, Beth felt more comfortable and wondered why she'd felt reluctant to be here. She looked around the room at the group of people she'd come to call friends. To think that, only a few months ago, she'd been on the other side of the world, caught up in a controlling relationship and unable to see a way out. Her thoughts were interrupted by the sound of her name.

"Beth? Do you agree?" Jo was asking her.

"I'm sorry. I was miles away." Beth smiled ruefully. "What did you say?"

"I was just pointing out to the men," Jo said, throwing the three men a look, "that not all violence is physical. In fact, some of their best mates may be abusing their wives."

"Steady on," Tom interjected. "No need to make it personal. Beth, Jo seems to think you can shed more light on this."

Beth felt herself redden and her throat constricted. It was as if Bryan were here in the room with her.

"Only if you feel you can," Ellen said gently. "Would you like some water?"

"No. I'll be fine." Beth took a sip of wine and straightened her shoulders. "Jo's right. It can happen in the best of homes. No one can ever know what goes on in another's marriage, behind closed doors. Physical abuse. Well, there's visible evidence, of course, though I believe many find excuses."

"Doors and steps have a lot to answer for," Jenny said grimly.

"You're right there," Tom said. "I see it when they finally decide to separate or divorce, when the violence finally gets too much. But what you're talking about is subtler. How do…?" He gave Beth a strange look.

"That's my story," she said in a small voice.

"You didn't know?" Jenny was quick to ask, her eyes turning towards Ellen as if for assistance.

Beth could feel Tom's eyes on her, but couldn't bring herself to meet them. A vestige of the shame she'd thought gone forever rose to almost choke her. "I…," she began, then stopped, unable to go any further.

"Sorry." Tom pushed back a lock of hair threatening to fall into his eyes. "I never guessed. This puts a different complexion on things."

Beth knew he was talking about Bryan, his death, the debts, and her reluctance to return to Sydney. She wished the floor would open up and swallow her. She looked around furtively. How could she get out of here? And if she did, how could she ever face any of them again?

"It's okay." Ellen's gentle voice cut through Beth's whirling thoughts. "You'd already told most of us. It's only a surprise to old Tom here. No reason why he should have known before now. But it's important he does. You were right to say what you did. It's *your* experience that can help us understand. Understand what many of the women have had to suffer. Maybe even understand why they have difficulty leaving. Would you like another glass?"

Beth looked down to discover the glass she was clutching tightly had tipped over and spilled most of its contents onto the wooden floor. "Oh, I'm sorry. I'll…"

"No worries." Jenny appeared in front of her with a cloth in one hand, a wine bottle in the other. "Better wipe it up, though, before Ben decides it's for him.

Beth smiled through incipient tears, and took a gulp of wine, determined to get hold of herself.

"Now where were we?" Jo said. "If you feel up to it, Beth, maybe you could share some of what you think these women experience?"

"Be right back." Beth carefully placed her glass on the floor and unsteadily walked out. Once in the kitchen, she stood by the window and gazed out into the darkness. Why had she become so upset? Where was the anger she'd felt on the drive up? She took a couple of deep breaths, trying to remember that these were friends, people she trusted. She felt something soft rubbing against her ankles and, looking down, saw Mike's dog.

"Hello, there. Have you come to find me?" She could hear the murmur of voices from the other room. Were they talking about her? They should be. She'd left rudely in the middle of a conversation. The old Beth – or Elizabeth – would leave altogether, go home and avoid them all in future. But she wasn't that person anymore. A steely resolve that Beth didn't know she possessed rose up to give her the strength to walk back into the group.

"Sorry about that. I just needed a minute. Thanks for sending Ben to find me," she indicated the dog padding behind her. "Now, you asked about me." Beth took a deep breath, then another gulp of wine. At this rate she'd be too tipsy to drive home. "It's difficult to explain," she said. "Domestic violence can happen so slowly, subtly that you wonder if you're imagining it. Then, one day the penny drops, but by then you've accepted the behavior, become a party to it, acquiesced in the role you've been given and you're expected to play. Then the feelings of guilt seep in, guilt and shame." She dropped her eyes. "It's not the woman's fault, but often she may think it is, think it's something she's done to deserve it. That's what makes it so hard to leave. That and the fear of everyone knowing. That's why…" She dared to look up to meet the circle of eyes. "That's why I stayed, even though Mum encouraged me to leave. But where would I have gone? I had no money of my own. It all belonged to Bryan. I belonged to Bryan. And there was my mother. Bryan was paying for her nursing home. Where would she…?" She wiped her eyes. "For many it's children. They can't leave them. I was lucky. Mum had some money squirrelled away. That bought my escape."

"Hmph. You're right. Could be anyone we know." Tom's face reddened, and he pushed back his hair again. "So, where do we start?"

"Madeline House was Maddy's last wish," Jenny said. "It's up to us to make that wish into a reality. We've had everything moved out ready for painting. Maddy knew the place needed a facelift, but she loved it just the way it was. However, now…" She hesitated, and Mike put his hand over hers. Beth was touched by this demonstration of his love for her, wondering what it would feel like to have someone so caring in her life.

"But she had such lovely pieces," Beth couldn't help saying, "Didn't she want them to stay there?"

"No." It was Ellen who replied. "I know what Maddy wanted, too. She wanted the place to have a fresh, new feel, to make the women feel renewed, at peace."

"That's right. Though we did save some special pieces. They're waiting in our garage, ready to be returned." Jenny appeared to have recovered her equilibrium. Beth remembered the empty spaces and scratches on the floor. "The painters will be in next week and will brighten up the dark wood," Jenny continued. "Then we'll fill it with some modern furniture, nothing too weird, but modern and comfortable. We want it to feel like home not *a* home, if you know what I mean."

"Right." Beth was still trying to get her head around the whole concept. "But I'm not sure what I can do to help."

"Right now, none of us are really sure what our roles will be – apart from Jenny and Tom that is," Jo said. "I guess we're here because we care."

"And that's enough to be going on with," Ellen replied.

Beth turned to look at Tom. There was certainly more to this man than she'd given him credit for. He shifted uncomfortably in his chair.

"I'm just the simple legal guy," he muttered, reddening again and pushing his hair back.

I wish he wouldn't keep doing that, Beth thought. It made her want to run her fingers through it. Where had that thought come from? It was her turn to redden, but no one appeared to notice.

"But you'll be offering your services free to the women – those who need it?" Ellen said.

"Yeah, guess so." Tom smiled and drew out a folder of papers from a satchel which had been sitting on the floor. "Well, now we're all here, I have the Trust papers ready to sign. I need Jenny and Mike's signatures and a couple of witnesses. Ellen?" He looked around the group as if expecting someone else to volunteer. "Beth?"

"Oh, I don't think so. I…"

"I will," Jo said. "No problem."

While the papers were being signed, Beth took the opportunity to collect the now empty glasses and carry them into the kitchen. Once there, she stood holding onto the edge of the sink, her head swirling with memories. She didn't know how long she stood there, but suddenly she became aware of a hand on her shoulder and a warmth coursing through her that had little to do with the touch itself.

"Are you okay?" Tom's voice echoed in her ear. "I'm sorry. I didn't know."

Beth turned to meet his concerned blue eyes. "How could you? No, I'm fine, thanks. It's just that, talking about it brings it all back. I've been trying to shut it away, to forget, but…"

"It's not so easy, is it?"

"No." Beth moved away from the arm which threatened to wrap itself around her shoulder. "I'll be right. It's good of you to…" But she wasn't sure what she wanted to say. Tom's presence was reassuring, comforting even. But she wasn't ready for another man in her life.

As if recognizing Beth's indecision, Tom removed his hand, leaving her feeling an emptiness. She regretted her hesitancy. What a fool she was being. The man was only trying to be kind.

Beth looked up again. "Thanks."

"I came to let you know we're packing up," he said. "And to tell you to leave the washing up. Mike's offered to stack the dishwasher when we've all left."

"Right."

The pair stood there looking at each other. Beth made the first move, finding she had to squeeze past Tom's bulk to reach the doorway.

"Sorry." He moved aside to allow her to pass, but their arms touched as she did so, and a tremor of something unidentifiable shook her. As she looked up, their eyes met, and Beth experienced a sudden quiver of excitement, gone in a flash.

"There you are," Jenny greeted Beth as she joined the others. "We thought the pair of you had gotten lost in there."

Beth smiled awkwardly. Had they been talking about her and Tom? What had they been saying? The last thing she wanted was to become an object of gossip or pity.

"Jenny's only joking," Ellen was quick to say, clearly noting Beth's embarrassment. "Don't mind her. We sent Tom in to fetch you because we're planning to get together at Madeline House in two weeks to decide on color schemes and such. The men won't be much good for that, so we thought the four of us," she waved her arms to encompass herself, Jenny, Jo and Beth, "could do it. Are you in?"

"Sure," Beth replied regaining her equilibrium. Color schemes she could cope with.

After agreeing to meet the three women at what was now to be called Madeline House on Monday week, Beth made her farewells and got into her car. She drove back down the winding road, the moonlight glistening on the water to her right and the forest rising up like a forbidding wall in the darkness on her left. As she negotiated the curves and bends, Beth went over the events of the evening in her mind, hesitating when she came to Tom's presence in the kitchen. Why had she felt so at ease in his company? Until now, she'd treated him warily. Something had changed. Was it only the news of his involvement in the women's refuge? No, it couldn't be that. She'd known he was involved before tonight. She puzzled over the problem for the remainder of the trip without reaching a solution, but as she closed her eyes that night, it was the look in Tom's eyes and the feeling of his hand on her shoulder that filled her thoughts.

Sixteen

Beth tossed and turned all night, unable to sleep, but when she opened her eyes to the first rays of sunlight coming through the venetian blinds, she realized she must have slept after all. Stretching her arms above her head, all the anxieties of the previous evening seemed foolish. Tom was a good man, a friend, like the others were friends. She had nothing to worry about. Any attraction had been a figment of her overactive imagination. Beth rubbed her arms, remembering the sensation when they had met his in the doorway, then, chastising herself for foolish thoughts, she leapt out of bed. Today was a work day, and Jo had asked her to take an inventory with a new client. This would be the first time Beth had been trusted to do it alone, and the last thing she wanted to do was jeopardize the trust of her new employer.

A little cry outside the sliding glass door leading into the garden drew Beth's attention, and she opened the door to see the white cat she'd become used to, waiting for attention. It was the same cat she'd seen the day she first viewed the house and had been arriving every morning as regular as clockwork for her morning feed. Beth had come to love the little creature while wondering who it really belonged to, or if it was simply a stray which traveled between houses being fed a little in each one. Beth bent down to stroke the cat, filled up the food bowl she'd purchased especially for the purpose, and watched affectionately as the little pink tongue lapped it up. Fixing herself some toast with cheese for breakfast, along with a cup of the herbal tea she'd come to enjoy, Beth planned her day. The client lived outside Florence, on the road south, so she'd have to pass close to Old Town on her way. If she set off early enough there would be time to pop into Ellen's shop on the way. After last night, she felt in need of some of Ellen's encouraging words to bolster her this morning. It was strange how her opinion of the Native American woman had undergone a complete about-face. While at first Beth had felt awkward in her presence, now she craved the peace and tranquillity which Ellen seemed to carry around with her.

"Anyone here?" The bell clanged above Beth as she pushed open the heavy door and gazed into the shop. At first it appeared to be empty. A candle sat behind the counter as usual, the delicate scents of chamomile and geranium filling the air. As the door closed noisily behind her, the only sound Beth could hear was the low hum of a car passing outside. She was about to turn and leave, when the door opened again, and Ellen's tall figure appeared behind her carrying two cups of take-away coffee.

"Oh!" Beth started. "You're expecting someone. I'll go." But before she could move, Ellen handed her one of the cups.

"I had a feeling you'd come this morning. This one's for you."

Dropping her purse on a nearby chair, Beth grasped the warm cup in both hands. "How did you…?" she began, then stopped, remembering Ellen wasn't like other people.

"You seemed a bit spaced out last night. Thought you might need to talk."

"Talk?" Until this minute, Beth hadn't known she did. Her decision to visit Ellen had been instinctive, not carefully thought through. But now she was here, she did want to talk, though wasn't sure where to begin.

"Last night," she started. "I felt… I felt embarrassed… and angry. There we were talking about women in abusive relationships, and not so long ago, I was one of them." She paused, her mind darting off in different directions all at the same time. "But now I'm not. And…" Beth looked down into the coffee, which she hadn't even started to drink. "Now I'm ready… ready to move on." It wasn't till she'd said the words that she realized exactly what she meant. She tried to clarify it for Ellen, who was giving her an encouraging expression. "I'm not afraid anymore. I don't want to hide when…"

"When a man looks at you or talks to you?" Ellen suggested.

"That's it exactly," Beth said wonderingly as Ellen managed to put it into words for her.

"So how do you feel now about Tom?"

"Tom? He's a friend – a good man. Seems to be kind and caring."

"That'll do for now," Ellen said, as Beth furrowed her brow in surprise.

"He's a lawyer. He's helping me work out some legal stuff."

"Right."

Ellen seemed about to say more, but finished her coffee instead, dropping the empty cardboard cup into a bin.

"That's all. Really," Beth insisted, while wondering if she was being too forceful. "I'd better go. I've taken up too much of your time."

"Not at all. Do you see a load of customers beating down the door? This is my quiet time of day, when I usually do my paperwork, get caught up on things. I'm glad you agreed to help with Madeline House. It needs you." Ellen stood up, her eyes seeming to bore into Beth. "You will take care, won't you? There are big changes ahead for you. Some stuff you may not be prepared for."

Beth left with a shivery feeling of unease. Surely there could be nothing more to come? She'd had enough surprises to last a lifetime. Relegating her concerns to the back of her mind, Beth focussed on enjoying the trip. She hadn't driven down this way before and was surprized to see so many stretches of water on her left, while signs to the sand dunes proliferated on the right hand side of the road. She stopped to check directions, then turned into a wide driveway which led down to a large house situated on the edge of a lake.

Stepping out of the car, Beth drew in a breath. This was exquisite. While she'd admired Tom's house on the lake, it was nothing compared to this one. The building rose to three levels, each with several arched windows. She was so engrossed in the view of the lake stretching out before her, the mass of water birds swimming in formation, and the few small fishing boats which seemed to be perched on top of the surface, that she failed to see a tall blonde woman walking towards her.

"You'll be from the estate sales. I'm Yvonne Walker. You'd better come in." The woman stalked off, clearly expecting Beth to follow.

Beth hid a smile and did just that, wondering at the exotic dress of the woman, who was wearing a calf-length skirt slit to the hip, topped by an almost see-through chiffon blouse with a revealing neckline. From the back, she could have been in her twenties, but when she finally turned to face Beth at the door, Beth saw that, despite the heavy make-up, she was clearly of Beth's own age.

"I'm Beth, Beth Carson. Do…?"

But, before Beth could say any more, the woman threw open the door and ushered Beth into the house. "Here it is. I suppose you'll do your thing. I need to leave, but I'll be back in a couple of hours. Will that be time enough?"

Beth gazed around the large open area, her eyes glazing over at the number of knick-knacks, paintings, overfilled bookshelves, and what appeared to be antique furniture. It was a treasure trove of traditional American household effects.

"It's beautiful," she breathed.

"It's okay, I suppose. The old dear never threw anything away, so most of it's been here since the year dot."

"Were you close?" Beth almost whispered, unwilling to sully the atmosphere with a loud voice.

"Close? No." Yvonne almost sneered. "Aunt Leona wasn't close to anyone. She hid herself out here. It's a blessing she's gone, and we can clear the old place out." Ignoring Beth's stunned expression, she added, "You'll be all right, won't you?" and without waiting for a reply, walked out. Beth heard a car starting up, then there was silence broken only by the sound of the birds and a distant motorboat on the lake.

The morning passed swiftly as Beth catalogued the items to be sold and tried to estimate their value. Jo would make the final decisions in a day or two, but she'd suggested Beth try her hand at this facet of the business. She was finding it fun to guestimate. She'd brought along her iPod and listened to some relaxing music, allowing her thoughts to wander.

Suddenly her mind was jerked back to the present. She'd been flicking through a box of photographs when something familiar struck her. She picked up the last few she'd been looking at, and gave them more attention. There it was – a group photo of several young men lounging on a beach. Beth peered at it. What was it that had made her want to look twice? She was working in a dark corner of the room, so moved to the window to see it more clearly. Yes, there he was – the same young man. Maddy's Rick and her mother's…? A bubble of excitement welled up. Maybe the answer was to be found here, in this pile of what Yvonne seemed to imagine was rubbish. Beth put the photo aside, determined to ask more about it when Yvonne returned.

By the time Beth heard Yvonne's car pull up and the door slam, she'd almost forgotten about the photo, so absorbed had she become in sorting out all of the assorted knick-knacks from the glass-fronted cabinets. The old lady had been quite a collector, and the items should prove popular with Jo's customers.

"How are you doing?" Yvonne swept into the room and looked around at the disarray.

"It may seem a bit of a mess right now," Beth said from her position on the floor, "but by the time the sale comes around, it'll all be set out beautifully. Jo and her team really know what they're doing."

"And you're part of that team, are you?" Yvonne's voice held a smirk, forcing Beth to rise. But even on her feet, the other woman towered over her, putting Beth at a distinct disadvantage.

"I really don't have time for this." Yvonne's gaze swept the room, including Beth in her scorn. "Can I let you have the key, then you and Jo can finish at your leisure? I suppose I can trust you?"

"Of course, but before you go…" Remembering, Beth moved to the side table on which she'd laid the photo. "Do you know who these guys are?"

Yvonne barely glanced at it before replying, "Haven't a clue. Interested in the menfolk, are you? But these would be long gone. I hear you've set your cap at Tom Harrison. Well, let me tell you, you've no chance there. He's taken." And with that, she dropped a key on the table and made her exit so hurriedly Beth was left stunned.

What had Yvonne meant? Set her cap at Tom Harrison? She barely knew the man. Beth neatly managed to forget their almost date at the casino. She sat at the table, remembering his kindness, his comfortable way of listening, his… She chastised herself. She'd just been told he was taken. Then she recalled a conversation she'd heard. Now where was it? She cast her mind back to the fair. That's where it was. She'd been standing in the queue at the barbecue and some women had been talking about… Tom. That was it! And Yvonne had been mentioned too, but Beth couldn't remember exactly what had been said. Well, it didn't matter, she reminded herself. The last thing she was interested in was becoming involved with another man.

*

In a brief lull between clients, Tom ruminated on what he was going to do about Simone. It had been almost two weeks now, and she showed no sign of returning home, deftly changing the subject each time Tom broached it. Not only that, she was determined to poke her nose into his affairs.

Her veiled references to Beth as 'that woman' were beginning to irk him. It was almost enough to make him arrange to see more of the woman. Almost, but not quite. Although now he knew a bit more about her history, he could see what a difficult time she'd had and admired her resilience. It wasn't everyone who'd make a journey to the other side of the world at her age. He scratched his head. Her age? What was he thinking? Why, she was younger than Janet would have been if she'd still been alive. Anyway, the last thing the poor woman needed was another man in her life. She'd just left one, and lost him too. And he'd left her in a real pickle. Which reminded him. Tom checked his emails. No, still no reply from the Sydney firm.

His mind wandered back to Simone. A pity his son-in-law hadn't a bit more gumption. What Simone needed was a firm hand. Maybe she'd respect Ed more if he took a stand more often. He pulled on his ear as a plan began to hatch. Yes, that's what he'd do. Checking his watch, he reckoned he had just enough time before his next appointment. He picked up the phone.

*

Dinner was almost over. They were all seated round the table, the boys wrangling as usual over the size of their ice creams, and Simone regaling Tom with some imagined slight she'd experienced in the superstore, when there was the sound of a car drawing up.

"Who…?" Simone threw an accusatory glance at Tom, who pretended ignorance. "I'll go," she said, rising as if to ward off the interloper she expected to find waiting at the door.

"Eat up, boys. I have a surprise for you," Tom said, smiling.

"Another one?" little Tommy said, sliding down from his chair and winding himself around Tom's legs. "Where is it?"

At that moment they heard Simone's voice rising in anger, then another deeper one, then silence.

"It's Daddy!" Tommy loosened his hold on his grandfather and ran towards the door, little Sam following him unsteadily.

Tom followed the pair at a more leisurely pace, and by the time he reached the front door, the two were in their father's arms while Simone stood facing them, hands on hips. "It's Ed," she said, needlessly.

"So I see. Good to see you, son," Tom said, shaking Ed's hand. "Come to fetch your family home?"

"Dad!" Simone's voice had an edge to it which Tom didn't like – one he'd been familiar with during her teenage years and thought she'd grown out of.

"Have you eaten, Ed?" Tom asked, knowing the other must have come straight from work to have reached here at this time. "Simone, can you put up a plate of something for the lad? There was some of that cottage pie left, wasn't there?"

"I think so, Dad," Simone said churlishly, while Tommy grabbed his dad's arm and began pulling him toward the deck.

"Come see Grandad's boat. We can all go for a ride."

Ed raised his eyebrows at Tom.

"Simone's not keen," Tom said, "but I promised the boys we'd go out fishing before they go back home." He emphasized the last two words. "Now that *you're* here, maybe the four of us can go – boys together, eh?" He tapped his nose, knowing his daughter wouldn't approve. "You'll stay the weekend won't you?"

"Well, I did tell the office they wouldn't see me till Monday."

"Good man." Tom threw an arm round Ed's shoulders. "Let your dad have some dinner first, then we can show him the boat," he said to Tommy. "Let's see what Mom's fixing for him."

"Okay, Grandpa Tom," Tommy agreed. "But Sam's too little, isn't he?" he added, trying to push his little brother aside.

"I think there's room for both of you," he was saying as they entered the kitchen. Hearing his last words, Simone turned with a start.

"You're not still on about that fishing trip?" she asked, setting a plate of cottage pie down in front of her husband.

"Ed's agreed to stay the weekend," Tom said, in an attempt to deflect her attention.

There was no reply, but the clashing of dishes in the sink signaled Simone's displeasure.

"Brad and Brooke are coming over on Sunday," she said without turning round, "And didn't you say something about Brooke's mom?"

Shit! Tom had conveniently managed to forget his promise to start on Louise's wedding plan. Her – Louise's – intention had been to arrange a tête-a-tête with him on his own, but Simone's presence had forced her to turn it into a family affair. Now there would be Ed, too. Maybe he could manage to leave the three women to thrash it out among themselves and take the boys out fishing. The thought must have transferred itself to his facial expression because, no sooner had it crossed his mind Simone asked, "What are you hatching now, Dad? I hope you're not trying to slide out of the afternoon. I'm looking forward to meeting Brooke again – and her mom. Louise isn't it?"

"Yes, Louise," Tom replied. As he did so, an image of the elegant, but hardboiled Louise crossed his mind side-by-side with one of Beth. He compared the worldly man-eater with the simple vivacity of his new friend, knowing which one he'd rather spend his Sunday with.

"You haven't met Brooke yet, Ed," Simone interjected. "She's a bit young, but seems to suit Brad. She…"

"Will run rings around your brother," Ed said. "Just as you have done."

"That's not fair. Why…"

Seeing the argument developing and conscious of both his own presence and that of the boys, Tom intervened.

"You'll see for yourself, Ed. Now, boys," he turned to his grandsons who had remained silent during this interchange, "how about we show Dad the boat?"

"Good idea,' Ed said. Thanks, honey. Great cottage pie." He took the boys' hands and headed out to the deck, one child hanging off each arm, with Tom leading the way.

Once the boat had been duly admired, the boys were happy to run around, allowing the two men to have a private chat.

"Thanks for your call, Tom," Ed said, kicking up some gravel with the tip of his shoe. "It's been hard, but you know your daughter. I've always found it easier just to give in to her. This is the first time I've taken a stand, and…"

"She ran off home," Tom finished for him. "Guess Janet and I didn't do such a good job of raising her. She practised on Brad, and he always followed her lead, I know it's difficult to change her view that she's always right."

"She usually is," Ed said, ruefully, "but I'm not her little brother."

"And you're not like Brad," Tom replied. "He's always needed someone to help him make decisions. Don't get me wrong. He's a good lawyer. Has no trouble making decisions in his work life, but he misses his mom. She could always steer him right. Brooke's good for him. But, as I said, you're no Brad. You have a mind of your own, and I'm surprised you two haven't come to blows before now. Simone's my daughter, but I'm with you on this one."

"Thanks, Tom."

"Now let's get these two scallywags to bed, and I'll take an early night too. Give you young things a chance to sort out your differences."

"Scallywags, scallywags," shouted the two boys, picking up on their grandad's word, as the four made their way back inside.

"Bedtime," Simone greeted them, disapproval in her voice.

"I'll do bed and bath duty tonight," Tom said, before she could say more. "Leave you to…"

"We need to talk." Ed spoke before Tom could finish.

"And a story, Grandpa Tom?" Sam asked.

"Two!" demanded Tommy as they climbed the stairs.

"Two it is," Tom agreed, glad to leave the bigger kids to their own devices and instead spend time with the two innocents.

While Tom read not two, but three stories to the boys, he could hear the voices downstairs – Simone's more strident, Ed's quieter, but firm. Gradually he was aware of Simone's voice lowering, then silence. He hoped this was a good sign and the pair had come to some sort of agreement or compromise. No doubt he'd find out in the morning. Tom shook his head as he made his way to his room, glad he kept a secret bottle of Jack Daniels in the bedside cabinet for just such an eventuality. He wasn't game to disturb the couple tonight. What was it with couples these days? He and Janet had rarely argued and never let the sun go down on a quarrel. But here were Ed and Simone, then there was the story Beth had told last night, not to mention Madeline House, which demonstrated the need for yet another women's refuge in the area. Had things changed so much, or had he and Janet just been lucky?

Settling down on his bed with a glass of his favorite nightcap and the latest Michael Connelly, Tom was conscious for the first time in years of the emptiness of his king-sized bed.

When he finally turned out the light, it was with a sigh of regret for what he'd lost and an ache of something unidentifiable. He cursed as he closed his eyes, hoping the continued silence downstairs was an indication Ed and Simone had resolved their differences and his life could return to normal.

Seventeen

Tom rose early on Sunday morning, drawn outside by the bright sunlight and the sound of the birds. It was early, so pulling on his old track pants and a sweater, he went out to his boat, intent on spending an hour or so on the lake before the family arose. It was very peaceful there, the only boat out at this time. The sun glistened on the surface of the lake, its reflection almost blinding Tom. The only sound was the warbling of the water birds as they swooped around him. Tom threw back his head and breathed in the fresh air. How he loved the lake, especially in the early morning. At a moment like this he was able to almost forget the couple who'd still been arguing when he went to bed the night before. He hadn't heard them later and hoped the silence signaled some sort of compromise had been reached, but was doubtful, knowing full well how obdurate Simone could be. At least Ed's arrival had taken her mind off Tom's life.

That brought Tom's own thoughts to the Australian woman. It had been a shock to hear the story of her marriage. Although he'd felt there was something in her past, something she was running from, it had been difficult to hear of the emotional abuse she'd suffered at the hands of her husband. It made her current predicament even more troubling. He hoped he could help her resolve it. He really admired the way she'd opened up about her experience at Mike and Jenny's the other night. It couldn't have been easy. And it can't be easy for her to start a new life in a new country. She certainly had guts. His thoughts had carried him along to almost the center of the lake, and by the look of the sun, it was time to return home.

By the time Tom reached the house, he could see four heads in the kitchen. He entered with some trepidation, but Simone smiled at him. "Pancakes, Dad?"

"Sounds good." Tom relaxed as he slid into the bench and met Ed's eyes with his own raised eyebrows. Ed nodded slightly.

"We're going home today," young Tommy announced. "And we have to go on your boat first."

"Sure, young fellow. Let's have breakfast, then see what Mom says, shall we?"

"What Mom says about what?" Simone turned from the stove.

"Thought we might take the boat out for a bit after breakfast, if that meets with your approval." Tom helped himself to orange juice from a jug on the table. "Me, Ed and the boys. Of course, you're welcome to come too if you want."

"No, I'll stay here. I might check out some things." She smiled over at Ed, settling Tom's concern. "And there's lunch to prepare – or had you forgotten?"

Dang it, he'd clean forgotten the forthcoming lunch party.

"You had, hadn't you? Oh, Dad!"

Tom decided to ignore her last remark. "What do you want to check out?"

"Ed's persuaded me to take a good look at the website for our local school, and I've agreed to make a visit to check it out. Then we'll make a decision together."

"Good to hear. So the boat trip's on, boys. But only if you eat up all your breakfast. We sailors need to be well-provisioned. And seems we need to be back for lunch."

"You been out already this morning, Tom?" Ed asked pointing to Tom's disheveled state.

"Hell, yes. Couldn't waste a good morning like this. I'll run upstairs and shower and dress before you're ready to serve. Okay, Simmy?"

"Okay, Dad," replied Simone sounding happier than she had since arriving.

*

By the time Tom showered and returned downstairs, the aroma of pancakes mixed with maple syrup was filling the kitchen, and he could hear the two boys bickering over the bottle of maple syrup. "Here, fellas," he said, grabbing the syrup before it spread its gooey mess all over the table and the two boys. "Let me."

"So," Tom said, when they were all settled at the table, "a boat trip, lunch, then…?" He glanced at his daughter. "You'll be going back to Portland?"

"Yes," Simone said, affecting to dismiss her earlier bad humor. "I'll pack while you're all out on the lake, then we can be home before dark."

"Right." Tom thought it best to leave it there and spent the rest of breakfast joking around with the boys, while Simone and Ed looked on indulgently.

"About lunch, Dad." Simone stopped in the midst of loading the dishwasher. "I thought I'd cook a roast, but…" She frowned.

"No need to worry. You have enough to take care of this morning. Let's go out. I can make a booking at Driftwood Shores. How would that be?"

Simone appeared troubled. "You don't think…"

"I don't think anything, nor will they," Tom said, knowing quite well what his daughter meant. When Janet was alive, she'd no more think of taking guests out to dinner than fly. Simone was like her mom in that respect. But she'd already pulled out all the stops for Brooke. They could let someone else take care of it this time. "It's a great spot, right on the beach. Give Brooke and her mom a taste of the beauty of Florence. We may not be the metropolis of Eugene or Portland, but we have a lot to offer. We're no backwater."

"Nice one, Dad." Simone reached up to drop a kiss on Tom's forehead. "That'd help."

*

"Thanks, Tom," Ed said. They were out on the lake, and the boys were trailing their hands in the water, loving every minute of this special trip. "If it hadn't been for your call…" He slapped Tom on the shoulder, then smoothed back his hair.

"It's nothing. I know my daughter. She can be very stubborn. Don't know where she gets it from. Sometimes she just needs a prod. Thought you turning up might do the trick. She was too far into it to back down all by herself."

Ed sighed. "I love her, you know, but sometimes… There's this thing with Brad too."

Tom laughed. "You mean her reaction to his engagement? She'll get over it. Brooke's a tad young, but she'll be good for Brad, and Simone will come to see that in time. Be interesting to see how she reacts to the mother." He grinned.

The remainder of the trip on the lake passed uneventfully, and once over, the two little boys climbed out of the boat with much laughing and giggling. "Thanks, Grandpa Tom," said Little Tommy, echoed by Sam as they ran and tumbled across the grass towards the house.

Not only did Tom make a booking for lunch, he sent a text to Brad telling him to meet there, and the party from Eugene arrived first. When Tom walked in with Simone and Ed, the two boys running ahead of them, the others were already seated in a table overlooking the beach. In the kafuffle of seating everyone, Louise adroitly managed to place herself next to Tom. He wasn't sure how it had happened, as the three of them had already been seated when Tom and the others arrived. Tom saw Simone raise her eyebrows as Louise proceeded to engage him in a private conversation. He shifted uncomfortably in his chair, wishing the whole damn meal was over.

Although the gathering had ostensibly been arranged to make wedding plans, nothing was finalized. Brooke was eager to hear about Simone and Ed's wedding, details of which Simone grudgingly provided. Tom guessed she didn't want her brother's wedding to be a replica of hers, but that seemed unlikely as Louise had plenty of ideas of her own. "But we can sort it all out between us, can't we Tom," she said finally, making coquettish eyes at him and touching his arm playfully for the umpteenth time. It was a relief when it was over and they were able to say goodbye, with the parting remark from Louise: "You'll be in touch, soon, Tom, won't you?"

Simone rolled her eyes, showing Tom that she still viewed Brooke with distaste and now included Louise in her poor opinion. "You want to watch out for that one, Dad. She's on the lookout for husband number two. She and Brooke are two peas in a pod."

As Tom waved the little family off, he sighed with relief, confident Simone and Ed would work out their differences. He surveyed the pristine kitchen – Simone had cleaned up after breakfast; he was sure he'd have trouble finding everything again – and made his way to the study. Once settled at his computer though, he found it difficult to concentrate. Not for the first time, he wished Janet was still with him. She'd have known what to do about Simone and Ed, and might have handled it differently. Well, he reasoned, he'd got the result he wanted, hadn't he? They were back together. Simone had managed to swallow her pride and compromise. But for how long? His daughter wasn't the easiest person to get along with, and her job in the busy finance department of their local hospital didn't lend itself to the development of many negotiation skills. He sighed. Even though she'd returned home, he hadn't seen much in the way of loving behavior between her and Ed, not on her side anyway. It was all about the boys, her work and, he realized, her anger at her brother and frustration with Tom himself.

*

A week passed without any further communication from Simone, encouraging Tom to think all was well there. He couldn't help worrying about his headstrong daughter. Janet would have known how to handle her, whereas he…

"What do you think, Janet?" he asked the photo sitting on his desk, a replica of the one in his office. "Were we too soft with our Simmy? Or did we give her too much responsibility too young?"

His eyes turned to a family photo taken at Brad's graduation. What a happy group they were. He remembered that day as if it was yesterday. Brad, his gangly son, grown up at last, but he'd retained that reserve he'd always had as a child, the reticence that had encouraged Simone to boss him around, and she was still inclined to do it. He guessed that was why she'd taken against Brooke. He sighed again. Kids! Did you ever stop worrying about them?

He opened up his emails, and as if his thinking had brought it into existence, there was an email from Brad. He scanned the screen – just the usual stuff about work, some bits about a theater outing he and Brooke had had, then at the bottom, the rider, that almost took his breath away.

Why haven't you been in touch with Louise? She and Brooke have been waiting for you to contact her re the wedding. Louise feels it's your place to get in touch with her, not the other way round. They've been making plans here, but they really need your input. Brooke thinks you should invite Louise to dinner and discuss it over a nice meal in a civilized fashion. It would do you good to get away from Florence for a bit and chill out. She's a great lady and she likes you.

Shit! Shit! Shit! Tom dragged his hand through his hair. This wasn't his son talking. These were Brooke's words. Maybe even Louise's – like mother, like daughter. Brad was marrying them both. Unable to sit still, he rose to make himself a coffee. As he waited for it to brew, he gazed out across the lake wishing he could just go out there and forget all this family stuff. But he couldn't. He took his mug back to the office and stared at Brad's words again. They weren't going to go away, nor was Brad's desire to see his dad and his future mother-in-law becoming friends. Well, Tom rubbed his chin, he guessed friends was okay, but nothing more. Louise was just like the women he spent his work life avoiding here in Florence. She was a predator, albeit a gentle and pretty one, but a predator never-the-less. And now she was being aided and abetted by her daughter and his unsuspecting son.

He read Brad's words again remembering he'd agreed to have the wedding here, so it wasn't too far-fetched to expect that he and Louise meet to discuss arrangements. In fact, he had a vague recollection he'd agreed to just that. He probably even had her number. Maybe they could meet somewhere innocuous over coffee to work out what needed to be done. Surely it wouldn't take long? He drew out his wallet. Yes, there it was, on the back of one of his cards. He looked at it for a few seconds. He took a gulp of his strong black coffee, sighed, and picked up the phone.

What seemed like an hour later, he hung up, his mind a confusion of invitations, guest lists, flower arrangements and his so-called lawn. It seemed there was more to planning a wedding than he'd envisaged, and Louise wanted his input at every stage. Surely he could manage to get out of much of what she'd suggested? He didn't know how it had happened, but he'd found himself agreeing to lunch at a place in Eugene called Café Soria in a few days' time.

Tom pushed his chair back from the desk, picked up his mug, and went to the kitchen for a refill. He dragged his fingers through his hair as he walked slowly back to the office. Now he'd let himself in for a meal with that blasted Louise. Well, at least it was in a restaurant. He'd managed to evade the not so subtle hint that she'd love to 'treat him to a home-cooked meal', so he'd be able to leave when the meal was over, with no invitations to anything further. He sat down with a thump. Maybe he was maligning the woman. She really hadn't said or done anything to make him think… Maybe she stood a tad too close, behaved a little too friendly for a first meeting, but, hey, they were going to be related. It was probably just her way. Some women were like that. He shuddered. Maybe he'd become too insular, too used to his own company. "What do you think, Janet?" he asked the photo. "Have I turned into a grumpy old man? Do I need to get out more? But I did take Beth out to dinner. That went okay. She wasn't angling for a relationship."

Thinking of Beth Carson forced Tom to scroll down his emails to check if there was a reply from the Australian lawyer. Yes, there it was – from Blackwood Associates in George Street Sydney. He opened it and scanned the page. All the usual polite stuff, then the meat. They confirmed his client was obligated for the debts, the amount of which had yet to be determined. The estate and assets also had to be valued, blah, blah, blah. Then, towards the end, a surprise. Since Bryan Flynn had originally come from England, they intended to advertise there for any relatives. He was yours faithfully, John Blackwood.

Tom scratched his head. This seemed a bit odd. Beth hadn't mentioned that her husband was English or that there were any other relatives. But then, he hadn't asked. He'd assumed… But surely it wouldn't make any difference? Beth didn't seem concerned about any inheritance. Her fear was that there wouldn't be sufficient funds to cover the debts. But this might put a different complexion on things. Wrinkling his brow, he picked up the phone, then replaced it. It was Sunday. What would she think if she received a call from him outside business hours? He'd have Gwen call tomorrow to make a proper appointment.

*

Beth was enjoying coffee in her little conservatory. She loved the white wicker furniture left by the former owner and the hanging baskets of blooms made it seem like summer even though a brisk breeze blew outside. Apart from the worry of Bryan's debts, she felt happy. She finished her drink and rose, determined to put all thoughts of Bryan and Australia to the back of her mind. She was loading the dirty mug into the dishwasher when the phone rang.

"Jo!" Beth was surprised to hear from her employer on a Sunday. "What's up?"

"I know I'm probably the last person you want to talk to on your days off, but Rob's playing golf and…" she hesitated. "Remember that photo you mentioned… at the Williams place?"

Beth racked her brains. The only photo she could think of was the one of the group of men where she thought she'd recognized one as Maddy's fiancé. But had she mentioned it to Jo? She couldn't remember. Jo's next words made her realize she must have.

"The old one with the group of guys."

Beth could immediately picture it, but she really hadn't taken time to examine it carefully. Now she wished she had.

"I was doing a final evaluation yesterday, and I came across it and a box of newspaper cuttings. Yvonne doesn't seem to want them, and I can't see anyone buying them so… I don't usually do this, but I have them here."

"You do?" Beth felt a bubble of excitement begin to build up. This was something to take her mind off Australia. "What…?"

"How about we meet for lunch? Mo's sound good to you? I'll bring them along and you can take a look. May be some answers for you there."

"Yes, please!" Beth couldn't disguise her eagerness.

"In about half an hour?"

"See you then."

Beth leaned against the white metal rail as she waited for Jo to arrive. The light breeze ruffled her growing hair, and despite the coolness of the day she felt a warm glow as she gazed out at the fast-flowing Siuslaw River. Fancy Jo taking the trouble to extract the photo for her, and some newspaper cuttings too. She couldn't imagine what they'd reveal. Maybe nothing to link the man to her mother, but it would be interesting to see them. And lovely to see Jo outside work, too. The office was so busy, and they were both out on sites much of the time. They rarely had time for more than a few words together most days. She was so glad she'd found Jo and Green Heron Estate Sales. Her days were busy and interesting, and she usually arrived home too exhausted to think of Bryan, even though he was still there, like a ghoul hanging over her. Even the thought of him darkened the brightness of the day. She shuddered, then turned to see Jo hurrying towards her and waving.

When the two were seated by the window and had placed their orders, both choosing the famous clam chowder again, Jo opened the brown envelope she'd been carrying and placed the photo on the table.

"This *is* it, isn't it?"

Beth picked it up. There they were – a group of young lads, clearly out for the day. They were sitting on some logs on the beach, their trousers and sleeves rolled up, shirt collars open, and all were holding cigarettes. It was a happy gathering.

"Looks like it was taken before the war," Beth said. "This one," she pointed to a handsome fellow in the middle of the picture, "is Maddy's fiancé – the one whose photo my mother had. I wonder who the others are."

Any further conversation was hindered by the arrival of two steaming sourdough bowls filled with thick white broth. Jo put the photo aside as the pair tucked into the hot soup.

"This is so delicious," Beth said, spooning up a piece of fish and breaking off some of the bread.

"Don't you have it in Australia?"

"Maybe we do, but I've never come across it, and certainly not soup served in bread, though I do recall a fad for dip served like this some years back. What are in the newspapers you brought?" she asked, curiosity getting the better of her.

"Later. Best if you see for yourself."

There was silence as the two women finished their meals. Once their plates had been cleared and Jo had a Bud Light sitting in front of her, while Beth had opted for a spiced cider, Jo placed the box on the table and opened it. Beth peered in, initially unwilling to touch the yellowed papers it held.

Jo picked one up and handed it over. "This is about Pearl Harbor when we were drawn into the war, then these…" she rummaged through the other papers, taking out a whole handful. "They all talk about the local boys who went off to 'do their bit' as they say."

Beth took the papers, but while they were no doubt of historical interest, she couldn't see how they added to her knowledge about the mystery of how her mother knew this Richard, or Rick. She laid them down again. "Thanks, but don't…"

"Just wait," Jo said, reaching deeper into the box. "Here it is." She drew out another cutting, which was less yellowed than the earlier ones, and passed it to Beth who took it, bemused.

"Local men to go to the Philippines. R and R in Australia," Beth read, with a tingle in her gut. "So that's how…"

"Maybe."

"But Mum lived in the country. There wouldn't have been any American soldiers based there." She shook her head. It was still a puzzle.

"You can have them if you like," Jo said. "No one else will want them."

Beth was about to refuse, when she thought better of it. "Jenny might," she said. "I'll take them with me. Might read them a bit more too. I'm unfamiliar with that part of our country's history. The photo too, if I may?" She peered at it again.

Besides the one who appeared to be Rick, there were three other young men. "I wonder…," she said. "Of course, they'd be pretty old now, but…"

"They might still be alive and living here in Florence," Jo finished for her.

"Well, see you tomorrow," Jo said, as they prepared to leave. "We have a busy week ahead. And don't forget we're meeting at Madeline House in the evening."

Beth arrived home and dropped the box on the coffee table. Her earlier excitement had turned to disappointment. The newspapers hadn't been what she'd hoped for, whatever that was. She wasn't sure herself. But the photo. That was a bonus and might even lead to something. Why on earth hadn't she or Jenny thought of this before? Richard Turner might not have any family left – she didn't count Yvonne who showed no interest at all – but the young man must have had friends. Beth sat looking at the photo till the light became too dim for her to see it clearly. If the opportunity arose, she'd bring it up with Jenny next evening.

Eighteen

"So, what do you think?" Jenny threw open the door to Maddy's empty house and stepped in, stopping in the middle of the room and turning to face the other three women before her shoulders sagged and her face crumpled. "Sorry," she mumbled as her eyes began to fill with tears. "I didn't… I haven't…"

"It's okay, honey." Ellen stepped forward and wrapped her arms around Jenny, while Beth and Jo looked on.

"I'm sorry." Jenny extricated herself from Ellen's grasp and looked at the other two. "It's the first time I've been inside since it was cleared. The place is so empty." She closed her eyes and took a deep breath. "But I think it still has traces of Maddy – the aroma of her coffee, the dusty scent of her dried flowers." She opened her eyes again and smiled. "Sorry again. I'm getting carried away. It's just an old, empty house."

"Not at all," Jo said. "I've seen a lot of these so-called empty houses. They still hold something of the owner, something that lingers. Call it their spirit or what you will, but it's there. It's here. Let's just all take a moment to remember Maddy." The four women joined hands and closed their eyes.

Suddenly Jenny felt Maddy's presence strongly. It gave her strength, just as Maddy had done when alive. "I'm okay now," she said, opening her eyes and smiling through her tears. "You're right, Jo. Maddy's still here in spirit, and she wants this to happen. I brought over some coffee. Let's make a brew, and we can discuss what needs to be done."

By the time the four were seated on the back deck, the sun was sending shadows across the yard, and they could hear the doves cooing in the bushes.

"She loved sitting out here," Jenny sighed.

"And so will the women who come to stay," Ellen said. "It's what Maddy wanted and she'd hate to see you so sad."

"You're right." Jenny mentally gave herself a shake. "We're here to make decisions about what needs to be done to prepare Madeline House for its new occupants."

"You mentioned something about color?" Beth's voice was tentative, as if she felt she had no right to speak.

"Yes." Jenny turned to face her. "The house is rather dark. It hasn't seen paint for many years. It suited Maddy, but we do need to brighten it up. What do you suggest?"

"Well, if it were me… I mean, if I were one of the women…" Beth coughed, and Jenny remembered Beth could very well have been one of them if things had been different for her back in Australia. "I'd want to be in somewhere light and bright. The dark beams are great, but maybe we could paint the walls in white… or yellow? Something to bring hope, if that doesn't sound stupid."

"You're right," Ellen said. "Being the lightest hue of the spectrum, the color psychology of yellow is uplifting and illuminating, offering hope, happiness, cheerfulness and fun. It's the best color to create enthusiasm for life and produce greater confidence and optimism."

"Wow! I didn't know that."

"Trust you to know these things."

Beth and Jo spoke together, while Jenny smiled in silence. She knew her cousin's interest in such matters.

"And perhaps some blue too, maybe in the bedrooms," Ellen added. "Blue promotes peace, tranquility, and both physical and mental relaxation."

"Wonderful." Jenny took some notes on a pad she'd brought along. "Now, what about furniture?"

"Something with clean-cut lines," Beth suggested, clearly becoming braver with the acceptance of her earlier suggestion. "And easy to keep clean. And maybe some bright throw rugs for the wooden floor… to soften it. I noticed there were some there when I made my first visit, but they were part of the items which were sold." She stopped, as if wondering if she'd said too much.

"I kept a couple which were in good condition," Jenny said. "You're spot on, Beth. We need to soften up the wood. I wonder…"

"I know just the thing. There's a woman in our community who weaves these brilliant rugs from natural materials. I'm sure she'd be thrilled to help," Ellen said.

"Perfect. Now what else needs to be done?"

The group continued to discuss ways of furnishing Madeline House, with Beth becoming more and more uncomfortable when the talk turned to the women who would live there.

"You'd be willing to talk with them, Beth. Wouldn't you?" Jenny regarded Beth with a smile.

"Yes. I think so." Beth looked down at her hands, now clasped in her lap.

"Not for you? Not yet? Still too close?"

"Something like that." Beth was relieved at Jo's perception. She only hoped Jenny and Ellen would see it that way too – and Tom. Her own experience was still very raw. Sure, she'd opened up to the group, but regardless of what they might think, they really had no idea of her experiences. It was all words to them, but to meet other victims of domestic violence, it would be like baring her soul. "Maybe later. But I'm still happy to be involved in the planning and organizing part of it."

They were interrupted by the sound of a car coming up the track. It stopped outside and Jenny rose. "That'll be Mike back."

"Maybe we should wrap up here," Jo suggested. "You and Mike can discuss the details. I'm sure the rest of us don't need to be involved in the day-to-day stuff. Right, girls?"

"Right," Jenny said. "But let's set another time. There's still a lot to arrange before we can open." The others agreed to continue to meet every two weeks until they were ready to open. "And let's do it in style," Jenny said. "It's what Maddy would have wanted."

Beth was worn out when she reached home, and the box of newspaper cuttings was still sitting on the coffee table. Damn. She'd intended to take those with her, to try to get Jenny alone. But it wouldn't have been possible anyway. She pushed them to the side, determining to set another time with Jenny when they could discuss this in private.

She'd been preoccupied when she left, having received a call from Tom's secretary earlier in the day. The woman hadn't been able to provide any information, but had made an appointment with Beth to meet with Tom the following lunchtime. There must have been some news from Australia – from Bryan's lawyer. Her heart sank again. Would this never end? Would Bryan continue to wreck her life from his grave on the other side of the world?

*

"Take as long as you like. I can cope." Jo had stuck a pen in her mop of hair and looked like a crazy lady. "I hope it's good news." She smiled encouragingly, while Beth's stomach was doing summersaults just thinking about what Tom might have to tell her.

"Thanks." Beth smoothed down her shirt and patted her hair.

"It looks good."

"What? Oh!" Beth blushed and patted her hair again. "You mean this? I thought it was time I did something about it. Coralie had an early spot."

"Next to Ellen's shop, isn't she? She's good. You know she's married to Ellen's brother?"

"Really? It sometimes seems everyone here is related to everyone else."

"Small towns."

Beth left, wondering if the hairstyle had been too much. It wasn't that she wanted to impress Tom, was it? No. Her careful choice of outfit – a white sweater and black pants topped with a red woolen shirt – and the new hairdo were to give her confidence. If she was to hear bad news, then she wanted to look her best. Foolish really. As she drove across town to Tom's office she painted the worst scenario in her mind. That would be the one where the debts were enormous, the house was fully mortgaged and… and… She couldn't imagine anything more, but she'd be glad to have this interview over.

"So there it is," Tom said at last, having laid out the contents of the email from the Sydney lawyer.

"England? They want to advertise in England?" Beth was stunned and confused, then her anger took over. "What are they playing at? Bryan left England years ago, before we met. He was an Australian citizen. As far as I knew, he never even renewed his British passport. He had no ties there. His family are all dead. What do they hope to find? How can this help?" She closed her eyes in despair, only to sense Tom moving across the room towards her. When she opened them again, it was to find his face close to hers, a handkerchief in his hand.

"It's okay." She pulled a face. "I'm not going to weep on you. It's just so stupid."

"Look, it's lunchtime," Tom said. "I usually go out for a bite. When do you need to be back? Does Jo…?"

"She said to take as long as I needed," Beth said. "But I don't think she meant for me to go out to lunch."

"You've had a shock. Why not give her a call?"

Beth did just that. "She said that's okay," she reported as she closed her cell. She didn't repeat Jo's advice to 'Make the most of it – half the single women in town would love to be in your shoes'.

"Good. Do you like Mexican food?"

Beth was surprised. She'd seen lots of Mexican restaurants driving up through California, but hadn't expected one here in Florence. "Ye… es," she replied.

"I often lunch in Los Compadres. They do a good mixed plate. That suit you?"

"You're the local. I haven't found my way around the eateries here yet – apart from Mo's and…"

"The casino, I know. Not sure if that was such a good idea." Tom rubbed his hand over his hair, making Beth want to still it. She'd noticed he had a habit of doing that. Maybe a sign of nervousness or uncertainty, though what Tom had to be nervous or uncertain about, she couldn't imagine.

"No, it was fine," she said. "I enjoyed it." And she had. Despite the raucous sounds of the slots and the cheering and bells at the jackpot, the evening in Tom's company had been relaxing. He was good company, didn't presume any intimacy, and kept his hands to himself. She laughed to herself. What on earth made her think of that? "So? Mexican? Sounds good."

Ten minutes later, they were seated opposite each other on wooden bench seats with a basket of corn chips and two dishes of dip sitting between them. When the waiter arrived to take their orders, he delivered two glasses of light beer, a large one for Tom and a small one for Beth, despite her protestations that she'd never get any work done that afternoon if she had a beer with lunch.

"You can't eat Mexican without a Corona," he said, and would brook no argument. His high-handedness should have reminded Beth of Bryan and his manner of always choosing for her when they ate out. But, somehow, it didn't. It seemed more like a friend advising on the appropriate thing to do. When it came to ordering the food, however, Tom left her to make her own selection from the enormous menu.

"They're really all variation on a theme," he said, when she looked perplexed, and after reading more carefully, she could see he was right.

Beth helped herself to a handful of corn chips and sipped her beer while she studied the offerings, feeling bemused at being here with Tom on a work day. Going out for lunch was nothing new for Elizabeth Flynn, but those lunches had been dressed-up charity events where she always felt she was on show. This lunch was something different. It felt like two old friends sharing a meal. She was still musing over this when Tom's voice broke into her thoughts.

"Have you decided?"

Looking up, Beth flushed as she saw that the waiter was waiting for her order.

"I'm having my usual mixed plate," Tom said. "It lets you try a few different dishes, but it's a big plate. You don't have to eat it all, though." He laughed. "What do you think?"

"No. I'll have the…" Beth quickly scanned the page trying to work out which meal would be small enough for her to cope with.

"Might I suggest the mixed fajitas for the lady," said the waiter, clearly understanding her plight.

"Yes, please." Beth closed the menu and handed it back, not really sure what she'd ordered.

"Sorry, I'm not…" Beth waved her hand in the air.

"Have you eaten Mexican before?" Tom laughed.

"Not a proper Mexican meal. I've had nachos and tacos at a kiddie's birthday party, but Bryan…" she took a deep breath, "Bryan felt they were for poor people." Seeing Tom's expression at her words, Beth burst out laughing, and Tom joined her. As she wiped away her tears – tears of laughter this time – she felt good. It was as if she was beginning to lay Bryan's ghost to rest. If she could laugh at something he'd said, laugh at him, surely he couldn't harm her anymore?

"Well, let's eat like the poor people," Tom said, when they'd recovered. "But don't let the staff hear you say that. They'd be most offended. This is a top spot."

Despite her misgivings, Beth enjoyed her meal, and there was silence as the pair ate. It wasn't till they had both finished, their plates had been removed, and Tom was on his second beer – Beth wondered how he could down two beers at lunchtime and still function adequately in the afternoon – that she returned to the topic which hadn't been far from the front of her mind.

"But why contact England? What do they hope to find?" Beth twisted her hands under the table, her nails digging into her palms so hard she had to stifle a moan.

"I really have no idea. It is a bit odd, especially as you say he has no connections left there."

Suddenly another fear took hold of Beth. "You don't think…? Could they think…? Could Bryan have left debts there too? Before he came to Australia."

Tom's eyes widened. Clearly he hadn't considered this. "But that would have been… how many years ago?"

"Twenty-seven." Beth's voice was almost a whisper. It was twenty-seven years ago, she'd met and fallen madly in love with the handsome young English doctor. He'd literally swept her off her feet, bumping into her as she carried an armful of books up the steps of the university library. The books had gone everywhere, but she'd been prevented from falling by a strong arm around her. When she'd looked up, there he was – tall, dark and handsome with an exotic English accent, a dream come true. At first she hadn't noticed Bryan's controlling behavior for what it was. He was older, more experienced. She'd been happy to follow his lead, listen to his advice. It was only later, when she was more aware of what other people's relationships were like, that she recognized his demands had become unreasonable. She shook her head and raised her eyes to see that Tom was looking at her with a puzzled expression.

"That's a long time for anyone to wait for repayment. Is there any reason for them to suppose…?"

Beth shook her head again. "I don't know. I thought I did. Know him, I mean. I lived with the man for all those years. I can't believe he could hide things from me, but he did. I really didn't know anything about his financial dealings." She gave a bitter laugh. "Said I shouldn't bother my little head about it. As long as there was money in my wallet and enough on the credit card, why should I worry? And I didn't. Worry, that is. Well, now I know why he was so secretive. It wasn't because he thought I wouldn't understand. It was because he knew I'd understand only too well. But to have debts hanging over from back then? Surely they'd have caught up with him before now?"

"Maybe," Tom said slowly. "It depends. There could be a number of reasons why they weren't pursued. Maybe family?"

"But Bryan didn't have any family left there." Beth was losing patience with the conversation. They seemed to be going round in circles and getting nowhere. She sighed. "Oh, well. I guess they'll do what they have to do, and I'll have to wait. At least they won't be asking for any money from me in the meantime." Beth moved her hands to rest on the table and looked down at her neat fingernails, now unpainted, then across at Tom's large tanned fingers encircling the damp glass. For a moment she was tempted to stretch over and take hold of them. They looked so strong, so safe. But the moment passed, and she clasped her hands together.

"So, what now?"

"We have to wait. As I said, this Blackwood guy is still getting everything valued, then they'll set the debts against the assets from the estate and see what's left or…"

"What's still owing," Beth finished for him.

"Are you okay? If there's anything…"

Beth could feel a flutter of fear in her stomach at the thought of what they might discover. What if there were still thousands owing? Hundreds of thousands? Remembering some relaxation exercises she'd read somewhere, she took a deep breath to calm herself, then exhaled slowly. "No. I'll be fine. Thanks for lunch and for being so…" But she couldn't think of an appropriate word.

"I'll walk you back to your car." Tom threw a handful of notes on the table, and they left the restaurant. Neither had much to say on the way back. Beth was trying to digest the new idea that there could even be additional monies owing, owing to people on the other side of the world, and she sensed Tom was unsure what to say.

They parted with a handshake and a promise on Tom's part to keep her informed. Beth hopped into her car with a feeling of what she could only identify as disappointment, at what she wasn't sure. At Bryan, his lawyer, or Tom? Thrusting it all to the back of her mind, she started the car and pointed it in the direction of Green Heron Estate Sales.

"Everything okay? Nice lunch?" Jo greeted her, then not waiting for a reply, continued. "Had Yvonne Walker on the phone. She wants to see you."

"What?" Jo's words brought Beth up short. What on earth could the woman want now?

*

It felt like *déjà vu* when she drove up to the Walker house again. This time the Yvonne woman was waiting for her, hands on hips and a glower on her face.

"You thought I wouldn't notice, did you? You with your questions about old photos, and even men old enough to be your grandfather. Then you sneak off with my aunt's pearls."

Beth's mouth fell open. Pearls? She hadn't even seen any pearls. She drew herself up, prepared to defend herself, but before she could utter a word, Yvonne had continued her tirade.

"Not satisfied with stealing Tom Harrison from me – oh yes, I've heard about the two of you, sneaking around at the casino, stealing into his office when Gwen is at lunch. It won't do. You think you can arrive in this town and take over the most eligible bachelor. And now you run off my Aunt Leona's precious pearls. Well, you won't get away with it. Let me tell you…" She seemed to run out of words and stood gasping, her hand to her throat.

If Yvonne hadn't been so riled, Beth would have burst out laughing. Not only was she being accused of stealing some pearls she'd never seen, but of having an – affair? – with Tom Harrison. She couldn't pretend it wasn't an attractive prospect. Where had that thought come from? She might have considered him that way, but had been quick to dismiss it. She'd been sure Bryan had put her off men for good. Now, this angry woman was putting ideas into her head.

"Um, the pearls," Beth began.

"I'm calling the cops. Then you'll see how we operate here in Florence, how you can't just come in and expect to take over." Yvonne turned on her heel and went into the house, slamming the door behind her.

Beth stared at the closed door, wondering if she should try to explain, then realizing the woman was in no mood to listen to anything she might have to say, decided to return to the office.

"And what I don't understand is the bit about the pearls," she said later to Jo. "The stuff about Tom was bad enough, but I can handle that – more amusing than anything else. But the pearls – I never saw the damned things."

"Oh, dear," Jo said, her lips twitching. "I'm to blame there. I found them inside an old antique charcoal iron. God knows how they got there. Anyway, I'm not good with jewelry valuations and they looked valuable, so…"

"*You* took them." Beth pointed at Jo.

"I fear so. I wanted to have them properly valued. Guess I'd better phone her and own up. But the stuff about Tom. Don't believe her. Tom's been trying to avoid her and her ilk since Janet passed. Why, I haven't seen him look twice at a woman till you arrived in town."

"What? Not you, too." Beth shook her head. Why was everyone trying to pair her up? What was wrong with these people? Ellen and Jenny had dropped a few not-subtle comments too.

"How often do I have to say it? I've had enough of men to last me a lifetime. Here in Florence, it's a new start for me, a life of my own, and I have no intention of complicating it, not for Tom Harrison, not for anyone. Yvonne Walker is welcome to him." As she spoke, Beth thumped her fist on the desk.

"Okay, okay. Keep your hair on. But you have to admit he's pretty easy on the eye and one of the good guys. Most of the men his age are on the lookout for a nurse or a purse, whereas Tom… If I didn't have my Rob, why, I'd…"

Beth almost choked. "Enough!"

"Okay, won't mention it again. But remember, you won't be able to avoid him in this town, and tongues do wag. Have you done anything about the photos yet?"

"No. I need to catch up with Jenny. I still have those papers at home. I thought… maybe…"

"On your day off. Sorry, we've been a bit slack about that." Jo absentmindedly pulled on a stray lock of hair. "We should formalize something so you can make plans. It's not fair to you if I only tell you a day in advance that I won't need you. How about we set Wednesdays as your day off? The middle of the week is usually quiet, unless…"

"I know. Unless it's busy." The pair laughed. "But that'll suit me fine. As long as you know you can call on me whenever. It's not as if I have a hectic social life."

"But you do have a life outside this place. You should get out and about more, see the sights, go horse riding, go on a dune buggy, fishing, meet some people, whatever rocks your boat." She stopped, the glazed look in Beth's eyes clearly indicating she'd gone too far. She shrugged. "Well, you know what I mean."

"Thanks, Jo, I do." As she settled into her afternoon routine, Beth reflected that she knew exactly what Jo meant and that, it being Jo, she couldn't take offence as she might if it had been suggested by anyone else. Beth did need to get out more. She was living in a beautiful part of the world and should make plans to take in the local beauty spots. But first, she needed to arrange a meeting with Jenny. Beth wanted to see if she could resolve the mystery of how her mother had come to have postcards of Florence and a photo of Richard Turner among her treasured belongings – or had her mother even known they were there?

Despite Jo's best intentions, there was a flurry of activity in estate sales, and it wasn't till a couple of weeks later that Beth was able to set a time with Jenny. They arranged to meet in what had become Beth's favorite café in Old Town, and Jenny had suggested asking Ellen along too.

Beth arrived early and settled down to enjoy her special licorice tea with a cinnamon roll. She figured if she kept on eating like this, she'd need a new wardrobe. But since she hadn't brought many clothes with her, that might not be a bad thing, and her mum had always told her she was far too thin. Bryan had liked her that way. But Bryan and his likes or dislikes were no longer an issue. As she gazed at a pair of water birds splashing each other in the river, Beth wondered if Tom Harrison liked his women stick thin or if he preferred them with a bit more flesh, then castigated herself for such a foolish thought.

Fortunately, Jenny arrived, and Beth was saved from her thoughts wandering any further in that direction.

"Ellen'll be here soon," Jenny said, giving Beth a peck on the cheek before plopping herself down opposite. "Isn't it just gorgeous here? Quite my favorite spot in Old Town, and so close for Ellen. Did I tell you…?" But whatever she was going to say was forgotten by Ellen's arrival with two mugs of coffee and a plate of cinnamon rolls.

"Good to see you again, Beth. I see you've already started," she said, indicating Beth's half-eaten sweet.

"Yes, I succumbed. I don't know how you all manage to stay so slim with all this sweet stuff around."

"Isn't it dreadful?" Jenny said. "I felt exactly the same when I first came, but you get used to it and learn when to say no." She repudiated her words by picking up a roll and biting into it. "Not all the time, of course." She laughed. "Now, you said you had something to show me?"

"Yes." Beth picked up the box, which had been sitting on the floor, and placed it on the table. "It's about Richard – Rick –Turner. I've found out more."

"Maddy's Rick?" Ellen asked, through a mouthful of crumbs.

"The same. At one of our estate sales, Jo and I…" Beth decided a small white lie would be okay. "We found these newspaper clippings and a photo." She removed the lid from the box and took out a sheaf of the papers. "During the Second World War, it seems some of the local infantry battalions were sent to the war in the Pacific, and spent some R and R time in Australia. It still doesn't explain…" Her voice died away as Jenny took the papers and began to read.

Ellen leant to read over Jenny's shoulder. Beth watched silently and sipped her tea, enjoying its sharp flavor which combined well with the sweetness of the cookie. After a few moments, Jenny looked up. "But, how…?"

"What makes you think Maddy's Rick was one of them?" asked Ellen.

"We found this, too." Beth took the yellowing photo, now protected in a plastic bag, out of her purse and placed it on the table. Jenny picked it up and peered at the picture.

"That's Rick," she said. "But who are the others?"

"That's what I'd like to find out," Beth said. "Maybe one of them is still alive and can tell us something about Rick's time in Australia. Though, I still can't see how he and Mum could have met. Even if he were there, it would have been in one of the big cities. Mum spent all her life in the country, in Wagga." She sighed.

"They do look rather cute," Jenny said as the three examined the young men, one of whom was wearing a soft hat, while another had his trouser leg rolled up to display what appeared to be a suspender. "Wonder how much they'd had to drink?" She pointed to a couple of empty bottles lying on the sand beside the men.

Beth was about to pick up the photo again, when Ellen beat her to it. She peered at the group, then tapped one of the young men. "I think that's my dad," she said.

Jenny and Beth gazed at her in amazement, Beth's heart beating fast.

"He looks a lot different now, of course, but I remember seeing some photos in an old album, and I'm pretty sure. I'd need to check with Mom. Can I borrow this?"

"Sure. I was thinking Jenny might like to have it. It's no use to me. But your dad. Could he…?"

Beth saw Ellen's mouth turn down, but it was Jenny who spoke. "Ellen's dad… my Uncle Dick… he's in a nursing home. He's not…"

"What Jenny's trying to say is that most of the time Dad's in his own little world. He does have some lucid moments, and his long-term memory is lots better than short-term, but…" She shook her head. "I doubt if he can help. I'll ask Mom anyway. At least we can find out if it *is* him."

Nineteen

"How was Dad, today?" Ellen walked into the kitchen just as her mom was putting a casserole dish into the oven. Rita turned and steadied herself with the edge of the kitchen table.

"Not so good. He was back in the past again, back when we were at school. He thought… he thought I was his mother. Can you imagine? He seems happy enough, but I don't know…" Rita shook her head and sat down, leaning her head on her hand.

"I don't know why you still go there every day. It's been well over a year, now and…"

"He's your dad, Ellen. Where else would I be? Sitting here on my own in this empty house? Not that I'm complaining," she added, clearly seeing Ellen about to speak. "I know you and Ron have your own lives, and pop in regularly. He's not in town so much, but Coralie sees I'm all right too. Ron found a good woman there," she said, referring to her son's marriage to the local hairdresser, which had followed hard on the heels of Ellen's marriage to Travis. "You'll stay for dinner?" Rita levered herself up again and moved towards the pantry.

"That's why I'm here. Travis will be over in time to eat. Don't we always have dinner with you on Thursdays?"

"And Sundays too. And don't think I'm not grateful. But it's not the same as having your dad here, even though… I sometimes wonder if…"

Ellen bit her tongue, remembering how difficult her dad could be, even when he was well. As his health had deteriorated, Rita had found it hard to cope with his tempers and ornery behavior to the extent that, eventually, a nursing home had provided the only solution. All she said was, "It was for the best, Mom."

Rita sighed and continued to prepare vegetables while Ellen checked her cell for messages. She knew her mom preferred to do the cooking by herself. Her independence was important to her, as Ellen had learned to her cost when she tried to help on previous occasions. It wasn't till everything was on the stove that Ellen was able to say, "Now sit down, Mom. I want to show you something," She took the photo out of her purse and slid it out of its protective covering.

"What's this?" Rita wiped her hands on her apron, put on her glasses and peered at the photo lying on the table.

"Beth, you know the new woman working with Jo at The Green Heron…"

"I know who you mean, I haven't lost my marbles yet."

Ellen stifled a grin. "Well, she found this photo at one of their estate sales, and I wondered… he looks like Dad, don't you think?" Ellen pointed to the figure wearing the hat and pointing at the camera.

"What is it to her?" Rita's voice was filled with suspicion.

"One of the others… this one here," Ellen's finger went to one of the other young men. "He's Rick Turner, the one Jenny's godmother Maddy was engaged to. It's a complicated story, but Beth's mom had a photo of him too, and Beth's trying to work out the connection."

"Hasn't she anything better to do?" But Rita picked up the photo and gave it her full attention. "Yes, that's your dad," she said. "He and Rick were good pals back then. There was of crowd of them, always went around together. Before the war. The war ruined a lot of things." She laid the photo down again and removed her glasses. "What's she worrying about all that for now? It was a long time ago." She stroked the photo with one finger, almost caressing it. "We were different people back then. It doesn't do to hark back to the past. We can't bring it back."

"But, Mom. Do you think…? We wondered…"

But Rita had lost interest in the conversation. She rose and stroked her apron as if to remove any creases. "When did you say that man of yours will be arriving? He's bound to be hungry, sitting over that contraption of his all day."

At that moment they heard the roar of the Harley in the driveway. Ellen's face lit up. "Here he is now." Before she could rise from the table, the tall aging hippie, his fading blonde hair escaping from a short ponytail, but with a neatly trimmed beard, entered the room to envelope her in a bear hug.

"You too, Mom." Travis turned to Rita, but she warded him off with a wooden spoon.

"Act your age, you two," she admonished, but the smile in her voice indicated her approval of her son-in-law.

"Do I smell…?" Travis made the pretence of sniffing hard, while Ellen looked on at this clearly accustomed charade with amusement.

"Yes, it's your favorite," Rita said smugly, her earlier annoyance clearly forgotten in routine byplay. "Fried chicken with roast vegetables."

"As only you make it."

"Go on with you. Now go and wash the stink of that machine of yours off your hands before I dish up."

When he'd returned and the three were digging in to Rita's well-cooked meal, Travis pointed to the photo which was still lying on the side of the table. Ignoring the slight shake of Ellen's head, he began, "Did Ellen…?"

"Not you too? As I told Ellen, it's all in the past and should be left there. I recognized Dick, but that's an end to it."

"Leave it," Ellen mouthed and picked up the offending object, sliding it back into its cover then into her purse. "So," she said in a normal voice, "how did it go today?"

"Went well," Travis replied, heaping more of the chicken onto his plate. "Boy, this is good stuff, Rita."

Rita preened.

"Finished that chapter I was stuck on and got the edits for the last one back from Guy."

"Another book is it?"

"That's right, Rita. Got to keep the wolf from the door. Don't want to be dependent on Ellen here to bring home the bacon."

"Mixed metaphors," Ellen said. "Yes, this is good, Mom. You went to a lot of trouble."

"It's nice to have someone to cook for, and I won't always be here."

Ellen and Travis looked at each other. What did Rita mean? Was she sick? Was she thinking of moving? When Dick had gone into the nursing home they'd broached the idea of Rita moving into something smaller, but she wouldn't hear of it, saying they'd have to carry her out feet first.

"I just mean I'm not getting any younger, so enjoy my cooking while you can." Rita was so matter of fact about it that Ellen and Travis were lost for words.

Although Rita had dismissed the photo and Beth's quest out of hand, when Ellen and Travis finally rose to leave, she whispered, "Your dad… you might want to show that photo to him. You never know. There might be a spark." She sighed heavily. "You can never tell what might bring things back. Then again, he could just throw it back at you."

"Thanks, Mom." Ellen hugged her mother goodbye. "I'll try to pop in to see Dad in the next day or two. You'll be there?"

"Of course. Let's hope it's one of his good days."

Since Travis was on the Harley, he reached home before Ellen in her little car, so she was greeted with a welcome streak of light shining out through the open door. Inside, she found he had already poured two glasses of red wine and was waiting for her on the sofa.

"Sit down," he said, patting the seat beside him and holding a glass out to her.

"Thanks." She dropped down beside him, his arm snaking around her shoulders to loosen her long plait. "I love Mom, but sometimes she's real hard going. All that stuff about the photo. She didn't want to know. Acted as if Beth was mad, then…"

"She changed her mind. What's wrong with that?"

"It was so unexpected. And that talk about not always being there. I… After Dad… I don't think I could…" Ellen took a gulp of wine.

"Hey, where did all that come from?" Travis' fingers tangled in Ellen's long tresses and stroked her head. "Your mom's fine. I think seeing the photo might have brought back memories… memories of happier times, that's all."

"But…"

"She has to live in the present, a present where your dad isn't himself. Maybe she doesn't want to be reminded of how it was. She would have been around back then, wouldn't she?"

"They met at school, so yes." Ellen lay back enjoying the sensation of Travis stroking her hair.

"Do you think there's any point showing the photo to Dad? Is it possible it could jog his memory? Or will it perhaps aggravate him further? Remember…?" Ellen pushed herself upright and turned to face Travis. "Remember how angry he got when he saw our wedding photo?" Ellen could see the scene clearly. Saddened her father hadn't been able to attend their informal wedding ceremony, she'd taken in the photos, hoping for some acknowledgement of her special day. Instead, he'd thrown the photos on the floor and harangued them about something incomprehensible."

Travis hugged her tightly. "I don't know. Aren't you the one with second sight? Didn't you see some challenges ahead for Beth?"

"Yes," Ellen faltered. "But nothing to do with a photo or her mother." She pushed her hair back, grabbing a handful. "Oh, hell. I don't even know why she's so bothered about it, or why I got involved at all."

"Because that's the sort of person you are. You like to help others, even when it puts you in a difficult position yourself. That's one of the things I love about you."

"Hmm. I *will* ask Dad, but maybe what Beth needs is something or someone to take her mind off this business about Rick Turner."

"And you have that something or someone in mind?"

"I do," Ellen said, a gleam in her eye.

"Why do I feel I'm going to be involved in this too?"

*

"So I thought you should have a dinner party," Ellen finished.

Jenny held the phone away from her head and looked at it in surprise, only bringing it back to her ear when she heard her cousin start to speak again. "*I* should have a dinner party? Why not you?"

"Beth seems more comfortable with you, and besides, you and Mike are Tom's friends."

Jenny didn't answer, her mind was going round in circles. Then she found her voice. "I don't think it's such a good idea," she said. "Tom and Beth have a professional relationship. He's her lawyer. They may have met at the Madeline House meeting, but to throw them together at a dinner party. Well, it will be pretty obvious we're trying to pair them up. I don't know if either of them are ready for that. Tom's a pretty solitary fellow, and Beth's just come out of a bad marriage. Maybe we should let things take their course."

"Like you and Mike, you mean? Don't try to tell me Maddy didn't have a hand in getting the two of you together."

"Her accident wasn't deliberate, but she did her best." Jenny grinned, remembering how she and Mike had circled each other like a pair of suspicious dogs for a while, before she let her guard down and accepted his help. "And we weren't rushed into anything. To be thrown together at a dinner party." She frowned, as she tried to imagine the situation.

"Isn't there some Australian celebration you could hang it onto?"

"Not really. Australia Day is in January and…"

"I know. What about a birthday? Yours is in two weeks' time."

Jenny groaned. She should have known Ellen would come up with something. She was one of the most persistent people she knew.

"You didn't have anything planned, did you?"

"No…" Jenny said, any thoughts she might have had of she and Mike re-enacting their night at Crater Lake disappearing in the face of Ellen's forceful personality. They probably wouldn't have managed to get a room there, anyway. That first time, they'd been lucky – and look what it had led to. How could she deny Beth the chance of the same sort of happiness? "I'll talk to Mike," she promised. "Talk – that's all, mind. See what he thinks. He knows Tom better than I do. He'll know if he's even remotely interested in Beth. Will that satisfy you?"

"Great. A birthday dinner. Don't take too long about it." Ellen sounded gleeful.

"And meantime, you do intend to bring Rick's photo up with your dad? Mike's become quite interested in the Pacific part of the story. He's started researching already."

"Yes. I'll be seeing Dad soon. Just hope he's with it and not lost to the world."

"I'm sorry, Ellen." Jenny knew how difficult the past two years had been for Ellen, with her dad's declining health, and her mother's insistence on spending each day with him in the nursing home.

"I worry about Mom. She needs more of a life than that, but…"

"She loves him."

"God knows why. He's been a rotten old duffer for years and made her life a misery when he got sick, but I guess she has her reasons."

"Think about it, Ellen. He was to her what Travis is to you. Would you desert him just because he became old and difficult?"

"I guess not."

Jenny could hear her cousin sigh. "So, I'll let you know when I've spoken to Mike. Right?"

"Right. I'll expect a call soon."

"What did Ellen want?" Mike asked, looking up from the paper. "Here, have you seen this?" He held out the page he'd been reading.

"Which do you want me to do first?" Jenny asked, laughing.

"Ellen first." Mike dropped the paper.

"She wants me to invite Tom and Beth to dinner – on my birthday, along with her and Travis."

"Wants us to act as matchmakers does she?" Mike chuckled. "Maddy would love that."

"She would, wouldn't she?" Jenny paused, contemplating what her godmother might have said in her sardonic way. "Anyway, I said I'd check with you."

"We don't have anything planned, do we?"

"It's not that. It's this whole matchmaking business. Have we any right to try to throw them together? Do they even like each other? And if they do, surely it'll happen anyway without our interference?"

"Wow! That's quite a rigmarole. Well, I have no idea about Beth. I can't read women on these matters – as you well know." He grasped Jenny's hand and rubbed his thumb over the back of it, reminding Jenny of their misunderstandings in the early part of their relationship. "But, as for Tom." He pulled on his beard. "I don't think he'd be averse to…"

"Oh, you men!" Jenny pulled her hand away, but dropped a kiss on Mike's head. "Okay. I'll tell Ellen 'yes'."

*

Beth hung up the phone on her second call of the evening, a ripple of pleasure flowing through her. The first, from Ellen, had confirmed that her dad was one of the men with Rick Turner in the photo, and Ellen intended to ask Dick if he remembered Rick. She hadn't held out much hope, but Beth had her fingers crossed Ellen would find her dad in his right mind for once. She'd heard it did happen, and wasn't he more likely to remember something from long ago? The second call had been from Jenny, inviting her to a birthday dinner in a couple of weeks. Beth was delighted about that one. She valued what was becoming a close friendship with both Jenny and Ellen. The only part that bothered her was that Jenny had mentioned Tom Harrison would be there too.

Why did it bother her? Surely she didn't think they were trying to matchmake? Her and Tom? No, that was a joke. But what did she know about them? Both Jenny and Ellen had found their partners fairly recently. In their more mature years. And they were happy. It wasn't beyond the realms of possibility they might… No, that was a foolish idea. It was only a birthday dinner. And Tom? Beth considered. She knew he was widowed, led a solitary life, owned a house by the lake, enjoyed fishing, had a grown daughter and two grandsons, had had his local law practice for years, and was pursued by at least one of the local ladies. Wow! Now she added it up, she knew quite a bit about him, more than she'd expect to know about her lawyer. That was the thing about small towns, she supposed.

He was a bit of a hunk, too with his big build, broad shoulders, penetrating blue eyes, thick thatch of hair, the way his mouth would turn up unexpectedly, his habit of dragging his hand through his hair. His whole being emanated safety and security. But she wasn't ready for anything like that, she thought, without considering what "anything like that" was. Maybe someday, and when that someday came Tom Harrison was exactly the sort of man who could turn her knees to jelly. With a jolt, she remembered the sensation when their arms had touched. She'd felt – not 'knees to jelly' exactly, but she'd certainly felt something.

Enough! It was only a dinner party. She was making too much of it. She hadn't had to think twice before accepting. But it was to celebrate Jenny's birthday. What she needed to do was to decide on an appropriate gift and forget about all those other concerns.

*

"Heard from Ellen yet?"

Beth raised her head. She'd been engrossed in listing the items for the next sale and hadn't heard Jo walk in.

"Not yet. She was planning to see her dad on the weekend, so maybe…"

"We're not so busy here. Why don't you pop over to her shop and ask her? Maybe have a coffee too. I can manage here for a bit."

"Are you sure?" Beth was still not used to the casual attitude at work. There was no stress, no pressure, but the work got done.

She stepped out into the fresh air and breathed in deeply. She gazed up at the blue sky, the first she'd seen after a week of rain. Walking briskly along the boardwalk, she enjoyed the sight of several fishing boats moored there, their blue, red and white cabins bobbing on the water, their high masts reaching up into the sky. Above, birds were wheeling and dipping after any stray pieces of fish they could manage to find while they chorused loudly. Beth pulled her jacket closer to keep warm. The breeze was sharp, despite the sunshine, and it would soon be colder still, a far cry from Sydney. She remembered how cold it had been when she arrived.

She pushed open the door of the bookshop, the clanging bell announcing her arrival. Ellen was shelving some books.

"Hey Beth. Not working today?"

'Yes, but Jo suggested… Did you see your dad?" The words were out before Beth had time to think, then she regretted being so impatient. "I'm sorry. I didn't mean to… You look busy. Do you have a minute?"

"Why don't you come through?" Ellen led Beth to the back of the shop and into a tiny room which seemed to serve as an office. It held a desk, a couple of chairs and masses of boxes. "Take a pew," Ellen said, seating herself with her back to the desk. Her hands fell between her legs and her head drooped. For a moment there was silence, then Ellen raised her head again. "I did see Dad, I showed him the photo, but I'm afraid it was no good. He just looked at it blankly. It didn't mean anything to him. He didn't remember."

"Oh!" Beth felt her whole body sag. She'd hoped…, expected even.

"I'm sorry. But Mom did make a suggestion."

Beth felt a glimmer of hope reignite.

"The school yearbooks. Mom thought you could find Dad there… and Rick Turner… and maybe the others in the photo. It would give names, then maybe you can find out if they're still alive – and maybe more *compos mentis* than Dad."

"School yearbooks. I didn't think of that. They're not such a big deal in Australia, and I don't know if they go back that far. Does your mom…?"

"She said she has one somewhere, but she hasn't seen it for years. You might be better off trying the library. They'd have the whole set there."

"The library, of course. They probably have some old newspapers too." Beth's voice rose as her excitement grew.

"Good idea. Will you go now?"

Beth checked her watch. She'd already been gone from work for almost an hour. "Not now. Jo's a flexible boss, but I do have work to do. I'll check by later. Thanks, Ellen." Beth gave Ellen a peck on the cheek before hurrying back to Green Heron Estate Sales. She was humming to herself as she opened the door of the showroom where Jo was unpacking a box of books.

"Help me go through them?" she asked. "They're from the Walker estate. Yvonne wanted them to go straight to the second hand bookshop, but I always like to check through them first, just in case."

Beth remembered Jo's earlier comments regarding money and old documents she'd discovered in old books, so happily set to and helped Jo hold each of the books upside down. They'd almost reached the bottom of the load, when a flimsy piece of paper fluttered to the floor. Beth picked it up and began to read it. Her face blanched.

"What is it?" Jo left her own bundle to peer over Beth's shoulder. "An old address?"

"An Australian address," Beth said. "It's the old farm, where Mum grew up, in Wagga Wagga. How…? That means…"

"You're on the right track."

"But it still doesn't explain how an American infantryman from Florence – presumably on his way to the war in the Pacific – got hold of my mum's address in Wagga Wagga."

"And how it came to be in a book in Yvonne Walker's aunt's home.

Yvonne Walker, of all people. She's not likely to want to help you solve the puzzle."

"Ellen suggested the library, yearbooks, and maybe even more old newspapers."

"Pity it was only an address we found, not some old letters."

"Letters?" Beth's eyes lit up. "Do you think…?"

"No. Sorry to dash your hopes. If there had been any, we'd have found them by now. Ellen's right. The library's probably your best bet."

Twenty

Tom found the Café Soria easily. It was a building with a pink façade in the heart of town, the busy parking lot bearing testament to its popularity, even on a weekday lunchtime. Looking around, he quickly spotted Louise. She was seated at a window table as if carefully posed, dressed in some flowery thing with a shawl – or what Janet would have called a wrap – artfully draped over one arm, a glass of white wine in her hand. Her outfit blended in so well with the décor, she looked as if she belonged there, or had taken root. He smiled inwardly.

Once at the table, Tom bent down, hand outstretched, only to find Louise reach up to plant a perfumed kiss on his cheek.

"No need to stand on ceremony, Tom," she said. "We're almost related."

Tom coughed and choked down the first reply that came to his lips. "Louise. Good to see you," he lied. "Nice place this." He looked around at the lunch crowd, comprising mainly well-heeled women, like his companion. "A favourite spot of yours?"

"I often meet friends here. The food's so fresh – the Mediterranean influence, you know," she said with a tight smile. "I'm sure you have a favorite spot in Florence. You must share it with me sometime soon."

"Hmph. Have you ordered?" Tom picked up the menu and proceeded to study it as if his life depended on it. How was he to get through this lunch? What had Brad landed him in? Louise was another of the predatory females he spent his days avoiding, and he was trapped into planning a wedding with her.

Settling on a grilled rib steak, while Louise opted for the fancy-sounding Jericho prawns, Tom also ordered a beer to wash it all down. Louise held up her half-empty glass with a smile and Tom ordered a refill, then leant back. Maybe now they could get down to business, plan what Louise had in mind, and he could be off back to Florence, before… what he wasn't sure, but he didn't want to wait to find out.

But Louise was in no hurry to get down to business.

"So," she said, eyebrows raised and gazing at Tom over the top of her glass with what appeared to be a well-practiced flirtatious look. "Our two little chicks want to fly the nest and make a match of it."

Tom almost choked at the thought of thirty-five year-old Brad being referred to as a chick. And the said chick had flown the coop several years ago. Also, to maintain the metaphor the pair were already feathering their nest, that nest being Brad's flat here in Eugene. How Janet would have laughed. It's what he missed most, the lack of someone to laugh with. They'd shared a sense of humor and some good times.

"And they've brought us together too." Louise smiled and reached her hand towards Tom's. He hurriedly picked up his beer and took a long swallow. This could turn out to be the lunch from Hell. Fortunately, the waiter brought out their meals, and Louise was forced to withdraw her hand.

"You said you had things you wanted to discuss?" Tom asked.

"Let's eat first." Louise smiled as she pierced a prawn with her fork and lifted it delicately to her mouth. "Business after pleasure."

Tom shifted uncomfortably in his chair. Damn the woman. This was going to take longer than he thought. He'd had Gwen cancel his afternoon appointments and had been planning some quiet time on the lake. He glanced out the window at the blue sky interrupted by only a few high clouds. It was a perfect day, and here he was, stuck opposite Brad's overly charming future mother-in-law. Well, at least he could enjoy his lunch. He took another mouthful of the delicious steak and washed it down with a swig of beer. Maybe he could eat in peace. But this wasn't to be. Louise seemed to be able to talk and eat at the same time, and the woman had a lot to say. By the time he put his cutlery down on the empty plate, Tom felt he'd been battered by a barrage of words. He'd learned all about Brooke's childhood, Louise's fears she'd choose the wrong man – as Louise had, it seemed – and a litany of Brad's strengths. While it was good to hear his son praised, Tom was all too aware of Brad's shortcomings. But he listened with barely disguised amusement as Louise rattled on, clearly determined to show Tom his son in his best light.

"They are so obviously meant for each other," she concluded. "A match made in heaven."

As the waiter cleared away their empty plates and filled their coffee cups, Louise slipped out of her seat, pointing to the restrooms. "Back soon. Don't go away," she trilled.

Fat chance. Tom checked his cell. Three missed calls – Gwen, Rob, and Mike Halliday. What the heck? Gwen and Rob, he could understand. Gwen liked to keep tabs on him when he was out of the office, and he and Rob had a longstanding appointment at the gun club that night, but Mike? He scratched his head and checked voicemail – two messages. He pressed Play.

"Hi Tom. Mike here, Mike Halliday. Wanted to ask if you're free Friday week. It's Jenny's birthday, and we're having a bit of a do. Just a few of us. Can you ring me back?"

Tom furrowed his brow. This was unexpected. He knew Mike and his wife quite well and was involved with them in the Madeline House stuff, but it was mostly business dealings. He hadn't thought they were on the sort of terms to be invited to a family birthday. Seemed like he was beginning to have a social life. Louise today, Mike and Jenny next week. He checked the next message as he saw Louise walking back. Gwen wanted him to call into the office before he went home. Tom sighed and slid the cell into his pocket. He'd be lucky if he got out to the lake before dinner at this rate.

"Now," Louise said, taking a notebook out of her purse and clasping her hands on the table. "Here's what I think…"

For the next hour, Tom listened to the list of matters Louise believed needed his input, though it seemed to him that she and Brooke had already made all the decisions. Since there was little he could add, he found himself agreeing, nodding silently and wondering how soon he'd be able to leave. It wasn't till they were on their third cup of coffee that he managed to catch the waiter's eye and ask for the check.

"One last thing, Tom." Louise put her hand on Tom's arm as they were about to leave. "We still haven't really discussed the venue. We agreed on your lawn, but I need to see it again so we can work out where to put the marquee, and exactly where the ceremony will take place – to have the best background for photos. When do you think? We don't need the children, just you and me."

Tom felt trapped. He wanted to refuse. He knew he'd have no say in the matter. It was a done deal. But he couldn't escape the vicelike grip on his arm. He had to say something. "Can I call you?" he asked. "I need to check…"

"Of course." She relinquished her grip. "I know how busy you must be, a professional man like yourself. Maybe on a weekend? I'll look forward to your call." She rose on tiptoe to brush his cheek with her lips then with another touch on his arm, she walked away.

Tom got into his car with a sense of relief. He sat for a moment reliving the cloying presence of his lunch companion. Surely he wasn't imagining her interest in him as a man. He wasn't given to flights of fancy, didn't imagine every woman he met found him attractive. Take Beth Carson, for instance. Now there was a woman a man could have a decent conversation with. No hidden agenda there. He threw the pickup into gear and roared off. A quick stop at the office, then the lake beckoned with the sense of peace it engendered.

*

Beth couldn't decide what to wear. Since arriving in Florence, her wardrobe had been pretty much limited to pants and shirts, like many of the locals. But tonight was a special occasion, and she was dithering between a smart pair of pants, topped with a shirt, or a deep blue dress with a swirling skirt. The latter was an impulse buy, the legacy of a shopping trip to Eugene, but till now it had hung in her wardrobe waiting for an appropriate occasion. She held it up and contemplated the soft feel of the fabric. Yes, she decided, tonight she'd be feminine. She brushed aside the unwelcome thought that she'd like Tom Harrison to see her as a woman, rather than a client, and took the dress off its hanger.

Beth found she was humming to herself as she drove up the now familiar road. She was looking forward to seeing Jenny and Ellen again. That was all, she told herself firmly, despite the image of Tom Harrison which threatened to come between her and the windscreen.

"Hi there. Happy birthday." Beth hugged Jenny and handed her a gift-wrapped offering, hoping she'd like the blown glass ornament Beth had discovered in one of the local craft shops. Jenny immediately tore off the wrappings.

"Look, Mike!"

"Isn't that the one you were admiring?" Mike asked.

"It is indeed. How did you know? Thank you so much!" Jenny grasped Beth's hand and led her into the room where the others were already seated.

It appeared Tom hadn't arrived yet, so Beth took one of the empty seats and accepted a glass of wine from Mike. She had barely taken her first sip when the door opened again and Tom appeared. He was wearing a pair of pressed jeans teamed with an open-necked shirt in a shade of deep blue which was a perfect match for his eyes. Eyes which when they fell on Beth, immediately moved away. Hadn't he known she'd be here? Immediately she felt uncomfortable, then his face broke into a wide grin, and he took the seat next to her.

"Hello again. Seems we're the ring-ins tonight," he said *sotto voce* to Beth, before adding more loudly, "So is this it – the small gathering?"

"Just us," said Mike. "Were you expecting a bigger crowd?"

"We thought it would be nice for Beth to get to know us all better," Jenny said, hurriedly. "Away from any hint of business."

"I think we're being set up here," Tom said to Beth, gripping her hand tightly and squeezing her fingers to engage her compliance. "What shall we do? Spill the beans, carry on or cut and run?"

As Jenny and Ellen rushed to deny it, Beth caught sight of Tom's wink and decided to play along. "Maybe we should tell them," she said, twisting her wine glass and hiding a smile. "We wouldn't want to…" Then, seeing the strange expressions on the faces of their hosts, she took pity on them. "Only joking, but I hope you didn't have any ulterior intentions. Tom and I, we're… friends, that's all. It *is* your birthday, isn't it?" she asked Jenny, suddenly hit by the awful suspicion the whole evening might be a sham, designed to bring about a relationship between her and Tom as she'd first imagined.

"Of course it is, and I've cooked a special birthday dinner to prove it. It should be ready now." The group took this as an indication to move to the dining room, where Jenny bade them to be seated while she set out a veritable feast.

The evening passed pleasantly until, as they were enjoying Jenny's special pavlova dessert, Mike asked Tom, "Did I hear young Brad's found himself a wife? About time. He must be…"

"Thirty-five. Yes. Janet and I had all but given up on him settling down. Brooke's young, but she seems a nice girl, and they're well matched."

"And the wedding?" asked Jenny. "Will it be here in Florence?"

Tom dropped his spoon with a clatter. Everyone stopped eating and looked in his direction. Beth wondered what on earth was wrong. Jenny's question had seemed innocent enough.

"Yes." He paused, as if wondering how much to say, then continued, "That's just it. Brooke's got it into her head she wants to be married on my back lawn. Not that it looks much like a lawn at the moment, but she – and her mother…" He hesitated again. "They're both pretty determined ladies. Louise, her mother, wants to come over to check the place out again." Tom drummed his fingers on the table, then dragged them through his hair. "It's Brad's day. I want him to have the best, but… all this… this footling around. I'm not cut out for it."

There was silence while the group digested his words, then Ellen spoke. "Is it just the wedding or is it more? Is this Louise… is she…?"

"Is she after you, pal? Looking to make it a double wedding?" Travis asked.

They all laughed and Beth joined in, any embarrassment she'd felt earlier, well and truly gone. Then she had an idea. "How about…" Everyone looked in her direction. "How would it be if, when you arranged to meet with her…, if we all came along too – for moral support, or something," she finished, her voice dropping as she wondered if this was a crazy idea.

"Capital!" Travis said. "No need for you to deal with this woman on your own. That's what friends are for. Does she…"

"You'd do that?" Tom seemed dumbfounded.

"Of course we would," Jenny said. "Great idea, Beth. And maybe…" She looked from Beth to Tom and back again. "Maybe we could do even more. Get her off your back for good."

Why did Beth have the feeling she wasn't going to like what Jenny was about to say? Her heart sank a little as Jenny continued, "Since we'll be two couples and Beth. Why don't you two pretend to be a couple too?" She nodded towards Tom and Beth, her eyes gleaming with amusement.

"Oh, I don't think so," Beth said, smoothing the skirt of her dress and trying to look anywhere but at Tom. Surely Tom would be quick to dismiss this mad idea.

"What do you think?" Tom turned towards her, his eyes crinkling and his mouth turning up attractively. It was as if he hadn't heard her words.

"I don't think Beth likes the idea," Ellen said. "We understand if it's too crazy, but it could be fun. Is this Louise really so awful?"

"Awful? No. She's elegant, well-dressed, confident. She's actually quite charming, perhaps that's the trouble. She's too charming, and very determined. Used to getting her own way." He rubbed his hand across the top of his head. "It's difficult to say no to her." He turned towards Beth. "You know… if you could bring yourself to… It would make things a lot easier for me."

Beth twisted her hands in her lap and looked down. She could feel everyone staring at her, willing her to agree. It was preposterous. The woman was going to be related to Tom through marriage. How long were they supposed to keep up this masquerade? Tom must have sensed her concerns, because he said, "Just this one time. I can handle her later on, but the damned wedding planning's got me beat. If we can… if she thinks I'm even interested in someone else, she and Brooke may drop the idea. Hell, maybe I'm imagining the whole thing."

Suddenly something inside Beth began to feel sorry for Tom. It really wasn't too much to ask: to pretend to be his – whatever – for an afternoon. And it might be good for her too, force her to accept being close to a man, even if it was pretend. She made her decision. "All right. If everyone else thinks it's a good idea, but…"

"I'll keep my hands to myself." Tom held them up in the air to emphasize the point. Beth felt a flush pulse through her whole body. That wasn't what she was afraid of, or was it? She wasn't immune to the man. His closeness *did* make her feel uncomfortable.

"That's enough," Jenny said, but they were all laughing by now, and

Beth no longer felt awkward. "Now, we need to prepare for this. Beth can't just arrive at Tom's on the day and fit into the role. She needs some practice."

"What…?" Beth was already regretting her easy acquiescence.

"Nothing earth-shattering," Ellen said, joining in. "Maybe a trip out to Tom's home to become familiar with it, find out where everything is. That sort of thing. We don't need to be involved in that part. Tom?"

Tom shifted awkwardly in his seat. Clearly he hadn't considered any preparation would be required.

"Maybe…," Beth began.

"No, it's okay. Why don't you drop over for lunch on Sunday? We can set Louise up for next Saturday. I'll call her tomorrow. Thanks, guys." He sighed, visibly relieved to have it all taken care of.

"Can I bring anything?" Beth asked, bowing to the inevitable.

"No. I'll fix a barbecue. That okay with you?"

"Fine," Beth smiled. Men were much the same all over the world. When faced with the need to cook, they opted for a barbecue. She wondered how he fared when he was on his own. Maybe he ate out a lot. Well, she'd soon find out. She was going to have the opportunity to poke and pry in his cupboards. Now the die was cast, and the time arranged, Beth was surprised to find she was quite looking forward to visiting Tom's home again.

*

True to his word, Tom called Louise to set the date. She expressed her delight to hear from him, offering to bring something, and twittering on about how she knew what men were like on their own, that he probably wasn't taking care of himself properly, the importance of a woman's touch, and so on. Tom bore it all stoically, glad he wouldn't have to suffer her company on his own. He felt a sight twinge of guilt about the deception they were about to inflict, but his main feeling was one of relief. A faint warning voice asked him how he was going to explain Beth to Simone and Brad. Simone was already suspicious enough. But he'd figure that out if he had to. It was enough for now he had Louise sorted.

It was as if the pair of them had been privy to their dad's thoughts. First Simone called, full of her visit to the local school, which had proved Ed correct, though now she was claiming it as her own idea. Tom was glad to hear her so enthusiastic, but had to back-peddle rapidly when she suggested he pop up to Portland to see for himself. Pleading unspecified local commitments for the next couple of weekends, he managed to fend Simone off when she tried to gain more details, muttering something about Brad and the wedding. That seemed to satisfy her. Although she did make a veiled reference to 'that little woman' which he managed to ignore.

Then Brad called. Louise must have gone directly from Tom's call to make one to her daughter. Brad, too, wanted Tom to hear his approval, and his hope this might be the beginning of closer relations between the two sets of parents. Tom chuckled as he hung up on his son, having been as non-committal as he could about any 'relationship' with Louise. He could hear Brooke's sentiments in his son's words, and if he'd been facing another meeting with Louise on her own, on his home soil, he'd have been seriously worried. As it was, he'd be well insulated from her advances. He'd be accompanied by Mike and Jenny, Travis and Ellen and… Beth.

He poured a second mug of coffee and stepped out onto the deck, musing again on the idea that the slope of rough grass leading down to the lake could be called a lawn. For the first time, he tried to imagine it trimmed and set out with a marquee and all the trimmings. He failed miserably. To him it was, and always would be, a strip of uneven and uncared for grass. His thoughts turned to Beth and her surprising agreement to what had really been her suggestion. She was a game one, and much more his style than Louise. It wouldn't be difficult to pretend they were more than friends. In fact, it might be fun.

Twenty-one

"Welcome," Tom greeted Beth.

"I brought this." Beth held out a cakebox. "I know you said not to bring anything, but I noticed how much you enjoyed Jenny's pavlova." She reddened, wondering if she'd been too presumptuous.

"That the thing with cream and fruit? Thanks. I don't usually stretch to dessert." Tom took the cake and led Beth through to the kitchen, which she remembered from her earlier visit. She gazed around, feeling awkward, wondering if she should sit down. Tom solved the issue for her by heading for the cooktop where a pot of coffee was bubbling away. "You like a coffee?"

The last thing Beth felt like was a coffee, a nice cup of tea would have been more welcome, but she nodded her agreement and took a seat.

"This is…"

"You must…"

Both spoke at the same time, then stopped and laughed.

"You first," Tom said.

"I was about to say that this is a bit awkward." Beth turned her mug around and ran her finger round the edge. "What are we supposed to do?"

Tom slid a plate of cookies across the table towards Beth. "Help yourself. I guess I should show you around, get you familiar with the layout." He rubbed his chin. "It all seems a bit back to front, doesn't it? But needs must. You're still okay with the idea, are you? Because we can always…"

"No, I'm good with it. This Louise, she sounds a bit of a difficult customer."

"That she is," Tom sighed. "A nice lady, I'm sure. And Brad and she seem to get on real well. I'm glad. He misses his mom."

"You must miss her too," Beth said gently, tempted to put her hand on his arm and comfort him, but unsure of his reaction.

"Yes. It's been five years." He looked down into his coffee, then raised his eyes to meet Beth's. "But I've moved on, found a routine, a way of coping. And you? Do you miss your husband?"

Beth thought for a moment, rolling her finger over some stray grains of sugar on the table. Did she miss Bryan, or was her feeling only one of relief at being free? She answered slowly, "No. I miss the companionship, because regardless of his faults, Bryan was there, someone to talk to. But I don't miss the control he exerted. It was wearing. No. I'm relishing my solitude, my ability to make my own decisions."

"The solitary life has a lot of plusses," Tom agreed. "But sometimes, it's good to have someone there – someone to share things with."

"Mmm." Beth reflected that it had been a long time since she'd been able to share intimate details of her life with anyone. With Bryan in the early days, but not recently. It must be nice to be in a relationship in which each party felt safe and secure, able to share the most intimate details without fear of ridicule or abuse.

"Well," Tom seemed to galvanize himself, as if regretting such a personal conversation, "Drink up and I'll give you the tour, then we can have lunch on the deck."

Beth drained her coffee and followed Tom through the house as he pointed out various bits and pieces he thought it might be useful for her to be aware of.

When they reached the upstairs section of the house and entered the main bedroom, Beth couldn't help noticing the large king-sized bed facing the lake. She immediately imagined how wonderful it would be to wake up here with a loving man beside her, then quickly stifled the thought. She felt herself blush and stole a glance at Tom, hoping he wasn't a mind-reader. But he seemed unperturbed. "What a view to wake up to," she said to cover her confusion.

"Wonderful, isn't it? Look at this." Tom took hold of Beth's arm and drew her to the window, expounding on the beauties of the lake and its surrounds. His chatter gave her time to collect herself, but his touch was disturbing, disturbing in a way she'd almost forgotten. It stirred up feelings she'd thought had gone forever. She was glad when Tom dropped his hand, and she rubbed the spot he'd been holding, as if by doing that, she could ignore the sensation it had triggered.

*

What was wrong with him? Tom dropped his hand to hide the flash of desire he felt for this woman. He didn't want to scare her off. He felt himself beginning to sweat. This wasn't a woman like Louise or Yvonne or any of those other women he'd tried to avoid of recent years. This was someone who'd been hurt badly, who had no reason to trust him or any man. He should keep his distance if he didn't want her to flee. Flee? What was he thinking? Tom tried to analyze his feelings – something he didn't do often – and realized he was attracted to Beth. No, more than attracted. He wanted… Shit, what *did* he want? They were standing in his bedroom. The first thing he wanted to do was to get out of here.

"Time for lunch?"

"Yes." Beth sounded relieved. Surely she hadn't imagined…? Read his mind? He was a man, with all the weaknesses that entailed, but he'd never…

He led the way downstairs, the journey seeming to give them both respite from whatever they had experienced in the bedroom.

"Can I do anything to help?"

"No. All done," Tom said, taking a bowl of salad and a plate containing two large steaks out of the fridge. "Wine?"

"Yes, please." Beth ignored his refusal of help and fetched a couple of plates from the cupboard he'd shown her earlier and flatware from a drawer. "I should get used to looking as if I know my way around," she said in response to his expression of surprise.

"Right." Tom was startled at the way she seemed to fit into his kitchen. It was almost as if she belonged there, yet she was unobtrusive, quite unlike Simone's way of taking charge. He didn't realize he was staring, until Beth spoke.

"Is there something wrong? Have I…?"

"No," he said quickly. "It's just that… you look so…" He threw his hands wide to demonstrate what he couldn't find the words to say. "You look so at home," he finished with a wry grin. "I think we're going to pull this off."

"Of course we are," Beth said in a business-like manner, softened by a gentle smile. "Now, you do want these outside, don't you? And I *would* like wine – white if you have it."

Tom looked at his hand, which was still holding the fridge door open, and removed a bottle of chardonnay for Beth and a beer for himself. "Yes, outside on the deck." What on earth had gotten into him? He was becoming a blathering idiot.

Tom watched Beth take a seat at the table and tuck her legs under her on the seat. She was wearing something soft and green today, unlike the tailored pants he'd mostly seen her in. It made her look more feminine, more… He turned his back and occupied himself with cooking the steaks. That was a task he was comfortable with. It brought back the memory of Louise and her sudden appearance at his side at the same barbecue. Louise, that was what this was all about. He mustn't allow himself to become side-tracked by an attraction, real or imagined, to Beth Carson.

"Here we are." Tom delivered the cooked steaks to the table, and there was silence while they ate, punctuated only by the wild cries of the water birds. By the time Beth served generous helpings of pavlova, Tom was feeling more at ease in her company.

"So," Beth said, twirling her almost empty glass and pointing it towards the lake. "This is where the wedding is to take place? Can we take a look? The pavlova will keep."

"Sure thing."

Tom helped Beth down the few steps to the grassed area, taking care to avoid touching her any more than was necessary. If she noticed his hesitance, she was too polite to say anything.

"Do you ever cut it?"

Tom regarded his feet, which were deep in the long grass, then Beth's more dainty ones, almost hidden in the greenery. He rubbed his chin and smiled. "Not very often. Do you think I should?"

"Well, it's difficult to imagine a marquee with all the trimmings on this. And it slopes!" The last came out almost as a yell as Beth tripped and slid down a few steps. "It's okay," she said, before Tom could reach her to offer assistance. "Yes, I'd say you should definitely have it cut – before Louise sees it again, I'd suggest."

Tom knew she was right, but he rather liked its unkempt appearance. It fitted the lake.

"Oh, look," she said, pointing. "Isn't that one of the birds you told me about last time? A green heron." She took a few steps toward the lake, and fearful she might slip again, Tom took her hand, her fingers curling trustingly into his as they stood together watching the small bird. She's not unlike the bird herself, Tom thought. Like him, Beth seemed to prefer a solitary existence, almost secretive, and she often appeared nervous in company.

"You know," Beth said. "It could be rather gorgeous. To have your son's wedding here," she added as Tom furrowed his brow trying to figure out what she was talking about.

"Hmm." He gazed around. This was his private place. He really didn't want it overrun by a horde of wedding guests, not even for Brad's wedding, but it seemed that his opinion didn't count. "I guess so. Now we should get back to that meringue you brought."

"Mmm. This is good stuff," Tom was well into his second helping. "Could you maybe… would it be asking too much…?"

"You want me to make one for next weekend? I'd be delighted." There was a glimmer of a wicked grin. "Now, I should probably go home. I'll help you clear up first."

"No need. I can manage." Tom picked up the empty plates and, balancing them on one hand, lifted the empty wine glass and his empty beer bottle in the other. It was too much, the glass fell and shattered on the deck, narrowly missing Beth's feet. "Sorry to be so clumsy." Tom bent down to retrieve the pieces of glass only to have a large splinter pierce the soft web of skin between his thumb and index finger. "Damn!" Dropping the empty bottle and plates on the table, he grasped the cut with his other hand, but the bleeding wouldn't stop.

"Hold this on it." Beth held out a tissue. "Where's your first aid kit?"

"It's nothing," Tom began, but the blood was soon seeping through the tissue. "Downstairs bathroom, bottom cupboard," he said through tight lips. It was hurting more than it had at first. He sat down. What a thing to happen.

It seemed to take forever, as he held the tissue tightly on the cut. Were there tendons there? He couldn't remember much from the anatomy class he'd done years ago. At least it was his left hand, but one he used a lot.

Beth returned carrying not only his first aid kit, but also a bowl of water with steam rising from it. She set both down on the table and crouched at his feet. "This may hurt," she said, gently removing the tissue. The cut stung when open to the air, but her touch was gentle as her soft fingers swabbed the wound.

He looked at the bleeding mess, seeing what he thought was a tendon. He averted his eyes. "Is that…"

"No tendons there." It was as if she had read his mind. "I don't think it's too deep, but it is bleeding a lot. I can strap it up for you, or you may need stitches."

Tom peered down at the cut again. "No, should be right if you can strap it up. That'd be good." He watched her dainty fingers apply antiseptic cream, then bind his thumb and index finger together tightly with tape. It would be some time before he could flex that hand again.

"There, that should do it." Beth raised her eyes, which had been focussed on his hand. She was still holding it in her small ones. Her touch was tender, arousing a feeling that couldn't be denied. Before he could stop himself, his lips touched to hers. If he'd taken time to consider, he'd have drawn back immediately, full of apologies but, to his surprise, he felt an answering pressure. Beth's mouth was soft. His tongue explored it, then the pair drew apart.

Beth released his hand. "I…"

"I didn't plan that," Tom said, his voice husky with desire. Where had it come from – this sudden yearning? He wanted this woman, wanted more than a stolen kiss. He wanted to feel her naked body next to his. This is what he had sensed – and thrust out of his mind – when they stood in the bedroom. Now, all he wanted was to pick her up in his arms, carry her back there and…

Beth was speaking. "I think we both got carried away." She was already picking up the bowl and the soiled cotton and tissue. "I'll get rid of these." She disappeared into the house, leaving Tom gazing after her in dismay. He pushed his good hand though his hair. Had he ruined everything? Had his one precipitous act spoiled what was promising to be a good relationship? Blow the Louise business. That was make believe. He wanted more than a make-believe relationship with Beth. He wanted… What did he want? He'd been so sure his solitary existence was all he needed, but he knew deep down that this woman was worth more than a quick roll in the hay. This was a woman for keeps. But how could he retrieve what he now saw as a major *faux pas*?

"I've tidied up and stacked the dirty dishes in the dishwasher," Beth said from the doorway. "Is there anything else you'd like me to do before I go?"

Stifling the urge to lay bare his innermost thoughts lest she'd decide never to see him again, Tom merely replied, "No, and thanks for this." He held up his injured hand. "This'll keep me out of mischief for a bit." Tom wasn't sure, but he thought he saw a faint smile around Beth's mouth. But it was gone in a flash.

"Would you like me to pop over tomorrow… in case you need anything?"

"Would you? I'm not completely incapacitated, but…" Tom felt guilty at playing the invalid. There was nothing he couldn't do with one hand. It might be awkward, but manageable.

"I'm still not sure you shouldn't have stitches," Beth said, her voice serious. "I could come check your wound, if you like."

"Thank you, that would be great," Tom said, levering himself up. "I'll see you out."

Tom gazed after the little car as it rattled down the driveway. She was coming back. Maybe the relationship was retrievable after all.

*

Thoughts were whirling around in Beth's head as she drove home. Tom Harrison had kissed her, and she'd kissed him back. Then she'd taken fright and run away. She was ashamed of herself, acting like an embarrassed teenager. It had all happened too soon after her unworthy thoughts in Tom's bedroom. What if he'd read her mind? If he thought she wanted… what? What did she want? Was Tom like a lot of other men – happy to take what was on offer if a woman…? She shivered, but whether in fear or anticipation, she wasn't sure. Her fingers reached up to touch her lips, the lips he'd kissed. It had been quite a kiss. Just thinking about it turned her insides to jelly. She'd been so busy telling herself – and anyone else who'd listen – that she wasn't ready for another relationship, that she'd sworn off men, once bitten twice shy and all the other clichés she could think of. But fate, her heart – and her body – had other ideas. Tom was… a special kind of man. Her subconscious had recognized that from the start, and seeing him there – so vulnerable – it was as if something inside Beth had broken, as if the hard shell which had formed during all those years with Bryan had begun to crack. So, instead of pushing Tom away, she'd wanted to pull him closer, she'd wanted to… She felt herself blushing. But how did he feel about her? Was the kiss just a knee jerk reaction to having a woman tend to him, a momentary urge, or was it something more?

Twenty-two

"Hello?" Getting no answer to her knock at the door, Beth wandered around the house, following the sound of a lawnmower which seemed to be making heavy weather of its task. Sure enough, Tom was pushing the large electric contraption through the thick grass between the house and the lake. He stopped when he saw her and turned off the motor, the ensuing silence made all the more noticeable by the sudden clamor of birds.

"You came." Tom ambled over to meet her.

"How's the hand?" Beth noticed he was holding it close to his body. How on earth had he managed the mower and what had possessed him to use it with an injured hand? Her second question was soon answered.

"Decided might as well get started on this while I was laid up," Tom said. "Thought it was something that wouldn't need a thumb, but…" He held up his hand to show blood beginning to seep through Beth's careful dressing. "May not have been such a good idea. Maybe you could…" He reddened, clearly remembering the result of her care the day before. "I promise to behave," he said, a twinkle in his eye.

Beth's lips twitched. Behave, indeed. When all she wanted was another kiss, and another and… "Well, see you do."

"I should shower and change first," Tom said and Beth noticed he was dressed in a pair of old gray track pants and a shabby green sweater displaying *Oregon Ducks* in faded letters. This, combined with his untidy hair and unshaven face, gave him a defenseless look which made her want to put her arms round him.

"How about I make some coffee while you do that? And I'll fetch the first aid kit again. We can fix you up at the kitchen table." She didn't add they'd be safer in the kitchen where the atmosphere would be less likely to encourage a repeat performance, though, she thought, looking at his disheveled appearance that might not be such a bad idea.

Tom disappeared upstairs and Beth busied herself organizing coffee and first aid as promised, all the while trying to dismiss the image of Tom in his shower upstairs. From the kitchen sink, she could hear the water running in the ensuite directly above. It was difficult to keep her mind focussed on the job at hand, rather than picturing water flowing over Tom's naked body. The very thought made her tremble.

By the time Tom appeared in the kitchen fully dressed in a green tee shirt and khaki cargo pants, his hair still damp, Beth had gained her equilibrium and was pouring out two mugs of coffee. "Sit down here and put your hand on the table," she said, indicating the chair to her right and busying herself with the antiseptic cream and tape. "It may hurt when I pull off yesterday's dressing," she warned.

"I'm tough. I can stand it." Tom grinned, crinkling up his eyes, no doubt recalling yesterday's pain. "It feels a bit better today."

"But not good enough to be pushing a mower." Beth removed the dressing as gently as she could, enjoying the feel of his skin. She felt him flinch as she replaced the tape firmly and looked up, afraid she was causing him more pain, but Tom was smiling as he watched her fingers neatly trim the edges of the adhesive tape. "There! That's done. Now, I hope you'll take more care."

"Yes, ma'am." Tom gave her a mock salute with his good hand.

"I…"

"About yesterday," Tom began, not giving Beth time to speak. "I… It won't happen again."

Beth kept her eyes fixed on his injured hand, willing him to give some indication of his feelings, yet dreading what he might say.

"I know it was too soon. I'm not in the habit of…"

"Kissing strange women?" Beth raised her eyes to meet his with a smile and wondered how she could help him overcome what he clearly felt was an awkward moment. "It was…" She was about to say 'nothing' when she caught the gleam in his eye and changed it to, "… quite a kiss."

"I don't think you're strange. Different maybe."

"Different from what?" Beth was curious. This wasn't the sort of conversation she'd anticipated.

"Different from the women around here. You're more… feisty maybe… independent I guess. You're not out to trap a man. Quite the reverse. And I don't want to scare you off. Yesterday… you left… suddenly. I thought… I thought I'd ruined my chances with you."

His chances? Beth gasped. There was a peculiar fluttering somewhere in her belly. This was definitely *not* what she'd expected. "I thought you were spoken for – a certain Yvonne Walker?"

"Christ no! Sorry, that came out without thinking. No, she's one of the local ladies who…" Tom dragged his good hand through his hair. He was obviously too embarrassed to say more, but Beth guessed from his flaming cheeks that there were a few local women who'd like his shoes under their bed – to use a favorite phrase of her mother's.

"Hmmm.' Beth put her head on one side and regarded Tom with what she hoped was a roguish gaze. "So you've been running fast and loose among the local women and have now decided to try it on with a stranger?"

"No, no, you've got me all wrong. I'd never… Since Janet died, I…" Tom stopped as Beth, unable to keep up the pretense any longer, burst out laughing.

"Sorry, I couldn't resist teasing you a little. Of course I understand. It can't have been easy for you, since your wife died. And you have a son and daughter?"

"Yes, you met Simone. She hates the idea I might find someone else. Interestingly enough," he tapped his nose, "she has you pegged as 'that woman' based on your one meeting. And Brad. He's the one getting married soon." Tom pushed back his hair. "His fiancée's mother is the one we're trying to fool. Seems it might not be too hard." His mouth turned up in a mischievous grin, and he took Beth's hand. "What do you think?"

"I think you may be presuming too much. I *do* like you, and you're right in thinking I enjoyed our kiss, but…"

"But?"

"But I don't think we should rush things," Beth said, trying to calm the butterflies in her stomach and hoping she was making sense. "Let's start with next weekend's barbecue and take it from there. Though you're right, pretending might not be so difficult now." Her lips turned up in a secret smile.

"It's a deal. We should seal it — just to make sure we're not mistaken."

This time the kiss came as no surprise. As their lips met, Beth closed her eyes and gave herself up fully to the experience. Tom's lips began with a slow exploration of hers, a nibbling on the edges, but soon her lips parted to allow his tongue to explore. His mouth became more demanding, and her whole body ached for him as she melted into his kiss. The world around them was forgotten as Beth strained towards him, her hands cupping his head as his moved to her breasts. It was with a shock that she heard the distant and insistent clamor of a telephone, and they disentangled themselves.

"Saved by the bell." Tom picked up his cell, checked it then turned it off. "Simone. I'll call her back later. She probably wants to know what I've been up to this weekend. Wanted me up there in Portland, but I pleaded non-specific local commitments. For next weekend too. Guess I'll have to go up the one after that. Now, where were we?"

Beth slid out of his reach. "I think I should go. If this is how you behave when we're not rushing things…"

"Sorry, it's been a while…"

"For me too."

*

The week passed slowly, but the day of the barbecue finally dawned, and with it, Beth's apprehension grew. What if Tom regretted his actions of the previous weekend? He'd been injured. What if his behavior all stemmed for a desire for comfort, and now he was sorry he'd started anything with her? Deep down she knew this was all garbage. Tom was a sincere man. He wouldn't say what he didn't mean, wouldn't lead her on. They were both adults, not a couple of teenagers playing at love. Her thoughts drew to a halt. Love? Was she talking about love? On the basis of two kisses? Well, if not love then what? Desire? Lust? Certainly more than the attraction she'd admitted to earlier.

Deciding it was pointless to pursue this line of thinking, she rose and showered. Her hair was fine, she decided. The growth of the past few months plus hairdresser Coralie's tender care had brought back Beth's natural curl, so it required little more than a quick blow dry. But choosing what to wear wasn't an easy task. Beth needed to strike exactly the right note. While wanting to look good for Tom, she also must fit the sort of image which would indicate to Louise that she was serious competition. This whole subterfuge, which had seemed like fun when it was being arranged, was now feeling distinctly deceitful. Beth was starting to feel sorry for the unknown Louise. What was wrong with her hoping to form a closer relationship with the father of her prospective son-in-law? They were both widowed. It seemed an eminently suitable arrangement. Maybe Beth should step aside and leave them to it?

But, a small voice prompted her – it's not what Tom wants. He doesn't want Louise – no matter how suitable she might be, and he clearly doesn't think she is. He wants you, Beth reminded herself. And you want him. She shrugged and turned her attention again to her wardrobe, finally settling on a pair of flared white pants teamed with a hot pink shirt. She checked herself in the mirror. It was an outfit in which she managed to look both elegant and feminine – one which she hoped would wow Tom while making the required statement to Louise that she wasn't to be trifled with.

Satisfied, she went downstairs to swallow a slice of toast with a cup of licorice tea, then donned an apron to put together the pavlova Tom had insisted she provide for lunch, despite her protestations that Jenny did a much better one.

By the time she'd placed it on the passenger seat of the car, Beth's earlier concerns had disappeared. She was looking forward to seeing Tom again, and Jenny and Ellen. She wondered if they'd guess that she and Tom weren't pretending. And maybe Tom was mistaken about Louise. She might be a perfectly nice woman, merely trying to do the best for her daughter. And they mustn't lose sight of the real purpose of the day, which was to plan a wedding – a wedding of two people Beth hadn't even met.

"Glad you arrived first," Tom greeted Beth. He was waiting in the driveway as her car drew up and immediately pulled her into a warm hug, giving her a long kiss. "You look great," he said, lifting Beth off her feet and twirling her around.

"'Pav as promised." Regaining both her feet and her breath, Beth brought the cake out of the car. "Shall I put it in the fridge?" As she entered towards the house, she heard another car pull up. She was standing in the kitchen looking out at the deck where the table was already set with seven places, when she heard footsteps behind her. "Wow. You haven't left much for me to do, honey," she said, turning round only when she heard a loud gasp behind her.

"Who are you?" The high-pitched voice came from a well-kept middle-aged lady whose outfit, while elegant, would be better suited to a twenty year-old. So this was Louise.

"Louise, this is Beth – a friend. Beth, Louise," Tom said.

"Hi Louise, lovely to meet you." Beth took a few steps forward, hand outstretched.

"But…" Louise looked around wildly, then at Tom. There was a pause while she seemed to collect herself and paste an insincere smile on her face. But not before Beth had seen a look of what she could only describe as disdain pass across it. "Lovely to meet you too. Tom didn't say there would be another guest." Louise's emphasis on the word 'guest' left Beth in no doubt of her intention. There would be no friendly overtures here. It was going to be a case of 'battle lines drawn and may the best man win'. Of course, Louise intended to be the winner.

Seemingly oblivious of the tension between the two women, Tom continued, "There will be a few others too. I've invited along two couples I know to add their advice. I'm not so good on the wedding front, so I thought we needed a few heads on this."

"Of course." Louise's tone was icy, but she smiled sweetly at Tom and laid a possessive hand on his arm. "How nice, but there was really no need. I'm sure we could have managed perfectly well by ourselves."

"Well," Tom said cheerfully. "Too late now, here they come." There was the sound of two vehicles stopping in the driveway and doors slamming. This was followed by a loud, "Anyone home?" and Jenny and Mike burst into the kitchen, closely followed by Ellen and Travis.

The arrival of the newcomers and the ensuing introductions broke the tension, and the group moved out to the deck, where Louise took a position as close to Tom as possible, edging Beth to the outside of the group. Beth smiled to herself and said nothing. First round to Louise.

"Beth, sweetie. Would you help me fetch drinks for these good people? It'll be white wine for you, Louise, and beer for the guys, What about you, Jenny and Ellen?"

Beth was watching Louise as Tom spoke. Her mouth retained a fixed smile, while her eyes told quite a different story, revealing the shock and dismay which Tom's words had created. A glance out of the corner of her eye indicated to Beth that Jenny and Ellen saw it too. Both were trying to hide their amusement, but covered it up cleverly as each replied to Tom they'd prefer wine.

The lunch progressed without further mishap. There was really very little discussion, as Louise knew exactly what she and Brooke wanted on the day. She insisted on a large marquee and even managed to persuade everyone to go down into the partly cut grass and step out the measurements.

At last, she appeared satisfied all of her suggestions had been favorably received, and everything would go according to plan – her plan – though she was clearly disappointed she'd been unable to have the *tête-a tête* with Tom she'd been hoping for. "Well, that's it," she said, preparing to leave. "I suppose I should add all of you to the guest list?" She looked at Tom for confirmation, eyebrows raised, the fixed smile still in place. Beth thought her mouth must be aching by now, so immobile had her expression been all through lunch.

"Well, Beth certainly," Tom said, throwing arm around Beth's shoulder and dropping a kiss on the top of her head. "It's time she met all the family." Beth was shaken at this public display of affection, but decided to play along by gazing up into Tom's eyes.

"Right. I'll bid you all good day. It's been lovely to meet you." Louise gathered up her purse and headed to her car, while the others watched from the doorway.

"You did well," Jenny said, as three women cleared up in the kitchen, the men choosing to enjoy a final beer on the deck.

"Too well," Ellen, the more perceptive of the two said. "What's going on? Are you and Tom…?"

Jenny whipped round from the sink where she'd been rinsing plates. "What did I miss? I thought we'd…?"

"The hug, the kiss, the secret looks. It wasn't all pretense, was it? Fess up. There's more to it."

"More to what?" Beth asked, but she could feel her face giving her away. "I don't know what you mean." She turned away to put the flatware into a drawer.

"Really?" Jenny asked. "Are you and Tom…? Oh, it would be such a good match."

"You're both way off the mark." Beth turned to face them, her back leaning against the cupboard for support. "We're… We've just…" She hesitated, unsure exactly how to describe her relationship with Tom. It was still in its fledgling stage, and she didn't want to make more of it than there actually was, but these two women weren't going to be easily appeased. "We've found some common ground," she said finally. "Nothing more."

"So?" Jenny asked.

"I predicted this," Ellen said.

"We're planning on getting to know each other better. That's all."

Beth was saved from any further explanation by the men's return, and in the general melee of their departure, nothing more was said.

Left alone, Beth and Tom looked at each other. "That went well," he said. "We seemed to carry it off. Think Louise got the message."

"Loud and clear. But we may have done too well. Jenny and Ellen had a few questions and weren't easily satisfied. And what did you mean about my attending the wedding?"

Tom had the grace to look sheepish. "Well, it would have looked odd if I hadn't said you should be there. After all the hints we gave that we were a couple, I realized I can't turn up at the wedding on my own. Wouldn't do. Would leave it wide open for her. And by then, who knows?"

Beth winced. It was one thing to pretend to be Tom's partner for Louise's benefit, or for the two of them to form a tentative relationship – for that was all it was at this stage. It might never go any further. But to attend his son's wedding, to meet Brad and Simone as their father's new partner or significant other as they said these days. That was a different matter entirely.

*

Although enjoying her new-found companionship with Tom, Beth hadn't lost sight of her other concerns, the chief of which was the length of time being taken by the legal guys in Sydney to wind up Bryan's estate. Tom had suggested asking another Oregon lawyer called George – the one who'd originally dealt with the de Ruis estate – to try to winkle out more information seeing as he was in Australia. But since he hadn't held out much hope, Beth had refused. It would take whatever time it took and she would have to grin and bear it.

In the meantime, there was still the puzzle of the photo of Rick Turner to investigate. Beth had made a visit to Florence Library, been impressed by the beautiful layout, the silence, and the comprehensiveness of the collection. She'd spent almost an entire day there but without much success. She had managed to identify the two others in the group photo as a Jack Prentice and Alan Fenton, but hadn't been able to find them in the local phone book. That could mean they'd left town, were no longer alive, or were living in a nursing home somewhere. She was stuck and couldn't work out any way forward.

She'd also checked out more copies of the local paper which was called *The Siuslaw Oar* back then, and discovered a letter to the paper from a local whose son was extolling the delights of the hospitality to be found in Sydney for US soldiers on leave there. That didn't add anything to what she already knew. Maybe there was nothing to discover, but finding the Wagga address had piqued her curiosity. She couldn't leave it at that. There must be some way of finding out where it had come from – why it had been in the book.

Beth was having coffee by the river with Ellen and Jenny one Sunday morning, feeling completely at ease with the world, her cares far from her thoughts, when Jenny asked, "Did you ever get any further with your investigation of that old photo? I was making a photo book to celebrate Maddy's life the other night and remembered it."

"No, a couple of names is as far as I got. I have no way of tracing them. Would your mum have any idea, Ellen?"

"Maybe. I can ask her. She didn't recognize them from the photo, but it may be easier if we can give her names. Though these days her memory's not what it was either." She sighed and pulled on the end of her plait, a sign Beth had come to recognize as meaning she was worried.

"But I wonder..." Ellen tapped the table with her index finger. "Jenny..."

"Are you thinking the same as I am?"

"Anne and Bill Huggins. They'd be younger of course, but they've helped us before. Maybe..."

Beth looked from one to the other in surprise. "Who are they?"

"They were friends of my birth mother and father – who was Ellen's uncle. It's a long story. But the point is they've helped us out with some old history on a couple of occasions. They have good memories, and they'd be familiar with some of the old guys here in town. They may at least be able to tell us if they're still alive."

"I didn't find any death notices for them, but I couldn't check out every issue."

*

The phone rang just as Beth was cutting up some tomatoes for a salad. Tom was coming to dinner for the first time. They'd been seeing each other regularly, but so far she hadn't prepared a meal for him. She didn't know why, but was a little nervous about the evening ahead. Was entertaining Tom in her home taking their relationship to the next step? Would he like her cooking? By all accounts Janet, his wife, had been a very accomplished cook, while Beth knew she was pretty average. Bryan had liked plain food, so that's all she'd done for years. Tonight there was a roast in the oven. She planned to serve it with little potatoes and salad. Surely not much could go wrong there?

This was all going through Beth's mind as she picked up the phone, so it took her a second to recognize Ellen's voice. Her heart leapt. Did Ellen have news? Had her mother recognized one of the names? But she was disappointed.

"Sorry," Ellen said. "No luck. Mom did remember an Alan and Jack, but she thought one had been killed in the war, and the other had moved away. She wasn't sure which was which."

"Oh," Beth could hear the drop in her voice. "Then maybe... those people you mentioned..."

"Drew a blank there too, I'm afraid. They're out of town for a few weeks. We can try when they get back, but..."

Beth heard the doubt in Ellen's voice. She could tell she wasn't hopeful. "Well, thanks anyway. It's good of you to try."

"Anytime. I'm sorry."

Beth hung up and returned to her salad, her disappointment leading her to chop the tomatoes with more force than was necessary. By the time Tom arrived, she had recovered from her disappointment and was able to greet him cheerfully.

"Can you help yourself to a beer?" she asked. "And white wine for me, please. Right hand side of the fridge."

"Sure thing." Tom headed towards the fridge, then stopped in front of it. He appeared to be reading something on the door. "How do you know these guys?" he asked.

"Who?" Beth turned from the oven where she'd been checking the roast and peered at the door which she'd covered in a variety of notes held in place by magnets. They ranged from tradesmen's cards to odd notes and shopping lists.

"Jack Prentice and Alan Fenton."

"Oh those. They're the names of the men I found in the photo I mentioned – the guys with Rick Turner and Ellen's dad. I'd hoped I could locate them, but Ellen's just been on the phone and…"

"I had old Jack Prentice in my office not long ago."

"You what?" Beth almost dropped the fork she was using to prod the roast. Why had she never thought of mentioning the names to Tom? As a local lawyer he came into contact with lots of people every day. She'd been searching everywhere she could think of, and he was right there. "Ellen's mum thought he was dead or had left town."

"He came in with his daughter, Cathy Hinchcliff. I believe he did move away, but he's living with her now. He wanted to set up a living will. A lot of the old guys are doing that these days. Don't want to live on as vegetables."

But Beth heard no more after the daughter's name. So that's why she couldn't find him listed in the phone book. It was so simple and hadn't occurred to her, though even if it had, it wouldn't have helped.

"And is he…?" she asked, unable to believe her ears.

"He has all his faculties if that's what you mean. Quite a character, in fact. Would you like me to arrange for you to meet him?"

"You could do that?" But of course he could. Tom was well-known and respected and would be able to set up a meeting without any fuss.

"When would you like?"

"Wow. I don't know. Would next week be too soon?"

"Not at all. Maybe I can be more successful in helping you with this."

"Still no word from Sydney?" Beth's excitement at finding Jack Prentice was dimmed. "Why is it taking so long?"

Tom took the beer and wine out and poured a glass for Beth before replying. He rocked back on his heels. "There's no hurrying these matters. I know how difficult it must be for you. Even if the news is bad, it's better to know than to be imagining the worst."

"Sure. But I just wish…" Beth prodded the roast again to test it was cooked.

"Are you going to stab that to death or are we going to eat it? It smells wonderful. What can I do?"

"All done." Beth laid the fork down, "But maybe you can carve. It's something I've never mastered." Something Bryan had never allowed her to do, Beth realized. Just one more part of her old life still impacting on her.

"Happy to." Tom put his beer down and picked up the carving knife and fork. "Seems you've set yourself up real well here."

"It is nice, isn't it? If you've been here before, you probably remember some of the furniture from the previous owner. I managed to buy the pieces with the house and have added a few of my own touches." She looked around with pride. She loved her new home and had made it exactly to suit her own taste – a basic décor with few ornaments, only one piece of art made from driftwood graced the unused fireplace.

"Isn't that…?" Tom nodded towards the piece of wood, bleached by the sea and carved into the shape of a bird.

"It's by a local artist. I bought it when I was at the hairdressers. She has quite a collection on display there. I'm not sure what the bird is, but I fell in love with it on sight."

"It would be one of Ron Williams' pieces, and if I'm not mistaken, it's a green heron."

"Really? Williams. Is he any relation to…?"

"Ellen's brother and your hairdresser's husband."

"Right. Someone did say… Florence is such a small town."

"Coralie's been a real good influence on Ron. He's been carving these things for years, and it took her encouragement for him to make a business out of it. He now sells them all over and is gaining quite a reputation."

"And you say it's a green heron?" Beth went to pick up the carving and examined it more carefully. "Now you've told me, I can see it. I'm afraid I'm not as good at identifying the local birdlife as you are. I'll value it even more highly now. It'll remind me…" She blushed. Although Green Heron was the name of her place of employment, the bird itself would always be associated in her memory with the birds she had seen at Tom's place on the lake. She replaced it carefully.

"Okay. Finished here. Where would you like it?"

"I thought we could eat on the patio. I've already set up out there. If you put the slices on the platter over here, I'll bring out the potatoes and salad."

While they ate, Beth and Tom grew closer, sharing and laughing together. When they had finished eating Tom suggested they take their drinks to a stone garden bench set under a shady maple tree. Once there his arm snaked around Beth's shoulders and she snuggled closer to him, reflecting how quickly she'd come to regard this big man as her rock. They sat entwined until the air was becoming cool. Beth stirred and drew apart.

"Going somewhere?"

"Inside. It's getting a bit cool out here."

"I can keep you warm." And with that, Tom wrapped his arms more tightly around Beth, pulling her towards him, his lips finding hers with renewed urgency, one hand cupping her breast, while the other reached down to pull her hips closer.

"Your hand." Beth murmured. Tom muttered something from which Beth inferred his injured hand was far from the forefront his mind.

Beth could feel her breath quicken, as her body responded to Tom's touch. This was the most intimate they'd been. She'd known subconsciously that inviting Tom here, to her home, was tantamount to letting him know she was ready, but until this moment, she'd imagined she could always hold back. She knew Tom was a gentleman. He'd never force himself on her, not like… But it was *her* that wanted *him*, wanted Tom's naked body next to hers, wanted him inside her. Beth struggled to get closer, but their clothes were getting in the way.

"We're too old for this," Tom said, his voice hoarse with desire. "Where's your bedroom?"

Beth couldn't find her voice, so pointed towards the house. She was about to rise, when she found herself picked up in a pair of strong arms. She wrapped hers around Tom's neck and allowed herself to be carried inside.

Once in the bedroom, Tom dropped Beth gently on the bed, lay down beside her and began to unfasten her blouse. His lips caressed each morsel of skin as it was uncovered, until they found her nipples, and he took one, then the other in his mouth, rolling his tongue gently over them, making Beth writhe in anticipation. It felt so right, to be here, in her bed, with this man. This man who had come into her life so unexpectedly.

"More," she murmured. "I want…" She lifted her hips to help Tom slip off her pants and felt the cool air on her body as he stepped away for a moment to remove his own garments. He was soon back, his hands caressing her, rubbing his strong body against hers. Beth felt him harden against her, and she squirmed even closer. She wanted all of him. She felt the area between her legs become moist, ready for him, then he was pushing into her, gently at first, before building up a wonderful rhythm and thrusting into her till she cried out in ecstasy. As Tom withdrew, he stroked Beth's body and rained kisses on her closed eyelids. Beth opened her eyes, gazed up at Tom's face, so close to hers, and smiled lazily. She drew a finger down his cheek, stroked his bushy eyebrows, and sighed with pleasure.

The pair rolled onto their backs and lay silently, legs entwined. "You may have noticed my hand's just fine," Tom chuckled. He laced the fingers of his right hand with Beth's and held the other up in the air. "It's healing."

"You did go to the doctor, didn't you?"

"Yes, and I was correct. No stitches required, and he complimented you on your care."

"Mmm."

"Do you…," Tom began, but Beth had fallen asleep.

Twenty-three

"Simone, we need to talk. I've been…I've been seeing someone."

"Seeing someone? Oh, Dad, that's so seventies." Then his words appeared to sink in. "A woman? Not the ghastly Louise?"

"No," Tom chuckled, though Simone's assessment of Brad's future mother-in-law didn't bode well for future family relations. "But you *have* met her."

There was silence on the other end of the phone, and Tom imagined Simone mentally reviewing all the female acquaintances she knew. He decided to put his daughter out of her misery. "Remember the day you turned up with the boys? When you took time out from Ed?"

"Not that little gray sparrow of a woman? How could you? After Mom, how could you even…?"

Tom gritted his teeth. Damn Simone with her pre-conceived ideas. "Her name's Beth, Beth Carson, and I'd like you to meet her properly."

"Da…ad." Tom could hear the disapproval in her voice. He wasn't handling this well. He dragged a hand through his hair, wincing a little. Despite what he'd told Beth, his hand was still hurting and the doc had said it would take some time to heal. Simone's whining voice aggravated the irritation he was feeling.

"Damn it, Simmy. I do have my own life to lead, and I expect you and Brad to be supportive of my choices. Will you agree to meet Beth or not? I thought we could drive up to Portland on Saturday," he continued without waiting for an answer.

Suddenly Simone seemed to capitulate. "Sounds serious, Dad. Well, if you really want me to meet this… this Beth woman, I suppose… But Saturday. Let me check my calendar."

Tom waited patiently, hearing buttons being pressed at the other end of the phone. Gone were the days of the calendar stuck up on the kitchen wall, as he and Janet used to do. It had been easy to check timetables at a glance. Now people had everything on their cells. He shook his head in wonderment. Call him old-fashioned, but he still liked his desk calendar, and yes, there was a wall calendar hanging in the kitchen, received each Christmas from a fishing association he belonged to, though it was sadly empty of events these days.

"Okay, Dad. Saturday, you said?"

"Yep."

"That could work." She hesitated. "You never did check out the school with me," she said petulantly.

Tom sighed. He'd forgotten her request. So much had happened in his life since then. "Could we fit that in too? Beth will be with me, but maybe…"

"I don't suppose she'd be interested."

"She would." Tom mentally crossed his fingers and vowed to fill Beth in. He had no idea whether she'd be interested in his grandson's future education or not, but he'd give it a shot.

"The school will be closed, but we can drive by, and I can show you the website. Tommy's becoming excited about going to school. And did Brad tell you? He wants the boys to be ring bearers at the wedding. I'm to chat with Brooke about their outfits. I hope she doesn't want anything too outlandish." Simone chatted on, with Tom listening to only a fraction of what she had to say. Reminded again about the wedding, he realized he'd promised to arrange the marquee and hadn't done anything about finishing the grass. He flexed his injured hand, wondering if he could risk another attempt with the mower.

"So, Saturday," he heard Simone say. When should we expect you?"

"Umm…"Tom remembered he had still to raise the trip with Beth. He'd thought it better to get Simone onside first. "How about we arrive for lunch? Don't…" But there was no point in telling Simmy not to go to any trouble. He knew his daughter. She'd pull out all the stops to show Beth… what? Well, to show her something, the way women did. Look at the trouble she'd gone to for the lunch with Brooke.

Tom hung up, only to dial again. He smiled as he heard Beth's breathless, "Hi Tom," followed by silence.

"Hi yourself. I hope you weren't too tired today?" He chuckled hearing the smile in Beth's voice as she replied, "Tired – no, but maybe a little sore. My body isn't used to…"

"Sorry, I…"

"No. I'm not complaining."

"Then you may be up for a repeat performance soon? But I really wanted to suggest lunch – if you can get away. There's something I want to run by you, and I'd rather do it face-to-face."

"Should be okay. I'll check with Jo, but we're not too busy today. Where and when?"

"I was thinking we might grab a sandwich and find a spot on the boardwalk- unless you'd rather…"

"That would be good. Save time too."

After making arrangements to meet there at one o'clock, Tom hung up again. He wasn't sure how Beth would react to the proposal to meet Simone. Would she think it was too soon? Was he acting precipitously? They'd only made love for the first time last night, but it wasn't something Tom had done lightly. He hoped Beth understood that. There hadn't been anyone since Janet. He never thought there would be. He looked at Janet's photo and knew she'd understand, approve even. In fact, it almost looked as if she was smiling her approval at him right now. "I think she's the one, Janet. You'd like her. You'd be good friends. You…" Then he realized how stupid he sounded. Not only was he having a conversation with the photo of his dead wife – something he often did – but he was imagining her meeting and becoming friends with the new woman in his life.

By the time he joined Beth at the appointed time and place, carrying a brown bag lunch with a couple of cans of Diet Coke, he had worked out what to say. They greeted each other rather self-consciously with a quick hug and pecks on the cheek. Delving into the package he'd brought, Tom extracted two Reuben sandwiches and they sat eating companionably till Beth said, "You wanted to ask me something?"

"I did." Tom swallowed the last of his lunch and folded the paper bag carefully before continuing, "Can you get free Saturday?" he blurted out, his carefully prepared speech forgotten.

Beth appeared startled, and started to laugh. "Day or evening? We have an estate sale in the day at Yvonne Walker's aunt's place. I'm not sure she wants me anywhere near it. She certainly wouldn't if she learned about last night." Beth gave Tom a secret smile, and he took her hand and squeezed it. "I don't know if I told you she warned me off, told me you were spoken for."

Tom threw back his head and roared with laughter. "That's a good one. Well, I am now."

"Really? I mean…"

"Last night… It's not something I normally do. I want you to know that. It… it meant something to me… meant a lot. I hope…"

"Me too," Beth's hand tightened in his and Tom had the urge to pick her up and kiss her right there. "But back to Saturday…"

"I was thinking about daytime. I have to go up to Portland – Simone wants to fill me in on Tommy's school. She's been at me for weeks to go. I wondered if you'd come with me. You haven't been there yet, have you? And you could meet Simmy and Ed and the two young ones."

"I believe we did meet," Beth said dryly. "But she may have forgotten. I left pretty fast."

"No, she hasn't forgotten." Tom released Beth's hand to hang both of his between his knees. "She remembers it well. Simone's not one for forgetting. But I've told her…"

Beth's eyes grew wider. "You've told her what?"

"That we're … an item. Isn't that the current term?"

"Is that what we are?" Beth sounded amused.

"Well, I could hardly tell my daughter we were lovers. She probably thinks the old man is past all of that."

"I wouldn't say so." Beth was still smiling, and a slight blush was beginning to rise up her neck.

"So, back to Saturday. You're working? Any chance Jo can manage without you? I'd really like you to come. In fact, I've told Simone we'll be there for lunch."

"I'm not sure," Beth's lips pursed as if she was weighing things up. "I'll have to check with Jo. I do usually work on Saturdays, but maybe… Look, I'll see. Jo may be able to get someone else to help. She does have a few casual staff. Can I let you know?"

"Sure." Tom was beginning to wonder if he'd spoken with Simone too soon. What would she think if he turned up without Beth on Saturday? No, it would be all right. He was sure about that. Jo would see him right. Although nothing had been said, he had a strong feeling that she, along with Ellen and Jenny had been hoping he and Beth would make a match of it. If he was right, then Jo would do everything she could to move their relationship along.

Seeing Beth was rising and about to leave, Tom put a restraining hand on her arm. "Before you go…"

Beth smiled, and resumed her seat.

"That other business, Jack Prentice."

"You contacted him?" Beth beamed.

"I did." It gave Tom a good feeling to be able to find something to please her. "I didn't say much, only that I had a lady who wanted to talk with him about the past."

"What did he say?"

"He was thrilled. I don't think he has much opportunity to chat about the old days. His daughter seems to keep him on a pretty tight rein." He grimaced, imagining his own position if he ever fell into Simone's clutches in his old age.

"So?" Beth leaned forward eagerly, her lips slightly parted.

The temptation to kiss them was pretty strong, but Tom managed to ignore it and instead said, "He's agreed we can drop in on him on Wednesday around twelve. His daughter works that day, so won't get in the way – his words, not mine. You could do that in your lunchtime, couldn't you?" Tom coughed.

"Wow, thanks. Wednesday is usually my day off, so that would work well."

"Jack lives in the newer part of town. Can I pick you up?"

"I'll let you know where I'll be – and about Saturday too."

They both rose, and Tom pulled Beth to him, her head barely reaching to his shoulders. He hugged her and dropped a kiss on top of her head, enjoying the soft feel of her hair against his lips. "Till Wednesday."

"Wednesday," Beth repeated before walking away.

Tom gazed after her, wondering how she had become such an important part of his life in such a short time. How he, who had successfully avoided all female entanglements for so long, was now hopelessly involved with this woman.

*

"This is it." Tom parked outside a large timber-framed home with not only a double garage, but a double height one which presumably held the family RV – what Beth would call a motorhome back in Australia.

Beth stepped out and took a minute to examine the neighborhood. "Very flash," she said. "Looks like they have quite a bit of land; and is that…?" she pointed behind the house.

"Yup. It's billed as the golf course estate – quarter acre blocks with golf course access. Are you ready to meet Jack?"

Beth nodded and followed Tom to the front door, which opened before he had time to knock or press the bell.

"Was looking out for you." The man who stood at the door looked all of his ninety-something years. A weathered and wrinkled visage peered at them through rimless spectacles. He was bent over and appeared to have difficulty walking, but the eyes which met Beth's were lively and alert. "So this is the little lady who wants to hear about the old days. Come along in."

Jack led the way into a state-of-the-art kitchen and bade them sit down. "I'm afraid I can't offer you much. Cathy keeps me on short rations. My place is out back." He pointed to the back of the house. "Good view of the golf course, not that I ever played the danged game. But I can offer you a glass of water."

"That would be lovely," Beth said, already having taken a liking to this old man.

"Now how can I help? These days the old times are clearer to me than last week, so it'll be a pleasure to recall them in the presence of such a lovely young lady. Your young woman, is she, Tom?"

Tom nodded, while Beth blushed. Knowing they may not have a lot of time, she drew the old photo from her purse. "I found this photo, and I think you're one of the young men there." She laid it on the table.

Jack picked it up, holding it close to his eyes, before lowering it again. "Oh my. Never thought to see that one again. Cathy got rid of what she called all my old rubbish when I moved up here. No place in this show home for an old man's memories. Still, she's a good girl. Didn't have to take me in. Not every daughter would."

Beth fidgeted, wondering if Jack was going to get to the point.

Then he placed his index finger on one of the men. "That's me – cut a fine figure in those days, if I say it myself – and Rick Turner and Alan Fenton, they both bought it in the war." He shook his head. "Good men. No reason why I came back and they didn't." His finger traced the faces of the two men, then stopped on the third one. "Dick Williams. I think he's still with us, too. Lost touch over the years, after I moved down to California with the second wife. She and Cathy didn't get on, but once I was on my own again…"

Beth was itching for him to say more about the men in the photo, but knew she'd have to allow him to proceed at his own pace.

"Remember that day as if it was yesterday. It was taken over at the beach at Seal Rock. Alan had a fancy for a girl from up there, and we all hopped in his old jalopy and took to the road." He smiled and gazed off into space as if remembering his youth, a time when life was much simpler and he didn't have to bow to the demands of his daughter in return for a roof over his head.

"You were in the army with Rick Turner?" Beth asked, barely daring to breathe.

"Sure was – ninety-sixth Infantry Division. We shipped out to the Pacific together via Hawaii after training right here in Oregon. That was a time." He rubbed his hands together. "You never saw anything like it. Would have been forty-four as I recollect."

Beth leaned forward, unwilling to interrupt the flow, but anxious to get to the point. "And I understand you guys had R and R in Australia."

"We sure did. Real hospitable folks they were too. Opened up their homes to us."

"Beth's from Australia," Tom said quietly.

"Is that right? I thought I recognized something in the way you spoke. Australia, well fancy. And what brings you to Florence?"

"A few things, but one of them is this." She drew out the photo of Rick Turner. "My mum had this – must have kept it for years – and I'm curious to find out the connection. Were you both in Australia together?"

"All three of us: Alan, Rick, myself. These Australian women – treated us like gods. Of course Rick was spoken for. He'd met his Maddy and put a ring on her finger before we shipped out. The faithful type was Rick, not like some of the blokes." He chuckled, making Beth wonder if he had been one of those.

"I don't suppose you'd know how my mother got Rick's photo?" Beth held her breath waiting for his response, clutching Tom's hand under the table.

"Wa…all, let me see." Jack looked off into the distance again. "Seems we were all allocated to families for dinners and the like. Some home comforts and a bit of sightseeing. Rick, now… Yeah, I think he became pretty friendly with his folk, even ended up washing up for them." He chuckled again. "He was that sort of guy – missed home a lot."

"And that was in Sydney?"

"Sydney, Australia."

"But Mum didn't live in Sydney. She lived in the country, a place called Wagga Wagga."

"Now that rings a bell. It's an odd name for a place. Don't usually double up like that. But…" He scratched his head. "Now what was it? Give me a minute." He closed his eyes and sat perfectly still for so long that Beth thought he'd dozed off. Catching Tom's eye, she nodded her head in the direction of the door, wondering if they should leave. Tom shook his head and squeezed Beth's hand.

"I recall it now." Jack opened his eyes. "There was some arrangement with a school. They were studying the geography of the US, examining how we were going to win the war for them, no doubt. One of those ladies who was organizing us into host families – that's what they called them – was asking for volunteers to write to these schoolkids. Most of the guys weren't keen. We were more interested in gals our own age, not kids who were like our young brothers and sisters back home. But Rick might have gotten involved. It was the sort of thing he would do. Didn't have any young of his own, and was missing Maddy. Yeah, guess that's where I heard of that place with the weird name."

Beth leaned back in her chair and released Tom's hand. Could it be that simple? The dates worked. It hadn't occurred to her before, but her mother would still have been a schoolgirl in 1944. This could be the explanation she was looking for.

"But the postcards," she said. "There were postcards of Florence. How could he have sent them to her?"

"Bless you, Beth, isn't it? We all carried these with us. It was a way of reminding us of home and showing the folks over there what our country was like. Reckon Rick had them in his pack and sent them to your mom if he was corresponding with her."

"Oh." Beth felt deflated. She had built this Florence connection with her mum into a mystery when there really wasn't one. Just a lonely American soldier a long way from home, and a wartime school project in an Australian country town.

"Thanks, Jack. Really appreciate your help," Tom said, while Beth was still trying to come to grips with what was for her a disappointment. She wasn't sure what she'd expected, but not this.

"Thanks, Jack. I appreciate your time." Beth shook the old man's hand as they left.

"My pleasure. It's not often I get a chance to talk about the old days. There aren't many of us left, and the younger generation don't care. It's been a delight to be reminded of those carefree times – to meet someone who's interested. Any time you want another yarn – Tom here knows how to contact me."

"It's sad," Beth said, as they drove off. "He's not living alone, but he's lonely. He has such a wealth of knowledge, of history. You'd think his family would be interested."

"I see a lot of it. Old-timers who've come to live with their children, shunted into a small unwanted space and expected to stay out of the way. Often kept on minimum pocket money too." Tom sighed. "Not much we can do. They've made their choice, but sometimes there isn't much choice involved. Despite what it looks like, Jack's probably one of the lucky ones."

Beth reflected on the last years of her mother's life. Bryan would never have countenanced her living with them, so she'd been forced into a nursing home. Had she been happy there? Beth had always assumed so. Bryan hadn't stinted on that. It had been the best money could buy, but had it bought Audrey's happiness? Would she have been happier living with Beth and Bryan? To that, Beth could definitely answer 'No'. Audrey may have been aware of Bryan's treatment of her daughter, but to see it firsthand would have broken her heart. No, it had been the best solution, and there was nothing to indicate she'd been unhappy there.

"Do you think he's happy?"

"Depends on how you define happy. He has a roof over his head, meals provided and probably a bit of spending money. He has his health and is with family."

"Put like that…"

"Makes you feel better?"

"Yes. I was just thinking of my mother."

"She passed, didn't she?" Tom's voice was gentle.

"That's what started all this. If it hadn't been for…." She drew a ragged breath. "Well, I wouldn't be here."

"So I have a lot to thank your mother for?"

Beth smiled and placed a hand on Tom's thigh, which he immediately covered with one of his.

"See you Saturday?" Beth turned towards Tom before hopping out of the car.

"Saturday's a long way away. What say I drop round tonight with a couple of steaks and a bottle of wine? Can you fix some salad?"

Beth's heart gave a skip. She still couldn't believe how quickly she and Tom had become… become what? He was waiting for a reply.

"I'd love that. Around six?"

"See you then. Must dash. I have a full diary this afternoon, and Gwen will be after me if I'm late."

*

Tom was humming to himself as he entered his workplace, but the sight of his first client soon sobered him. Waiting for him, legs crossed to reveal more than he cared to see, her neckline exposing an expanse of bare flesh even on this cool day, was Yvonne Walker.

"Give me a few minutes," he muttered as he hurriedly entered his office and closed the door behind him.

"Guess you might need this, if you missed out on lunch." Gwen sniffed as she placed a coffee and a wrapped sandwich on the desk. "Madame's early, so no need to rush. Let her wait. Did you have a pleasant visit?" Gwen's innate good manners prevented her from asking more, but Tom knew she was bursting with curiosity.

"Visiting old Jack Prentice," he said, avoiding any mention of Beth. Gwen would find out soon enough. "Thanks, Gwen. How long have I got?"

Gwen checked her watch, a silver affair which she had been wearing as long as Tom could remember. "Mrs. Walker's appointment isn't for another fifteen minutes," she said.

Tom took a gulp of coffee and began to unwrap the sandwich. "Give me ten."

"Now, Mrs. Walker, what can I help you with today? Sorry if I kept you waiting."

"It's Yvonne, remember. And you're worth waiting for, Tom."

"Ahem." Tom cleared his throat. He wasn't in the mood for Yvonne's antics today, not with his mind full of Beth, who with her gentle ways and modest demeanor, was the antithesis of the woman sitting in front of him. He picked up his pen to indicate his readiness to make notes. "I thought we'd resolved your issues last time." He furrowed his brow in an attempt to indicate his frustration and puzzlement at her return.

"It's my aunt's estate," she began. "You know she passed recently and left me her home – the one on the lake?"

"I'd heard, but I wasn't her lawyer. I believe she dealt with Pete Markham."

"Yes, yes, I know that. But that's not why I'm here. It's about the estate sale. I've made arrangements with Green Heron Estate Sales. The sale's to be held on Saturday, and now, I'm not sure…" She smiled at Tom in a way that made him cringe. He had the feeling he wasn't going to like what she had to say next.

"They're a good firm," he said. "I've referred a lot of my clients there. Jo runs a tight ship."

"Jo's not the problem." Yvonne's voice took on a bitter tone, and her eyes narrowed. "It's that new woman she has working for her. She came out to do the inventory, and I don't trust her."

Tom supressed a grin and covered his amusement by scribbling on his pad. "That's a pretty strong statement. Why do you distrust her?"

Yvonne leant forward, her neckline gaping so much Tom had to avert his eyes. "There are things missing – a photo and a box of news clippings. I know it was her because she asked me about the photo." Yvonne sat back and stroked her skirt, as if satisfied.

"So why have you come to me about this? Have you spoken to Jo? Were they valuable items?" Tom knew exactly why she had come to him. He remembered Beth mentioning Yvonne had tried to warn her off. Now she was trying the same tactics on him with a twist, and quite a twist. "I think that's probably the best thing to do. Let Jo take care of it. She'd hate to think anything valuable had gone missing from one of her estates."

"Well," Yvonne seemed about to backtrack. "They weren't valuable exactly, not in monetary terms. I didn't want to bother Jo." Yvonne gazed at Tom, eyes wide. "I thought maybe you could…" Her voice tailed away. "It's the sale on Saturday. I don't want…"

"Why don't you just tell Jo you don't want Beth there, if that's what you're trying to say?"

"If that's what you advise, though…"

"As your lawyer that's my advice." Smiling inwardly, Tom laid down his pen and rose. "Now if that's all?"

To his relief, Yvonne took the hint and rose to leave too. "Thanks, Tom I wouldn't like anyone else to be taken in by her – the Australian woman, I mean. She seems to have appeared out of nowhere. Maybe you need to check up on her," she said as she sashayed out.

Twenty-four

"So," Beth said, "Did Simone really initiate this trip, or is it an excuse to introduce me to the family?" They were on their way to Portland, and something Tom had said on Wednesday at dinner stuck in her mind. The subject had changed before she'd time to process it properly, then they had been otherwise occupied, and there had been no opportunity to question him.

"*Mea culpa*. Am I so obvious?" Beth saw Tom throw a quick glance in her direction. "It wasn't all fiction. Simmy did ask me up to check out the school, but I suggested her meeting you and set up today to introduce you. You'll like her, and Ed's a great guy."

"But will she like me? Is she ready for another woman in your life? I guess she was pretty attached to her mum and must still miss her a lot. Will she be prepared to resent me? Not that I imagine I can take…" Beth suddenly realized Tom might misinterpret her concern, think she imagined more between them than there was. "I mean," she added hurriedly, "have you… what have you told her about me?"

"I told her I was seeing someone."

"Oh dear! That sounds so…"

"So seventies is what Simmy said."

The pair laughed, and no more was said about Simone or their relationship for the remainder of the trip.

Although they'd left Florence at nine they'd stopped for coffee and what seemed to Beth to be an enormous cinnamon roll on the way, so it was close to one o'clock when they finally pulled into the driveway of a tidy white ranch-style home on the southern outskirts of Portland.

"Here we are," said Tom. The front door opened, and two small bullets with blonde hair rushed out to throw themselves on him as he stepped out of the car. Smiling, Beth slipped out of the passenger seat prepared to greet the boys, who when they caught sight of her, tried to hide behind their grandfather. Tom grasped their hands, "This is Beth. Say hello properly. Beth," he drew forward the taller one, "this handsome fellow is my namesake, Tommy, and this scallywag," he pulled forward the other, "is Sam."

Beth bent down till she was almost level with them and stretched out her hands. "Hello Tommy and Sam. I'm a friend of your grandfather, and I hope I'll be your friend too." The pair stood looking at her shyly and keeping a firm hold of Tom. She straightened up still smiling. She hadn't had much to do with children this age, but these two were cute and looked a lot like Tom with their sturdy bodies and thick blonde hair. Suddenly she became aware of another presence and, looking up, saw the woman she'd last seen in Tom's kitchen.

"Simmy, this is Beth. Beth, my daughter, Simone." Tom was still ensnared by the two little boys so could do little else.

"We've met," Simone said, standing with her arms folded to preclude any handshaking or hugging should Beth try either. Well, that answered Beth's question. She was going to have her work cut out here. But while she was trying to work out what to say, little Tommy found his courage, let go of Tom's hand and ran over to take Beth's. Looking trustingly up into her face he asked, "Are you Grandpa Tom's honey?" This broke the ice and brought a smile to the face of all three adults. Even Simone couldn't maintain her distant mood in the face of such an ingenious remark.

"She sure is, Tommy," Tom replied for her, swinging Sam up into his arms. "Let's get inside and see what your mom has for our lunch."

Simone led the way into a kitchen, which although rivaling the one at Jack's place, had a homelier feel about it, with children's drawings having pride of place on the large fridge/freezer and several toys scattered around. The white walls set off the wooden cupboards, and through the window, Beth caught glimpses of an extensive lawn with the requisite play area for the boys complete with swings and a high cubby house.

"Would you like to freshen up?" Simone asked politely. "The bathroom is to your right." She pointed along a hallway, and Beth followed her directions, relieved to escape, albeit for a brief period. On her way back, Beth took the opportunity to take in the layout of the house, impressed by the high ceilings, open-plan rooms and large windows which filled the house with light. Beth's home in Sydney had been around the same size, but it had been a shell, devoid of anything resembling warmth. This house was lived in, loved. It was a home.

"You have a lovely place here," Beth said, returning to the kitchen where Tom handed her a glass of wine. She accepted it gratefully, glad to have something to do with her hands. "It seems pretty big."

"We have five bedrooms. Lots of room for Dad, as I keep telling him. I don't know why he wants to stay in the old house, when he could…"

"We've been over that, Simmy," Tom said, the warning tone in his voice telling Beth this was a well-worn argument.

By this time, they were seated at the kitchen table, which held a couple of iPads, several books, and a bundle of newspapers hastily pushed aside. Evidently they weren't eating there. The same thought had clearly passed through Tom's mind. "Formal lunch today, Simmy?" he asked.

Simone bridled. "We always use the dining room for guests, Dad. You know that. Just as Mom did." She threw a look at Beth as if to say 'beat that!'. "It's almost ready. Go fetch Daddy from the den, Tommy," she instructed the older child who ran off, his brother at his heels. "I don't know how Sam's going to cope when Tommy starts school," she said, gazing after the two. "He's his brother's shadow. Do you have any children?" she asked Beth as if remembering she was there.

"No. I was never blessed."

"Blessed? Well, I don't know I'd put it like that, but they're good kids." She smiled fondly, seemingly pleased by Beth's reply.

At that the two children returned, followed by a large brown-haired man wearing spectacles and a friendly grin. "Hi! You must be Beth. Welcome. I'm Ed as you probably guessed. Good to meet a friend of Tom's. You must be pretty special to brave this circus. We're dining in style today I see."

Simone glared at her husband and hustled everyone through to a large dining room overlooking the yard. The table was formally set with what appeared to Beth to be a good set of china and the appropriate flatware. Two bowls of salad stood in the centre of the table flanked by a platter of bread, and a heated trolley holding what appeared to be a roast stood to one side. Simone might be prepared to resent Beth's friendship with Tom, but she had clearly set out to impress.

"Wow, this looks delicious," Beth said, taking her seat. "You've gone to a lot of trouble."

"Pushed the boat out today, honey. I should bring Beth along with me more often."

Lunch passed without incident, the presence of the two children facilitating the conversation, and by the end of the meal, Simone appeared to have mellowed. "So you've met Brooke and her mom?" she asked as Beth was dipping into a delicious peach cobbler. "What did you think?"

"I haven't met your brother or his fiancée yet," Beth said, "but yes, I did meet her mother – Louise."

"And?" Simone seemed impatient for an answer.

Beth hesitated, unsure how to proceed. Should she give the polite answer, or be completely honest? She risked a glance at Tom, who raised his eyes to the ceiling. No help there. What did Simone want to hear? If she resented Beth, what would be her view of Louise? Beth decided to take a conservative approach. "She's a very elegant lady. I've only met her once, but she seemed…"

"A piranha." Tom came to Beth's rescue. "We all know that, Simmy. Beth came along to lunch with some other kind friends to protect me from Louise's clutches. We set it up so that she would imagine Beth and I were more than just friends." Tom grasped Beth's hand. "We weren't at that point, then…"

"Now you are," Simone said with a tight smile.

"Good for you, Tom," Ed said. "And you too, Beth. We're pleased for you both. Aren't we, Simone?"

Simone wavered. Beth could see her deciding how she would respond and held her breath. Did Simone still view Beth as another woman trying to entrap her dad, or was she willing to accept her as someone who mattered to him, who might be in his life for some time? Beth had only recently accepted the latter view herself, so it wasn't difficult to imagine Simone might have trouble with it.

"Your mom would have liked Beth," Tom said breaking the silence. Even the children, realizing something was afoot, had stopped their chatter and were looking at their mother with open mouths.

"Yes," Simone said, although she seemed to be having difficulty forming the words. "Mom would." She smiled at Beth – a genuine smile this time. "It's good Dad has found someone… someone like himself. I can tell he's happy. That's important to me. But first Brad, now you, Dad. I… Well, I guess this puts paid to any chance of you moving here."

"That was never going to happen, Simmy. You know that. But we'll still be in Florence. And Beth and I aren't rushing into marriage like Brad."

Beth gulped. Marriage? This was all going too fast. She felt dizzy and closed her eyes, hoping she wasn't going to faint.

"Dad!"

"Okay, hon. Only joking. Beth and I are only beginning to get to know each other. We have plenty of time."

Beth opened her eyes again in relief to find the conversation had moved on to education and the proposal to drive past Tommy's new school.

"I want to show you the website first, Dad," said Simone. "As soon as I clear up…"

"You go ahead. I can clear up, and the boys…," Ed said.

"Can I help?" Beth asked, keen to leave father and daughter alone.

"I can manage the dishes, but it would be great if you could take these two outside. They're full of energy and need to expend some of it if we're going to be sitting in the car."

"Sure thing. Can you show me your swings?" she asked the boys who, their earlier shyness forgotten, grabbed her hands and led her outside.

After her private time with Tom, Simone seemed more relaxed and, on the trip to the school, asked Beth about what she was doing in Florence. She expressed interest in her work at Green Heron Estate Sales, and Beth felt comfortable enough to relate the discovery of the photos and her mum's link with Florence. She kept quiet about her Sydney background, grateful Simone didn't appear interested in the

Australian part of Beth's life. Even though it was the weekend, they found the school gates unlocked, and the adults were able to wander around the grounds and peer into classrooms while the boys enjoyed running everywhere and scrambling up the climbing frames.

By the time they were preparing to leave, Beth was beginning to feel comfortable in Simone's company. It was a strange feeling to become involved with a man who had grownup children. Beth felt today had been a test, one which she'd passed, if not with flying colors, at least maintaining some degree of self-respect. But she still had to meet Brad. From what Simone had implied and what Tom had told her, Brad was very different from his sister. Tom had assured Beth Brad would love her and welcome her presence in his dad's life, but she suspected Brooke might be quite a different matter.

Brooke was Louise's daughter, and Beth's heart sank at the thought of what Louise might have reported back after the lunch. Also – and this is what concerned Beth most – from what she'd heard, Brad was completely besotted with his fiancée and quite under her thumb. What if that meant they'd both be influenced by Louise's opinion, which certainly wouldn't be positive?

Tom must have read her mind. "Only Brad to go, now," he said as they left Portland's suburbs and made their way down the highway.

"Mmmm. And Brooke, I guess."

"Well, they seem to come as a package these days. Brad's okay. You've won over Simone, so he and Brooke should be easy."

"Don't forget Louise."

"Louise? She's accepted the situation. Brad tells me she's set her cap at one of the local councillors. Suit her down to the ground. I'd never have been right for her – no social circle for her to lord it over in Florence." He grinned and patted Beth's thigh. "No, nothing to worry about there."

Beth covered his hand with hers and smiled. But she wasn't so sure. Tom was a lovely intelligent man, but could be pretty naïve when it came to women. No woman likes to think she's been slighted, and that's exactly what had happened to Louise. She'd made a very obvious play for Tom, only to be blocked by Beth and the other couples who'd all conspired against her. Beth didn't imagine she'd take that lying down, regardless of who might now be in her sights. The question was, would her annoyance be strong enough to turn Brad against Beth too?

Beth must have dozed off, because she was jolted awake by the car stopping suddenly. "What.., where…?" She gazed around, her eyes trying to become accustomed to the darkness. "Where are we?"

"At your front door. I think you may have fallen asleep."

"Oh, dear." Beth struggled into an upright position. "I'm sorry… I don't know…"

"It's been a long day for you, and tiring too – meeting all those new people, being on your best behavior. You did well. Shall I help you in?"

"No, I…" But, before she knew it, Tom was out of the car, had lifted her from the passenger seat and deposited her on the front step.

"Your key?"

"In my purse."

They were inside in a flash, and Tom's arms were around Beth again, this time in a warm hug. "You need to sleep. I won't stay."

"Uhhh."

"Sleep. You're dead on your feet."

"Mmm."

Tom gave a low laugh. "How about you come out to the lake for breakfast? I'll cook, then we can go out in the boat."

Beth barely heard him. She did hear the door close and managed to make her way to the bedroom where she undressed and fell into bed.

The next thing Beth knew was the sun shining through the open curtains, which she hadn't taken time to close the night before. She sat up, shielding her eyes from the glare, and tried to remember what Tom had said before he left – something about breakfast. But was he coming here? A shower would help. Five minutes under the powerful jet wakened Beth properly, but she was still trying to recall what Tom had said when her cell buzzed.

Good morning sleepy-head. Did you remember you're coming here for breakfast? Dress for the boat. It's a glorious day. Tom x

Beth smiled at the cell as she replied, then picked out a pair of jeans and a white shirt and sneakers as being suitable attire for a day on the water. Before leaving, she threw a pale blue sweater across her shoulders, and she was ready.

Tom was already on the deck when Beth drove up. As she left the car, she could smell bacon and onions cooking on the barbecue, evidence that Tom's idea of breakfast was a long way from her usual cereal and fruit.

"Thought you'd be here around now, so I made a start. Don't want to be too late in getting off." He indicated the boat tied up at the edge of the lake. Beth joined him to be greeted with a bear hug and a warm kiss on the lips. As their lips met, she felt herself tremble deep down inside, experiencing the joy his presence had brought into her life. She could get used to this. He made her feel so safe. Beth felt that, with Tom around, nothing bad could ever happen to her.

Breakfast was a fun affair. By an unspoken agreement, no mention was made of Australia, debts, children or weddings. They shared stories of their childhood. Tom recounted tales of growing up right here in Florence, then at the University of California's Berkley campus where he and Janet had met after what seemed like a plethora of student escapades. Beth shared her more sheltered life living on a farm on the outskirts of an Australian country town. She described the hot summers when they took to swimming in the dams and river to escape the heat, the red dust that seemed to infiltrate everything, the swarms of flies and locusts, then her excitement at traveling to the city to attend university.

"It's time," Tom finally said. "Don't bother about the dishes. Let's get you on the water."

They made their way down to the water where a wooden boat was sitting, the water lapping gently against its sides. "This is it!" Tom said, proudly stroking the craft.

Beth thought the vessel looked even bigger from here than it had from the deck, but it still appeared quite small to her, unaccustomed as she was to sailing and boats. "Does it have an engine?" she asked, knowing it was a stupid question even before Tom laughed and leapt aboard.

"Come up and join me." Tom reached out to help Beth board. She was amazed how different everything looked from here, though the rocking beneath her feet disturbed her, and she hoped she wouldn't be sea-sick.

"How long have you had it – her?" she corrected, remembering that, for some reason, boats were always referred to as feminine.

"Nigh on twenty-five years. She's a beauty, isn't she? Of course she wasn't always like this."

"No?"

"She was in pretty bad shape when I got her. Took a few years to restore the old girl."

"You restored her? Wow!" Beth didn't know what else to say. She knew nothing about boats and didn't want to reveal her ignorance any more than she had already, but she needn't have worried as Tom continued to speak.

"She's a classic mahogany runabout – a Chris Craft sixteen, sixteen feet, built around 1941. Many a collector would give his eye teeth for her or one like her. I put in new decks and frames, and a new 'no soak' bottom, plus a fully overhauled Hercules model 'B' engine that outputs seventy horsepower with stainless steel valves and hard seats. And she still has all the original chrome and gauges."

Beth's eyes began to glaze over.

"Sorry. Too much information. I tend to get carried away when I'm talking about my baby. Best I show you what she can do. There's nothing quite like being aboard her as she carves a path across the still lake. You'll see." Tom helped Beth don a lifejacket, revved up the engine, and they took off across the lake.

Despite her fears and much to her surprise, once she was seated beside Tom on the firm maroon seat, and they were flying along with the wind in their hair, Beth began to enjoy herself. By the time Tom brought the vessel to rest near the middle of the lake, she was laughing with enjoyment.

"What now?" she asked. "Do we fish?"

"Not today. Didn't pack the gear, but next time – if you're up for a next time." Tom threw an arm around Beth's shoulders, and she snuggled into him, enjoying the feel of his strong body next to hers and his lips on her hair. They sat without speaking, the only sounds the lapping of the water against the side of the boat and the calling of the birds as they flew overhead or swam close by. They were in a world of their own. It was magic.

They remained like that till the sound of another vessel approaching broke the silence. "Maybe time to go back," Tom said, removing his arm and leaving Beth with an empty feeling where the arm had rested. She shivered and pulled on her sweater, glad she'd remembered to bring it.

"Lunch?" Tom asked as he helped Beth on to dry land, his arm remaining around her shoulders.

"Yes, please." Beth found the trip had given her an appetite, even though breakfast had been much larger than she was used to. They were trudging across the grass towards the house, Beth stepping carefully on the uneven surface, when Tom stopped suddenly. Beth looked up and noticed a figure sitting on the deck watching them.

"Damn," Tom muttered under his breath. "It's Brad. What does he want?"

"Your son?" Beth raised her eyes to meet Tom's. "Were you expecting him?"

"No. I'd planned on calling him to set a meeting time, but… Oh well, now you'll get to meet him too."

Beth felt herself shiver. She wasn't ready to meet Tom's son. Their visit with Simone yesterday had been planned. She'd been able to prepare herself, but this? Beth tried to remember what Tom had told her about Brad. He was a lawyer like his dad, younger than his sister, engaged to be married, and what was more worrying, his fiancée was Louise's daughter.

"Dad!" A younger version of Tom rose to greet them as they climbed the steps to the deck. "Thought you must be out on the lake. And this is…"

"Beth," Tom said, hugging his son. "What brings you to here" Are you…" He looked around as if expecting Brooke to appear.

"I'm on my own today. Brooke and Louise are busy with wedding dresses, and evidently no men are allowed, so I thought I'd visit my old dad."

Beth could tell from Tom's expression that he didn't completely buy Brad's explanation.

"Been talking to your sister?" he asked.

Brad looked sheepish, shuffling his feet in the same way as she'd noticed Tom do when he was feeling awkward. "Simone did call," he said. "And Louise mentioned…"

"And you decided to come and see for yourself. Well this is Beth. What do you think, son?"

Beth wished the ground – or the deck – would open and swallow her up as Brad and Tom both examined her closely.

"I think you've done very well for yourself, Dad," Brad laughed and slapped Tom on the back. "Hi Beth, good to meet you. I hope you're managing to put up with this old curmudgeon."

Beth relaxed and smiled. It was going to be all right.

"We were going to have lunch. You'll join us?" Tom asked.

"A beer would go down well."

"I'll get it. For you too, Tom?"

Tom nodded, and Beth went inside, glad to have something to do. While she was fetching the beers and pouring a Coke for herself, she could hear the pair talking and laughing outside, clearly happy to be in each other's company.

"Brad's offered to cut the grass," Tom said when Beth emerged. "Doesn't think the old man's up to it." He flexed his left hand, which still appeared to be a bit stiff, even though the tape was now off.

"Well, it is my wedding," Brad said, flipping the top off his beer and taking a long gulp. "Sometimes it feels as if it's a stage play, and I only have to appear in the final moment to place the ring on Brooke's finger and kiss the bride."

"All weddings are a bit like that, son. It's the women who get excited about it. We just have to turn up and foot the bill, though Louise seems to be perfectly capable of doing that."

"They're not short of a dollar. Which reminds me. Louise wanted me to check with you about the marquee. She said you'd promised to see to that side of things."

"Blast. Completely slipped my mind. I'll take care of it tomorrow. I know there's somewhere local. They had a few at the fair."

"And Jo uses them for sales when she needs more space," Beth said.

"Consider it done. You can tell Louise it's in hand."

"So you're from Australia, Beth?" Brad asked, turning his attention to her. "What brings you all this way?"

Beth took a moment to answer, wondering how much to reveal and whether this was simple curiosity about a friend of his father, or if Brooke and Louise had primed him to find out more about her.

Tom put a comforting hand on her shoulder and replied for her, "Beth's mom passed away, and she wanted to make a fresh start."

So he wasn't going to mention anything about Bryan. That suited Beth. "My mum's family came from the US," she added. "I wanted to return to my roots." Crikey, where had that come from? It sounded like something out of a bad movie, but seemed to satisfy Brad.

"You mentioned lunch, Dad?"

"I planned on sending out for pizza. That suit you?" Tom gave Beth a shamefaced grin as if to ask for her approval too.

By the time they'd demolished two enormous pizzas and the men had finished off another couple of beers, Brad rose to leave.

"So you can fill Brooke in on Beth, now," Tom said as he embraced his son. "It would never have worked between Louise and me. I know she and Brooke might have hoped… I'm a simple fellow, you know. Those city types scare the bejesus out of me."

"I know, Dad. It was Brooke's idea, and I went along with it. You're both on your own. We may have encouraged Louise to think that… Sorry if…"

"I don't think she needed much encouragement, son. She's a man-eater for sure. I hope Brooke…"

"She's not like that, Dad. She's a lonely woman, and Brooke's a sweet girl. She keeps me focussed. You'll find out when you know her better."

"I'm sure you're right."

Beth listened to this repartee with amusement. It told her a lot about Tom's relationship with his son, and not a little about Brad and Brooke.

"And is she?" she asked, when Brad had driven off in a cloud of dust.

Tom linked arms with Beth as they walked back into the house. "Is who what?"

"Is Brooke sweet and unlike her mother?"

"That's a matter of opinion. My opinion – and Simone's – is that they're two peas in a pod. Brad's is different. We all see people as we want to see them, and I guess both Brooke and Louise are what Brad wants to believe they are. That's good enough for me."

"And how do you see me?"

Tom appeared to give Beth's question careful thought, before tipping up her chin and gazing into her eyes. "Why, you are the sweetest, cutest thing I've come across, and I can't believe my luck. And now my wretched son has finally left, we can continue where we left off." He bent his head to meet Beth's lips with his, and the kiss that began as a gentle peck became much deeper and led to the bedroom and an afternoon of lovemaking.

Twenty-five

Beth was quivering with anticipation. Tom had called to let her know he'd received an email from John Blackwood, and suggested dinner. He hadn't said whether it was good or bad news, but any news was better than this interminable waiting. On an impulse, she'd invited him to her home for dinner, relishing another chance to use the cooking skills which had been going to waste with only herself to cook for. And if the news was bad, she could retire quietly without having to drive home. Tom had sounded awkward on the phone, so Beth wasn't optimistic about the contents of the email from Sydney.

As she picked up a red wine and selected a couple of steaks on the way home, Beth hummed to herself. She intended to enjoy this evening. Regardless of the outcome of Bryan's estate and the weird need to advertise in England, it was almost over. Either she'd be celebrating or drowning her sorrows by the end of the evening. And there was always the anticipation of being with Tom again. It was only a few days since her visit to the lake, Brad's unexpected appearance and the afternoon which had followed. Beth grinned, her whole body suffused with warmth, remembering that afternoon. It had been dark by the time they'd disentangled themselves, exhausted and fulfilled. They'd lain together, face-to-face murmuring sweet nothings till hunger had forced them to rise. Maybe tonight would be a repeat performance. Beth had considered herself past such a display of passion, but she'd been wrong. Hadn't someone – Ellen? – tried to tell her this recently?

After a quick shower and change into a fresh pair of pants and shirt, Beth headed for the kitchen and began to prepare dinner. Remembering their Mexican lunch, she planned a black bean salad to accompany the steaks, along with some baked potatoes. Checking the temperature outside, she decided it would be warm enough to eat there again.

Although pretending to be calm while she fixed the salad and marinated the steaks, Beth's stomach was churning with worry. This was it. She was about to find out exactly how much was owing, exactly how big a mess Bryan had left, the extent of her liability. By the time she heard Tom at the door, she had imagined every possible scenario, including one in which mafiosa-type bagmen appeared from Australia to demand payment. She'd managed to discount that one as being in the realms of fantasy and the result of watching too much late-night television. Nevertheless, she was relieved to hear the doorbell and hurried to answer it.

Tom's arms grasped Beth in a warm hug, but she drew back, her eyes searching his face for some indication of what he had to tell her.

"Is it…" she asked in a shaky voice.

"Let's eat first," he said, taking both of Beth's hands in his.

"It's bad news, then?" Beth's voice rose, sure her worst fears were about to be realized.

"It's… unexpected news. Best you at least have a drink first. Sit down. I'll pour."

Beth perched on the edge of the sofa, tapping her feet, her hands trembling. When Tom returned and placed a glass in her hand, she was too confused to realize he'd poured a glass of the Jack Daniels Mike and Jenny had left one evening they'd visited. Tom sat next to her, an arm around her shoulder. Beth took a gulp, grimaced, and put it down. "Now. What's happened? Why do you look so…?" She couldn't think of a word to describe the strange look on Tom's face.

"I do have bad news. It's going to be a shock. I had an email from Blackwood. He had word from England." Tom paused. "Hell, there's no easy way to say this. Your… Bryan Flynn wasn't your husband. You weren't legally married. He had a wife in England."

Beth started to laugh hysterically. Not married? A wife in England? How could that possibly be true? "No," she said. Her glass dropped to the floor spilling its contents all over the carpet as she held up her hands, palms out as if to ward off the unwelcome news. "It's not true. Where did they get that idea? No," she repeated, clasping her hands in her lap, her eyes darting wildly from side to side. "I can't… Bryan…"

"I know it's difficult for you." Tom ineffectually patted Beth's shoulder and handed her his glass which was still full. "Have another drink.'"

Beth pushed it away and rose, beginning to pace up and down agitatedly. Her eyes blurred. She felt dizzy. She sensed Tom rise to stand behind her. She felt she was about to fall and putting out a hand to steady herself, found Tom's broad chest supporting her. She fell against him, and they stood like that for a few seconds before Tom held her away with both hands.

"Are you okay?" he asked.

"No. But I will be. Just give me…"

"Why don't you sit down again? What about tea? Sweet tea?"

"Mmm." Beth felt her tongue stick to the roof of her mouth. She couldn't make her mouth work. She tried to form the words she wanted to say. She opened her mouth, but no words came out. She was aware of Tom placing her in a chair and disappearing into the kitchen. She couldn't think straight.

Tom returned and placed a hot mug in Beth's hand. "Drink," he said. "You're suffering from shock."

Beth grasped the drink in both hands, taking comfort from its warmth. She raised it to her lips and took a sip. The hot, sweet drink had a revitalizing effect. Beth could feel it traveling to the tips of her fingers and all the way down to her toes. Tom sat beside her, hands on his knees, seemingly unsure what to do next.

Beth sipped the tea slowly without speaking, still holding the cup with both hands. She thought carefully about what Tom had said. Could it be true? Surely the lawyers in Sydney would have checked their sources. But it seemed incredible. How could Bryan have kept such a thing secret? How could he have married her if he already had a wife in England?

"Are they sure? Maybe it's a mistake. Maybe…"

"I think what you need is a good night's rest. It'll all look different in the morning. I'll help you…"

"But…" The immediate reality intruded, and she waved her

hand towards the kitchen where the dinner preparations were still incomplete. She couldn't face the idea of dinner.

"Don't worry, I'll put everything away." Tom guided Beth into the bedroom, helped her undress and tucked her into bed.

Beth lay there shivering, unable to sleep. Every time she closed her eyes she saw Bryan's face laughing at her, or his figure embracing a faceless woman. She tossed and turned, but must have fallen asleep at last. When she awoke, the room was in darkness, and she could feel Tom lying beside her. She stretched out a hand to make sure he was real and was reassured by the warmth of his body. Beth sighed and closed her eyes again. The next time she woke, the sun was shining through the curtains, and the space next to her was empty.

Pushing herself upright, Beth could hear water running. Tom must be in the shower. She rubbed her eyes, memories of the previous evening returning with a jolt. Was it true? Was Bryan married to someone else? Was he really a bigamist? Then what did that make her? A fool, that's what.

Beth almost ran into the ensuite and dragged the shower door open, startling Tom in the middle of his ablutions. "Where is it? I want to see the email from Sydney. I need to see for myself."

"Hold on." Tom turned off the water and stepped out of the shower, grabbing a towel. "It's back at the office. Why don't we have breakfast, then you can come with me. Is Jo expecting you?"

"Yes." Beth stood stock still, trying to work out what to do. "I'll call her, say I've had some bad news, and that I'll be in later."

"Are you sure you want to go to work today? I'm sure Jo would understand if…"

"No. I'll be fine." It was as if the night's rest had changed Beth in some way. "I just need to see for myself."

By the time Beth had showered and dressed, Tom had made coffee and toast and was searching in the pantry.

"This what you're looking for?" Beth reached past him to take down a box of muesli. "Probably not what you're used to."

"It's good." Tom filled a bowl and added milk, while Beth sat down with a slice of toast. Her throat was still closed up at the thought of food, but she knew she had to eat something.

"Tell me again – exactly what did Blackwood say." More clearheaded this morning, Beth was ready for more information. "Sorry, last night…" She waved her hand in the air in an attempt to explain her behavior the night before.

"You were in shock. I know." Tom carefully placed his coffee down and leant his elbows on the table. "What Blackwood said was that he'd had a reply to his advertisement in the English papers. It was from a woman called Cecily Bradshaw who said her sister was married to a Bryan Harvey-Flynn who had disappeared in 1998."

"What? Cecily who?"

*

Beth followed Tom into his office, fidgeting impatiently while he booted up his computer. "See for yourself," he said, moving aside to allow her to sit at the desk. Beth sat and scrolled down the email frowning when she came to the reference to the response from this Cecily Bradshaw.

"Cecily Bradshaw! What sort of name is that? This could all be a hoax. Someone who thinks there's money in it." She turned to Tom standing behind her. "It could be that, couldn't it?"

Tom placed a firm hand on her shoulder. "Read on."

Beth turned back to the screen and continued down the page. She gasped, reading that the Bryan Harvey-Flynn who disappeared had recently gained a medical degree, had married Cecily's sister Elaine while they were both studying, and had been about to take up a position in a London hospital. He had apparently left gambling debts behind.

"But it could still be a coincidence," she muttered. "No one can disappear in this day and age."

"Check the attachment." Tom's hand gripped Beth's shoulder more firmly. "Maybe that'll help."

Beth hadn't noticed the little paper clip at the top of the email. She held her breath and clicked on it to reveal a wedding photo. It was pretty small, so she enlarged it and examined the groom closely. It looked like… it could be… it was… it was Bryan! Beth's hands left the keyboard, and her eyes filled with tears. "It's him – the bastard!"

Anger boiled up inside, making Beth want to lash out, but the only other person there was Tom, and it wouldn't be fair to take her rage out on him. She clenched her fists, her nails digging into the flesh till she wanted to cry out. Her teeth bit into her lip until she tasted blood. Damn the man! If Bryan had a wife in England, what did that make Beth? Not his widow, for sure. If they'd never been married, then she was still single. It was an odd feeling.

"Are you okay?"

"Okay? How can I be okay when I've just discovered my marriage was a sham?" She stood up, fuelled by her anger. "I need to… I need to go to work."

"I don't think you…"

"Jo's expecting me. I need to do something. I can't think straight." Beth turned away from his outstretched arms. "Not now, Tom. I need to process this. Will you…?"

"I'll send a reply. See if I can get more information. Shall I…"

"Let me know when you do." Beth picked up her purse and headed to the door. Once there, however she stopped and turned, frowning. "Why did the *sister* contact Blackwood? Where's the wife?"

"I'll ask."

*

Beth threw herself into work for the rest of the day, her rage at Bryan's deceitfulness giving her so much energy that Jo wanted to know what had inspired her. "Don't ask," was Beth's terse reply, after which Jo kept her own counsel, apart from saying she was there if and when Beth wanted to talk.

By the time she reached home Beth was exhausted. She took a shower and, going into the kitchen, opened the fridge to see the remains of last night's meal. The two steaks still sitting in their marinade, and the wilting salad makings seemed to leer at her. She closed the door again quickly, unable to think of eating a proper meal. Instead, she brewed a cup of licorice tea and toasted a slice of bread, then sat down at the kitchen table, put her head down on her arms and relived the moments in Tom's office.

It was definitely Bryan in the wedding photo. She'd never been

Elizabeth Flynn. There was a bitter justice in the fact she'd reverted to her maiden name, become Beth Carson again. It was her name – always had been. The house was silent around her, in keeping with her mood. She didn't know how long she sat there till the ringing of the phone broke the silence. It would be Tom. Beth let it ring. She didn't want to talk to him, not now. All she felt was shame. Shame she'd allowed herself to be duped. And what about the debts? Bryan's debts. If she wasn't his wife, was she still liable? It was all too much to take in She'd worry about that later. Suddenly tired, she made her way to bed, but before doing so, took the phone off the hook and turned off her cell. She didn't want to talk with anyone. She just wanted to be alone.

*

Things didn't look any better next morning, but Beth managed to force down a soft boiled egg – her mother's standby when she'd been sick as a child. She started to dress for work, then stopped halfway. She felt dreadful. A glance in the mirror told her she looked worse. Her skin had developed a grayish tone, there were bags under her eyes and a host of wrinkles had appeared overnight. All she wanted to do was crawl back into bed and hide. Well, why not? She turned on her cell, sent a text to Jo, then turned it off again. She couldn't bear to speak to anyone. She wanted to be left alone.

Beth must have slept through the day, because when she opened her eyes again it was dark. For a moment on wakening she felt good, then she remembered and wanted to hide her head again. She forced herself up and into the kitchen where she saw the half-full bottle of Jack Daniels where Tom had left it two nights ago. For a moment she was tempted. Getting drunk would banish the shame, help her forget… But that wasn't Beth's way. She stiffened her back and raised her head, reaching instead for the coffee maker. The liquid she scorned so much was exactly what she needed.

Mug in hand, Beth became curious. She took out her laptop, booted it up and googled Cecily Bradshaw, then Elaine Bradshaw – nothing. Damn! Then she tried Bryan Harvey-Flynn. Here she had better luck. There were a few items about his sports prowess, and a clip about the disappearance of a promising young medico, then nothing. She stared at the screen as if she could summon up the whole story of the bastard's life. He'd been clever. She had to concede that. He hadn't changed his name completely so he could still use his qualifications, but to all intents and purposes he'd changed his identity. Bryan Harvey-Flynn had morphed into Bryan Flynn and he'd fooled everyone. Beth closed the computer and returned to bed. If she closed her eyes, maybe it would all go away.

*

Beth was awakened by a loud thumping at the door. She opened her eyes in alarm and checked the time. It was nine o'clock in the morning. She'd lost track of the days and only knew it was morning because of the weak sunlight shining through the windows. She didn't want to talk to anyone, see anyone. Maybe if she pulled the covers over her head and ignored them, they'd go away. The knocking didn't stop, and Beth heard Tom's voice calling her name over and over again. Cursing, she threw on a toweling robe, and not taking time to check the mirror or even brush her fingers through her hair, she trudged to the front door and opened it a crack. "Go away," she said and closed it in Tom's face. Beth leant against the closed door, taking deep breaths. The room began to swirl around her, and she sat down where she was, on the floor. It was Tom outside, the same Tom whose body had brought her so much pleasure only a few nights ago, the man who had renewed her faith in the possibility of a future, the man she'd now closed the door on. Part of her wanted to get up, open the door, welcome him with open arms, snuggle up to him and ask him to make everything right again. But she couldn't do it. She couldn't handle seeing or talking to anyone right now. Not even Tom.

"Are you still there, Beth? We're worried about you. Can you let me in?" Tom's voice did sound anxious, but allowing him in would be to allow in all the stuff she was trying to banish from her thoughts. It would open the box she'd firmly closed when she closed the computer. It would… Beth put her hands over her ears in an attempt to shut out Tom's voice. But it was no good. "I'm not going away till we've spoken.

You're not answering your phone or your cell. I need to know you're all right. I've had a reply from Sydney. I can fill you in. Beth? Can you hear me?"

It was no use. He wasn't going to leave.

"Give me a few minutes," Beth said, as she levered herself up and returned to the bedroom. She looked in the mirror for the first time in days and grimaced at what she saw there. Only a few days ago, she'd have been reluctant to let Tom see her looking like this, but now she didn't care. Pulling on an old tracksuit that was lying on top of the laundry basket, she dragged a comb though her hair, made a face at herself in the bathroom mirror and headed back to the door.

"Well?" she said, opening it wide.

"May I come in?"

*

Tom took in Beth's disheveled appearance. A rush of pity welled up, fuelling his affection for her. No wonder she'd gone off the grid. She'd had a shock – another, on top of what she'd already experienced in a few short months. It was to be expected it would hit her hard, but when she didn't answer her phone, and Jo rang him concerned she hadn't seen or heard from Beth in days, he became worried and decided to come here.

Taking silence for assent, Tom stepped in and closed the door behind him. Beth didn't speak. She turned her back to him and walked away. Tom followed her into the kitchen where he found her standing, holding onto the sink and gazing out of the window.

"Beth," he said tentatively, moving close but not touching. He could sense her anger, as if it was a living thing.

"Why are you here?" Even her voice sounded strange – strangled, tense.

"We were worried. No one has seen or heard from you for days. We wanted to make sure you were all right."

"Well, now you've seen me, you can go away again."

Tom rubbed his hands along his side. This was way out of his experience. He didn't know how to handle this side of Beth, but he did know he couldn't leave her like this.

"Why don't you sit down? Have you eaten? I'll make you something." Tom managed to lead Beth to the table, where she sat motionless, as if in a dream. He opened the fridge, which looked exactly as he'd left it the other night. Spying a carton of eggs, he took them out along with a container of milk. Scrambled eggs. He could do that.

"Now, you must eat something," he said as he placed the steaming plate of eggs down. He sat opposite and watched as Beth slowly took first one then another small mouthful of the food. It reminded him of when the children were little, and he and Janet had watched them carefully to ensure they were getting enough to eat.

Beth ate half of the meal before pushing the plate away. She gazed into space. It was as if Tom didn't exist.

"I heard back from Blackwood," he said, taking a sheet of paper from his pocket, but there was no change in Beth's expression. He might as well have been talking to the wall. "Beth," he tried again. "Are you hearing me?"

Beth turned her expressionless eyes towards him. "Tom? You can leave now. We're done."

Reluctantly, but knowing to stay would be useless, Tom rose to leave. He stood looking at Beth's downcast expression before her head dropped to hide it. "Will you do one thing for me? Please?" She lifted her head to stare at him blankly. "Will you turn your cell back on?" There was no answering glimmer to indicate she'd heard or understood. He'd done what he could and had a full diary of appointments waiting for him back at the office. Tom turned and left, closing the door gently behind him. When he reached his pickup, he sat for a time behind the wheel, looking at Beth's house and wondering how he could bring back the Beth he knew and was beginning to love, before he sighed and drove off.

Twenty-six

Beth didn't know long it was since she'd heard the door close behind Tom. Hours, days, a week? She stood in the kitchen and gazed into space. What had he said? Something about Blackwood? In the recess of the fog that was her brain, something connected. Blackwood. The name should mean something, but the linkage wasn't there. She wandered around the house touching objects, while the name Blackwood whirled around in her head. She had the feeling it was important, should be important, but where the memory ought to be there was an empty space.

Although she was up, Beth still felt unable to settle to anything. The call of her bed was strong and she was about to return to its comforting warmth when there was another knock at the door. This time it was less urgent, and the voice which accompanied it was lighter.

"Beth? It's Jenny. I'm here to listen, if you need to talk. Now or later." The words were followed by silence, and Beth wondered if Jenny had left. Strangely, unlike her reaction to Tom's arrival, Beth felt less threatened by Jenny, less wary of seeing her. She moved slowly to the door, opened it and stood unmoving as Jenny hugged her.

"Can we go in?" Jenny led the way into the lounge and took a seat. Beth found herself sitting too, feet together, knees together, hands in her lap as if waiting for something to happen. She looked at Jenny, focussing on her in a way she'd been unable to with Tom.

"If you don't want to talk that's okay. I'm happy just to sit here with you, if you'll let me. Of course, I can't imagine how you feel, but

I do have some inkling. A few years ago, I discovered I wasn't who I thought I was, that I'd been adopted. It was a shock and took a bit of getting used to. Mike helped. I discovered it's good to have a friendly ear at times like that. Then I set about researching to find out more – to discover my real identity, I suppose."

Beth felt the slightest flicker of interest. She knew Jenny was related to Ellen, but didn't know her story. As Jenny continued to recount her discovery and subsequent shock, Beth listened, casually at first, then intently. Jenny's experience was nothing like Beth's, but there was something about her story that touched a vulnerable place in Beth. It was enough to make her speak.

"I feel so ashamed," she began. "All those years I called myself Mrs Flynn. All that time I acted the part of Bryan's wife… and he already had one. I had no idea."

"How could you? You operated on what you knew, what he told you – and the rest of Sydney. There's no shame in that."

"Did Tom tell you?"

"We're all worried about you. Tom only told Ellen and me. Jo thinks you have a virus."

Beth tried to smile, but her lips refused to turn up. "That's good of him."

"He's a good man. And he cares about you. He's sorry…"

"I don't want his pity!" Beth almost shouted, then her eyes widened in surprise. Where had that come from? "I mean…," she said, then wondered exactly what she did mean.

"It's okay to be angry. I'd be furious if I discovered Mike had lied to me, and about something so vital, too. But don't you want to know more? To find out about his life in England? Aren't you curious?"

Through the fog that was still Beth's mind, she noted Jenny had carefully avoided mentioning Bryan's first wife, his real wife, his only wife.

"I did," she said. "Then it didn't seem to matter. I just wanted to forget. So I did. But then, every time I wake, it's still there. It won't go away."

"No, it won't," Jenny agreed.

Unexpectedly, Beth was beginning to feel better. It was as if, with her shouting at Jenny, something had cracked inside, breaking open the hard shell that had begun to reform around her when she heard of Bryan's deceit. She brushed her hair off her face, conscious of her disheveled appearance. She was wearing an old toweling robe, hastily pulled together with its belt. "What must I look like?"

"Well, I've seen you look better. Why don't you take a shower, get dressed in something more…" Her eyes raked Beth from head to toe. "And I'll make us both some tea."

Beth rose slowly, but for the first time in days, the old Beth was beginning to reassert herself. "Thank you, Jenny, I will. There's some licorice tea in the cupboard on the right and…"

"Don't worry. I'll find my way around."

Once in the shower, with the water cascading over her body, Beth's head began to clear. The darkness surrounding her was beginning to lift. She held her face up to allow the water to stream over it, enjoying the feeling of vitality it gave her. She'd master this. She wouldn't let Bryan win again. It had been a blow to her pride to learn of his dishonesty, but Jenny was right when she'd said it didn't change who Beth was. She was still the same person she'd been when she imagined herself a widow. She was still Beth Carson. She'd always been Beth Carson. Elizabeth Flynn had been a mirage. Pursuing this train of thought led Beth to consider the way she'd treated Tom, and she winced at how she'd shut him out.

"That looks better," Jenny greeted Beth when she emerged dressed in a pair of tailored jeans teamed with a pink and white striped shirt. "Sit down here." Jenny pulled out the chair beside her at the kitchen table where two steaming mugs of herbal teas were waiting alongside a plate of macadamia nut cookies. "I found these in the pantry. I hope you don't mind."

"No." Beth sat down and bit into a cookie, surprised to discover she was hungry. "Tom," she said.

Jenny sipped her tea and raised her eyebrows.

"I must… Hell, what must he think of me? We were just becoming…" She dragged her hand through her newly brushed hair, making it stand on end."

"He'll understand."

"But I…" Beth bit her lip, remembering how she'd refused to let him speak.

"How do you feel about him?" Jenny didn't beat around the bush, and her blunt question took Beth by surprise.

"I… I like him," she stuttered. "But his life is complicated too. He has two children – grown children – and grandchildren. They are adorable, but… I don't have any experience with either. And there's his son's wedding, and… he's my lawyer," she finished.

"You've met Brad and Simone?" Jenny asked in surprise. She clearly hadn't realized how far Tom and Beth's relationship had progressed.

"Briefly. Brad's good, though there's Brooke and Louise."

"And Simone?"

"I think she's okay. She was pretty standoffish at first, protective of her dad. I can understand her point of view. I arrive from nowhere, then… Christ, what'll they think when they learn…?" Beth's voice began to break at the idea of everyone discovering her situation.

"Is there any reason why they should?"

Grateful for Jenny's matter-of-fact approach, Beth considered. "No… I guess not."

Beth sipped her tea, several thoughts competing for her attention. "You mentioned earlier… You asked if I was curious. I think I am. Tom did say something about another email from Sydney, but I'm afraid I…" Beth placed her mug on the table and rubbed at an imaginary mark on the surface.

"Is this it?" Jenny held up a piece of paper which had been lying on the table. "Did Tom leave this for you?"

Beth took the paper, holding it cautiously by the corner. She began to read, scanning quickly down the page. "It's from the Sydney lawyer – John Blackwood – Bryan's lawyer. He…" she read it again, puzzled by the contents. "He says his only contact has been with this Cecily woman who is…." Beth looked up. "I guess she's Bryan's sister-in-law. How odd." Her eyes focussed on the paper again. "The wife…," Beth was unable to keep the bitterness out of her voice, "is dead." She dropped the email on the table, unwilling to read further. "So that's that."

"Does it say when she died?"

"What does it matter?" Beth had become tired of this conversation, but knew she still had something to do. "I guess I should contact Tom." It wasn't a task she was looking forward to. "When he left… I was pretty rude. I don't know if he'll find it in himself to forgive me."

"Only one way to find out." Jenny hesitated as if unsure of how much to reveal about her own life. "I… Mike and I… we had our misunderstandings too. I'm glad we managed to work things out. Life's too short to let things go. When you get to our age…" She laughed. "Heck, here am I trying to offer advice when I almost made a right royal mess of my own life. If it hadn't been for Maddy and Mike, I'd never be where I am today. I can only tell you not to let too much water flow under the bridge before you mend it."

"It was only a few days ago," Beth said, unsure what day it actually was. But it felt much longer since she'd heard the door close behind Tom. Even through the despondent haze that enveloped her, it had felt like the door closing on the chance of a new life, a new beginning. And it had been her choice.

"I should go, now," Jenny said, picking up the dirty mugs and carrying them to the dishwasher. "Shall I put these in too?" She indicated the egg encrusted dishes which were still lying in the sink, along with several dirty mugs and plates.

"Oh, you shouldn't have to do that." Beth half rose, but Jenny gestured to her to sit down again. "But thanks. I've been lazy lately."

Beth waved Jenny goodbye and went back inside. She knew she had to contact Tom, but dreaded speaking to him. She equivocated, arguing with herself about the best course of action. But first, she had to do something else. She set up her laptop and began to compose an email to her mother's lawyer. She wanted to check the ins and outs of the legal system back in Australia. While she'd been talking to Jenny she'd had a flash of insight. Maybe, if she hadn't been Bryan's wife, she wasn't liable for his debts. Maybe this other wife, this Elaine Flynn was liable, and while Beth didn't wish indebtedness on anyone, it would certainly ease the burden on her.

Once she'd composed the email to her satisfaction and sent it off, Beth took out her cell and sat looking at it, telling herself all the reasons why she shouldn't just ring Tom and apologize. She finally screwed up the courage to make the call, only to have the office phone answered by Gwen, who apologized that Tom was engaged all afternoon, but could she take a message? "Yes… no…I'll call back." Beth closed her cell feeling all kinds of a fool. Was he really busy *all* afternoon? Had he instructed Gwen to fob her off if she rang? Then she chastised herself. Tom wasn't like that. He was honest and sincere. Those were the qualities that had drawn her to him. But what to do now? If he was really busy, she didn't want to call his cell. She turned the phone over in her hands. Maybe she could leave it till later? No, she'd take the coward's way out and send a text, then it would be up to him. Her fingers flew over the keys. *So sorry. I was unbelievably rude. You were so kind. I read the email and am ready to talk. Please call me when you're free. Bx.* Beth pressed *send* before she could have second thoughts, closed the phone and clasped it to her chest as if she could send her feelings for Tom with it.

*

Tom farewelled his final client for the day and checked the notes Gwen had left, which included one saying Beth Carson had called but hadn't left a message. Gwen added the comment that she had sounded confused on the phone, so she hoped Beth was all right. Tom started to pick up the phone to call Beth, then stopped midway. He rubbed his chin. He didn't want to exacerbate the situation. Beth had told him to leave in no uncertain terms. Her call to the office could mean anything. And she hadn't left a message or called back. No, best leave it alone.

Unusually for him, Tom felt a reluctance to drive straight home. He experienced a need to be surrounded by people, but didn't want to make conversation with anyone, so his usual haunts were out. Driving aimlessly, he found himself on the road out of town with the Three Rivers Casino looming up to his left. Taking it as a sign – though of what he was at a loss to understand – he drove up the long driveway and parked. He could grab a bite to eat here and would be surrounded by strangers.

Once inside, he was cocooned in the warmth and clamor of the building. Maneuvering his way between the rows of slots, he stopped at an empty one to play a couple of dollars before heading for the bistro. He ordered a beer and sat staring into the amber liquid. This had been a mistake. It brought back memories of the night he'd brought

Beth here. Thinking of Beth made him pull out his cell, as he debated whether to call her after all.

Blast! There was a message he hadn't noticed earlier. He read Beth's text with mounting relief. This sounded more like the Beth he knew. He began to press her number then stopped, his finger hovering over the keys. He needed to see her, to assure himself all was well, that she'd recovered from the depression into which she seemed to have sunk, the depression which had led to her sending him away in such a summarily fashion. Forgetting his hunger and leaving the still full glass of beer on the table, he leapt up.

Parking outside Beth's house, Tom was relieved to see a light shining out through the curtains. He hesitated. She had asked him to call, but Tom had never been one to do as he was told, especially when he thought he knew better. Throwing caution to the wind, he made his way to the front door and took a deep breath before giving it a gentle knock.

"Did you… Oh!" Beth's eyes widened at the sight of Tom. Clearly she hadn't expected him to turn up like this. "I thought Jenny had come back," she said.

"I got your text."

"Right."

The two stood there in the doorway gazing at each other, till Beth moved aside. "You'd better come in."

Tom was pleased to see Beth dressed and with her hair arranged in its usual style. They sat opposite each other, and Beth looked down at her hands. "I'm sorry."

"So you said. You said you read the email."

"Yes. She's dead." Beth's eyes were dark pools of grief. Then she seemed to rouse herself. "Wine? I think I still have that bottle of red."

Remembering how he sealed the bottle before placing it in the fridge, Tom nodded. This was more difficult than he'd expected. Beth appeared normal, but she had erected a barrier between them that he wasn't sure how to scale. He stood up and paced around as he waited for her return.

When at last they were both seated again with a glass of wine, the conversation became easier.

"So Jenny dropped round?"

"Something else I have to thank you for."

"I didn't do much." Tom shifted uncomfortably. "A couple of emails, a word in the right ear. I thought Jenny…"

"Was exactly the right person." Beth finished, smiling at last. She drew her fingers through her hair, giving it an attractive tousled appearance and making Tom want to stroke it. "I was in hell, ashamed, humiliated, embarrassed. By the time she arrived I was ready to scream. Well," she grimaced weakly, "at least that was better than killing myself. And no, I didn't guzzle the Jack Daniels, though it did cross my mind before…" He saw her give a shiver and, without thinking, joined her on the sofa, one hand on her shoulder. Beth put her hand over Tom's and met his eyes. This time, he saw something else in them, a spark of the old Beth's indomitable spirit. "Being depressed is not for sissies. If Jenny hadn't come when she did, I don't know…" Beth covered her eyes with her free hand.

This time, Tom didn't hesitate. He took hold of Beth's hand and pressed it to his lips, moving his other hand to stroke Beth's slender neck. "It's all going to be all right. *You're* going to be all right," he murmured into her hair.

Beth fell against him with a low moan. "It was so awful. I've never felt that way before. Not even…" Tom's lips met hers, his mouth nibbling on hers and whispering words of comfort.

After what seemed like an age they drew apart, Tom gently stroking tendrils of Beth's hair back from her forehead. "Shall we…"

"Mmm."

Tom picked Beth up and carried her to the bedroom, her arms wound around his neck. This time their lovemaking was leisurely. Tom wanted to ensure Beth's pleasure, taking time to be certain she was fully aroused before entering her and was thrilled when she took the initiative to stroke and fondle him too. Her moans of pleasure took him to even greater heights of sensual delight. Their bodies writhed and twisted as both reached a climax. As they fell apart, spent and satisfied, Beth stroked Tom's face, her fingers tracing his lips. He opened his mouth to nibble them and she smiled.

"I thought… I thought we'd never be together again," she whispered.

"I'd never have let that happen," he said, although for a time that had been his fear too. He stretched out his legs, his toes touching hers, and took her in his arms again, raining kisses down on her upturned face. "You can't escape me that easily."

Tom was surprised at his own words. He hadn't expected to feel this way again, or so quickly. He'd been attracted to Beth, wanted to get to know her better, and now he couldn't imagine a future without her. "Now I have you again, I don't ever want to let you go." He pulled Beth closer, reveling in the sensation of her soft body against his. This felt right. He'd been on his own far too long.

*

Beth struggled to sit up. It was dark outside. Both she and Tom had fallen asleep, exhausted after their lovemaking, and now she was hungry. She rose cautiously, taking care not to disturb him, and made her way to the kitchen. She didn't bother to turn on the light, feeling her way to the fridge. She knew she'd be able to find something to eat by its light alone. She scanned the shelves and settled on a package of mixed cheeses she'd bought some time back. Checking the use-by date to ensure the contents were still edible, she lifted it out, leaving the fridge door open while she rummaged in the pantry for some crackers to accompany them.

"Oh!" Beth almost jumped in the air as a large arm encircled her waist, and she was pulled against Tom's warm body. She turned, smiling. "I thought you were still asleep. Hungry?"

"For you."

"No." Flustered, Beth drew back a little. "I mean for food. I'm fixing some crackers and cheese. Would you…?"

"Sounds grand. Shall we take it back to bed? Maybe with more wine?"

Beth beamed at the idea of what was tantamount to a midnight feast. "If you can grab a bottle and a couple of glasses…" But before she'd finished speaking, Tom was heading for the wine rack.

Back in bed, they propped themselves up on the pillows and shared not only biscuits, cheese and wine, but some olives and nuts, Tom had managed to unearth. The horrors of the past few days behind her, Beth took time to consider her position. "I've contacted Ann," she said. "You know – Mum's lawyer. I'm hoping she can find out a bit more about Bryan's wife."

Tom stopped, about to throw a handful of nuts into his mouth. "Are you sure you want to know?"

"Yes." Beth was very definite about that. Now she'd accepted the fact she wasn't Bryan's legal wife, she had to know the truth, the whole truth. All of a sudden the stray thought she'd been trying to pinpoint floated to the surface. She turned to Tom. "Could it affect liability for his debts?"

"If she was alive when Bryan died?" Tom rubbed his chin. "Depends on the law in… where is it?"

"New South Wales. Ann would know, but first I need to know when Elaine Harvey-Flynn died."

"Well, you don't need to know right now, and maybe we should try to get some more sleep. It'll be morning before you know it, and sounds like you're going to have a busy day ahead of you."

Sliding the leftover food onto the bedside tables, they nestled under the covers, Tom fitting himself snugly behind Beth, his arm around her waist and his lips in her hair.

Twenty-seven

There was no reply from Ann next morning, and Beth chastised herself for being impatient, remembering the time delay between Florence and Sydney. Of course it would take her some time to search for the information Beth had requested. Meantime she reveled in the unusual pleasure of Tom's company at breakfast and, more unexpectedly, in the shower. It was surprising they managed to leave the house fully dressed and ready for work before nine o'clock.

"Tonight?" Tom asked, kissing her chastely on the brow before getting into his car.

"Tonight?" Beth was still tired from her interrupted sleep and wasn't sure if she could cope with another such night.

"I promise I'll let you sleep." Tom's lips curled up in their infectious grin as if remembering their night of intimacy.

Beth blushed. "Okay."

"I'll see you around six. And don't worry about dinner, I'll see to it."

By the time Beth reached the warehouse, she felt more awake and was looking forward to working again. She'd allowed her melancholy to take over her life these past days, remaining locked in a misery of her own making. Getting out of the car, she raised her face to the sun and took a deep breath. She was in charge of her life once more and vowed that never again would she give in to the sort of sadness she'd been caught up in. Bryan had lied to her. He'd treated her like a fool. So what? She was still the same person she'd been a week ago, maybe even stronger. With a spring in her step she strode into the warehouse.

"Good to see you. Feeling better?" Jo was sitting at her desk, her usual mug of coffee in her hand.

"Yes, thanks. I'm sorry, I…"

Jo waved away Beth's apology. "Think nothing of it. Tom said you had a virus. Can't help that."

Jo was so consoling, Beth bit her lip. Jo was a good employer. It wasn't fair to lie to her, to keep her in the dark.

"It wasn't exactly a virus. I was in shock."

Jo raised her eyebrows, put down her coffee, and leant her elbows on the desk.

"I discovered I wasn't married. I mean Bryan was. He was still married to someone else."

Jo's eyes widened. "A bigamist? Well, well. No wonder you were in shock. Bet you wanted to shoot the bastard."

Beth smiled weakly. "I can't. He's already dead."

"Of course."

Then the pair seemed to see the funny side of it and burst out laughing, Beth's laughter almost hysterical. At last, tears streaming down their cheeks, they stopped. Beth held on to the edge of the desk for support.

"Sorry," Jo said. "I shouldn't have…"

"I think that's what I needed. I was feeling pretty good when I walked in, but now… Yes, I would like to have shot him. However, I still have to work out who's liable for his debts."

"But surely you're not, if you weren't legally married? And anyway, how can they reach you over here?"

"It's not that simple. At least, I don't think it is. I do need to find out more. But not today. What do you need me to do?"

Jo filled Beth in on the day's activities, which included a visit to a new deceased estate and unpacking several boxes from the previous weekend's estate sale. It wasn't till late afternoon that Beth had time to think about herself, then it was to anticipate another evening in Tom's company.

Dinner that evening was a subdued affair, Tom and Beth hugged and kissed, but true to his word, when they fell into bed it was to sleep in each other's arms. When they awoke, Beth couldn't help feeling so relieved to be lying here with Tom, instead of in a lonely bed here or anywhere else. Whatever it was that had brought her to Florence, whether her mother's postcards from a lonely US soldier or fate, it had been the right thing for her. She sighed contentedly as she rose, evading Tom's arms with a grin.

"This is getting to be a habit," she said when the couple were sitting over breakfast.

"A good one." Tom took the last bite of the Spanish omelette Beth had prepared. "It's a long time since I've been so well looked after."

"So it's my cooking…" Rising to clear the table, Beth flicked a tea towel in his direction, knowing full well he understood her joke.

"Come here." Tom drew Beth down onto his lap and nuzzled her neck. "You know that's not it. You're a wonderful person. A beautiful soul."

Beth glowed. She was still getting used to this sympathetic, caring man. She snuggled close then struggled free. "I need to…"

"Yes, I need to be off, too. This may be the day we…"

"Do you think so?" Beth knew exactly what Tom was referring to. While she'd been waiting for a reply to her email to Ann, Tom had been expecting a response from John Blackwood. Surely they'd have valued Bryan's assets by now?

"Let's hope." Tom rose and took Beth in his arms again. It was strange how his very presence had a calming influence on her. It was as if once she was close to him, no one and nothing could harm her. She moved away reluctantly when his arms dropped. "Be in touch." He kissed Beth's cheek before going out the door, leaving her touching the spot where her skin still felt the imprint of his lips. Was it love she felt for this man? Neither had mentioned the word. She had been burnt too badly before and Tom… he'd loved his wife, probably still did. So what did that make Beth?

Beth decided to check her emails one more time before leaving, and there it was, the one she'd been waiting for. She opened it nervously, scanned it quickly, then sat down to read it more slowly.

What a shock! I really feel for you. I did as you requested and have checked out the English end. Found the marriage so there's no doubt on that score.

Never was. Beth scrolled down the page.

I further checked on Elaine Harvey-Flynn and discovered the notice of her death on August 5th, 2010. I double-checked and it's the correct Elaine

Harvey-Flynn. This would explain why her sister is the current contact. Cecily was her only living relative – apart from Bryan.

There was more in the same vein, with a potted biography of Elaine, but Beth didn't need to read any further. So Elaine had pre-deceased Bryan. What did that mean for Beth? Ann failed to mention anything about liability for debts. Beth needed to talk with Tom. She checked the time and realized she should be at work. She closed down her laptop. She wanted to tell Tom, to ask his advice, but he had work to do too and couldn't drop everything to satisfy her wishes.

The morning seemed to drag despite the visit to a house in a part of town unfamiliar to Beth. She and Jo drove up the highway, then turned off to the right and continued to climb. Their destination was an old property perched on top of the cliff with a magnificent view out to sea. The house itself was packed with belongings. It looked as if everything had been stored for generations, with each one adding to the collection.

"I see why you brought me," Beth said as she and Jo took a break and were standing on the wide veranda overlooking the ocean.

"Yes, too much for one person. I knew the old guy who lived here. He was the last of his kind. The family who inherited it are distant relatives. They just want rid of what they see as a load of old rubbish, but there are some real gems here. It's sad."

Beth agreed, thinking of her own mum's belongings. Bryan hadn't been willing to give them house room, and what could fit into her room in the nursing home was limited. As a result, much of the stuff of Beth's childhood memories had gone to various charities. At least these things would find new homes.

Having decided they'd done enough for the day, Jo locked up, and they began the drive back down the coast. They had almost reached Florence when Beth's cell rang. Glancing at it, she saw Tom's number and gave Jo an apologetic look before pressing to accept the call. Beth could see Jo's grin when she said, "Tom?"

"Dinner," said Tom without preamble. "Can't talk now. Pick you up at seven, I've booked a table at Driftwood Shores."

"Driftwood Shores I…" but he was gone. Beth held the phone to her breast. She wanted so much to talk with him. She'd hoped they could meet for lunch, but now she'd have to wait till later. She met Jo's enquiring gaze. "It was Tom," she said unnecessarily. "We're having dinner at Driftwood Shores."

"Mmmm. Very nice. You'll enjoy it. So, it's true then, you and Tom?"

"I guess so." Beth could feel herself redden. "He's… We've…"

"No need to explain to me. It's high time he found himself a good woman." Jo regarded Beth warmly. "I had a feeling there was more to you than meets the eye. This'll certainly put Yvonne Walker's nose out of joint."

Beth could feel her blush deepen. "Don't mention her. She'll never believe there wasn't anything between us when…"

"When she demanded you be taken off her sale?"

"Mmm." Beth had forgotten Jo was involved in Yvonne's jealous rage.

"So, Driftwood Shores. Hmmm. Must be planning something special. Want some shopping time?"

"No, I…"

"Well, take some time for lunch. Be back by two."

Beth bought herself a sandwich and sat by the river to eat it, but her enjoyment was hampered by her need to share the information she'd learned with Tom. She could hardly wait till she saw him again. Rising and dropping the wrapping from her lunch into a bin, she was walking back lost in thought, when a voice startled her.

"Thinking deep thoughts?"

Beth looked up and realized she was passing the bookshop, and Ellen was outside setting up a display.

"Sorry, I was lost…"

"Is everything all right?"

"Yes. I…," Beth began, then stopped. Did she want to broadcast her date with Tom to the world? Well, Ellen wasn't exactly the world. "I…," she stuttered.

"You and Tom." Ellen laughed. "I didn't need my psychic powers to work that one out. It's written all over your face."

Beth blushed.

"But it's not over, is it?" Ellen said more seriously. "You've overcome one hurdle, and a pretty big one at that, but there are still some matters to be resolved. Hang in there. It will all work out. Don't lose faith."

Beth swallowed hard, her mouth suddenly dry. It was as if the sun had gone behind a cloud. She'd forgotten Ellen's gift for prediction. What did the woman see? She opened her mouth to ask, but Ellen had disappeared inside again.

*

"You look very nice tonight."

"Thank you."

Beth and Tom were seated by a window, which looked down on the beach. It was deserted at this time of night and a strong breeze was whipping up the sand to send it hurtling across the shore. Beth was wearing her blue dress again and felt very feminine and almost happy, only her lingering worry about Bryan's debts clouding her mood.

"I need to tell you…," Beth began, "I heard from Ann. She…"

Tom held up his hand as if to stem her flow of words. "I have news too."

Beth's heart lurched. She clasped her hands tightly. So this was it. She was going to find out whether Bryan's debts were going to bankrupt her or…"

"You've heard from Sydney? What…?"

Tom signaled to the waiter and a couple of glasses of wine appeared as if by magic. "You first," he said.

As Beth recounted Ann's email, Tom looked concerned. He pulled on his ear, then took a gulp of wine.

The waiter interrupted to ask if they were ready to order, but to Beth's relief, Tom waved him away. Food was the last thing on her mind.

"I don't think that changes anything," Tom said at last. "I heard from John Blackwood this morning, and there's both good and bad news."

Beth was perched on the edge of her seat, her knuckles white from gripping her hands so tightly. She leant forward as if she could force Tom to speak faster. She had to know.

"They've valued your… Bryan Flynn's assets and set them against the debts they're aware of." He coughed. 'Seems that, apart from the mortgage, many of them are gambling debts, and Blackwood's not convinced all of the creditors have come forward. It may be that…" Tom hesitated. "Some of them may have criminal connections."

Beth felt an icy shiver travel up her neck to lodge itself in the back of her head. This was worse than she'd feared. Could she have criminals come after her looking for repayment of debts incurred by that swine?

Tom was still talking. "According to Blackwood, the best thing to do is to sell the house and contents as quickly as possible. There won't be a final accounting till that's settled. He's of the view the Sydney housing market is close to its peak, and it seems there are a number of valuable paintings and other pieces of art which could fetch good prices if they're sent to auction." He looked at Beth as if for confirmation.

"Yes," she said, her hands loosening their grip sufficiently to allow her to raise her glass and take a sip of wine. She remembered how Bryan had loved to collect those pieces, most of which had never appealed to her. She'd never been privy to the purchases, but supposed they must be of value. Bryan had too much pride and valued his reputation too highly to have bought anything mediocre. She'd sometimes wondered if he actually liked the artwork he collected or if it was all for show. She focussed on Tom's words again.

"It would appear that, even though you weren't legally married…" He cleared his throat. "In the eyes of the law in New South Wales, you are regarded as his…" Tom gave Beth an apologetic glance. "His *de facto* and as such, liable for all his debts."

"Oh!" Beth slumped down in her seat. She'd been afraid of this outcome, though, she reminded herself, she'd still have felt responsible even if… "Would it have mattered if she – Elaine – had still been alive… or had died after Bryan?"

Tom reached over to still Beth's hands, which were now drawing circles on the table. "There's no point in tormenting yourself with what might or could be. We need to work with the situation as it is." His fingers tightened on Beth's, comforting her with their strength and promise of safekeeping.

Beth met his eyes, her own widening as his meaning sunk in. "We? You'd…?"

"We're a team, you and me. At least, I'd hoped… I know you don't want to rush things between us, but I can't hide my feelings. I can't let you go through this alone when I… Hell, Beth, I want you in my life.

Not as a friend, I want more than that."

Beth thought she caught the glimmer of a tear in Tom's eye and felt a trace of moisture in her own. What had she done to deserve this? She met the pressure of his fingers with an answering force. "If you're sure, I…" She smiled through her tears – tears of joy, of relief, relief she no longer had to bear this burden alone. "But…"

"We can take our time to work out the details, but not too long. After Janet, I never thought I could care for another woman. But none of us can predict how life's going to turn out. It feels so right with you, Beth. I can't imagine a future without you. I love you."

Beth's breath caught. Tom's words were whirling around in her head. Had she heard correctly? Her eyes blurred and she clung to his hands. She looked into Tom's eyes and the wealth of tenderness there almost choked her. A warm glow began to spread from the pit of her stomach to engulf her entire body.

"Can you bring yourself to…?"

"I love you too, Tom." Until she said the words, Beth hadn't been fully aware of her feelings. Now she knew. She'd come to love this gentle giant of a man and was willing to trust her future to him. Coming to Oregon had been the best decision she'd ever made.

A wide beam spread over Tom's face. He appeared to be lost for words and only gripped Beth's hands more tightly. They sat gazing into each other's eyes, oblivious to the buzz of the restaurant going on around them.

"Ahem." The waiter's voice jolted them back to the present, and they grinned like a couple of children caught out in some mischief.

Ignoring the menu and keeping hold of Beth's hands, Tom raised his eyebrows at Beth and asked, "Fish?"

She nodded.

"We'll both have the fish of the day," Tom said to the waiter, then turned his attention back to Beth.

Beth didn't know how she got through the meal, or what she ate. By the time they returned to her house, she was filled with yearning for this man, this man who'd come into her life so unexpectedly and turned it around.

Twenty-eight

Beth dressed carefully and smiled to herself, filled with anticipation for the evening ahead. It was two months later, and the opening of Madeline House was to be celebrated by the cocktail party to end all cocktail parties. Jenny and Mike intended to make the evening one all of Florence would remember – a fitting tribute to Madeline de Ruis. While the group of friends had been involved in preparing for the opening, it was Jenny and her partner who had taken the responsibility for planning the evening's celebrations.

As Beth brushed her now almost shoulder-length hair, she reflected how much her life had changed in the short time since she and Tom revealed their feelings for each other, and how they were now regarded as a couple by all their friends. Moving back through the bedroom she picked up the photo of the two of them taken only two weeks earlier at Brad's wedding. Her eyes glowed remembering the day. It had been a perfect September afternoon with only a slight breeze rippling the lake. Brad, Brooke and Simone had all accepted her as Tom's new lady, while Louise, despite several glowering looks, seemed happy on the arm of a silver-haired gentleman who appeared enamored by her.

Beth sighed as she replaced the frame on her bedside table. Tom was such a dear. He'd been urging her to move out to the lake, but she was in no hurry to take that next step in their relationship. For now, it was enough they'd admitted their love, and while she slept over at his house several nights each week, Beth liked to maintain the independence of her own home.

"Ready, honey?" Tom's voice from the other side of the house interrupted her thoughts.

"Coming," she called, making one final check in the mirror before joining him in the living room.

By the time they parked outside Madeline House, there were already a number of cars filling the driveway, and light was flooding out of the house, even though it was not yet dark.

"Doesn't it look good?" Beth pointed to the sign on which the words

Madeline House

In memory of Madeline de Ruis

had been carved, surrounded by flowers and birds. "Ellen's brother made it."

Once inside, Beth headed to the kitchen to see how she could help, but was chased away by Jenny who assured her all was taken care of.

"The caterers have it in hand," she said, passing Beth a glass of sparkling wine. "Get out there and circulate."

More people had arrived when Beth was in the kitchen, and as she made her way across the room towards Tom, who towered head and shoulders above most of the crowd, she found herself waylaid by a number of locals she'd met through her work. It surprised Beth how many people recognized her and welcomed her contributions to the community. She had a grin on her face when she finally reached Tom. Mentioning her astonishment to him, he responded with an arm around her shoulders and a warm squeeze.

"They can see what a warm and loving person you are," he told her. "People here are quick to recognize those qualities. You fit in well."

It was while she and Tom were chatting with Ellen and Travis, that Beth felt Ellen's warning hand on her arm and saw her looking towards the door. Following the direction of her friend's eyes, Beth drew her breath in sharply. Standing in the doorway, surveying the room stood Yvonne Walker. While Beth knew Yvonne remained a client of Tom's, she hadn't set eyes on the woman since the time she'd accused Beth of being a thief.

"What's she doing here?" Beth whispered to Tom, drawing closer to his side.

"She probably received an invitation like everyone else," Tom replied *sotto voce*. "Don't worry, she won't…"

But it seemed that she did intend to speak to Beth, because after gazing around the room for a few moments, Yvonne's eyes appeared to settle on the group, and she began to weave her way unsteadily toward them, accepting a glass of wine from a waiter on the way and tossing it down in one gulp.

"I think she's a bit tipsy," Ellen said, as Yvonne approached, replenishing her glass from a passing waiter. Tonight she was dressed even more bizarrely than usual in a bright red calf length dress, emblazoned with sparkling beads, slit almost to the hip on one side and showing more cleavage than anyone of her age ought.

"Beth Carson," she said loudly as she came closer. "I need to talk to you."

Beth clung to Tom's hand, relishing the security of his fingers curling around hers.

"I don't…" Beth began, but Yvonne interrupted.

"I want to apologize. I know I behaved badly towards you. I have no excuse," she said, slurring her words.

Tom made a sound almost like a snort, and Beth threw him a reproving glance.

Yvonne waved her hands wildly, her glass almost tipping over. "I see what you people are doing here. My mother…" Her voice began to break. "My dad… Mom couldn't leave. You're doing a good thing, and I wanted to tell you, I…"

"It's okay, Yvonne," Beth said, trying to stem the flow of words. "No need to…"

"But there is." Yvonne suddenly appeared to regain her composure. She drew herself up to her full height. "There's something I need to tell you." She took a deep breath. "That photo you were interested in. I *do* know who was in it. Richard Turner was a distant cousin of mine. He came to live with Aunt Leone when he was a child. His parents were killed in car crash. He had no other relatives, and Aunt Leone was some sort of distant connection who had no children of her own. I was always jealous of him, of her love for him." Her eyes glazed over, and some of the old bitter Yvonne shone through. "Even when he died, she couldn't forget him. I thought I'd managed to destroy all the photos of him, but it seems I missed that one. His folks came from Minnesota or thereabouts. His mother was a Sherwood."

Yvonne tottered, and Travis reached forward to prevent her falling, while Beth's mouth dropped open. Sherwood – that was her mother's maiden name. Could…? She tried to speak, to ask Yvonne for more information, but the words stuck in her throat.

"That's all I know," Yvonne said, and walked off clutching the glass to her bosom.

Beth raised her eyes to meet Tom's. "Sherwood," she said. "That's… My mum… My grandparents… Minnesota …" She could barely get the words out. She thought she was going to burst with excitement. "Do you think Rick Turner could be…?"

"We may never know," Tom said. "But it's a good thought, and it may explain why your mom kept those items. He could be some sort of distant relative of yours, or maybe your mom had some other sentimental reason for keeping them. But if it makes you feel good to believe he is a relative, then go for it."

"I did tell you…" Ellen's gentle voice broke in. "You were meant to come here – and not only to connect with Tom. Though I do believe that was part of it. Whereas Jenny is Maddy's link to Madeline House, you may be Rick's link to Maddy."

"Maddy would have liked that."

Beth turned to realize Jenny had joined the group and been privy to the latter part of the conversation.

"I did feel the house had a special meaning for me," Beth murmured, almost to herself.

"Let's drink to Maddy and her Rick," Jenny suggested.

The three women raised their glasses, and made the toast together. "To Maddy and Rick –and Madeline House."

THE END

Acknowledgements

As always, this book could not have been written without the help and advice of a number of people.

Firstly, my husband Jim for listening to my plotlines without complaint, for his patience and insights as I discuss my characters and storyline with him, for confirming for me the male point of view, for a final proofing to check all my US terms and spellings, and for being there when I need him.

John Hudspith, editor extraordinaire for his ideas, suggestions, encouragement and attention to detail.

Jane Dixon-Smith for working her magic on my beautiful cover and interior.

My writing group, the Inkstained Groupies for their support and encouragement, my critique partner, Helen, for her continuing patience and my beta readers, Louise, Maria and Toni for their willingness to read the draft of this novel.

Annie of *Annie's books at Peregian* for her ongoing support and advice.

About the Author

After a career in education, Maggie Christensen began writing contemporary women's fiction portraying mature women facing life-changing situations. Her travels inspire her writing, be it her frequent visits to family in Oregon, USA or her home on Queensland's beautiful Sunshine Coast. Maggie writes of mature heroines coming to terms with changes in their lives and the heroes worthy of them.

From her native Glasgow, Scotland, Maggie was lured by the call 'Come and teach in the sun' to Australia, where she worked as a primary school teacher, university lecturer and in educational management. Now living with her husband of thirty years on Queensland's Sunshine Coast, she loves walking on the deserted beach in the early mornings and having coffee by the river on weekends. Her days are spent surrounded by books, either reading or writing them – her idea of heaven!

She continues her love of books as a volunteer with her local library where she selects and delivers books to the housebound.

A member of Queensland Writer's Centre, RWA, ALLIA, and a local critique group, Maggie enjoys meeting her readers at book signings and library talks. In 2014 she self-published *Band of Gold* and *The Sand Dollar, Book One of the Oregon Coast Series,* and in 2015 *The Dreamcatcher, Book Two of the Oregon Coast Series* and *Broken Threads.*

Sign up for the author's mailing list – keep up-to-date with news and new releases and get a **FREE** copy of *The Sand Dollar, Book One of the Oregon Coast Series.* http://maggiechristensenauthor.com/

The Sand Dollar

Maggie Christensen

A well-kept secret and a magical sand dollar. Can Jenny unravel the puzzle of her past?

What if you discover everything you believed to be true about yourself has been a lie?

Stunned by news of an impending redundancy, and impelled by the magic of a long-forgotten sand dollar, Jenny retreats to her godmother in Oregon to consider her future.

What she doesn't bargain for is to uncover the secret of her adoption at birth and her Native American heritage. This revelation sees her embark on a journey of self-discovery such as she'd never envisaged.

Moving between Australia's Sunshine Coast and the Oregon Coast, *The Sand Dollar* is a story of new beginnings, of a woman whose life is suddenly turned upside down, and the reclusive man who helps her solve the puzzle of her past.

The Dreamcatcher

Maggie Christensen

Dreamcatchers trap bad dreams – but sometimes nightmares escape.

Ellen Williams, a Native American with a gift for foretelling the future, is at a loss to explain her terrifying nightmares and the portentous feeling of dread that seems to hang over her like a shroud.

When Travis Petersen – an old friend of her brother's – appears in her bookshop *The Reading Nook*, Ellen can't shake the idea there's a strange connection between her nightmares and Travis' arrival.

Suffering from guilt of the car accident which took the lives of his wife and son, Travis is struggling to salvage his life, and believes he has nothing to offer a woman. But Ellen's nightmares come true when developers announce a fancy new build, which means pulling down *The Reading Nook* – and she needs Travis' help.

Can Ellen and Travis uncover the link between them and save her bookshop? And will it lead to happiness?

A tale of dreams, romance, and of doing the right thing, set on the beautiful Oregon coast.

Band of Gold

Maggie Christensen

A relationship after a failed marriage. Can Anna love again? Does she dare?

Anna Hollis believes she has a happy marriage. A schoolteacher in Sydney, Anna juggles her busy life with a daughter in the throes of first love and increasingly demanding aging parents.

When Anna's husband of twenty-five years leaves her, on Christmas morning, without warning or explanation, her safe and secure world collapses.

Marcus King returns to Australia from the USA, leaving behind a broken marriage and a young son.

When he takes up the position of Headmaster at Anna's school, they form a fragile friendship through their mutual hurt and loneliness.

Can Anna leave the past behind and make a new life for herself, and does Marcus have a part to play in her future?

Broken Threads

Maggie Christensen

A story of loss, grief and the struggle to survive against adversity.

Jan Turnbull's life takes a sharp turn towards chaos the instant her eldest son, Simon takes a tumble in the surf and loses his life.

Blame competes with grief and Jan's husband turns against her. She finds herself ousted from the family home and separated from their remaining son, Andy.

As Jan tries to cope with her grief and prepares to build a new life, it soon becomes known that Simon has left behind a bombshell, and her younger son seeks ways of compensating for his loss, leading to further issues for her to deal with.

Can Jan hold it all together and save her marriage and her family?